The Eternity Stone

Across Time & Space series

The Eternity Stone
Mountain of Glass
Desert of Fire
Desert of Ice
The Hidden Door
Whiter Than Snow
City of Light

Fairytale Memoirs series
The Mostly Forgotten Memoirs of Rose Red
Viola Sends Her Regrets
Gifted

Standalone books
Breaking the Glass Slipper
Unshakeable
Tyger
Take Me Home

For information on new and upcoming books,
go to **mmarinanbooks.com**

The Eternity Stone
ACROSS TIME &
SPACE BOOK ONE

M. Marinan

Silversmith
PUBLISHING

First published in New Zealand in 2017
This edition published 2023
by Silversmith Publishing

A catalogue record for this book is available from the National Library of New Zealand

Original cover paperback ISBN 978-0-9951108-0-9
This cover paperback ISBN 978-1-99-001418-5
This cover hardcover ISBN 978-1-99-001419-2

Dedication

To everyone who listened to me chatter about 'my book'
without seeing any proof it actually existed – thank you
for your patience and ongoing encouragement.

And to the person who supported me all the way in a very
hands-on fashion (yes, you, Kate!) – an extra big thank you.
We finally made it!

Contents

Prologue

The town of Upper Iversley was special, although at first glance you wouldn't think so. It sat in a green valley in the Anglish county of Leister, looking small and tidy and quaint in a quintessentially Anglish way, but with a marvellous secret component that made it so very unique.

But that secret wasn't what made it special.

The town itself was made up of only a dozen or so houses. The lines of the buildings were curved and precise, neatly fitting around the figure-eight-shaped road with its two central round-abouts and strategic trees in the centre of each half.

The whole village, or 'town' as the locals generously called it, was perfectly clean and perfectly balanced: grass precisely two inches long, houses a uniform light yellow – except for Solomon's down the end, which was more of a grey colour. Everyone knew that man hadn't cleaned the place in ten years.

But that wasn't what made it special either. There were dozens of similar villages in this part of the world, each complete with their own 'Solomon' for the other inhabitants to comfortably complain about.

The streets themselves were a bit more unusual. There wasn't a single visible vehicle, nor a decent route in or out of the place. Dozens of people walked purposefully around the figure-eight streets, in and out of the houses and small buildings, and into the nearby woods – far more than expected for so few dwellings.

But while unexpected, that wasn't what made it special either.

No, what made Upper Iversley special were the newest inhabitants, who had just come down from the cloudless blue sky like a meteor shower, and who planned to stay a long, long time.

Forever, in fact.

IN THE BEGINNING

The grounds of Renwick Castle, Iversley, Angland
1556 AD

"My lady? My lady, where are you?" The maidservant's call echoed through the thicket edging the castle grounds.

Rather than responding, Anne sucked in a breath and pressed herself deeper into the greenery, tucking the wide skirts of her gown in against her legs. She had no patience for Maura's fussing today, no matter how kindly 'twas meant.

It had been a difficult morning.

"My lady!"

The woman was starting to sound frantic, and Anne pushed back a pang of guilt. Being ordered to marry a much-older stranger – again! – was never welcome news, but 'twas not right to take out her misery on her maidservant.

After all, Anne was a grown woman of sixteen and a noble-woman-born. Her husband Wilbert was gone, the Eternal One rest his soul, so it should not matter that the queen who'd ordered his execution now ordered his widow's remarriage.

Yet it did matter, to Anne at least. But when had anyone cared what *she* wanted?

Maura's footsteps crunched on nearby leaves. "Wicked, redheaded wretch," she muttered. "Some lady you are, Anne of Covington. Taking any excuse to make mischief!"

Anne's guilty feelings withered and vanished, and she stood in complete silence as her ill-mannered maidservant stomped right past her hiding place.

Then once she was gone, Anne stuck out her tongue in the woman's direction. Mayhap she would take out just a little misery on Maura after all.

But as if to punish Anne for her own ill manners, an orangey-red lock of hair slipped out of her coif and into her mouth. She shoved it back inside the headcloth in annoyance.

"Saints' eyeballs," she murmured to herself. "One hour to think, 'twas all I wanted. 'Tis not as though if I tried to run off with the gypsies."

Sir Robert had given her the news of her new betrothal just one hour past, and truly, she'd tried to take it well. But then she'd had the sudden urge to be violently ill.

She'd told Maura and the assembled others that she needed a moment of privacy, but what she'd *really* wanted was some peace and quiet. True, these woods that bordered the castle might be filled with ghosts, fair folk and even a few bandits, but today she'd risk those dangers.

By the Rood, all she needed was one single, solitary hour of peace…

❧❦❦❧

Mountbatten Manor, Iversley, Angland
1818 AD

"Star's a fine mount, Mr Seymour," the stable boy said. "Steady and fast. But she gets spooked by squirrels."

George raised an eyebrow. "Squirrels in particular, or any small, furry creature?"

"Only squirrels, sir. She'll be fine with anythin' else, but if you see a squirrel, 'old onto your seat." The boy looked concerned. "I can change the saddle if you don't mind waitin'; it's just the only other mount available is ten years old and we usually use 'er for teachin' children."

So basically George had the choice between an ancient and incredibly slow horse, and one that would try to throw him if they came across a squirrel suddenly. Not a rabbit, not a cat, just a squirrel. "I'll risk the squirrel," he said firmly. "I expect to be back within a couple of hours."

As promised, Star was a fine mount, lively and obedient. And with no squirrels in sight, George rode her over the fields that bordered his neighbour's manor, heading for the woods. These were large grounds, and they also bordered George's own family estate.

Well, not *his*, his older brother's. As the second son of the late Viscount Morley, George was in line to inherit precisely nothing. Not even a title.

Not being fond of the other options available to him, George had tried to make his own way in business. But his attempt at true independence had ended up in a shipwreck, humiliation, and an empty bank account.

Oh, and an absent fiancée. Once mustn't forget the fiancée.

Scowling at the reminder, George dug in his heels and set Star into a gallop past the ruins of the old castle that sat between the two estates. He would see exactly how lively the horse was – barring any squirrels, of course.

❦

The road between Little Brimley and Whiteside,
Leister County, Angland, 2012 AD

"Some adventure this is turning out to be," Ash muttered, pulling her well-used sedan off to the side of the rutted country road. A sign by the small carpark read '*Scenic walk: 30 minutes return*'. "I could have stayed at home for all the excitement I've had."

Home being the Southern Isles, a former Anglish colony on

the other side of the world.

A few months earlier, nineteen-year-old Ash had left that small, green country for the distant shores of Angland.

She'd had grand plans. She'd find a great job and a flat in Lunden city, save loads of money, meet exciting, glamorous people, and travel all over Europa.

But so far, she'd found an admin job quite like the one she'd had back home; a little house also quite like the one back home – just more expensive; and she'd travelled in between the two small towns where she lived and worked. No savings. No glamorous friends – no solid friendships of any kind, actually.

It was just like normal life, only everyone had a different accent.

Ash sighed. "Probably should've moved to Lunden after all." Because right now, all she had to look forward to was last night's reheated lasagne.

She looked again at the sign advertising a thirty-minute scenic walk, then got out of her car. Life might be dull and disappointing, but at least she could manage some exercise.

She pulled her woollen hat over her messy dark hair, then a moment later, grabbed her mini pepper spray out of her handbag and tucked it into her pocket.

Better safe than sorry.

Two hours later, Ash was lost. Somehow she'd wandered away from the loose gravel path – she'd stumbled over her own feet, then when she'd picked herself up, she'd been lightheaded and didn't recognize a thing.

She'd tried retracing her steps, then retracing the retrace when that didn't work. It didn't make sense, because the area wasn't even very big…

To add insult to injury, the walk hadn't even been that scenic. Angland was flat and boring compared to home, and Leister County no exception. Green grass, brown mud…trees, and more trees.

Except…

Ash paused, looking around her with a frown. She still felt a little lightheaded from her earlier stumble, and it was long enough past her dinner that she felt very cranky, but the surrounding trees didn't look at all familiar. They were more jungle-ish than the forest she was used to. And now she was walking up a hill – that *certainly* hadn't been there before.

Oh, Deias. She was so lost.

After checking a large rock for bugs, Ash sat on it with her head in her hands. A small, unfamiliar-looking bird watched her from a nearby tree. It stood out brightly against its surroundings with its pine green feathers, crested head and red chest. *A festively themed bird*, she thought, although it was the wrong time of year for it.

The newly named festive bird cocked its head to the side and stared at her with what she imagined was a smirk. Ash waved a hand at it, but it didn't move, clearly aware of who had the upper hand. Hint: not her.

She sighed. Even the animals seemed to be against her today. "Don't you know staring is rude?"

"My apologies," a reply came in distinctly Anglish tones. "I thought perhaps you might direct me to Iversley?"

Ash jumped in surprise, almost falling off her rock, and turned to see the new arrival. Behind her stood a boy in his late teens. About her age or a little older, he was fair-haired, slightly rumpled, and dressed like an extra for a Jean Austen film.

He smiled at her ruefully. "I didn't mean to startle you. I was thrown off my horse, and the blasted beast bolted. Squirrels, you know."

"Squirrels?"

"The horse," the boy explained. "She's easily started by squirrels. But never mind that – I've lost my bearings, and the day is short. Would you be so good as to tell me in which direction I might find Iversley?"

He looked sane enough – more so considering he'd actually asked her for directions – but then so did plenty of serial killers. Ash stood, carefully taking a step back. "I don't know where that is, sorry. Is it a street name?"

He frowned. "No, it's the village near here, with the manor of the same name. It should be very close. I hadn't ridden for more than twenty minutes when I was thrown."

Deias, his voice was as posh as one of those films too, Ash thought. "There's no manor or village around here that I know of. The nearest town is Whiteside, and that's a fifteen-minute drive north." She paused, debating how much to say, then added, "Perhaps you can help me, though. Do you know which direction the main road is?" If she could find it, she'd walk back to her car.

There was a long pause where the boy's heavy eyebrows lowered in distinct irritation. Then he said again, very slowly and clearly, "I...vers...ley. It's the village nearest here, just ten miles east of Markfield. Do you know where it is?"

"No...I...don't," Ash replied just as slowly. "Do you know where the main road is? Or any road at all! I'll get a taxi."

He looked as disgruntled as she felt. "By Jupiter, you're not making any sense at all."

"At least I'm not dressed like an escapee from a period drama," she snapped. "What are you, an actor?"

Mr Posh's jaw dropped. "You're a bold lad, to speak to your betters so! What's your name?"

Lad?

Betters?

"None of your business," Ash retorted, getting to her feet and backing away slowly. She reached carefully into the pocket of her autumn jacket and wrapped her fingers around her mini can of pepper spray – just in case. "Now if you'll excuse me, Mr Darcy, I'm going back to my car." Wherever that might be.

But he stepped closer, now looking furious. "My name is not

Darcy, and I do *not* excuse you. Whatever your game is-" And then he made the mistake of grabbing her arm.

Ash shot him full in the face with the pepper spray. He screamed, bent double, and held his hands to his burning eyes.

She didn't wait to see how well it worked.

She ran.

And ran, and ran. After about fifteen minutes of running (the last five spent limping and wheezing, as Ash was *not* used to that level of exercise) she figured that he wasn't going to catch up.

She stopped to catch her breath, feeling guilty and wondering if she'd overreacted. Yes, the guy had tried to grab her, but he'd seemed kind of nice at first. Just…odd. And she didn't want to permanently blind him, or cause him to get hit by a car in his helpless state…

Except he'd be lucky to find the motorway, because she sure wasn't anywhere near it. Her impromptu sprint had taken her so far into unfamiliar ground that it didn't seem like the same country anymore. The vegetation was even more foreign here, with twisting trees growing only feet apart, and tangled vines trailing between branches and over the forest floor.

The air was different too; warmer and somehow thicker, almost misty instead of clear and cool. It brought to mind movies she'd seen of parallel universes and supernatural doorways, and small people with big hairy feet...

More likely she was walking in circles. The woods weren't supposed to be that big. Theoretically you could walk through them in forty-five minutes.

That doesn't explain the change in scenery, her inner sceptic whispered.

That couldn't be right; she must have stumbled into a very large area of exotic trees. With…exotic birds. Angland had hummingbirds, right…?

Her mind started to replay stories she'd heard of people

who'd 'just gone for a walk' in the woods, unprepared for the elements, then got lost and died in the forest. Ash had always thought those people were complete idiots. Who did that?

But now she had, and the one person who could have possibly helped her, she'd maced in the face.

(Which was really his fault, Ash reminded herself self-righteously. She had no problem with historical recreation, but it shouldn't involve random, unsuspecting passers-by.)

Oh, well. She'd just have to do it alone. Pick one direction; walk in it until something happened.

Worst case scenario, she'd have a good reason to miss work tomorrow…

Anne was beginning to regret her hasty decision to hide from Maura. If she'd not hidden, she could have claimed that she'd needed some fresh air – 'twas the truth after all. Then she might have retained her dignity and gone back inside the castle to face her impending marriage.

Instead she'd hidden, and then she'd gone further into the woods, far enough that she didn't recognise the surroundings. She'd tripped on her too-long skirts and almost twisted her ankle, and now she was well and truly cross with herself…and more than a little frightened.

Some creature made a call, and Anne shivered. By the Eternal One, she was trembling like a leaf. It seemed she wasn't as courageous as she'd imagined, not when she was so easily frightened by an hour lost amongst the trees, a mere mile or so from her home.

Although considering most of the tales of ghouls and fairies had come from Maura, mayhap this *was* the woman's fault after all.

Anne tried to remember the Church's stance on supernatural beings, but couldn't remember much more than that if it had horns and a forked tail, it should be avoided.

As for mysterious, silent, pale figures moving through the woods…?

The girl was tall and reed-slender. Her dark hair was loose down her back, and bare toes peeped out from under the scandalously thin fabric of her long white gown as she moved silently through the trees.

Through the trees.

Anne went cold from head to toe, and the hairs stood up on the back of her neck.

Then the spirit-girl turned and looked at her. Her eyes widened and her mouth opened in a silent scream.

Anne sucked in a deep, shocked breath. 'Twas a…

"GHOST!" she shrieked, turning and running full-speed in the opposite direction.

✦❦✦

Crunch.

"Argh!" Ash spun around to confront the new terror, then realised she'd just stepped on a stick. "It's just a forest," she told herself aloud. "Stop being an idiot. There's nothing out of the ordinary here." Except for the guy in the fancy suit, who was probably now an enemy for life.

There was another *crunch* and a shuffling noise, and Ash bit back a whimper. She wrapped her arms tightly around herself and picked up the pace, looking about to see who might be following her. *Please, oh please let it just be a squirrel…*

Was that *breathing* she could hear? Her pepper spray was only good for one shot. Hades.

She quickly looked around for a suitable weapon, and a fist-sized rock at her feet caught her eye. She slowly picked it up off the ground, then pressed back against the nearest tree as silently as possible.

And then when she saw a flash of colour to her left, she swung the rock-

"Please!" the girl cried out, throwing herself to her knees with her arms shielding her head. "I meant no harm!"

Ash stepped back and lowered the rock, having caught herself just in time.

The child – no, not a child, just a small teenager – was peering up at her through raised hands. She babbled on, "By the Saints, I'd have vowed you were another ghost, and one is enough for a lifetime, do you not agree?"

Another ghost? Eek. "Did you say ghost?" Ash asked the girl cautiously.

"Yes, I saw one just a moment ago; a horrible tall woman in a nightgown!"

Ash just stared at her.

The girl amended, "Well, mayhap she was not so very horrible, but she looked at *me* as though she was afraid! What should a ghost have to be afraid of, I ask you?"

She looked really serious, alternatively offended and scared, and Ash immediately forgot her own fears of moments before. "I don't believe in ghosts," she replied kindly but firmly. "You must've seen something else."

"Oh, no. Verily, 'twas indeed a ghost, and these woods are surely haunted. Z'wounds, Maura was right." The girl frowned. "I do so dislike when Maura is right."

There was a brief pause where Ash pondered who Maura might be, and decided she didn't care enough to ask.

The girl rattled on, "But enough of this bibble-babble. Direct me towards Renwick Castle at once, as I must return home anon or my reputation shall be ruined and Sir Robert shall be *very* cross with me!"

Ash raised an eyebrow. Bibble-babble, eh? This one must be going to the same costume party as Mr Darcy, although dressed from a different era.

She was a tiny thing, all dark eyes and pale, pale skin, and the top of her head barely reached Ash's shoulder. Her vibrantly red hair was escaping from some sort of headpiece, and she wore a green velvet dress with a straight, bosom-crushing bodice and bulky skirt.

She also smelled like she hadn't bathed in a month.

Ash stepped a little further back. Talk about overdoing the historical accuracy. "I can't direct you to any castles," she replied firmly, "or villages, or anything at all. I'm lost too. And that makes three of us today – four if you count the ghost. So maybe we could stop playing games like we've escaped from a Renaissance fair, and help each other?"

❧❦❧

The tall boy's words ceased to make sense to Anne once he got past 'three of us today', unless he'd been counting the ghost, which seemed unlikely. So while he was jabbering nonsense about lost 'cahs', she stopped listening and focused instead on her new companion's odd appearance.

The woollen cap and rough blue breeches were the least of the oddities, for Anne could not decide which class he belonged to. 'Twas clear he was not nobility, but not a vagrant either, since they rarely ate enough to grow that tall. Mayhap a yeoman, but not too wealthy...

But his language! He'd said *bloody*. Anne felt guilty even thinking the curse word, as a lady should never use that kind of language.

Very well, that was a lie. She *did* use that kind of language, just not in front of anyone who mattered. Whoever this was, didn't count.

The boy's accent was odd too; very soft, with clipped vowels. He mustn't be Anglish, Anne decided, especially wearing that strange garb – the thick black jerkin of some incredibly fine weave shone with a silver light where the sun hit it. She'd never seen that type of fabric before, even at court in the days when her family had been welcome there.

And the jerkin's fastening was so strange, like a long silver snake running from the high neckline to the hips. The aforementioned breeches were overly tight and of a coarse, dark blue material, worn along with flat, thick-soled slippers and a short-brimmed cap.

Most certainly not Anglish, Anne decided. One of those Northmen, mayhap, to grow so big?

But aside from the obvious, there was something not quite right about him. His voice was too high, for a start. Such a large man should have a strong, deep voice. Mayhap he was a eunuch? 'Twould explain the soft skin and odd manner.

Anne surreptitiously checked his codpiece, and 'twas as flat as a slice of manchet bread. Her eyebrows shot up. Surely eunuchs didn't have it ALL cut off?

In quick succession, all the other visual oddities added up. No cods, an odd bulge to the chest, fine features and soft cheeks, that high voice…

…Her eunuch was female.

❧❦❧

"By my trowth! You're a woman!" the little redhead burst out accusingly.

Ash was stunned. "How…how could you possibly think otherwise?"

The girl put her small hands militantly to her corseted hips. "You're dressed as a man, and you're vastly tall. By the Eternal One's truth, I've never seen any good woman dressed as you are." Then she added for good measure, "It's not decent. I can see your *legs*!"

"That's a problem…?"

Ash looked at the girl again. *Really* looked at her. Judging by the costume, this girl was aiming to appear as if she was from Tudar times: wearing a dark cloak over an ornate dress, with a tiny waist, stiff bodice, and square neckline. Ash had never seen anybody so ornately dressed outside of the movies. It brought to mind a painting of Queen Eliza the First, minus the ugly ruff and layers of jewels.

It was a great costume, marred by the frazzled hair escaping from the hairpiece and the slightly crazy look in the girl's eye. Her language didn't seem quite right either – less thee's and thou's than Ash would expect from a real Tudar woman.

But then it *was* only a costume. And the girl *did* seem to be lost, just like Ash…and the pepper-sprayed Mr Darcy.

Ash tried again. "I'm sorry I offended you with my, er, legs. But I think we can help each other. Where are you supposed to be right now?"

"As I said, Renwick Castle! 'Tis nearest to the village of Iversley, and if you've not heard of *that*, then I can't see what good you'll be."

Funny, Mr Darcy had said almost the same thing – and Ash *still* hadn't heard of Iversley.

Several minutes later, Ash hadn't learned anything new, and both she and the redhead had grown increasingly exasperated. The only thing they could agree on was that they were both lost somewhere in Leister County.

The girl also refused to tell Ash her real name, instead insisting she was 'Lady Anne of Covington' – because no one ever wanted to be the servant or the peasant, did they? She may as well have called herself Queen Henrietta the Sixth, for all it meant to Ash.

"Fine," Ash said at last. "I'll play along, *Lady Anne*. I left my…horse and cart at yonder, uh, highway. Prithee direct me towards it?"

Now the redhead stared at her as if she was crazy. "Might you be touched in the head?"

Pot, speaking to kettle. "So says the girl dressed five hundred years out of fashion."

Lady Anne smoothed down her velvet skirts indignantly. "I'll have you know I had this sewn just a month past, in line with the most recent fashions of the royal court!"

"Of course you did," Ash shot back sarcastically, throwing her hands in the air. "And you're looking for a castle that doesn't exist, *and* you've never heard of *anywhere* useful-"

"Wait." The redhead froze suddenly, her eyes wide. "I have an idea."

*One month earlier, not far
from our intrepid heroines' meeting point*

Ten feet underground a man worked silently in a bunker. Arrogant, brown-skinned and shiny-bald (because science couldn't fix everything, and he genuinely believed it was a sign of his great virility and intelligence) he watched a wall full of screens, each showing a very slightly different scene of the same forest. His hand rested over a button on a device, like a game show contestant sure that they knew the answer before the question arrived, but while his fingers twitched from moment to moment, he never pressed the button.

No, they'd be missed.

No, too old.

No, that was a couple, and he didn't want both of them. He needed more variety in his studies. Urgh – really? Didn't they *know* they were being watched?

Well, likely not, he conceded. That was the whole point of what he was doing, that they didn't know. Impatiently he skimmed past that scene, watching the seasons change across the many screens like an old nature holographic in fast-forward.

No, no, *chaos* no. Just twelve. He just needed a measly twelve subjects to show his patrons that his work was worth doing, and he hadn't thought it would be so difficult. Ironic, really, considering that the last study had gone far more easily. Or perhaps he'd just been less fussy.

But although he felt impatient, he was disciplined enough to stick with it until finally, *finally* he'd met his quota. Now to set the timer…

❦

The oddly named, oddly dressed girl didn't look impressed by Anne's pronouncement. Instead she looked baffled. "You think we *what*?" she asked in her strange accent.

"'Tis evident," Anne explained patiently. "We've wandered into the land of the Fey from our own homes. Does this look at all like your home? Because I vow that I've never walked these woods before, and I've picnicked many a time."

Ash's jaw dropped, and Anne continued thinking aloud. "And it explains so much; even the poor ghost."

"Not horrible anymore, is she?" the girl muttered.

Anne ignored her. "Everyone knows that fairyland – that's the same thing as the land of the Fey, you see – is simply brimming with enchantment! So the two of us were unknowingly snatched away from our homes, and that poor spirit found herself able to make a brief connection from the realm of the dead."

Now she was truly making sense of things. Anne found she surprised even herself sometimes. "Oh, bother. I ought to have asked her about Wilfred."

"Who's Wilfred?" Ash looked reluctantly fascinated.

"My late husband, the Eternal One rest his soul." Anne gazed thoughtfully off into the distant misty trees. "I've some burning questions I would have put to him, if I'd simply known."

Like, did the Eternal One prefer the Universal Church or the Protestor?

Did Wilfred mind that she was remarrying, and that she'd been quick to convert when the new queen came to power, even though he'd been stubborn enough to die over it?

And did it hurt having your head cut off?

Now Anne could see what had happened, she felt a little ashamed of how badly she'd reacted to the ghost's presence. She still remembered the last, terrified look on the wraith's face. Why should a ghost be afraid of a person? How very odd.

"How very odd," Ash said, and after a moment Anne realised that she'd not been reading her mind, but voicing an opinion. "I've got another suggestion. Either I tripped and hit my head hard enough that I'm imagining all of this, or else we were both shot with drugs and brought to a new location for some unknown purpose." Now she looked panicked. "What if someone's watching us right now?"

"Of course they are," Anne agreed. She felt far more cheerful now she'd come up with an explanation for their presence here.

"They are? Who?"

"The Fey," Anne explained again. "The wee folk." By the Rood, the girl was dim-witted. But at least she was impressively large, and would perhaps scare off any attackers by her size alone. Except for trolls. And boggarts. And ogres… "The elves."

"*Elves?*"

"Indeed, elves! I've heard tales that time does not pass the same way in their land, and they are known to take humans who catch their fancy, if they are fair of face or in some way talented." Anne considered Ash critically. "Mayhap you are a musician?"

"The wee folk," Ash repeated flatly. "You think we're being watched by fairies, who've stolen us away for some unknown reason."

Anne set her hands on her hips and lifted her chin. "Do you have any better ideas?"

Yes, Ash did have better ideas, and she'd just voiced them, but they didn't make her feel any better.

She sighed heavily. "Talking with you is making me crazy. Look, why don't we just start walking? We can work it out as we go."

Lady Anne sniffed. "Very well."

"Fine."

Sigh. That warmed-up lasagne was sounding pretty good right now.

They chose a direction that seemed about right – downhill – and picked up a pretty good pace. Ash had read somewhere that if you headed downhill you'd eventually find a river, and if you found a river, you'd eventually find civilisation. That probably didn't apply to people who'd got lost on a thirty-minute walk, but it was all they had to work with.

As they walked, she made conversation with her new companion. It was entertaining, if a little crazy. The girl's knowledge of history was better than Ash's own – except for the obvious issue with the vocabulary. "So, Queen Marian, is it?" she queried. "Didn't she have six husbands and kill them all?"

"That was her mother, Henrietta the Eighth," Anne corrected. "And she couldn't have killed them all. That would be unlawful. She only killed two."

"And the rest died to get away. Right," Ash agreed cheerfully. She was almost enjoying herself now, as long as she didn't take it too seriously. "So, Anne, this was all in what, the fifteenth century?"

"Queen Marian's reign began in fifteen-fifty-four. My lady."

Naturally. "Oh, I'm just Ash. You're the lady, you said."

"Yes, I *know*. You must address me as 'my lady'. Calling me by my first name is certainly unacceptable for a new acquaintance, even if they were of an equal class. Which you are not."

Ash let out a small, sad sigh. "Right, forgot we were playing this game. *My lady.*"

Apparently satisfied, Anne continued. "Where on earth are you from that you don't know the ruling monarch?" She stopped walking and studied Ash with a gimlet stare – quite striking with her dark eyes against her pale skin. "I shall guess – Germanica?"

"Not even close. Think far, far south."

Anne tried again. "Espaine."

Ash laughed. "Think of going across oceans; ancient colonies."

"Normandy?"

"No!" Realising she was getting sucked in to the fantasy, Ash found herself explaining. "I'm from the Southern Isles in Pacifica. You know, Angland's old colonies from when it decided to shove people on all parts of the globe?"

Anne wrinkled her little nose. "That's silly. Why would the fairies snatch you from all the way over there?"

"Good question," Ash answered flatly. "Come on, we need to keep walking. Do you recognise anything yet?"

The girl shook her head. "I don't know these trees, and we're yet to find even a stream. Is aught familiar to you?"

"No. Not yet." Although Ash had been trying hard to find a familiar landmark, there was nothing. All trees – some familiar, some not – and those random birds flitting around, and not a clearing in sight.

Trees… "Hey, I've got an idea."

By Jupiter…the *pain!* George felt like he'd had poison poured in his eyes: a horrid, peppery, blinding poison wielded by an ill-spoken lout.

How *humiliating*.

By some mercy the pain had receded a little, but his eyeballs still felt like over-spiced boiled eggs, and it put him in a foul mood. He hadn't been in a good mood even to start off with, but this just made it worse.

George tried to open his eyes again, then decided it still hurt too much, so hunkered back against the tree trunk he'd stumbled into when he'd been so brutally attacked. Of course, the villain might come back to finish him off, but that would be a fitting end to a too-short, ill-spent life.

Ill-spent if one asked George's father, which of course one couldn't because he'd died six months earlier. He'd taken the time to disown George first, though. He hadn't really needed him, not when George's older brother was there to inherit everything and to be the 'good' brother.

George, on the other hand, had managed to shame the entire family through his involvement in trade before he even reached his twenty-first birthday.

He huffed out a sigh. Half-blinded, miserable, horseless – it seemed as good a time as any to ponder the actions that had brought him here.

But really, he didn't see what was so shameful about earning a living. He'd been quite proud of his success when the shipping venture he'd founded from his small inheritance had finally started to bring in an income. He hadn't needed the allowance from his father, although it hadn't hurt.

Anyway, he wasn't close to his family anymore, not after the Clarissa Incident. That was why he was currently staying with his neighbour, Dorian Wythe, rather than with his family.

Wythe was a childhood friend who hadn't judged George for

the last few years' happenings. He was also the owner of Star, the horse who was skittish around squirrels.

Well, George couldn't say he hadn't been warned. But he hadn't even seen the squirrel that had caused him to end up on the ground, lightheaded and nauseous, with the horse long gone.

And when George had picked himself off the ground, he hadn't recognized the landscape at all. Had he been paying so little attention that he'd strayed off Wythe's estate and onto entirely unfamiliar land?

The day had become uncomfortably hot as well. Not quite what he imagined the jungles of the Indies to be like, but rather warmer than an hour ago. And he'd wandered around that unfamiliar land, sweating under his high collar, until he'd run into the ill-spoken, poison-wielding lout.

It had been a bizarre encounter. The boy had been so oddly dressed, with such an odd way of speaking, even before he'd shown himself to be so vicious.

Very well, perhaps George shouldn't have grasped the boy's arm, but he'd been frustrated over the nonsensical conversation and over being lost in the first place.

Scowling, George blinked his stinging eyes and slumped to sit on the ground. A hard shape poked into his hip. He patted at it in confusion, then reached into his coat pocket and pulled out a small pistol.

Through his blurred vision he could see the scrolling decoration on the pistol's grip. He vaguely recalled pocketing it for his journey to Iversley, in case of highwaymen, but he'd had no need of it. He hadn't even loaded the blasted thing.

George considered it briefly, then with a resigned shrug, slipped it back into his coat pocket. At least if he ran into that lout again, he wouldn't appear defenceless.

SPECTRE

"Can you see anything?" The redhead's voice came up through the branches, unseen but unmissable, and not exactly helpful. "Well?"

Ash struggled her way past yet another stabbing twig, trying to get a glimpse over the forest canopy. The road should be easily spotted, if only she could make it high enough, but unlike in the movies this tree wasn't easily climbed and didn't have a convenient lookout point. "Just give me a minute!"

Finally she made it as high as she dared – jokes aside, she wasn't a lightweight – and shoved aside the leafy branches for a better look. "Huh."

There was no highway in sight. There was a gray haze in the distance that could be a city, but otherwise it was all green. There was no sign of the castle that Anne had mentioned, nor village, nor ruins of any kind; not that Ash's view was all that good.

"What is it? Tell me!"

"Hold your horses," Ash muttered, struggling her way back to the ground. "Phew, that was hard work. I haven't climbed a tree since I was a kid."

Anne gave her an odd look. "Since when have you been a young goat?"

"Oh for- we're going the right way, OK? There's a clearing a few miles downhill. It looks pretty flat, but there might be a dip further down." Ash found it hard to believe she'd strayed so far from her car, and her idea of being drugged seemed more likely. This was not the part of Leister County she was used to.

"Did you see the castle?"

"No castle, sorry."

"How about any elves?" Anne asked hopefully as they began to walk again. "Elves like forests, or so I hear."

"There are no elves! No ghosts, no boogey men, no trolls, alright? Just trees-"

"*Ash…*"

Ash stopped mid-step, caught by the girl's tone, and saw that Anne had frozen in place, her face even paler than usual. She was staring at Ash's left shoulder. "What is it? Do I have a bug on me?"

Anne raised a shaky hand to point. "*Ghost!*"

Ash spun around. Behind her was a bearded man with a sword and two long plaits, looking rather like a Viking who'd lost his horned helmet.

He also happened to be transparent.

Ash's eyes bugged. She wanted to scream like Anne, but nothing would come out.

The Viking's eyes were just as wide at the sight of her. For a moment they mirrored each other, arms akimbo, mouths dropped open like a couple of goldfish.

He's as scared as I am, Ash realized.

Or perhaps not. With a snarl he swung his ghostly sword right at her, so fast she didn't react until it had passed right through her midsection. Then *poof!* He vanished as quickly as he'd appeared.

In shock, Ash stood unmoving for a moment longer. Then she looked down at her unharmed waist, then back at where the Viking had been. There wasn't a trace of him left behind, not even any ghostly ectoplasm. It was almost disappointing.

Finally, she turned back to Anne. "What just happened?"

The girl swallowed. "What a shame; I forgot to ask it about Wilfred. Do you think we'll see another?"

Not if they were lucky. Ash shook herself, frowning. "It must've been a trick. A 3-D light show or something, because ghosts don't exist. See, he went right through me."

Anne was still carrying on her own conversation, seeming to have recovered quickly from her second ghostly visitation. "But mayhap the ghost would not have known Wilfred. It didn't appear very friendly, did it? Forsooth, I'd think it tried to kill you."

"It wasn't a ghost," Ash said firmly, to convince herself as much as Anne. Although if it had been one, it would've been the murderous sort horror movies were based on.

Lucky there were no such things as ghosts.

"You truly are stubborn! You do not even believe your own eyes?"

It had given her a fright, that was all, Ash told herself. She *knew* it wasn't real. Her own father was an alter-power theorist, into all things supernatural and unlikely, and even he'd admitted there was no real proof for ghosts' existence. (Much to Ash's mother's embarrassment, it hadn't stopped him from trying to find some.) "I'll believe them, right after I believe you were born in fifteen-fifty-six."

"Fifteen-*forty*. I'm hardly an infant."

And so they were back to arguing – and that in itself made Ash feel safer. "Alright, Lady Anne. Pick up those skirts and pick up the pace."

"Mind your manners!"

Ah, that was more like it.

❧❧❧

Meanwhile, not very far from where Ash may or may not have met her first ghost, George made an interesting discovery. He did this by stubbing his toe hard on a hidden object in the grass. Once he'd stopped swearing and jumping up and down (it had been a *very* trying day), he took a closer look.

It was a trapdoor. Painted the same green colour of the

surrounding grass, the round metal frame rose a mere inch from the ground, with a pull-away latch. He gave it an experimental pull and the lid suddenly slid aside and disappeared into its frame, leaving a round hold straight into the ground.

How very clever; he hadn't even had to push the lid. Perhaps it operated on springs?

Inside the hole a ladder disappeared into the darkness below. Even though the outside of the door was dirty, the hinges and ladder were shiny bright: they must be regularly used, he deduced.

George cleared his throat, then called into the darkness; "Hello down there!"

Silence.

He tried again, more loudly. "Good day, is anybody there?"

His voice echoed back up at him, but no one replied. That was good enough for him, so he began to carefully climb down the ladder, his feet easily gripping each metal step.

After about fifteen steps (or two body lengths, George estimated) the ladder stopped. He gingerly felt for the floor. Ah, there it was, hard and secure under his searching foot.

But just as his second foot touched the ground, it seemed that the sun came out.

He squinted against the sudden brightness. "Who's there?!"

There was no answer, and no one was visible in the small chamber the light revealed. It was just a square room with a table in the centre, and with some sort of miniature forest model covering the table's full surface.

It certainly wasn't an underground barracks as he'd considered. It was far too small for that: probably only five or six people could comfortably stand. There was only one seat by the table.

George glanced around curiously, noting that three of the main walls were covered from top to bottom with pictures. Unframed and rectangular, the pictures fit as closely together as the tiles of his courtyard back home, although oddly enough they all seemed to show the same thing.

Or at least very similar: beautifully detailed paintings of the outside woods, with only slight variations in each. It seemed that the entire forest must be represented here, and so realistically it was like a window into a miniature world. He could almost see the leaves moving in the wind.

He noticed an image with people in it – the only one that had anything besides trees. A familiar youth stood next to a short young woman in a very old-fashioned green dress. A girl, really.

But why was she painted into a picture with the poison-wielding lout?

George peered closer. The quality of the work was so good he couldn't even see the brushstrokes…

Good grief! The girl moved! He stepped back in alarm, doubting his eyes, before leaning in again. The little figure, only as tall as his index finger, was definitely moving. What trickery was this?

Even though he was raised Protestor, George crossed himself.

But his fascination soon outweighed his concern. He considered how in his own lifetime, machines had made things possible that would have been considered sorcery a century before. Perhaps this was just a very complicated mechanism?

In the picture, the two figures were more animated now. The girl appeared to be shouting at the stone-faced lout, who stood with his arms crossed.

"What a shame I can't hear you," George murmured.

"*It wasn't a ghost.*"

The voice was small and soft, but George leapt out of his skin, looking around frantically to see who had joined him. But the room was as empty as before, and the small figures in the images carried on their conversation.

"*By the Rood, you're as stubborn as an ox and twice as foolish!*" a different voice returned, the words matching the redhead's moving lips. "*It was a ghost! Ghost, ghost, ghost!*"

Ghosts? I bloody well hope not, George thought crossly. There was enough to contend with today without adding that too.

But someone *must* be here, watching him. How else could the timing have been so perfect for him to suddenly hear this conversation?

He probably should have taken that as a sign to leave the underground room, but he was too fascinated. Surely another few minutes down here wouldn't hurt.

Feeling voyeuristic but not sorry, he leaned in to listen once more.

"It must have been a hologram," the lout was saying in his soft voice. *"There's no such thing as ghosts."*

The girl was almost hopping now. *"I have never heard of a hollygram, but I know what I saw, and I know where we are!"*

"For Deias' sake, Anne, we're not in fairyland! If you seriously believe that then you've got something wrong with your head!"

Well, George would have to agree with that one.

"Lady Anne!"

The boy sighed. *"Whatever. Lady Anne, Queen Anne; stick on a fake beard and I'll call you Evan the Terrible if you want. Just drop the game, will you? It's hard enough being lost without this as well."*

The girl was red-faced with fury, her fists held tightly at her sides. *"There is no game, and you are the biggest fool in Churchendom if you cannot see we're no longer in Angland. But I've had enough of your lack of respect for your betters. I shall find my own way out."* And with that, she picked up her skirts and stomped across the image, heading towards the right side.

The boy threw up his hands in exasperation, then walked after her.

"Stop following me!"

"We're going the same way!"

George watched as the tiny figures made their way to the edge of the picture. For a moment they disappeared, then they were marching from the side of the adjoining picture as if nothing had happened. And it hadn't for them, he realised. He must be seeing what was happening up in the forest, maybe even right now. How was that even possible?

A blinking red light caught his eye. On the table in the centre of the room was a three-dimensional model of the forest, accurate in detail down to the tiny, individual leaves on the trees. A map of sorts, perhaps.

But if that was the case, then where was Iversley? The forest according to this map was quite sizable, and thickly wooded. He didn't see any type of civilization represented at all. Just trees, trees and more trees. Oh, and a stream running down the centre of the whole thing.

The light he'd seen was made up of three thin shafts, shooting up about a hand span from amongst the foliage, blinking red. They didn't seem to be attached to anything, and next to each shaft of light were some words, floating eerily above the tree line.

Two lights were moving very slowly towards the edge of the tableau. They read in a boxy, barely legible text, 'A.O.C 1556' and 'A.J.O 2012'.

There were other lights scattered over the map, but these were yellow and didn't shoot up in the air like the others. They didn't move, either. Their text was faint and almost unreadable, but one not too far from the two red lights read, 'H.R.B 986'.

Initials, perhaps, although what the numbers were for, George had no idea. But the lights seemed to represent the locations of The Poisoner and the redhead. How very useful.

The last light was alone in the centre of the table. It read, 'G.W.S 1818'. Now those were *his* initials – barring the Honourable Mister.

"And that's the date," he said aloud. But then he considered that the other numbers couldn't possibly be dates, since that would mean – well, that he had travelled through *time*.

Ha, ha. How very, very silly.

He looked around again at the bunker, and thought of the

amazing mechanisms that allowed moving pictures and the words to come right to his ears, and the door that had slid open with barely a touch. And the still-ongoing argument between the girl dressed like she was from Tudar times and insisting she was a lady, and the tall, soft-voiced lout.

Time travel. Ha, ha…ha?

"Where are we going?" Ash asked, sounding bored.

"I know not where *you* are going," Anne snapped back. "*I am* searching for a way out of these cursed woods."

And then to emphasize her words, she picked up her voluminous skirts and ran ahead of the other girl.

That lasted not long at all before she was forced to slow. She could feel her cheeks were flushed from the unaccustomed exercise and her coif was coming loose from her hair. Making the pretence of waiting for her companion, she stopped to catch her breath and arrange her headpiece.

A few seconds later, Ash came up behind her. The girl had been walking, Anne noted, and had almost kept up with Anne's run. That was somewhat demoralizing, but clearly speed came with the territory of overlong legs.

"Are you happy now?" Ash asked her.

"As a matter of fact, I am satisfied," Anne lied. "See how far we have come. There is the break in the trees just ahead, as you said." She had only noticed the trees thinning just before she spoke, but Ash didn't know that.

Ash shrugged. "Fine then. Let's take a look." Then she muttered something about a 'ren fair' and 'cah-park', but it didn't make any sense to Anne, so was happily ignored.

As they approached the break in the trees, they saw that it was actually the edge of a cliff where the hillside sharply dropped thirty feet into gently rolling grassy hills. In the valley directly below was a town, and unlike any town Anne had seen before.

"By the Rood and all the saints, that's not Iversley!"

"Not Iversley," Ash agreed dryly, "but it sure isn't Whiteside or Little Brimley either, or anywhere I've visited. Look at what the people are wearing!"

Anne looked. There seemed to be a large number of people for the number of buildings, since there couldn't be more than two dozen strange, rounded cottages set out in a curving grid-like pattern.

The men and women walking purposefully around and disappearing into the buildings were dressed a little like Ash, but even more scantily. Both genders wore tight breeches, but the women wore vests to lend them a little decency.

The weather was mild, but not enough to warrant almost nakedness! Anne shouldn't stare, really, but she hadn't seen that much bare skin since she'd watched the castle lads swimming in the millpond last summer.

"They're so dark," Anne commented, trying to decide if she found such a trait appealing. 'Twas unfamiliar, for certain. "Like gypsies or Moors, don't you think?"

"What's a moor?"

Anne waved a hand. "Foreign. Dark."

"Oh. Well, this lot have a good tan, and that's unusual for Angland." Ash went back to watching. "Where do you think they're all going?

Exactly what Anne had been wondering. But mayhap they weren't Moors, mayhap they really were elves. But Anne had always imagined the fey folk to be stunningly beautiful, all pale with skin white as milk. Mayhap these were brownies?

She kept those last thoughts to herself. Even though she was clearly Ash's social superior, Ash didn't seem to know it. She could be terribly condescending when she thought Anne was being foolish, and had made her disbelief of fairies and such obvious.

But then Anne saw something that made all thoughts of brownies and elves exit her mind.

George didn't know what to think. All he could remember was the argument he'd overheard once in his club, where two ancient scholars had fervently argued over the possibility that men might be able to travel through time even as one would ride from one village to another. He'd chuckled when he'd heard them, but now…? It felt terrifyingly real.

"No," he said aloud. "It's not possible."

By Jove, he must have hit his head when he'd fallen. Actually, he couldn't remember falling at all, just that one moment he was on the horse, and the next he was on the ground. His head hadn't hurt then either, but there had to be *some* explanation for all of this.

The surrounding land wasn't at all familiar, not at all like what he knew of this part of the country. In fact, he was tempted to think that he wasn't near Iversley at all. Perhaps he had been abducted, struck so hard that he couldn't remember it at all? Could would-be kidnappers have left him in this place?

Why they would bother, he didn't know. His father had cut him off, so no ransom there, and of course practically his entire fortune had just been lost at sea in the stupidest gamble since Lord Emmersdale bet his trousers on a roll of the dice. But how else would he have got to this unknown place? He certainly hadn't walked himself here.

So assuming that he had been brought here by unknown enemies for an unknown reason, then who must this underground room belong to? If it was the Frencine – then with advanced machinery like this, they certainly shouldn't have lost the battle of Waterlôe three years before.

George looked back at the elaborate model on the table. On

closer inspection, the pieces didn't resemble the models he was used to. He reached out to touch a tiny oak tree, then gasped as his finger went right through. It seemed to be made of coloured light.

Incredible, but also rather beyond anything he could explain away as clever mechanisms. If he was truly honest with himself, that feeling in the pit of his stomach was fear.

Time to leave. Or rather, time to have a chat with someone who could give him some direction. And this time, he would be sure to disarm the lout before he got a shot off with that poison spray.

With one last glance at the map to check the couple's location, he climbed back up the ladder. The mysterious light disappeared as he left.

Walking in the direction the two had gone, it wasn't long before George saw them in the distance. They weren't arguing anymore, though. Instead they lay side by side on their bellies, facing away from him and peering over what seemed to be a cliff marking the edge of the flat forest floor.

A certain A.O.C and A.J.O, if those initials had been correct.

They hadn't even heard him approaching.

George quietly pulled out his pistol and crept closer. Then when he was just ten feet away, he said in his deepest, most intimidating, ideal-for-scaring-small-children voice; "You there. Turn over slowly. No fast movements or I SHALL shoot you." That was of course a lie, but they didn't know that.

Both turned in shock, the boy with horror evident on his somewhat effeminate features when he saw who was holding the pistol. "Oh *no*," he groaned. "It's you."

"Regretting your earlier actions with that bottle of eye-poison, are you?" George said with grim satisfaction. "No doubt you're wondering how I found you. I-"

"Hush!" the redhead cut in. "They'll hear you!"

George actually turned to look over his shoulder to see if she'd been speaking to someone else. It was just him, of course. "I beg your pardon," he repeated irritably, "but I *am* holding a pistol, pointed at you, and...I shall do something terrible with it!" He waved the weapon threateningly, but was disheartened by their lack of response. Could they tell it was unloaded?

"Alright, we see you have a gun," the boy interrupted wide-eyed. "Now would you *please* get out of sight before they see you?!"

"They...?"

The boy nodded towards the cliff, then turned away from George as if he wasn't even the real threat.

Perhaps he wasn't.

George stared at the two for a long moment before deciding that their fear was real, and it was directed at whatever lay just out of his sight, at the foot of the cliff. "If this is a trick to distract me in order to take my pistol, I assure you it will not work!"

"We care not about your silly pistol," the redhead said, rolling her eyes in a way that reminded him of his younger cousins. "Come see over this ledge – but keep your head down!"

If it was a trick then they were both marvellous actors, and George was curious enough to risk coming closer. Giving them both a wide berth so they couldn't suddenly try to disarm him, he crouched down and shuffled to the edge of what turned out to be a decent-sized cliff.

Set in a grassy valley below was a small town. Certainly not Iversley, by Jove, nor any of the half a dozen almost identical towns in the same area of Leister County. It didn't even seem *Anglish.*

Iversley never had sterile, tub-like houses with shiny curved roofs. Anglish towns never had swarthy men and women walking around half-naked in scandalously brief vests and tight trousers. He'd be surprised if *anywhere* in civilized Angland or even Europa had that. (Well, perhaps Italie. They were a little 'different' for all of their good weather.)

And the Iversley he knew certainly didn't have...

"Giants?!"

"I *told* you we were in fairyland," the redhead told her companion smugly. "Now do you believe me?"

Giants. That was the only word for them, really. All easily twice the height of the townspeople, the three huge men were sitting or standing in the straight, wide streets of the town. They weren't doing anything, just watching the humans go about their business.

The humans didn't seem afraid, but George couldn't shake the idea that the giants almost seemed like guards, or supervisors at the very least. They also seemed bored, and as he watched, one scratched at his neck then sneezed.

Very, very ordinary, except for the size. Oh, and the green skin tone of one, which wasn't usually seen on humans without the help of a bucket of paint.

George turned to the others in shock, wanting to confirm that he wasn't seeing things.

The redheaded girl saw the unasked question in his eyes and nodded tersely. "Yes, there truly are giants. 'Tis a fearsome thing, is it not? And here I was thinking Ash was huge!"

"I told you," the boy muttered. "I'm not that tall. You're just small."

So his name was Ash, was it? George tried to think of some clever insult that would link up the concept of burning eyes, revenge and the boy's name, but decided it wasn't precisely the time for it. "I can't believe I'm seeing this. It has to be some kind of trick."

"It's not *my* trick," Ash said defensively. He looked a little guilty, and it made George feel better. "This is as confusing to me as it is to you."

And somehow George doubted that the boy had even seen the bunker at all. Giving him a narrow-eyed stare, George turned back to study the scene below.

If David's Goliath had been that size, then he definitely understood why the boy had been hailed a hero. Comparing the giants to the humans around them, he suspected that the tops of the humans' heads would reach their belt buckles.

Of course, he could be mistaken from this far away. George hoped desperately (and pointlessly) that he was. Perhaps these humans were from a pygmy tribe, and the so-called giants merely tall men? But then the surrounding trees and buildings would have to all be pygmy versions too, because the giants were far too large in comparison.

And it didn't explain why the one with the white braids hanging down his back was *green*. A pleasant apple-green shade, but green nonetheless. That wasn't normal for this part of Leister County.

The giants, all apparently male, were dressed in a manner reminiscent of some old warrior tribe. He couldn't quite place the style…slightly Viking?

"They look like Ronan the Barbarian, don't they?" Ash commented in a low voice. "All that leather and long hair."

"Ronan who?" Anne queried. "I've never met any barbarians. I've never left Angland."

"It's a tee-vee show. Or a move-ee. I forget which. You haven't heard of it?"

"You're not making an ounce of sense," the girl announced, and George turned away grimly. Ash wasn't making any sense to him either, but all he could think of was '2012'.

Ash frowned, then turned to study the scene again. "Never mind."

George hadn't had a close look at his attacker before now. He seemed unthreatening now, but that could be a combination of George's (pointless) pistol and the shock of seeing such unusual people in the town below.

George also noted that the boy seemed content for strangers to call him by his shortened first name – a sure sign that he was of one of the lower classes, perhaps a groom or a footman or similar. If he hadn't been a servant, he would have been called 'Mister' or simply by his last name as a mark of respect to his station. His manner was also overly familiar, and George mentally counted it as another mark against him.

The boy also had rather delicate, soft features, and seemed to be retaining a little childhood plumpness late for his age. Eighteen, nineteen perhaps? Though he had the confidence of someone older. Smooth, lightly freckled cheeks, dark green eyes, tendrils of black hair escaping from under a soft white cap.

And his ears were pierced twice on each lobe! That was something George had never seen before. It seemed so *savage*. By Jove, but the boy was feminine-looking. The unusual diamond ear studs only added to the effect.

Ash saw him looking, blushed, and turned away. George was reminded of how on first meeting the lad he'd been accused of staring. And now he was. He turned his gaze back to the scene below.

One of the giants, a monolith with dark, shoulder-length locks, lifted his gaze in their direction. Although George knew he should have been sheltered from view by the trees, for a moment their eyes met. He saw the reaction on the giant's face.

George sat up abruptly. "They've seen us. That big dark one."

"They're all big," the boy muttered, but he got up. "We should leave. I don't want to wait around to see if they're friendly or not."

The others wholeheartedly agreed. The three of them moved quickly away from the cliff, back in the direction they had come from.

"Where shall we go?" the redhead asked plaintively. "Surely they know these woods better than we do. They'll find us for certain, and I don't care to have my bones ground to make someone's bread!"

George got *that* reference. "I know a place they can't get us," he offered, crossing his fingers that the giants didn't know about it. "But we should move now."

"I thought you were lost," Ash said suspiciously. "That's what you said before."

"I was," he countered. "And after you threw poison in my face, I found a safe place where those giants couldn't even fit their leg in. I'm offering to lead you both there."

The girl – Anne – had already leapt to her feet. "By the Rood, the sooner the better!" Then she asked Ash plaintively, "Whyever would you throw poison in this kind man's face? 'Twas a most cruel thing to do."

George had already set off at a trot towards the bunker, but he glanced over his shoulder to see Ash's reaction.

"It wasn't *poison*. It was just pepper spray. He startled me. It was supposed to act as a temporary deterrent."

Deias forbid George ever startle him again, if that was the boy's reaction.

"Oh. I'd rather thought pink was your natural eye colour," Anne commented to George, picking up her pace to match his. She practically had to run. "Or that you'd been weeping. I'm pleased to hear 'tis not the case."

"I don't weep," George retorted, both amused and offended. "I'm Anglish. Now if you don't mind, I'm trying to find my way."

The girl dropped back to trail with Ash, and as he tried to navigate back the way he'd come, he heard their whispered conversation.

"I don't know if we should trust him," Ash was saying. "We don't even know his name."

"George Seymour," he called back over his shoulder. "The Honourable Mister, younger brother of the seventh Viscount Morley. And if you're wondering who you should trust, might I point out that *you* attacked *me*?"

Ash might have said something like, "Oh Deias, not another one," but then more clearly, "George, is it? You're pretty good at holding a grudge."

"Mister Seymour to you," he snapped. "Ash."

"If we're being formal, then it's Miss O'Reilly to you," Ash snapped back.

George took several more steps before what he'd heard finally set in, and he actually stopped in his tracks, causing the small redhead to walk into his back.

"Oof! Are we here?"

"What?" He looked around, realising they were, in fact, quite close. But it was Ash that had his attention. "Did you say *Miss*?"

Ash lifted his- (her?) chin, standing up straighter and tidying his- (her?) jacket. "Oh, don't pretend you couldn't tell."

George was shocked speechless. But then it made sense – she was either a very effeminate young man, or else a girl dressed in men's clothes. "Then why, madam, are you dressed like that?"

"Why are *you* dressed like *that*?" Ash countered.

"Like what?"

"That's precisely what I said," Anne added confidentially. "But she won't explain what she means."

"Oh, but you're wearing a costume," George said to Anne. Obviously. "Ah…aren't you?"

1556. 1556…

Anne sucked in a breath so that she almost looked like a fish, and her voice came out very frostily. "No, I am *not*. But mayhap we can discuss this further when we're not being pursued by giants?"

He jolted, suddenly remembering what they'd been doing. "Of course."

The trapdoor was barely twenty feet away from where they'd stopped, and just like the last time, the door slid open with barely a touch. "Come along quickly. We'll be safe down here."

The two girls (*two, two,* he reminded himself) looked down the dark hole dubiously.

"You'd rather risk the giants?" George asked. He turned and began to climb down the ladder into the dark, and for a moment it seemed that they wouldn't follow.

But only a few seconds after he'd stepped on the ground and the lights had come on once more, he saw Ash's feet appear down the ladder. She was wearing rather elaborate shoes, some sort of purple leather in contrast to her otherwise plain appearance, and an inch of trim ankle showed as she climbed down.

He looked away hastily just as she came out into the room, her eyes narrowed at the brightness. "Oh. It's a bunker. Are those surveillance cameras?"

"I don't know," he replied in confusion. "Are they?"

"Well, they certainly look like it," she replied, her lips curving upwards. "But then of course Mr Darcy wouldn't recognise a TV screen."

She meant *him*. "The name is Seymour," he corrected, moving towards the ladder where he could hear the other girl climbing down, but was yet to see her. "Are you well, ma'am?"

"Lady Anne," the girl's voice echoed down the tunnel, and then she too was struggling her way out into the artificial light. "I've decided you may call me by that name, as you are the brother of a viscount. Although I can't say I've ever heard of your title."

"It was granted to my ancestor in sixteen-forty," he explained as he helped her down the last few steps. "Mind your step." But it was a moment too late, and the girl stumbled. He caught her, and she smiled sunnily up at him, reminding him briefly of Clarissa. It must be her age and height more than anything else, and the reminder made him feel big and stupid all over again.

"Sixteen-forty?" Anne – *Lady* Anne queried. "You must mean *fifteen*-forty. Ooh, it's bright down here, isn't it? Where's all that light coming from?"

"No, I definitely meant sixteen-"

But she'd already lost interest (again, rather like Clarissa after all) and had seen the screens. Her jaw dropped. "Witchcraft!"

"You almost sound happy about that," Ash said with a hint of humour. "The dark enchantment of cameras and film."

"You know what this is?" George asked her abruptly. "This place."

Ash shrugged, poking at the light-map on the table. "Well, the screens are obvious. This here must be a holograph, a better one than I've seen before. But what do you think these lights mean?"

He cleared his throat. That was the key question. "Well. That was how I found you. If your initials are A.J.O, then one of these would be you." He pointed to the red lights, now clustered very closely in the centre of the map."

"Ashlea Jane O'Reilly," she agreed. "That's me. And twenty-twelve, that's this year. Well…" She frowned. "A.O.C is Anne, of course-"

"Lady Anne!" the other girl shouted across the room.

"*Lady* Anne," Ash agreed, rolling her eyes. "And you must be G.W.S. What does the W stand for, Wilbur?"

"William," he corrected. But she still hadn't commented on the numbers paired with his initials, and he felt like he couldn't breathe.

"Eighteen-eighteen. That's what you're dressed as." Ash indicated to his very ordinary riding wear with some relief. "And Anne- Lady Anne- is dressed as fifteen-fifty-six. Oh, this is finally making sense. We're all playing a part, although it would have been nice to know what the game was a good half-hour ago, and you both could have told me once you realised I didn't know about it. And the giants – just special effects. Of course."

But there was no 'of course' about it, and with every word she spoke, George's head grew blanker and blanker. Not only did half her words not make sense, but what she was implying? It wasn't possible, no matter that the thought had run through his mind earlier.

"O'Reilly?" Lady Anne said, finally catching up with the conversation. "Is that not an Eirish name?"

"Yes, what of it?"

The redhead shrugged nonchalantly. "Well, it does explain why you're so uncouth. You can't help your heritage."

"*I* can't help myself? What about you, motor-mouth?"

"Please, speak Anglish," Lady Anne replied snootily.

Ash looked an inch away from snarling, but George was still twitching. Why weren't any of them noticing that if it was a game then they were all playing with different rules? What was *wrong* with them?

⚜

They were shut in an underground bunker that reminded Ash of a spy thriller film, and the further they got away from the 'giants', the less real it felt.

She didn't know how she'd got here – and she was getting sick of being mistaken for a boy just because of a loose jacket and some plain trousers – and that tactless little redhead was driving her mad. Anne seemed unable to speak two sentences without throwing in an insult, and when Ash considered how long the other two had drawn things out without explaining...? It made her fume.

"That's enough," Ash said abruptly, turning away. "As fun as this all isn't, I do have to work tomorrow. I'm going back out to see if I can find a way to my car."

Anne stopped her rant about expected behaviour and looked anxious. "But what about the giants?"

"About those..." Ash shook her head, feeling as foolish as Anne had called her, although not for the same reasons. "Yeah...well, I'm not sure about those. I want to go back and take another look, a close one, you know? People can do all sorts of things these days with special effects."

"These days?" George was standing in the corner of the room with his hands clenched into fists, and with the oddest look on his face. "And what days would these be?"

Ash took a large step back. He was starting to sound hysterical, and she didn't really know him. The younger brother of a viscount – now that was original, but there was no way in Hades she believed it. "I'm not playing that game anymore."

"Game!" he exploded, waving his hands in the air. "If there's a game here then I'm not the one playing it! What year do you think it is, *Miss O'Reilly*? Well?" He barely gave her a chance to answer, continuing on, "Because last I knew it was eighteen-eighteen, and the numbers on the map say something quite different, and *nothing* is making any sense anymore!"

He finished with a heavy huff, still wild-eyed.

Ash opened her mouth to reply…what? That he was a liar? That he was crazy? But if he was a liar, then he was a fantastic actor, and if he was crazy, then she *really* didn't need to be antagonising him. And the fact did remain that she was lost. Maybe working with a couple of crazies for a while wouldn't do her any harm.

"Now that makes sense," Anne said approvingly to George. "We've each been snatched from our own times and pulled into this land of enchantment." She paused thoughtfully. "And if 'tis the elves that created this place, then it wouldn't be considered witchcraft, would it? 'Twould be fairy magic."

George turned to Ash. "Ignoring the part about elves, she believes me. What about you? Don't people believe in time travel where you've come from?"

Ash found her voice. "Some people think it should be possible, but no one's ever been able to do it. To *prove* they did it, I mean."

"So that's a no, then."

She looked down at her feet, clad in her favourite purple leather shoes. They were now worse for wear since she shouldn't have worn them walking. Shouldn't have gone walking at all. "I didn't think your time believed in fairies," she said instead, still looking at her feet. "It seems rather far-fetched."

"Not necessarily fairies," he replied, white-faced but calmer now. "Just someone else that we don't know and don't understand. Lady Anne might call them fairies, but perhaps we'd know them by another name." He shrugged. "Who's to say that time travel isn't possible for someone in – I don't know, the distant future or the distant past?"

That made sense, as long as you were talking about complete impossibilities. Improbabilities rather – time travel had been one of Ash's father's favourite ideas, and he was convinced that with the right level of alter-power, you could do *anything*.

Sure, and if you found a way to reach the moon, you could end world hunger with all the cheese you'd harvest.

"It probably is," Ash replied instead. "But for me, for today, I can't accept it. So I'm going to go, and you two can…discuss your family trees, or compare Pommy accents. Perhaps you're related."

She turned and moved towards the ladder, setting her hand on the first strut as if to climb, but the door's lock slammed into place above her. She hadn't noticed before whether it was open or closed, but the sound was unmistakeable.

She turned slowly back to face the other two, feeling cold and scared and a bit angry. "Let me out. *Now.*"

"I didn't do it," George replied, still pale-faced.

Next to him Anne shook her head. "Nor I. It must have been the-"

"Don't say elves!" George snapped, and Anne looked affronted.

"Not elves," a new voice said. It was a man's voice, confident and extremely ordinary, but they couldn't see its origin. "Just me."

DOCTOR WALKER
AND THE
LIES OF JEAN AUSTEN

A figure began materialising over the table/map, starting from the head down. It was transparent and glowing faintly like Ash imagined a celestial being would…or special effects in just about any modern film.

It began with a head, bald and shining and arrogantly handsome, and then moved down to a neat jacket with long sleeves, and…well, whatever was beneath that couldn't be seen, because it disappeared into the table at about waist height.

Within seconds the colours had corrected, and then the man stood there in front of them. Or half of him did, anyway. Now he looked as solid as any of them, except for a hint of lagging when he moved.

"I'm afraid I can't let you leave," he said apologetically. "There's rather more at stake than whether you get home to your lasagne, Ashlea. So if you wouldn't mind?"

He gestured to the space in front of him where the other two still stood, and Ash slowly moved away from the ladder. He was tall, and his purple jacket and shiny brown skin made Ash think of a particular chocolate advertisement, and that just made her feel hungrier. She didn't need the reminder of the not-so-great dinner she was missing. "Hey, how did you know about the lasagne?"

"You'd be surprised at what I know, Ashlea. Or should I say Ash?"

"Isn't that a man's name?" someone muttered – she thought

it might have been George – but Ash ignored it.

"You're a hologram, aren't you? Being projected from somewhere else?" He nodded, so she continued, "Would you mind explaining who you are, and what on earth is going on here?"

"Ah, yes. Well." The figure cleared his throat self-importantly, then began. "I am Doctor Osvaldo Walker, world-renowned sociologist and one of the rare few to have access to an inter-periodical matter movement device, that is, a time-travel device. You three are fortunate enough to have been selected for a study of, aha, *historical* proportions."

"I knew it," George muttered from beside her.

But Ash had quite a different perspective. "No, *I* knew it," she snapped, pointing her finger shakily at the holographic figure. "I knew I'd end up somewhere like this, with someone who should seem trustworthy spinning me a tale that I can't help but believe, with the whole thing being secretly recorded, of course.

"And then at the end of it, it'll go live on the internet or for some stupid reality show, and everyone will laugh at how I was the idiot who believed in time travel. Well, I won't do it." Rant finished, she set her hands on her hips. "So you're the idiot, aren't you? Because you picked the wrong person to play games with."

The other two stood in baffled silence, but Dr Walker looked at her almost with approval. "I expected that you'd respond like this, you and the Grecian from 26 BC, but for quite different reasons. You, because your culture is notoriously slow to accept anything that seems even slightly supernatural, and the Grecian because he would have thought me a god, and not accepted that he'd simply time-travelled." He smirked, straightening his purple jacket once more (although it didn't need it). "Although I can understand the mistake."

Ash still wasn't convinced, although she had a growing dislike of this half-person. "I don't know about any Grecian. There's just the three of us – and you're trying to convince us that we've time-travelled."

"I knew it," George said again more emphatically. "It was the only explanation!"

"Not quite," the doctor corrected him. "Your companions came up with explanations that made sense to them at the time, although they hadn't had the advantage of seeing my little room here. They were wrong, of course, which can be forgiven as they didn't know any better. Now they do, a degree of acceptance is required." He looked at both girls sternly.

"I do not understand," Anne blurted out. "How is it that you-"

"No, I'm not an elf, fairy or any kind of supernatural creature. I am a mere human like yourselves. Well, rather more intelligent and advanced in every way, but otherwise, like yourselves. Although as I previously said, I do understand your confusion."

"I was not going to ask that," Anne said, lifting her chin. "I merely wished to know where your legs are."

They all looked down at the point where he disappeared into the table.

"I'm a recording. I don't *need* legs," he explained irritably. "I can make myself fit full figure on the table, but then I look like a leprechaun and no one takes me seriously."

"Indeed," George said. He looked either angry or amazed, or maybe a bit of both. "Then perhaps you'd be so kind as to tell us why we're here?"

The hologram nodded. "Since you've asked and it suits me to do so, I will tell you a tale of- *Ashlea O'Reilly, that door is not going to work until I tell it to!* So you may as well come and listen."

Ash backed away from the exit ladder and tried to look interested. "Of course. Please go ahead."

The hologram looked pleased to have an audience. "Very well. My tale begins nineteen months ago, not five miles from this very point, where an eminent and respected scientist, that is, myself, was gifted with the opportunity to use a very rare, highly restricted time-travel device. Of course, knowing I should only have it for a maximum of ninety days as is the usual rule in such cases, I proposed a plan, a study of *historical* proportions, as I said earlier, ha ha. The selection process was arduous and time consuming..."

Rather like his speech, Ash thought, but didn't interrupt.

And he talked, and talked, and waved his arms around a little, and generally looked very pleased with himself.

About ten minutes later he finished with, "And that's how we came to this point."

Ash looked around the room. Her brain was hurting, and George and Anne looked as vacant as Ash felt. It wasn't that she was stupid, but the words the doctor used didn't make any *sense*. "Could you repeat that please, in very simple words?"

"In *Anglish*?" George added with a pained expression on his face. "As succinctly as possible."

Dr Walker reared back as much as the table setting would allow him, distinctly offended. "Indeed. What of you, little Tudar girl? Do *you* also need it explained again?"

Anne shook her head. "It made perfect sense to me, although I confess I am disappointed that you are not a fairy creature. You would have made a marvellous brownie."

He looked unsure of whether to be offended, but finally smiled. "Of course I would have. Then perhaps you would explain it to your less able companions?"

"OK, she is *definitely* in on this," Ash muttered, looking at the girl with folded arms. "Go on then. Make sense of what he just said."

Anne lifted her chin. "Very well. The year is twenty-one-fifty-five...and we've been taken along with nine others from different time periods for some form of testing, I'm not certain what. I didn't understand that part. But something has gone wrong and there aren't but three of us."

Dr Walker nodded approvingly. "Indeed. And while the study's intent was to see the natural interactions when each subject was brought out of their environment, as the transfer failed for most of the others, I have had to, as you say, 'wing it'. And thus you are here, speaking with me. Are there any questions?"

Ash opened her mouth to speak, and he added quickly, "You can have one each. Go on, Regency man."

George looked baffled. "Why do you call me that?"

"Because that's how future generations will summarize your time period. Now you, Millennial girl. What's your question?"

"I say," George interrupted. "That wasn't my question! I had another one."

"And yet you asked it, and I answered," Dr Walker shot back. "Don't test me on this, or I'll leave you where you are. Millennial, your question?"

He meant Ash. There were so many things she could have asked – the first one being 'do you really expect us to believe this rubbish' – but instead she found herself saying, "You do realise this is kidnapping, don't you?"

Dr Walker looked at her down his long, walnut-brown nose. "Is that really the one question you want to ask?"

"No!" Ash quickly corrected, "When are you going to let us go home?"

"Oh, he let *her* ask a second question," George muttered, but Dr Walker ignored him.

"I will send you home to the very moment you left – *after* you've done what I require."

George had grown progressively angrier since the appearance of the…whatever this person was. He claimed to be human (although the fact he stood *in* the table was distracting) and with every word he spoke, he made George feel more and more trapped and helpless.

"What you require?" he burst out finally. "What can we

possibly do for you that you can't already do for yourself?"

"Well," the doctor agreed, "it's true that I know more about the universe and the mysteries of the human mind than all of you will in your lifetimes combined, but there is a question I do need answered at this point. It pertains to why *you three* are here, but the others stopped partway through their transfers."

"Oh, Hades," Miss O'Reilly murmured. "It doesn't involve probing, does it?"

The doctor shuddered theatrically. "I've no interest in touching any of your diseased, ancient bodies, not at all. To think, the viruses, the bacteria…"

"Excuse me," she retorted, looking as offended as George felt. "I don't have any diseases! I'm very healthy!"

Dr Walker held up a hand and began to count on his fingers. "To start with, you carry HSV-1 also known as the cold sore virus, Cytomegalovirus, the varicella-zoster virus also known as chicken pox – do I need to go on?"

"Please don't," she said, slumping her shoulders. "I get it. I'm gross."

He waved a hand dismissively. "Don't feel bad about it. Most ancient peoples of this area are short, unattractively pale, and disease-carrying. It's not just you."

"That's quite enough," George interrupted. He had no particular love for Miss O'Reilly, but the arrogance of the man was infuriating, and that last statement had insulted all three of them. "The ethics of this whole thing aside, what is it you need from us? To the point, if you will."

"Very well." The man steepled his hands in front of him, looking at the three of them seriously. "Something has happened in the last two weeks, something that disrupted the proper transmission of all twelve of you, and something which has prevented me from updating this recording. I need-"

"Wait," Lady Anne interrupted. "You said there were others that didn't come all the way through. Was one perhaps a tall, screaming lady with a thin nightgown, and another a man with a sword and a big beard?"

"Miss Xanthia Nightingale, and Harald Red-Beard," Dr Walker agreed, then sighed. "What a shame. The dynamics would have been incredible."

"No ghosts, then," Lady Anne said with some disappointment.

And thank Deias for that, George thought emphatically.

"Dynamics?" Miss O'Reilly interrupted. She had this angry, intent look on her face – an expression she'd carried almost the whole way through this experience, George noted. "The Viking tried to kill me! If he'd come through the whole way I'd have been cut in half! What kind of insight would that give you?"

"That Millennials are too slow to dodge a poxy Viking with a sword?" Dr Walker suggested. "Never mind. Now what I need of you all, is to find out what went wrong in the last two weeks-"

"A Viking?" Lady Anne squealed in horror. "A Northman? All they do is kill and plunder and destroy! The Eternal One save us from the wrath of the Northmen!"

"Oh, for Chaos's sake!" the man finally shouted. "Harald Red-Beard was a settler. A settler, not a raider, which was why he was in the damned area at all instead of up in the fjords eating lutefisk. He was in the right place at the right time with no one to notice he was missing, as were all of you!

"Now will you all just shut up for a minute so I can talk? Almost two years of preparation went into the study, and now circumstances outside of my control have left me with *you* lot. And it's not as if I can just restart the experiment now. I'll have to work with what I've got." He glared at them. "Fortunately my great mind can make use of even the feeblest materials. And let me remind you, I choose whether to send you home. So you'd better cooperate, is that understood?"

George understood that the man had lost his veneer of kindness, if it had ever been there, and that in this case they did *not* have the power. "Understood," he clipped out, and the two girls nodded their heads.

"Good." Dr Walker calmed. "Now this is what I want you to do…"

In the small town nearby, a young man strolled nonchalantly out of one of the larger, more impressive houses to stand in the centre of the figure-eight. Most of the others had gone inside now the day was coming to a close, and he stood relaxed, hands in pockets while the last Noble walked past, looking down at him curiously from his much greater height.

The young man gave the dark-haired Noble a reverential nod. "My lord Hadur."

The huge Noble narrowed his eyes, then nodded back. "Islo, servant of Kadeon."

Hadur continued walking to the far end of the village, but Islo knew it was his cue to move on. He quickly checked around him for the visitors – his informant had insisted that they'd be here around about now – but there was no one out of the ordinary, and certainly not *that* out of the ordinary as he'd been told.

Not today, then. He'd be back tomorrow, and if the visitors weren't there…that was their problem. He'd done his part.

So Islo stretched as though he was just enjoying the cool evening air, then turned and sauntered back into the building he'd come from.

Back in the bunker, the three 'lucky selectees' stared in dismay at the tall, purple-coated figure.

"But if you don't know what's gone wrong," George pointed out, "then how are we supposed to find out?"

"That's your problem. Go and find my real self, if you need to. Just do it, and do it within a reasonable time. Then we can talk about returning you home."

"Why do you keep saying 'my real self'?" Ash exclaimed. "Why can't you just tell us now?"

"Or do it yourself," George added.

"Well, aren't you a clever little tag-team," Dr Walker sneered. "Did you know, Regency man, that Millennial females have a romanticised view of gentlemen of your time period? Due to your silly films and the lies of Jean Austen, no doubt.

"But as for why I say 'my real self', it's because that's what I mean. I'm a recording, you imbeciles. I told you that at the start. All I can tell you now is what my true self knew at the time of the recording, that is, two weeks ago. And my *real* self hasn't come to update the recording since. So anything that's happened since then, I don't know about."

There were several seconds where Ash flushed with embarrassment over the comment he'd made regarding Regency gentlemen, and also tried to take in what he'd said. A recording. "But how can you be talking to us if you're a recording?"

"I'm a *clever* recording. I carry the personality and knowledge of the original, at the point in which the recording was made. Now is that understood, or do I need to explain it again?"

There was a long silence, then Anne started to cry. "I don't want to go to the village. What if the giants eat us?"

"There aren't any giants, fool," the doctor snapped. "Everyone's taller than you here. Deal with it."

And then everyone lost their tempers.

"Mind your manners!" George snapped back. "This is a lady you are speaking to!"

"And there are too giants," Anne insisted. "We all saw them. Huge, and one had green skin and long white braids!"

The hologram had begun to flicker as though static was disrupting the signal, and the lights in the bunker flashed on and off as if in sympathy. "That's just ridiculous. And *you* mind your manners-" and whatever he would have said next was lost to static.

Meanwhile Ash slowly began to creep back towards the ladder. The lights lit it up to its round door at the top, but it was impossible to tell if it was locked or not, and chances were that Dr Walker (if that was his real name) was controlling it. As she moved she kept listening with half an ear to the conversation below.

"They would too notice if we were gone!" Anne was saying amid tears. "I'm to marry one of Queen Marian's favourites within the week!"

"And I'm the brother of a viscount!" George roared. "People notice if we disappear!"

"Not when the Tudar girl is running from an unwanted marriage?" Dr Walker taunted. "And you, Regency man, just had a dreadful business disappointment that cast you into the depths of despair... Even the Millennial would be just one more missing foreigner, forgotten within six weeks when the next news item came up!"

"By Jove, you've planned this well," George declared. "But you won't get away with this!"

Dr Walker had planned it well – they'd all planned their stories well, whether George and Anne were lying or crazy. Oh Hades, what a mess.

Ash had been blasted with so much nonsensical information that she didn't even know what to believe or not to believe. OK, she *didn't* believe that she'd time-travelled, but there was no doubt that someone was playing an elaborate game with her.

Only it didn't feel like a game. As she'd thought earlier, if it was a game, either Regency Man and Tudar Girl were both amazing actors, or they were both crazy...

The aforementioned crazy people were still in the middle of a massive argument with a flickering projection. The two males were shouting at each other and waving their arms in the air, and

Anne had stopped crying and was now looking under the table as if she could find the hologram's legs.

Ash quietly climbed to the top of the ladder and pushed on the door. It was stuck fast, and she felt around as if to find a release latch. This whole place seemed secure enough to outlast the apocalypse…except for the unfortunate lack of toilets and food stores.

Suddenly Dr Walker's voice rose over the din. "Get down from there, Millennial! You're damaging private property!"

Not yet, she wasn't. Ash shoved at the door with her shoulder, trying to put her whole weight against it.

It was a mistake. Her foot slipped and she fell hard, hitting the far side of the tunnel, bouncing off and then stumbling all the way down. It was a miracle that she didn't land on her head on the hard floor but instead slapped her hand against the wall as a last bid to catch her balance.

"Ashlea Jane O'Reilly," a pleasant woman's voice came. "Date of birth June thirteen, nineteen-ninety-three. Anglish. Eirish. Italien descent."

Ash looked in alarm to where her hand still pressed against the wall. She'd landed against a plain white square just the right size for her outstretched fingers, and the outline shone red.

"What did you do?" Anne cried in alarm.

"I don't know!" But Ash didn't move her hand away. It must be some kind of sensor…

The pleasant woman's voice continued, "Do you wish to take authority of this structure?"

"No!" Dr Walker shouted. "No, take your hand away!"

Ash looked at the others.

"Say yes," George urged.

Anne nodded.

Ash turned back to the sensor square. "Yes," she replied just as pleasantly. "I would like to take authority."

Suddenly the whole room went dark, right down to every

single screen. Dr Walker was gone, and Ash couldn't even see her hand in front of her face.

Anne started screaming, and Ash heard the exasperation in George's voice. "By Jove, don't we have any lights in here?"

Ash cleared her throat. "Um. Lights, please."

The lights flicked on.

"Also display the map of the forest. And the surveillance screens." Ash paused. "But don't let anyone else in without my permission."

"Understood," the voice responded. "Do you have any further requests?"

Ash was starting to enjoy herself now. Maybe it was all a big game after all, but for the moment she was winning. "Why, yes I do. Are there any bathroom facilities?"

A previously unseen door slid open just next to the exit, displaying a bathroom in shiny steel tones. It reminded Ash of something from a spaceship, but was no doubt a copy of the average Tokyo bathroom. "Excuse me," she said with dignity to the other two. "I'll be just a minute."

Two and a half minutes later, Ash opened the door again to find George and Anne standing directly outside, both staring at her with intent expressions.

"By the Rood, you've returned," Anne exclaimed in relief. "I thought you'd been eaten up by the steel wall. You said you'd be a minute, but I'm certain you were longer than that."

"I told you, it's just a doorway," George told her, but Ash could see equal relief on his face. "What happened? How did you make Dr Walker leave?"

Feeling a little awkward over them standing *right there*, Ash moved out of the doorway and told it to close after her. "Um...just the sensor. It's touch activated."

George followed her across the room, looking very intent. In the small space and with everything that had just happened, it was a little overwhelming. "I don't know what that means, but I don't believe you understand the import of what we are facing here. That *man* wants us to go down to that village that we just fled from, and…what are you doing up there?"

"Seeing if I can open the door." But Ash hadn't even reached the top of the ladder this time when the door slid open, revealing the darkness outside. "Oh."

"Is there a problem?" he asked, then answered his own question. "Oh. I hadn't realised it was that late. It was first thing in the morning when I was taken."

"Right." Ash closed the door again, then climbed back down the ladder, resigned to her fate. "I think we're going to have to stay the night. What are the chances that there's food and bedding in here?"

✿

Anne thought that Ash had meant the comment as a jest, but as it turned out, the girl had been right. There was food – of a sort – and bedding – of a sort, as two oddly curved, narrow pallets slid out of the wall once requested, as though enchanted. Although Ash might insist 'twas no enchantment, Anne saw no difference.

"Twenty-one-fifty-five, my arse," Ash said rudely. "This isn't too far off anything I've already seen back home." It sounded like even after everything they'd experienced, Ash still didn't believe she'd left her time behind.

Anne exchanged a weary glance with George. The crudeness of the common folk sometimes had to be overlooked, especially when dinner was at stake.

But unfortunately *getting* to the food was the hard part. They made awkward seats on the floor, Anne spreading out her wide skirts so that they covered several square feet of space. She looked up to where Ash was sitting cross-legged on the ground in those almost skin-tight trousers, then quickly glanced away again. It was scandalous, simply scandalous, and Anne felt *embarrassed* for the girl, especially with Mr Seymour in the room. Did she not know how indecently she presented herself?

Mayhap not. Unconcerned, Ash passed out odd little parcels along with flasks of a flavourless liquid, then told them to remove the parcels' packaging and eat up.

Easier said than done. After several minutes of prodding at the grey slab she'd been given, Anne gave up in despair. "By the Rood, I cannot get through the food's covering. Plas-tik, did you say?"

"I think that *is* the food," Ash replied, putting down her own piece in disgust. "Hades, they might have the technology down, but their food sucks." The other two stared at her, and after a moment she corrected herself. "The food is very bad."

"I quite agree," Anne said desolately. "'Tis simply dreadful. Oh, for a slice of honeyed manchet bread, or even an apple."

"I was thinking more of a solid Anglish meal," George commented thoughtfully. "Soup to begin with, then three types of meat, potatoes, and freshly baked bread, with some kind of fruit tart to finish. Apple, perhaps, like yours, my lady."

"Good Deias," Ash muttered, putting her own food aside. The girl had circles under her eyes to match their dark green colour, and she'd taken off that little flat cap to display wavy dark hair bound in a dishevelled bun. "This is a bit much, isn't it? I don't know how I'm going to explain this at work tomorrow."

"Didn't you hear the man?" Mr Seymour asked, putting down his half-chewed slab. "He'll send us straight back to the moment we left, once we've done what he wants."

And risked the giants, Anne thought in dismay. It almost made her lose her appetite. "I do not wish to go back," she admitted. "But for my sister Elspeth, I have nothing. My husband has just passed, and I'm to be married once more to another stranger."

Ash spat out the drink she'd just taken. "Chaos, are you

saying you've already been married and widowed? You look about fourteen!"

"I've passed sixteen years," Anne said with dignity. "I did mention my late husband to you when we first met, but you appear to have forgotten. And would you be so good as to watch your language? 'Tis uncouth and common to swear so." She thought about it, then added kindly, "But as I said before, mayhap you cannot help yourself. Our time spent together can benefit you, then?"

The other girl must have been struck silent by Anne's graciousness, because she just sat with her mouth open for several long seconds before closing it. "I thought the husband was part of the game," she murmured as if talking to herself. "And there are so many things I could say right now, but I'll just leave it at that, shall I? I'm tired; I'm going to bed. Use the bathroom if you want to, but don't be freaked out by the automatic flush."

None of the last part made sense, so Anne decided it meant agreement. Ash moved to take one of the narrow pallets where it disappeared into the wall, sitting on it and beginning to remove her loose plain jacket as if 'twas nothing at all. Anne looked at Mr Seymour anxiously. He hadn't seemed to notice yet – that the woman was disrobing or that she'd taken the bed clearly intended for those of higher rank – but it was surely a matter of time.

"Ash!"

The girl paused, her jacket half off her freckled shoulders. Underneath she wore the barest pink chemise, some sort of striped lacy thing, and it showed everything, even her *armpits*. "What is it now?"

Well, there was no need to be foul-tempered. "You mustn't disrobe in public," Anne whispered urgently. "Most certainly not in front of a man."

Anne's whisper didn't have its intended effect, because the man in question looked up, and his face went blank for a moment before flushing pink and glancing away. "Oh! I beg your pardon."

Point proven. But Ash just rolled her eyes as if it didn't even matter. "Come on. As if I'm going to sleep in that jacket. It's full of buttons and zips that stab into me if I lie on them. Anyway, it's just a shirt. What's the big deal?"

"You're not wearing a corset," Anne whispered. "That's the problem! Now put that jacket back on immediately! You look like a harlot!"

"I look like a what?"

"A trollop! A loose woman! You *must* cover yourself!"

"Oh for the love of-, mind your own business, Anne! I don't tell you to pull up that dress of yours or to take a shower, although you *clearly* need one!"

"I couldn't take a shower, I wouldn't know where to find one or even what that is!" Lady Anne sounded shrill now, but was still clearly trying to keep her voice down. "But I do know what is right and decent, and this is not it!"

The two women continued to argue over what constituted suitable clothing, but George couldn't get that one idea out of his mind. No corset. Miss O'Reilly wasn't wearing a corset, and while it had meant that with the jacket on she'd been able to be mistaken for a male, without the jacket her figure was left so natural and unobscured that...

George coughed, abruptly standing. "Forgive me," he interrupted, still averting his eyes. "I would not enter a debate about something as *feminine* as women's clothing except that it appears that I am partially the cause of the debate. Might I assure you that while, ahem, *corsets* are quite common and expected in both my and Lady Anne's time, I see that they are, ah, not in yours. In which case, I should not wish to...enforce my beliefs upon you."

"So good of you," Miss O'Reilly said with a definite hint of sarcasm, although he noted that she'd pulled the blanket up around her shoulders. "What a gentleman you are."

"Naturally," he agreed. "I was raised as such, and to treat all women with respect, no matter their class."

"So kind," she muttered. Oddly, she didn't sound like she meant it.

"Not all men are so lenient," Lady Anne said, looking at him with approval. "Mayhap in our unusual circumstances you are right to think so."

"Of course." George looked at the remaining narrow bed. Although it was dark outside in the forest, it had been full daylight when he'd been taken, and he wasn't nearly ready to sleep yet. "I believe I'll explore this room further, with your permission, my lady."

"Oh yes," she agreed. "I'd like to see what further marvels it holds. I've never seen such wonders in my life."

"I quite agree." He'd already worked out how to get the room to respond to his own voice as well – by placing his hand on that white square – and there was just so much here he'd never even imagined.

They explored the far side of the room for a while in comfortable silence. George had never spent so long alone with two unmarried women, and at home it would be considered a little scandalous. Although he could have slanted it that Ash was Lady Anne's chaperone.

He glanced over at the taller girl's back, covered in one of the dark blue blankets that came with the room. She'd been still for some time now, but didn't have that relaxed breathing that came with deep sleep.

"Tell me," Lady Anne asked curiously. "Are you of any relation to James Seymour? The third husband of Queen Henrietta the Eighth, that is."

"Fourth cousins a couple of times removed." It was one of George's mother's favourite subjects: how the family was related to royalty. She'd found links to thirty-eight kings of Europe, and that was only in the last eight generations. Well, it was good she had a hobby, especially now her husband was gone.

"Oh. Did you hear..."

"How he passed away?" He hid a rueful smile. What was old news to him would be all new to Anne, and he realised with some shock that he'd have to take care in what he said. "Henrietta's six husbands are well known to all, my lady."

"Oh?" Lady Anne glanced at him under her eyelashes. "And what of her daughter, Marian? Did you know that they call her Bloody Marian for all the deaths under her rule?"

Actually, George's knowledge of history was excellent. "Anyone in particular?"

"My late husband, the Earl of Longford." Lady Anne looked sad for a brief moment, then shrugged. "He would not convert to the Universal Church, you see. He was a staunch Protestor and would not accept any other way. But at least he was old, and had a full life before he was executed."

"A full life?" he echoed in horror. "How old was he?"

"Thirty-two, mayhap thirty-three. Old enough for grey hair."

George lifted a hand self-consciously to his own temples. His older brother Edward had the same fair hair, and at twenty-nine was already beginning to grey. He'd only just married to a widow of George's own age, and this girl was talking as if Edward must be coming to the end of his life. By Jove, the world had changed. "I see."

Urgh. George made a note to himself that when he returned home, he wouldn't court any woman more than five years younger than himself. After all, he didn't plan to marry until he was at least thirty himself. He amended that to ten years younger – he wasn't interested in twenty-five-year-old spinsters, after all.

They pulled open yet another drawer, this one filled with clear globes. Each held a different leaf or insect in its midst, and the carrier acted like a magnifying glass.

"It feels like it ought to be heavy, like glass," George

commented, weighing one in his hand. "But it's as light as cotton."

Lady Anne picked one up and it slipped from her hand to land on the hard floor. He cringed, waiting for the smash, but instead it sat where it had landed. "How odd. It's changed shape to fit where it fell." And indeed the globe was now flattened on one side, but as she picked it up once more it became again a perfect sphere.

"Incredible."

"Marvellous, yes," Lady Anne agreed. "If only I could take something back with me afterwards, or no one shall believe me."

Something pricked George's memory, and he looked down at her curiously, at her rumpled clothing so carefully put together but also so very, very old-fashioned, and even the tiny frame that must have come from poor nutrition as a child. "Did you say your husband was the Earl of Longford, who lived in Renwick Castle?"

"Yes, that's right."

"What is your full name, if you don't mind me asking? The 'C' doesn't stand for Covington, does it?"

"Why, yes it does," she replied in surprise. "Do you know my family?"

His interest in history meant he'd learned a few things, yes. "Perhaps. I do recall there have been several women of the same name, though. One of them was quite notably burned at the stake as a witch along with her Moorish lover." He frowned, trying to remember more details, then saw the look of horror on her face.

"Not from your time," he corrected quickly, realising how his careless comment had affected her. "I'm certain of that." No, the Anne of Covington who burned was the third earl's wife, or perhaps the fourth. He was quite, quite sure. "Anne is a common name."

Lady Anne relaxed. "Indeed it is."

George had no idea how much time passed as the light didn't change, but at some point he reached the last hidden drawer, then looked up and saw that both girls were sleeping. There was something about seeing others sleep that made him feel tired too, so he made an awkward bed with his jacket and lay down on the floor. He could explore more tomorrow.

George slept. When he awoke some time later, the whole room was very dim, lit with just the faintest of pinkish light. Someone was moving quietly nearby, and he thought, *the servants are up already. I've a few hours more to sleep.*

But then he tried to roll over and realised that his bed was dreadfully uncomfortable. It felt like the floor, in fact, although someone seemed to have given him a blanket at some point.

"You can take the bed," the servant said in an odd accent, the vowels all flattened. "I've slept enough."

The little oddities added up, and all of a sudden George remembered the events of the previous day. Had that *really* all happened? "Screens on," he muttered, and then suddenly the whole room was flooded with green light as the forest was displayed from fifty different views.

Yes, it was real all right. Time travel, complete with giants, bald doctors, and women dressed as men.

"Not now, Maura," Lady Anne muttered from her bed. Her head covering had come off overnight, displaying violently orange-red hair that stood up on the side of her head. "I said I wanted to sleep in if there's late mass."

"I take it you're ready to get up," he heard Miss O'Reilly say. He turned to see she was wearing her jacket and cap once more, although this time she wore her hair in a short braid over one shoulder. "Just tell the computer to lock up after you, will you?"

"Are you leaving *now*?" George asked in dismay, lurching to his feet faster than was comfortable at this time of the morning. "We should go together. Dr Walker said he'd return us after-"

But she was already climbing the ladder, and he heard the door slide open. A shaft of daylight streamed in. "Perfect, the sun's just coming up. I'd better get moving."

"Miss O'Reilly," he tried again, more sternly this time. "We must not separate. We need to work together."

"Sure we do," she called down. "Have a fun life, Mr Darcy, and maybe wear sunglasses next time you startle someone holding pepper spray, alright?"

Suddenly Lady Anne was awake. "Ash isn't leaving, is she?"

"Not if I have something to do with it." Pushing aside the remnants of sleep, George scrambled up the ladder after the girl. She was tall, and she'd made it quite far before he could catch up. "Miss O'Reilly! *Ashlea!*"

She sighed and came to a halt. "What do you want?"

"What do I...?" George shook his head in dismay. He didn't know what he wanted, except that there were only three of them, and Miss O'Reilly seemed a little more comfortable in this time period than he or Lady Anne. "You're going the wrong way for the village," he replied finally. "You'll need to go downhill."

She shoved her hands in her pockets, shrugging. "I'm not going to the village, so that hardly matters, does it? I'm going to get to a high point, then find my way back to my car. And it better still be there when I find it."

"By Jove," he said in amazement. "You still don't believe we've time-travelled, do you? You think this is all some kind of elaborate jest, with yourself as the target. That's remarkably..." Pigheaded? Stubborn? Self-centred? "...*determined* of you."

She smiled tightly. "Isn't it just. But incredibly, I cannot believe I have time-travelled, which makes you either crazy or a liar, and either way I don't feel the need to stick around. Now if you'll excuse me..."

She turned to walk away, and behind George Lady Anne emerged from the tunnel, blinking in the light like a mole in daylight. "But I'm not ready to go yet," she said plaintively. "I need someone to help me dress. I don't have my maid."

They both watched as the only other female present strode away at great speed, and George sighed. There went the chaperone. "I can't say I've had any experience fixing ladies' hair, but I'll do my best."

High, high above the forest, someone else watched the entire scene. The distance was immense, but the man's vision was good enough to take in every detail even through the covering trees, and he clucked his tongue in dismay. "Stubborn girl, Ash."

But then he'd seen that coming, and so this argument and separation had been expected, even planned for.

It was just an argument, and considering all the things they *could* have said, not even a bad one. But it had separated them, and while George Seymour hadn't realised the importance of what he'd been saying, he'd been right. They *did* need to work together, and they needed to get to that meeting point.

Seeing wasn't always believing. In Ash's case, and for so many from her time, it would take a good slap upside the head before a truly new idea could be accepted. It wasn't enough for her to just see the change. She needed to experience it.

The watcher looked uphill to where the trees were rustling as if parted by a great force moving through them, then smiled, clicking his tongue. A small, brightly coloured bird came to sit on his shoulder, and he nudged his chin towards the scene below.

"Go on then, 'festive bird'. Give her a show."

SEEING IS BELIEVING

Ash strode across the damp ground, avoiding the occasional patch of mud. It had rained overnight, but then it was Angland, wasn't it? If it stopped raining for more than a couple of days, people started calling it a drought.

"It *is*," she said aloud, almost viciously. "It *is* Angland, and it is twenty-twelve, and I just have to find the right direction to get home."

That was assuming she hadn't actually been kidnapped after all. There had been that moment on the walking path where she'd stumbled, and then when she'd got up again, couldn't find the path. The idea that she'd been shot with a tranquillizer and then put *here* didn't seem too far-fetched anymore, although it would be a hard sell as an excuse for lateness to work.

Besides, there were so many other things that didn't fit. The one that hit Ash the most was the way Anne and George, or whoever they really were, spoke almost normally. Ash had seen enough period dramas to know that a few hundred years did make a difference in speech. It had to. She should barely be able to understand 'Lady Anne', if those Shakespeare plays were any example.

A bright flash of colour caught Ash's eye. It was the same kind of bird she'd seen earlier, right before she'd met (and assaulted) George. The green and red one with the beady-eyed stare. It flitted across the trees right in front of her face, stopping to stare at her in the way it had before, and then moved once again, close enough for her to almost get feathers in the face.

"Sheesh." Waving a hand as if to scare it off, she tried to take another step forward, but now it dove down to hover in front of her, almost like a hummingbird.

"*Peep.*"

Ash moved right to go around it; the bird moved right as well. She moved the other way, and it blocked her again…

"Fine, I get it," she told it irritably. Deias, even the animals were against her here. "I'm too close to your nest."

She moved as if to go the other direction, planning to take a detour around the area, and that was when she saw the footprint.

❧

Lady Anne sat on the single chair in the bunker, staring down at the map of the forest in front of them. "So this direction here," and she pointed to the far right of the map, "you say this is where you found us overlooking the town. I wonder why it doesn't display the town at all?"

"It's because we weren't supposed to see the town," George replied confidently. The style of the text he'd read last night was very different from what he was accustomed to, but it had given him enough of a picture to see what had happened. "We weren't even supposed to find this room, but it seems that Dr Walker allowed it just because the others had failed to arrive with us."

At least that was what George had assumed. If the man could bring them across time as he had, then surely he could also control whether they'd found the bunker or not.

"Oh." Lady Anne wrinkled her nose. George had offered to help her with her hair, but she'd declined, not that he blamed her. The stiff white cloth that had covered her hair yesterday was worse for wear, and every few minutes she'd reach up to straighten it, reminding him rather of his younger sister Amelia, back when she'd first had her hair put up like a lady. She probably didn't even realise she was doing it. "What I don't understand is how we're supposed to fix this. A device for travelling through time – I've never seen *anything* here before. How would I know how to make any changes? Ash might have, but she would run away, wouldn't she."

They both looked down at the map again, where the three little red beacons of light appeared to be clustered around the same area once more. "She didn't get very far, did she?" George said hopefully. "Perhaps she'll come back."

"Or mayhap she will not."

"Hmm. I had the impression that it wasn't the device itself that malfunctioned, that it may have been something external. Perhaps if we…"

Lady Anne looked up at him hopefully. "Yes?"

Really, George had *no idea at all*. But he was going to make something up, because the alternative was to admit defeat. Then suddenly the door slid open to the bunker, and familiar shoes were stomping their way down again.

"Alright, I'm back," Miss O'Reilly declared. She'd lost her cap somewhere, and she wore a general air of frazzled dishevelment. "I'm ready to play along."

"Play along?" Lady Anne asked in surprise. "With what?"

The older girl waved her hand vaguely. "With whatever is needed to get me out of here and back home, the sooner the better."

For a moment George was stunned, and he wondered if he'd somehow missed something important. "I thought you'd…" …decided they were 'crazy or liars'. "What made you come back?"

Miss O'Reilly shuddered. "I'll just call it a close encounter." They stared at her, and finally she sighed. "Alright. Well, first there was the footprint…"

It had been the biggest footprint Ash had ever seen on *any* creature, let alone a human. A shoe print, really; a metre in length and with a sole patterned like a honeycomb. She would have figured it was some fool stomping around with giant boots (and good luck not falling over doing *that*, unknown imaginary fool) except then she'd seen the giant.

It had been the same dark-haired one she'd seen in the town the day before, and he'd been less than ten feet away from her, moving purposefully through the trees and underbrush in the direction of the town, pushing greenery aside as he went like – well, like a twenty-foot tall giant in a forest.

He didn't seem frightening close up, although Ash couldn't shake her original impression of vaguely Viking clothing. He was human-like, though, right down to the way he scratched his backside as he'd walked.

She hadn't been able to move. *It's a trick, it's a trick,* she'd told herself over and over, but then the stupid festive bird still following her had let out an almighty SQUAWK and had caught the giant's attention. He'd turned and seen her, and they'd exchanged a stare across the short distance.

"It's a trick, it's a trick-"

But then it turned out Ash still had her habit of thinking out loud, because the giant had cocked his head to the side curiously. **"What's a trick?"** He'd had a very deep voice to go with his very large self, and looked like he could have done with a shave.

"Um…" And for some reason she hadn't been able to reply to that.

The giant had studied her for a few moments longer, then grunted. **"Who do you belong to?"**

"Um…myself?" she'd squeaked out, and he'd just kept staring.

But then finally he'd shrugged, then turned and walked away. Just walked away, shoving trees aside as he did, and never looked back.

"And then once he was out of sight I turned and ran here," Ash finished telling the others. It still felt like it *couldn't* have happened, but it had. Who had said that seeing was believing? Well, she wasn't so sure about that in general, but today…

"Does this mean you no longer believe us to be madmen or liars?" George asked, one eyebrow raised quizzically. He looked an inch away from saying 'I told you so'.

"Hey, I'm not saying I buy all of it, alright? The time travel thing…" She couldn't think about it, because it made her stomach clench in knots. "Don't ask me to believe that. Don't even *talk* about it."

"That is simply foolish!" Anne said loudly. "How can one-"

"I can't, OK? I *can't* think about it, because people who start to believe that kind of thing are thought crazy or really, really naïve." Like her father. Poor Dad. "But I'll go to the town with you. I won't do myself any favours looking for my car, I can see that now."

There was a silence, and Ash saw the moment when the others seemed to give in.

"I suppose we ought to leave then," George said in resignation. "Miss O'Reilly, you said that the giants weren't dangerous-"

"That one wasn't, anyway. And please, call me Ash. Only really old people use last names."

There was another long pause, because she seemed to always be pushing the boundaries with these two, then he sighed almost silently. "Ash is what you clean from a chimney, and is hardly a name for a lady- a woman. Although I'm accustomed to Ashley being a *male* name, perhaps I may call you that instead?"

"It's actually spelt with an A," Ash explained. "A-S-H-L-E-A. Not the male way, although it's pronounced the same."

George paused, looking a little pained, but finally gave in. "Very well…Ashlea. And you may call me George, if you wish."

Deias, if you wound the guy any tighter he'd pop. Ignoring what had felt like insults to her social status and name (and the fact she'd been thinking of him as George anyway, pretty much from the moment she'd known *his* name) she nodded. "George. Right."

She looked at Anne, who lifted her chin snootily. "I believe we were discussing giants," Anne said, pointedly avoiding the subject of names. "Although what I wish to know is why that one would ask who you belonged to? 'Tis an odd question."

"Rather like a pet," George added with a frown. "Or a farmer with sheep."

"I don't know." That *had* bothered Ash, but there were so many things that bothered her about the last eighteen hours that she couldn't focus on just one right now.

"It's probably a feudal thing," Dr Walker called from the tabletop. "With my extensive knowledge of societies-"

Anne let out a belated scream, making the hologram roll its eyes. "Oh, come on. Don't pretend you didn't know I was here the whole time."

"We *didn't* know," Ash insisted. Her heart was still pounding from the shock of his entry, and she'd had enough surprises for the whole year. "Do you have a secret camera?"

Dr Walker looked offended. "Of course not. I'm not a spy. I had audio only, but it was enough. Tudar girl, did you know that the fourth Countess-"

"That's enough," George cut in suddenly. "So you've got an opinion, do you? You've heard what we've said. Must we still go down to the town?"

"Of course you must. I'm just a recording; I can hardly carry out the study, can I?" He took on a distant, noble expression. "You'll need the full brilliance and wisdom of my true self for that. No, you must go to Iversley."

"Iversley?" Lady Anne burst out. "That strange little town is *Iversley?*"

George sympathised. *That* was Iversley? It was less than half the size that he had known it to be, and he hadn't seen any sign of the Great Houses still being there, of his home...not a single landmark was familiar. If the town they'd seen was Iversley, then his home was gone. His friends and family – warts and all, with some of them more wart than anything else – were gone. He felt a sudden lump in his throat, and struggled to keep his voice level as he responded. "I must say it's changed since I last saw it."

"Of course it has," the doctor replied arrogantly. "It was razed to the ground during the Great War and then rebuilt. In Ash's time it was barely even a town at all."

"The Great War?" Ashlea echoed, just as George burst out, "Razed to the ground?"

Dr Walker waved a hand dismissively. "Not *your* World War One, Millennial. Another Great War. And don't change the subject. Wars come and go, but giants, now…" He took on that distant expression once more. "That would be a truly ground-breaking study, aha, and I do use that pun intentionally. How on earth did giants develop from the societies we are already aware of? Did they use time travel themselves? Are they from the distant past, or perhaps the distant future? Did they-"

But George wasn't listening. He was thinking about the town of Iversley, razed to the ground. It would explain why he hadn't seen any familiar landmarks; they'd all been destroyed. Perhaps the very land itself had been changed too.

It was interesting how much could change in a day, he mused. He'd been ruined in a day – or rather, one day had shown the result of a year of bad luck and perhaps poor decisions. And now in the space of a few moments, he'd skipped over three hundred years.

Three. Hundred. Years. How many generations of his family

had lived and died in that nearby town? Not his own descendants, that was for sure. George had no children. He was as red-blooded as the next man, but he knew that the world was not kind to illegitimate children, and so had been very careful not to create any.

Unless he had managed to get back home, and had married and so forth, but how could he know?

It was disturbing to think that his own flesh and blood could be so close. He could look them in the face and never know their relationship to him.

The other two seemed just as subdued. It seemed Miss…*Ashlea* didn't entirely accept what had happened to them, but at least enough of it was getting through to impact her mood. Lady Anne in particular seemed very quiet.

"So what you're saying," Ashlea asked the man, "is that two weeks ago when you were last updated, this area was giant-free."

"Yes, of course it was giant-free." The hologram sighed and rubbed his eyes. His image had started to flicker like a flame in the breeze. "Maybe the giants arrived, or maybe some people simply-…grew. There must be more to this than I thought. Do try to find the real me in the town; I'll be around there somewhere. Make sure you go right in to the government buildings, or perhaps the hospital, and you'll find me. Unless I died." He frowned suddenly. "That shouldn't bother me, as I'm a recording and don't have feelings, but I must say it does.

"Of course!" He perked up suddenly. "I am simply exhibiting the emotions that my true self would feel if he heard that he had died. Not that he *has* died, simply that he may have."

Government or hospital? That couldn't be difficult to find – there were only a dozen buildings in total. "Which of the buildings are the government ones?"

"Near the centre of the city, off Mineglove Street," the doctor replied promptly. "And the hospital isn't far from there. It has an enormous sign – you can't miss it, and your translation devices will help you understand the language." He paused. "Or perhaps that's only audio translations. Oh, well. You'll find out soon enough."

The three of them exchanged baffled glances. "Translation devices?" Ashlea echoed, touching her ear. "What translation devices?"

"And how can there be a city centre?" Lady Anne asked with a laugh. "There are but a dozen dwellings in the whole town."

Dr Walker stared at the three of them, then rolled his eyes quite rudely. "You really don't know anything at all, do you?"

⁂

"Fancy a whole city being beneath the earth," Anne commented in awe as they walked away from the now sealed underground room bunker, heading downhill towards the new, unrecognisable Iversley.

They'd heard the lid lock with a distinctive *click* afterwards – the walking doctor making it clear that in some ways at least, he still had control. Six centuries may have passed, but men had not changed all that much, it appeared.

But 'twas what he had revealed that still had Anne reeling. "How would they breathe? How would they have light without burning the place down? Like a whole city of mole people…"

She shuddered, tempted to be afraid until she remembered that the locals had looked perfectly normal. Except for the swarthy skin, scanty garb and enormous size of some of them, that was.

Mr Seymour however seemed almost amused. "A city of troglodytes. Fascinating. It does at least explain where they were all going, doesn't it?"

Anne was going to say that the doors must be too small to fit any of those giants, but then Ash spoke instead. "Aren't you guys bothered that he stuck something in our heads? Translation devices – where I'm from, this would be kidnapping and assault."

"So you do believe it," George said triumphantly. "And my name isn't Guys. It's George."

"I didn't- I know what your name is. Guys just means- ...people. And I'm not saying I believe it, just that if it was true, then it would have been assault. Implant with a...useful item." Ash frowned, apparently as unclear of what she was talking about as Anne. "Although if it was real, it might actually be useful..."

Anne lost interest in their conversation, instead choosing to watch the scenery around her as she tripped along, holding up the front of her full skirts so that she didn't stumble. By the Rood, she'd not had this much exercise in...how long had she been a countess? Two years of walking quietly and demurely, and being a lady...which she was, of course. But this was such a *change*, and 'twas not all bad.

Anne decided in that moment that she may as well enjoy the time she had here. She settled into a steady rhythm, walking quite far ahead of the other two (who were so caught up in debate that they didn't seemed to realise that they were both vastly tall, and so could walk faster if they wished to), and marvelled at how she'd ended up in this place.

Mayhap 'twas not truly enchantment that brought them here, but 'twas something so far beyond her understanding that it *felt* like enchantment. Even now as she walked along, she quite felt like she was in another world rather than simply her own land in six centuries' time.

Past George and Ash's squabbling behind her, there wasn't *quite* perfect silence: there were birds and the sound of the wind in the trees, but not a hint of human occupation. There was no one talking or shouting or fighting (besides those two), no dogs barking, no one asking her questions (the servants) or telling her what to do (her late husband or mother-in-law).

She was almost alone, and that almost *never* happened in a castle the size of Renwick. No one was watching her and expecting her behaviour to always be perfect, or acting scandalised if she accidentally let off wind. 'Twas oddly liberating, knowing that she could be as cross as she liked, ignore all those lessons in appropriate behaviour, because there was no one around who would care or even notice.

So with more than a little glee, Anne took off the wrinkled, stiff, overly-starched coif she wore every day, and quietly dropped it off the side of the path. Heavens above, she'd already broken so many rules on this adventure, what was one more?

And as she approached the cliff overlooking the town, she found she was now more excited than afraid…

❧

"Good cattle is a sign of wealth and position," George was saying as they walked along, waving his hands emphatically. "Why, to simply say that horses are smelly and impractical – where I'm from, such a statement would unintentionally show one's station in life." He paused. "If one's speech and dress don't already show such, that is."

Ash still didn't understand how he called horses 'cattle' and cattle…well, whatever he called those. It was probably the same as how he hadn't understood 'guys'…or pretended that he didn't, anyway. But the part of her that believed all of this was an elaborate joke was growing quieter and quieter, and while she didn't dwell on the idea of George and Anne being time-travellers, she didn't argue with it either.

"Hardly anyone rides horses anymore," she replied instead. "They're not allowed on the roads because they'd panic if they heard a car. Only…" *Only rich people have them*, she was going to say, then realised she'd be proving his point.

George didn't seem to notice, luckily. "What are these 'cahs' you keep talking about?" he asked, pronouncing it without rolling the 'r' like she did. "Is it an animal, or a machine?"

"It's a…" She tried to think of how best to explain a car to someone who had never seen one before. "Like a horseless carriage that can go faster than any horse could manage."

"How fast?"

Ash thought about it. How fast *could* they go, or how fast were people actually supposed to drive them? She decided to go for the second option. "Easily 120 kph, which is what, sixty-five miles per hour?"

"That's incredible!" George exclaimed, forgetting to be supercilious for a moment. "I would love to see one of those!"

Ash bit back a smile. He was cute when he was enthusiastic – it was just a shame he could be such a pig. "You might get a chance after all. If Dr Walker was telling the truth, then I'm sure the town will have something similar." Or better, most likely; like flying cars. If the town had those, *then* she'd believe they'd time-travelled.

Up ahead Anne came to a halt, her silhouette standing out against the sunny valley like an upside-down tulip. She'd been going at quite a pace considering that she was seriously hampered by those massive skirts, restrictive corset and short legs.

She'd lost her head cover somewhere along the way, Ash noticed. It made her look younger, and perhaps a little more approachable.

"Considering your over-long legs, you two walk as slowly as crippled crones," Anne called out. "Come, before we lose the light."

It must have been Anne's idea of a joke, because it was barely eight in the morning by Ash's guess. Not that she could tell without a watch. She usually relied on her phone for the time, but she'd left it in the car since it had been out of battery.

"The town is almost empty," Anne noted as they came closer, pointing. "Look. But how in heaven could the giants have fit into those doorways?"

It was a good question. Now Ash could see down into the town below, and it looked as tidy and shiny-roofed as yesterday.

Fewer people – maybe three or four men and women moved around the wide central street. But there was one distinct difference from the day before.

There were no giants.

"Where could they be?" Ash murmured. "It's not as if they could fit in the buildings…" Unless, in the best horror movie tradition, the giants were behind them. Ash shuddered and checked surreptitiously. They looked to be alone, thankfully, but it didn't answer the question.

"It doesn't matter," George said flatly. "We have nowhere else to go."

He was right, unfortunately. They had to go forward.

❧

They slowly made their way down the cliff face, George graciously taking the lead so that if the girls fell they'd have a soft landing.

"This would better suit goats than any decent human," Lady Anne grumbled.

George did sympathise somewhat; the girl was significantly hampered by her thick skirts. He was finding it hard enough in his snug breeches and hessian boots. They were *the* fashion, but not practical for cliff-climbing.

At the bottom they stopped at the edge of a wide grassy field, clipped short and neat and a healthy green. Not two hundred yards from them the first of the houses began. There were still no giants in sight, and that bothered George. Where had they gone?

He glanced at the girls at his side. They were obviously nervous; Lady Anne's eyes were wide and Ashlea was jittering in place.

"Come on then," he encouraged, sounding rather more confident than he felt. He did have to set the tone for the females, after all. But by Jove, he hoped *they* couldn't smell fear…because he would be reeking of it.

But the giant hadn't hurt Ashlea, and so by rights, it wouldn't hurt them either. It was just getting that belief from his head to his shaking hands.

They reached the outskirts of the town within a few minutes. Close up, the townspeople were all brunette, their skin in shades of brown from light golden through to walnut. They were also very tall; the men that George saw probably averaged six-foot-three, and even the women could look George in the eye.

And they did, too. As the three travellers came and stood at the edge of the road, the people watched them curiously, and a couple of them even smiled politely. But apart from that, no one seemed to be bothered by their presence. It was strangely comforting that no one was screaming, 'Stop! Intruders!', but it wasn't getting them anywhere.

George really should just use one of the opening lines he had been mulling over ever since he'd learned they'd have to go to the village.

Do you come here often?

Could you please direct me to the nearest giant killer?

Or even the desperate and probably untrue, *Don't eat us! We're stringy!*

How about, *Can you direct us to Dr Walker's residence?* Ah, that would do. It was actually even true, and didn't give away too much about them that people couldn't tell by looking at their clothing and colouring.

"Shall I just grab some random person to ask?" Ashlea asked, with unexpected perfect timing. For her part, Lady Anne had been uncharacteristically silent.

George shook his head, startled by the image of her seizing some poor bystander. Perhaps people really *did* behave differently where she was from. "Goodness, no. I don't believe they'd like that. But I'm the man, so I'll do the talking. Just give me one moment." Ashlea let out a strange sputtering noise, but he ignored it, studying the various options before them. Who looked the most likely to come to their aid?

A boy watched them from the shadow of one of the buildings. He looked perhaps a year or two younger than George, and was tall (but weren't they all?) with neatly cropped, straight black hair brushed over his golden brown forehead. He wore a light brown outfit in similar colours to George's own clothing, with neat trousers that came only to mid-calf, and a vest. He seemed to have forgotten his shirt, and jacket, and cravat…

Even across the short distance his gaze was curious, perhaps even overly familiar, and even as George thought that, the boy stood, moving directly towards them.

"Is he coming up to us?" Ashlea whispered beside him, rather redundantly.

Within five seconds the boy had reached them and was standing (looming) with a friendly smile. "Ah, travellers. What a wonderful, but unusual, occurrence. Would you come to my home for some breakfast?"

All three of them were struck silent by that, because it was really the last thing they'd expected to hear. "Breakfast?" Ashlea echoed. "That's very kind."

And unexpected, George thought.

The youth winked at her, grinning far too familiarly. "I am known for being kind. Won't you come in?"

Lady Anne was staring up at him with an awestruck expression that reminded George of his sister when shown a beautiful new dress, and George realised that he too had been silent far too long. "That is most kind," he agreed. "Mister…"

"Islo." He grinned again, and something sparkled in one tooth. "Just Islo. We don't use titles around here."

They didn't? "Mister…George Seymour," George replied, unable to break the habits of a lifetime. "And might I introduce to you Lady Anne, and Miss Ashlea – or Ash – O'Reilly."

"Ash, George and Anne. Nice to meet you."

"Actually, it's Mr Seymour," George tried to say, but Ashlea nudged him in the side, mouthing something like, *'don't aggravate him'*.

Aggravate? Since when was he ever anything but perfectly polite?

Islo was still speaking. "Won't you come in? We don't know the Noble policy on visitors, so we don't want to test it."

"Noble policy…?" Ashlea echoed.

There was a long silence where Islo looked at Ashlea again as if waiting for her to say something – heaven knew what – then finally sighed. "Come on, please. Before we start attracting attention."

"Whose attention might we attract?" Lady Anne asked, almost running to keep up with the youth's longer strides as he turned towards a nearby building.

They followed a curved side path that wound past sharply defined gardens to a wide door in the wall of a large building. Perhaps four storeys tall, it had an architectural style that George found completely unfamiliar.

"The Nobles, of course." Islo smiled down at her. "I like your dress, Anne. Isn't it a bit hot for this weather?"

If he offered for her to take it off, George was going to punch him, friendly local or not.

"Well, I was not expecting such warmth," the girl replied lightly, barely pausing as they stood at the door to one of the larger houses. "'Tis a cool autumn. Which nobles do you refer to? Are they not generous towards strangers? For we are not truly strangers to this area. Forsooth-"

"Anne," Ashlea cut in, giving her a meaningful look. "Save it for Dr Walker."

"*Lady* Anne," the younger girl hissed, then gave the startled Islo a sweet smile. Notably she wasn't requiring *him* to use her title. "We've been here before, as I was saying. In Iversley."

Islo studied the three of them from head to toe, intently

enough that George almost bristled. "You'd be time-travellers, then. I knew it."

They exchanged startled glances.

"Why would you think that?" George asked cautiously.

Islo grinned. "Let's see…you're all pale as milk, dressed like you're going to a costume party, and you look more than a bit lost. Now won't you come in? Illegal immigrants or not, I won't leave you standing on my doorstep." He turned and disappeared inside the wide doorway, and with nothing better to do, the others followed him in.

The inside of the building was as well-lit as the bunker had been, with the same unidentifiable light source. Apart from that aspect, it was the complete opposite. They turned out to be standing in a spacious lobby, at the base of a flight of dark wooden stairs leading to a second level. The occasional picture graced the pale yellow walls and thin, fine carpet covering the entire floor.

Glancing at the walls, George noticed a familiar portrait. The square-jawed young man was more faded than he was used to, but the expression and the hair and the powdered white skin was perfectly recognizable.

"By Jupiter," he gasped. "What's *that* doing here?"

MEET THE FAMILY

Inside, the large, comfortable space reminded Ash a little of an expensive hotel. There were paintings over the walls, as well as vases and statuettes – everything that screamed 'wealth', and didn't seem to fit with the casual, long-haired Islo.

Strangely, there were also what looked like family photographs from Ash's time- *argh*, she meant home – full of generic, smiling white families, which apart from their general good looks, didn't resemble Islo at all. But it was his last words that caught her attention.

"Oh, we're not illegal immigrants," she explained hastily. "We're here on- on a government project." Because that's what it was, wasn't it? Time travel – *argh, argh, if it was true…*

"Illegal or not, I don't mind. I'm guessing you didn't get yourselves here, so it's hardly your fault, is it?"

That was a good point. "It's really not our fault," Ash agreed fervently. "Do you know Doctor Walker?"

"Nope."

There was an awkward pause.

"Doctor *Osvaldo* Walker?" she corrected.

Islo shook his head cheerfully. "Never heard of him."

Then there must have been far more people underground than she'd imagined, because she'd been picturing a 'city' of a hundred or so people.

"But he said he was very famous," Anne said anxiously. "A tall man, with brown skin…"

"In case you haven't noticed, love, all men here would be tall with brown skin compared to you," Islo said kindly. "I've never seen anyone as tiny as you. And your skin…"

"What *about* my skin?" Anne countered, but she was definitely blushing.

"It's perfect," he replied with another grin. "Right down to those tiny speckles on your nose. Is that your natural hair colour?"

Anne immediately slapped a hand to her nose, mortified. Obviously Islo didn't realise that mentioning her freckles wasn't a compliment, and Ash had to hold back a smile.

"Yes," Anne replied with a slightly nasal twang. "I assure you it makes no difference to my temper."

Islo laughed. "Why would it?"

"Red hair means the devil's own temper…?"

He laughed again, and leaned over her. "I'm sure whatever temper you could summon up would be adorable. Do you want to demonstrate?"

Anne looked flustered, and Ash finally stepped in. "We get it," she said. "You think Anne's cute. Now not to look a gift horse in the mouth, but you invited us here for breakfast. Which you didn't have to do, we get that, but I'm also thinking there's something you're not telling us…?"

Islo stared at her, and Ash thought she saw real confusion in his expression. He started to smile, then it faltered when he saw her face. "Uh…what can I tell you that you don't already know?"

Just about everything, actually. "Where are the giants?" Anne piped up. "Surely they can't fit through the doors."

"Of course not. They change size."

There was yet another silence, then Ash echoed, "Change size? How is that even possible?"

"Never mind that!" George called from across the room. Whatever he'd been doing, he'd been so caught up that he didn't notice Islo hitting on Anne. "Who is *this*?" He stabbed a finger at the generic ancient painting that hung incongruously between two black and white photographs. It was a faded portrait of a man in a curly white wig, with a massive jacket and high boots, and dogs at his feet.

Islo shrugged. "You'd have to ask my mother."

But George was practically vibrating. "That is *my grandfather!*"

Now the younger man did a double take. "Really? And your name is George...Seymour?"

"Yes! And yes!"

"Huh. Interesting."

"Interesting," George muttered. "Miraculous, more like it. And did I hear you say before that you *don't* know who Dr Walker is?"

"I did indeed," Islo agreed. "But my parents will probably know. They know just about everyone here. Come on, they're just having breakfast. We can join them."

In perfect timing, a door slid open across the way. Anne quickly followed him through, her skirts briefly getting stuck in the narrow space, and Ash went to follow. But George was still standing behind, staring at that same painting.

"Aren't you coming?" she asked.

He shook his head, but it was more an expression of shock than of disagreement. "It's my grandfather. Imagine that, they've got a painting of my grandfather."

Ash watched him. He really did seem sincere. *Really* sincere. She sighed, patting him on the arm. "So they do. And if you're really lucky, maybe you'll be related."

The breakfast was nice, mostly familiar. There was fruit, bread, some weird paste thing that was apparently made from 'spoike' – Ash didn't ask, she just avoided it. Islo's parents Teron and Georgiana were also nice, and arguably familiar.

Well, not to her. To George, who looked as stunned as if he'd been slapped upside the head with a cold fish.

"How on earth can we be related? We don't look a thing alike!"

"You did say you were from the early nineteenth century," Teron said placidly. Middle-aged and with slightly darker skin than his son, he wore a matching jumpsuit to his wife, except where she wore gold, he wore forest green. "A lot can change in more than three centuries."

"Yes, but…" George looked lost. He stared down at his plate of perfectly round, red-tinted bread in confusion. "I didn't expect it to be as different as that. What happened to the title?"

"I'm sure Islo told you we don't use titles," Georgiana said. Yes, that was her real name – a family name, apparently, and it matched her slightly fairer colouring. Unusually for what Ash had seen of the town, her hair was a soft brown that was almost blonde. Rather like George's. "So what happened to it doesn't matter."

George looked like he would have argued, so Ash quickly interrupted. "We really do appreciate you having us over for a meal on such short notice. The family connection is a bonus."

To her, anyway. Regency boy looked like he was choking on his spoike to be actually related to someone who wasn't lily-white. Clearly he didn't have much knowledge of slavery in the Amyricas…

Georgiana smiled at her. "But of course we would welcome you, family connection or not. It's what my Lady Alfeior would have wanted. She is most welcoming to strangers, and especially travellers, even if the old bureaucracy was not."

Funny, Ash thought; because Islo had been in a real hurry to get them out of sight. He hadn't known about the 'noble' policy, but his mother seemed far more certain.

"*Lady* Alfeior?" Anne burst out, putting down her glass of bright-yellow something. "Did you not just tell us that titles are no longer used?" And she'd looked really offended at that, too.

Islo's parents exchanged glances. "For *Nobles*, dear," Teron explained kindly. "Nobles use titles. We do not."

"But *I'm* a noble."

Georgiana laughed aloud, and even Islo smiled a bit.

"No you're not, dear," Teron countered. "And you'd be wise to remember that while you're here."

"But I *am*," Anne insisted. Her cheeks were pink, and her red hair was coming loose from its moorings once more, but Ash couldn't help feeling a bit sorry for her. "I was born daughter of an earl, I married an earl, and I am betrothed to one once more. I *am* a lady, and a noble born."

Now the silence became a little dangerous. "As I said," Teron repeated gently, but his tone was most serious, "humans do not use titles here. Only the Queen's people do that, and we are not they. Do you understand what I'm telling you?"

"For frack's sake, he means the giants," Islo cut in. He'd lost his jolliness as soon as they'd sat down with his parents, and Ash wondered if he was younger than she'd first thought. His height could be misleading. "The giants are called Nobles, and they have titles. Lord and Lady. We don't. That's all."

"Speak with more respect for your betters," his mother scolded him, then smiled apologetically at the visitors. It was clear that the 'betters' she meant were not the three in the room. "My son has been a little slow to embrace any changes here in Iversley, a fault which we hope to soon remedy."

Teron gave him a stern glance. "Your Lord Kadeon goes too lightly on you, boy. Disrespect must be quickly trained into obedience."

Islo stared mutinously down at the table, and Ash suddenly felt very, very uncomfortable, but also like she was just at the edge of some great discovery. "So the Nobles," she asked carefully. "You are each…assigned to one?"

"Pledged, Ashlea dear," Georgiana replied with yet another pleasant smile. It was as if the exchange with her son had never happened. "We pledge ourselves, and happily so. If you saw what power they held, you'd do the same."

"There'll be time for that," Islo muttered, and suddenly his mother turned on him.

"Mind your mouth, boy!" Then with an apologetic smile to the others: "If you've eaten enough, I'll have the bathing chambers made ready, and some suitable clothing found." She made a polite, dithering gesture towards the three of them. "You cannot go into the city like that, my dears. Your colouring makes you stand out enough."

"That's very kind," Ash said again, because the other two didn't seem to be saying anything. "But I was wondering about that. Where we're from…a lot of people are pale, like us, and some are very dark. But everyone we've seen seems to be somewhere in the middle…?"

"Simple genetics," Teron replied. "Small population, diverse genetic pool, and of course the anti-inbreeding policy they brought in after the Great War, and everything shifting underground here in Iversley. Besides, we were very isolated for a long time. Still are, and self-sufficient too." He held up the glass of something-yellow. "The lemoranges that the juice is made from were grown not two miles south of here, in the orchardery buildings. Perhaps we'll show you, if there's time enough."

"Forgive me," George said, suddenly finding his tongue. "We didn't see any buildings of note, just these dozen or so homes…?"

The man smiled at him briefly. He seemed to spend a lot of time smiling, Ash noted, and probably even meant it. Still, she found it disconcerting. "But then only we lucky few live above ground. Everything else is grown below, else why waste the space?"

"Why indeed," George echoed, but was clearly not getting it.

Ash thought of the models of glasshouse buildings she'd seen back home, and thought that if these people had really learned how to grow fruit underground, then she'd be impressed.

Flying cars, underground fruit, perpetual tans…Well, she

hadn't seen the first yet, and was still expecting to spot a pasty white Anglishman like she was used to. Anti-inbreeding policies indeed…

And now she was starting to sound like George. It was probably the stress. "I am *sooo* late for work," she whispered to herself.

But not quietly enough. "What do you do for work, Ashlea?" Georgiana asked politely.

"At the moment I do admin at an accountancy firm, which is just about as exciting as it sounds."

"Admin?" Georgiana queried.

"Um… a secretary," Ash tried.

"What's that?" Islo asked. "And what's an accountancy?"

George muttered under his breath, "Now that explains the trousers, although not the attitude."

Ash put down her drink, showing great inner strength by not tossing it into George's lap. "You know, I think I am ready to wash, if that's alright with you?"

⁂

The house was a decent size, and appeared to be very clean considering, but the breakfast had been lacking in meat and eggs; not even a kipper in sight.

And no servants. No matter what the woman (family or not) had said, George considered that the basic mark of a well-run, well-bred home. At least a couple of servants – perhaps a cook and a general below-stairs maid, as well as an above-stairs maid and a strong footman. You never knew when you'd need something heavy lifted.

But they didn't have any *at all*. Instead they had small round black things that ran all over the walls and the floor and pushed themselves flat as paper when you moved by – clean-bots, someone had called them.

None of their customs made any sense to him, either. He'd gone to pull out a chair for Ashlea as she'd been the closest woman to him and he'd been wanting to make a point of treating her the same as Lady Anne, but she'd promptly pulled out one of the dark-coloured chairs and seated herself. He'd felt a little silly and definitely put out, standing there with his hand in mid-air. But he'd recovered himself and pretended that he'd just been going to brush off his waistcoat.

The lower classes weren't used to gentlemanly behaviour, he reminded himself. Of course she *could* seat herself, and as someone who was more of the servant class (he thought?) he wouldn't have been expected to seat her back at home.

But by Jove, he wasn't at home, and he had no idea of the etiquette of these situations! He kept trying to do the right thing, but it would help if he actually knew what the right thing was.

But that wasn't what bothered George the most – it just added to his general sense of discontent and displacement that had grown from the time he'd arrived in the town. He couldn't believe the family had given up the viscountcy, even assuming that it *had* passed this way and they weren't just making fun of him for being clearly so naïve. Why would anyone choose to give up their title?

Why would anyone choose to pledge themselves to a giant, was the more pertinent question.

For power, he heard Georgiana's voice echo.

Or perhaps it was his imagination. What kind of power could giving up a title lend? Surely you'd have less respect, less authority-

Not that kind of power, George's mind told him, and images of golden light flashed through his head, ending in a sparkle so bright it hurt the back of his eyes. Urgh, he must be heading towards one of those horrid headaches that would set in on occasion, right before his melancholy episodes. He'd had a truly dreadful one when…Clarissa had left…

His former fiancée's lovely face sprang to mind, but it was

mocking him. *Everything you did was to prove me wrong*, she seemed to say, *but you just proved me right, didn't you?*

Nonsense. They'd never had *that* conversation…

"Oh, look at this," George's possibly-great-great-great-niece said, interrupting his dark thoughts as she pointed at something in the middle of the table. "I've found the picture. This is you, isn't it, George?"

It was. Now, filling the centre of the sizeable table, was a portrait of George that he'd commissioned just two years ago, right after Clarissa had broken off their engagement and he'd begun his shipping business at the tender age of eighteen. He'd lounged in a casual pose, a false expression of boredom fixed on his face, and surrounded by expensive items that he'd hired just for the occasion.

Looking at it now, all George could see was the insecurity and false confidence he'd been trying to project at the time. He wondered if the others saw it too.

"Yes, it's me," he croaked.

"An excellent likeness," Lady Anne said approvingly, unaware of his inner turmoil. "Although 'tis somewhat faded, is it not?"

"Three hundred years will do that to a body," Teron said jovially. "Could be worse, couldn't it? If you're Georgiana's great-great…great, great, great, great uncle, you could truly look your age."

"More like a dozen greats, surely," Georgiana corrected. They turned to look at her, and she shrugged. "Three hundred years, twenty-five years a generation, that'd be a dozen, yes?"

The others chatted amiably amongst themselves. Ashlea had vanished a while ago to bathe, and Islo had also gone who-knew-where. He remained along with Lady Anne and the two parents, who were probably his brother's distant descendants. At least the family line didn't die out, even if they'd thought of the title as garbage and had disposed of it.

They got new names, new titles, a woman's voice whispered in his mind. It was as sweet and golden as honey, if a voice could be that pleasant, but it reminded him so closely of Clarissa that he wanted to throw his oddly shaped utensil across the room. Why was he thinking of her now? He didn't *want* to think of her!

Don't you want something real, George?

You'd be the one to talk about real, he thought viciously, then realised he was replying to his own thoughts and decided to focus once more on the conversation. That way lay madness, and he would *not* entertain it any longer, even if his mood was becoming increasingly foul.

"So my grandfather moved back to Iversley about fifty years ago after the radiation cleared," Georgiana was saying when he began to pay attention again, "and we got permission to build, being some of the original landowners, and here we still are."

George looked down at his crumb covered plate, unsure of what they were discussing. He changed the subject. "Tell me ma'am, how exactly are we related?" he asked.

"Through your older brother Edward, according to my wife's research," Teron replied, showing he didn't know what 'ma'am' meant. "We were lucky to have here in Iversley one of the last remaining genealogical records from the last thousand years. Debretts' Peerage, Hello Celebrity Lineage…"

George smiled tightly. It was a comfort to know that although Edward had no children when George had last seen him, his marriage would bear fruit.

Edward had been recently married to a young widow. Not the usual for anyone in line for a title (they tended to prefer maidens for practical purposes – that way you knew you weren't getting someone already 'enceinte') but apparently it had been a love match as well as socially advantageous. The lady was a duke's daughter, so Edward had actually married upwards. So now George knew that must have lasted at least long enough to have an heir, if this woman was telling the truth. Lucky Edward.

As for George himself – he would have appreciated knowing that if Georgiana was his distant descendant, then he must make it back home in order to have children, mustn't he? As it stood, to his family back home, he might have just disappeared one day and never returned. They likely would think him dead, if he didn't return, or perhaps think that he had been too ashamed to face them after his business failure, and had run off to the wilds of Canadia to be a trapper or something.

Had he gone back?

"I probably shouldn't ask this," he said to Georgiana, "but did you find any information on my life?"

The lady raised an eyebrow. "Do you mean, any information on the date of your death?"

He nodded sheepishly. She was very perceptive, this great-grand niece of his.

"Nobody should know the time of their death," she said firmly. "It would stop you living your life to the fullest. Regardless, it was not available. I had only your name and the date of the portrait."

Are you afraid of dying now, George? Of leaving behind nothing but an embarrassing memory?

He told the imaginary thought to shut up. It had hit too close to home. Hades, where were these thoughts coming from?

Georgiana added, "I must say that you're not what I expected from looking at that portrait. I thought you'd be arrogant, but you're very friendly. You're not even wearing a wig. It's nice to know one can be proud of family."

George thought that was supposed to be a compliment, so took it as one, even though he wasn't feeling at all amiable at this moment. It was a testament to his acting skills, then – and as for the wig, simply a matter of fashion. A modern man like himself didn't wear a wig; they had a short and neat Brutus cut. As did he, much good had it done him. "Thank you, ma'am. But perhaps I might also bathe now, if it suits?"

Maybe with a little privacy he could get back to normal.

Anne finished sipping the glass of sweet juice. Lemorange, they'd called it. It tasted not at all like anything she'd tried before, but 'twas much better than the water that was available.

She couldn't believe they actually *drank* water here. The vase sat on the table along with the rest of the breakfast food, and the water was clearer and brighter than any she'd seen before. Still, she'd imagined it must be for feeding any animals or washing hands, because at home, drinking water was a guaranteed way of becoming ill.

Islo's parents had told her this wouldn't make her sick, but she wasn't going to take the risk. Besides, when they'd said that, Islo had this odd look on his handsome face. 'Twas not outright denial, but 'twas enough to make her cautious.

But the choice of beverages was not the biggest shock in this place. There were a thousand little things, from the colouring of their skin, to their garb, to the slight wrongness of their Anglish speech, to the *smell* of the place. 'Twas not unpleasant, but 'twas different. Somehow…lacking, too clean.

Empty, rather. Anne had grown up in castles: Morag Castle up in the small county of Covington as a child, and then Renwick Castle for the last couple of years. They were always busy and noisy and full of smells both good and bad. This place was sterile. That was the word she was looking for, and it fit.

With that being said, the oddness of the smell and beverages was nothing compared to that other, dreadful thing. They didn't use titles. No titles!

And Islo's parents (that looked just like Moors although they swore that they were Anglish) had told her emphatically that she,

Lady Anne of Covington, about to be Countess of Longford twice over, could not use her title. And why? Because she was only *human*.

What did being human have to do with using a title or not? 'Twas a part of who she was, whether she was human or fairytale creature or a winged pig. By the Eternal One, the unfairness of it made her furious.

But she kept the fury inside, because in spite of her feelings she was no fool. Here in this place of wonders there might also be terrible danger. If she wouldn't risk drinking their clear, shining, diamond-like water, then she wouldn't voice her displeasure about refraining from using her title. For now, anyway.

But then breakfast appeared to be over, and Anne followed her host up a slightly frightening set of moving stairs to the second level of the building. This house wasn't small, mayhap seven or eight bedrooms, but certainly not as large as Renwick Castle.

It had no Great Hall, to begin with; nowhere for all the people to meet for celebrations, or to hide in case of attack. No enormous kitchens heated almost to Hades-level by the large fires, pots big enough to feed a hundred set over their glow, and all the while the hounds moving around, snuffling in the rushes that covered the floors and squabbling over scraps.

She felt a pang of homesickness for that place. She'd lived there ever since her wedding day, and in spite of its large size she knew everything and everyone there. For all of its flaws and even without her husband, 'twas what she thought of when she heard the word 'home'.

A door slid open in the upstairs hall, revealing a room with two enormous beds, and yet more of the strange decorations set about the house. The beds were wide and very flat rather than the mounded shapes Anne was accustomed to, and were draped in royal blue. Expensive in appearance, and the mattresses so large that a thousand geese must have given up their feathers to fill them.

"Your friend is currently using the washroom," Georgiana explained, "but I think she's nearly done. You wash up, and I'll bring you some clean clothes."

Her *friend*, was it? And Anne didn't miss how the woman flicked her eyes critically over Anne's gown. Georgiana wanted her to *change*? Anne sniffed. She obviously didn't know that Anne had this gown specially made by the Queen's own seamstress. As if she'd trade it to wear one of those scandalous outfits they seemed to favour.

"That is kind of you," she replied graciously, "but I shall require no change of garb. I am quite comfortable as I am."

Just then another internal door slid open, revealing Ash. She was wearing a short fluffy robe that *exposed her bare legs below the knee!* and her hair was loose around her shoulders. "She means we can't go outside dressed as we are, Anne. We'll need to change." Then to Georgiana, "Do bring clothes, thank you, and perhaps long sleeves and a long skirt for Anne if you have one?"

The lady of the house smiled with relief and left, and Anne turned on Ash furiously. "You do not speak for me, least of all in the matter of clothing! Would you'd have me prance around half naked as you do? It's simply disgraceful!" She stared down at the other girl's pale legs, which were shining strangely in the light. Were they…were they *hairless*?

"Disgraceful," Anne repeated, but she was strangely mesmerised. "What's wrong with your leg hair?"

"My disgraceful leg hair is all shaved off," Ash replied with a twist to her mouth that spoke of hidden laughter. "And if you went home with me, you'd see a lot worse than someone's calves."

"Then I am most blessed not to return home with you."

"But we really do need to change clothes," Ash said. "Both of us. We'll stand out too much otherwise."

Anne considered that. While she disliked agreeing with Ash on such matters, the girl might just have a point. "Very well, I'll change my garb for as long as the locals require, but not because you asked me to. Now show me to the wash bowl, if you will."

"Sure."

Anne followed Ash into the adjoining room. 'Twas smaller than the bedroom, and inside was rather similar to that back in the underground room they'd stayed the night in. That room had had similar odd and marvellous devices for removing one's waste, but this one was larger and more beautiful. Half of the room was taken up by a glass-encased cubicle, and the walls were covered in coloured tiles and strange metal appendages. There was also a narrow grate set into the shiny white floor.

"There's no wash bowl," Ash told her, although Anne had already realised that. "You'll need to have a shower. It's quite nice, really, a sort of mist. It tingles."

"As long as it does not damage my gown. 'Tis velvet, and quite expensive."

Ash laughed. "You can't wear your dress into the shower! You won't get clean. You'll have to undress completely."

Undress! "As if I would stand in the nude and let myself be…shower," Anne retorted, wrapping her arms around herself. "I am not the same kind of woman as you. I am a good, Churchian woman," (although one that did tend to swap between the Universal and Protestor churches depending on which monarch was in power, but Anne thought that the Eternal One probably didn't mind), "-and I do *not* allow such indignities. You may act as my maid, but do not think to encourage me in such actions. I shall not do it."

Ash closed her eyes briefly as if in pain, then she looked down at Anne. "Please, let me explain."

"I cannot see that there is anything to explain!"

"Oh, believe me, there is."

Ash looked down at the small, fragrant Tudar girl, and tried to work out the best way to tell someone that they needed a good wash without causing terrible offense. There didn't seem any way to say it, whether at home (strategically gifting bottles of deodorant?) or here.

But then Anne said, "Oh, cease staring at me in that manner. I shall not take a scolding from you, you lowborn speckle-face!"

Speckle-face? The insult to Ash's freckles was the last straw. "That's it," she snapped. "I was trying to be nice, but now I'll just say it. You smell, Lady Anne of Covington. You smell like you haven't washed properly in weeks, and your clothes are part of the problem. You need a proper wash for the sake of everyone around you."

Anne gasped in shock, and her cheeks flushed deep red. "I do *not*! Take that back!"

And now Ash had embarrassed her about it, and she was starting to feel guilty. Just a little. "I'm sorry, I didn't mean it like that. What I *meant* to say was that clearly where you're from people tended to wash much, much less than where I'm from, and I'm quite sure here as well. I usually wash fully every day, so it's really obvious when people…don't. The reason you don't notice is that you'd be used to it," she finished lamely.

"So what you are telling me," Anne retorted icily, cheeks still red, "is that I reek like a pigsty but I cannot smell it because everyone back home also reeks like a pigsty."

"Not a pigsty. More like…a student near exams reusing their clothing too many times."

There was a long silence where Ash wondered if Anne would flounce off in a huff, but suddenly she turned her back. "Help me untie the laces."

Victory! But… "Say please."

"Z'wounds, do you wish me to beg? *Please*, Ash, aid me. I cannot untie these by myself."

Eh, Ash was unlikely to get anything better than that. She

began to try to unpick the tightly tied ribbons running down the entire back of the dress. Not only were they tight and small, but they looked like they'd been put there to stay. No wonder Anne hadn't wanted to get undressed, if it was this much work. "Deias, for a pair of scissors…"

"Don't you dare!" Anne snapped, and Ash felt a little guilty once more. Heavens knew the girl was rude and arrogant, but it didn't make it alright to embarrass her. "And if it turns out you were simply being spiteful, I shall find some dreadful means of revenge."

"I wouldn't expect anything less." And Ash didn't even hide the smile this time.

"Humph." Anne was silent as Ash loosened the ties all the way down the narrow waist to the flaring skirt, then started on the arms. "For your information, I change my undersmock daily. 'Tis a matter of pride. And mayhap you were the only one to notice. My mother used to say that women have better noses than men. So it stands to reason…"

That Islo hadn't noticed? Ash was a second away from saying it, but this time she bit her tongue. Anne clearly had a crush building, and while she might act tough, chances were her ego was fragile.

"You could be right," Ash agreed instead. "Thank Deias I've finally got the strings undone. Let me show you how to use the shower."

"You're not done yet." Anne began to slip out of the dress, revealing another layer of clothing. "That was only my gown. I still need help removing my kirtle and petticoat, although I can do my smock by myself."

So Ash helped, and it was an education in why women were better off wearing pants. No one needed this amount of clothing. They should sell the fabric and clothe the homeless population of Lunden with it. "I don't know how you managed to run so far with this dress so tight," she muttered, trying to undo the kirtle –

the corset-like thing that squashed the girl's torso flat.

"Practice, I suppose." Anne shrugged out of the red dress that she'd called a petticoat, finally left in only a light, white, long-sleeved gown. Ash had seen people wearing less than that single layer, and yet it was only the *underwear*? "That will suffice. Now how do I do the shower?"

Ash was so relieved Anne was actually washing that she didn't correct the girl's grammar. When Georgiana returned a few minutes later trailed by what looked like a hovering coat rack, the washroom door was closed and the faint hum of the shower could be heard through the door.

It wasn't *really* a shower, Ash allowed. It had a lot of similarities, but she'd bet that it used a lot less water, and she'd come out practically dry. And yes, tingling.

Their host saw the piles of heavy velvet and cloth lying on the bed, and frowned. "I thought your friend would wish to wash her clothing while she bathed. Did you not know you can wear clothing into the cleanser?"

"No, I didn't know that." And it meant Anne had been right, damn it.

"Well, don't worry. I'll send all the clothes to the processor, and they'll be done in no time." And even as Georgiana spoke, the other end of the coat rack began lifting the piles of clothing and clipping them in a row. Georgiana began unloading the new clothes: what looked like tunics in shades of sky blue. "These new-blues will be just right for your first meeting. They are somewhat adjustable. Now you don't have any issues with wearing trousers?"

"Not me. Anne, however-"

"Ah, yes." Georgiana held up a long-sleeved dress that would have fit a ten-year-old. "It belongs to the neighbour's daughter, but I'm afraid we didn't have anything to fit her otherwise. If she wears trousers underneath I trust it will suit her ideas of decency."

"It will," Ash agreed firmly. She'd make sure it did. "New-blue, did you say?"

"Yes. It's what one wears the first time they meet the Queen."

And now Ash just about swallowed her tongue. "We're going to meet a *queen*?"

"You did want your questions answered, did you not? There's no better source of wisdom in all the world, and certainly not in Iversley. Now move along, my dear, because our appointment is in less than an hour."

"But-"

"I'll be back in twenty minutes," Georgiana called, heading out of the room with that robotic coat rack once more trailing behind her. "Do be ready, please."

"Alright," Ash replied weakly, sitting down on the bed with a thump. The Queen. They were going to meet a *queen*? Now she *really* wished she'd had that haircut.

Ash was still sitting on the bed when there was a slight knock on the door, and then Islo came in. "You're still not dressed?"

What, couldn't a girl get some privacy in this place before she went to meet a monarch? "I was just about to get dressed," she replied, grabbing the pile of clothes Georgiana had allocated her, and heading for the door on the other side away from the bathroom.

"That's the wardrobe," Islo called.

At this point Ash didn't care. At least she was unlikely to be interrupted.

✒︎✒︎

Anne had finally decided to do the shower not because she needed to or Ash had said so, but because she wouldn't want her hosts to be offended that she didn't use their facilities.

Truly. She was that thoughtful.

Ash had to show her how to use the device as it was unlike

anything Anne had ever seen. Actively wetting her whole self all at once, on purpose? It simply wasn't done.

But when Anne finally gathered her courage, removed her smock and stepped under the spray, she wondered why she'd ever turned it down. 'Twas heaven in a glass box. 'Twas an odd sensation, like being in a very small, hot rainstorm, but so pleasant that she stayed in much longer than she'd intended.

While she was in there she decided to use the 'Revolutionary Made in Iversley of All Natural Ingredients Hair Cleanser and Glosser'. It had an unwieldy name, but came out the top of the tube like beaten cream, and smelled of lilacs. She liked it so much that she used it all over, right down to her toes. She left the fruity cubes of soap alone though. They smelled just like the juice she'd had earlier, and she had visions of flies or hungry mice chasing her down the street.

The water ran a little dark at first. Anne wondered if her skin was coming off, but that was silly. Her skin was white, barring eleven tiny freckles on her nose that she could never quite get rid of. Mayhap 'twas actually....*dirt*?

Mayhap Ash had been just a little bit right, and this thorough bathing wouldn't do her any harm. It wasn't as if Anne didn't wash back at home. People did *own* baths – or at least there was supposed to be one at Hampton Court Palace, for medicinal use by Queen Marian once a year. As for Anne, she would wash with scented water from a bowl most mornings. Although 'twas good, it couldn't compare to total immersion like this.

Afterwards she wrapped herself in the thick, fluffy robe provided – which went almost to her ankles, thank heavens – and stepped back into the bedroom, prepared to brave Ash's 'I told you so'.

But the other girl was nowhere to be seen. Speaking of which, neither was Anne's precious velvet dress. Instead, neatly laid out on the bed was some kind of garb that no doubt she was expected to wear.

Anne sighed. She'd loved her velvet. It had been very expensive, and showed her rank in that only certain levels of nobility could wear it, although she'd been careful not to overstep by choosing a subdued dark green. However, this garb was blue, which of course was a colour only worn by the highest nobility.

Back home, anyway. Here she knew the rules must be different. Dr Walker had worn purple – which only royalty would be allowed to wear back home – and there'd been no doubt that he wasn't royalty. He hadn't worn enough jewels, for starters.

"Lost in thought?" someone asked, and Anne gave an undignified little shriek. It was Islo, and he'd been sitting in the corner of the room quietly enough that she hadn't even seen him.

"You should not be in my room," she scolded him, though she felt that familiar blush rise into her cheeks. He really was very handsome, in a way she'd never seen before and never thought she'd appreciate. Handsome men were supposed to be pale and elegant and *Anglish*, but somehow Islo managed to be more so than anyone she'd seen before. Although he was, in theory, Anglish.

But then she hadn't really experienced much of life.

Islo just grinned. "Actually it's my room."

"Truly?" It didn't *look* like a man's room…

"Only in that all the rooms are mine," he replied with a laugh. "I live here. How did you like the shower? Was it to your liking?"

"Oh, it was most odd, but lovely," Anne assured him. "I should like to try it again before I leave, if possible."

"I'm sure it will be possible. Maybe I can show you some of the best settings for the spray."

It was not so much what Islo had said, but the way he'd said it. Anne might be young and from an entirely different culture, but she wasn't completely naïve. "Am I correct in assuming you are proposing more than just a shower?" she asked carefully.

His grin didn't falter. If anything it became wider. He had a dimple set in one golden cheek, and his brown eyes sparkled. By the Rood, he truly was as handsome as an Espanish prince ought to be. (In Anne's brief experience at Court, 'twas the footmen who were dark angels, and the nobles tended to look like bloated toads. Islo did *not* resemble a toad.) "If the proposal is welcome, then yes."

Ooh, *scandalous*. Anne was actually being propositioned by a man – and one not entirely of the Anglish persuasion either.

Didn't he *know* she was betrothed on the Queen's command?

Didn't he *know* that by giving in to any temptation, she'd give up her good name forever, and that if Sir Robert or any of the men heard about it, they'd no doubt kill him because as a Moor and a foreigner (as they'd see it anyway) he didn't have the right to even *think* about approaching her…?

But Islo didn't know about any of that, because she hadn't told him. And none of those things would happen, because no one back home would hear a single word about this adventure, more's the pity. And that meant that really, truly, Anne was free to make some uncommon choices if she so wished.

Oh, by the Eternal One, she'd never been so tempted in her life. The other girls whispered of kisses with handsome lovers, and she'd just got a man twice her age with a short life expectancy, and another to come. And no one would ever have to know…

"Still thinking?" he teased. "Perhaps you need a little persuasion…"

He stood as though he would have come closer, and Anne made a decision. A very, very difficult one, but one she knew was right. "I'm sorry, but I cannot. I am betrothed, and besides, we are not married. 'Twould not be right."

"Married?" Islo's eyebrows shot up, and he sat back on the bed with a plunk. "You need to be married before you-"

"Yes," she confirmed with a nod. "Because as we all know, a man doesn't buy the cow if he can get the milk for free."

"He doesn't…?"

"No, he does not," Anne said with more passion. "Further-more, this milk is already spoken for, so oughtn't to be on sale at all. Which means the cow mustn't act as though it is on sale, because that would not be fair to the potential buyer and to the true owner of the cow, would it? Even if the potential milk buyer is as handsome as an Espanish prince ought to be, without one of those noses that looks like a banana."

She moved close enough to gather the garb left on the bed, then turned to move back to the washroom. There was enough room in there that she could clothe herself, or at least try to. "I believe I have made myself clear. I am most flattered by your regard, sir, but it can never be."

And with that last, poignant statement, she gave him a longing glance and shut the door behind her.

"What...?"

Then Anne thought of one more thing, and opened the door again. "Oh, and while Ash might appear a harlot due to her garb and manner, I do not believe she is as round-heeled as she seems. If you were thinking of turning your attentions to another, easier route, that is." Well, handsome as Islo was, she had to be practical.

Then she closed the door again, and set to getting dressed. And a few seconds later when Ash came charging across the room and shouted at the washroom door, "YOU DON'T KNOW A THING ABOUT MY MORALS!" Anne found herself snickering a little.

It wasn't quite revenge for the embarrassment of being told she reeked like a chamber pot, but it helped.

***

Furious, embarrassed and perhaps a little bit amused, Ash turned away from the closed washroom door to where Islo sat on the bed, his jaw dropped like a stunned mullet.

She'd partially heard the conversation between him and Anne

while she'd been changing into her surprisingly comfortable clothing, but it wasn't until Anne made that last parting comment about Ash that she'd decided to come out into the light, as it were.

And somehow she'd found herself shouting at the closed washroom door. Was that Anne *laughing* on the other side?

Stupid, rude girl. Ash hoped she didn't even know how to flush the loo, and serve her right.

Islo had managed to change the stunned expression into a winsome little smile. "So, do you-"

"No!"

"Not even-"

"NO!"

He looked disappointed, but shrugged casually. "It was worth a try. After all, girls of your time do have quite a reputation."

Of her *time*. Whatever she thought about it, they were all playing the same game, and playing it well. Ash glared at him. "Really? Well, even if I was interested - which I'm not – I don't fancy being anyone's second choice, thank you very much!"

Islo raised his hands as a gesture of peace. "I meant no offense. You are very pretty…"

Just not as pretty as Anne, apparently. Not that she had wanted to be hit on first or at all, but, well, it would have been a little flattering.

"…but I've never seen anyone with Anne's hair colour before. Red hair is extremely rare here. Besides, you're kind of…old."

"Old? I'm nineteen! How old are you?"

"Seventeen." There was a pause. "Next year."

It was fair to say that his height had made him look older than he really was. Not that Ash cared. Ash tried to gather her dignity. She was angry at what Anne had said, and insulted that Islo had so readily believed it. And being second choice to little Anne? This trip so far was *not* good for her ego.

"Age aside, didn't you know that Anne is from a very morally rigid society? She'd never consider sleeping with you, even if you were the king himself." Ash considered what she'd just said in light of history lessons. There seemed to be a different standard for kings. "Okay, maybe if you were him, but otherwise absolutely not."

He shrugged sheepishly. "I understand. She might be really cute, but there's no chance. Er, that thing about the cow…?"

Heh, that *had* been funny. "Basically she's not available, so don't even try it."

"I got *that*. Um…would you mind not mentioning this to my parents? They wouldn't be very pleased with me."

Ash delayed her reply, enjoying Islo's anxiety, then shrugged. "Sure. I'll tell Anne not to say anything to George either. If he decides to defend her honour and shoots you in a duel, we'll have nowhere to stay, family or not."

He smiled crookedly, unsure if she was joking.

She wasn't. After all, George *did* carry around that pistol, and he'd seemed free enough with it when Ash had got on his bad side. "But maybe you can answer a question for me. Your mother said we've got an appointment to see the Queen…?"

"Yes." Islo's expression became blank.

"Why would a queen want to meet *us*?" Ash asked in confusion. "And what queen are we talking about here? The queen of Angland?"

"Angland's a republic. She's the queen of…" And here he paused and gave her another of those strange, knowing looks. "Of the Nobles, and of *us*, for now."

"Oh." She imagined those enormous, possibly unnatural giants having some kind of leader, but could only picture a larger version of Boadicea, complete with plaits and leather. "Should I be worried about this?"

He shrugged. "It's not as if you can get out of it. And they don't hurt anybody, though you might end up with another change of clothes." That didn't make any sense, but he continued,

"Was that a serious question?"

"Of course!" Ash replied in surprise. "Why wouldn't it be?"

He gave her another of those *looks* that she didn't understand and was starting to feel annoyed about, then said lightly, "Because you seem really familiar. Regardless of age, doesn't it feel like we know each other?"

She stared at him. Was he serious? "Not really, no."

"But doesn't it seem like we've met before?" he persisted.

"Nooo…"

He sighed, shrugging. "Maybe I met someone who looked like you, then."

Oh. Was he still hitting on her? But it hadn't seemed that way. "Maybe I've got that familiar kind of face," she answered instead. "I don't really look like anyone, so I look like everyone."

"You look like-" he began to say, but then Anne came out of the bathroom and a moment later Georgiana came back, and the conversation was finished.

"The new-blue fits," Georgiana said with satisfaction. "But then they usually do. Are you comfortable?"

"Very, thank you." Physically, anyway. The fitted sky-blue vest looked shapeless, but once zipped up the front proved to be quite flattering, especially paired with the sleek trousers of the same colour. As someone who was naturally more Marilyn Monroe (she wished!) than slinky supermodel, she appreciated this feature. Everything else was a mess, though. "I noticed everyone wears similar outfits here, all in one colour. Is that just the fashion?"

Georgiana laughed. "Oh, aren't you a dear."

Was she? And that wasn't an answer. Ash had noticed from the start that the locals were monochromatic. Islo had been wearing light brown, Georgiana gold, and her husband forest green. No patterns, no jewellery, no accessories. It was a bit funny-looking in Ash's opinion, but then with the fashions of her ti…at *home*, who was she to criticize? Practically everyone wore jeans casually, and it was hard to find any business suits that weren't grey or black.

"So it *is* just fashion?"

"We wear our colours with pride, Ash, for they are significant," the lady replied firmly, not answering the question at all. "All except new-blue, of course. Now come along, or we'll be late, and we don't want that."

By this time Anne had come back out of the bathroom wearing her more modest version of the same outfit, and Islo had slunk off somewhere, probably to avoid more mentions of unbuyable milk.

"I don't suppose we do," Ash agreed glumly.

They followed Georgiana down the escalator (and who needed one of *those* in a house?) to what had to be a lift. Teron was already waiting along with George, and the latter wore a similar outfit to Ash's as well – new-blues for everyone. If he was anyone else, she would have guessed that he worked out; but he didn't seem the type to be sweating at the gym. Lots of riding on squirrel-shy horses, perhaps? It was a shame he wore the long sleeves, she thought idly, since he looked like he would have nice muscular arms.

No! No perving at Mr Darcy, she scolded herself. And she shouldn't be calling him Mr Darcy anyway, because if she wasn't careful she'd find herself saying it to his face again, and they didn't get on well as it was – and he did not look like he had a sense of humour at the moment.

George didn't meet her eye, or Anne's, instead seeming almost jittery. His jaw was tight and his eyebrows low and grumpy-looking, and his whole face alternately pale and flushed. His whole persona was grumpy, in fact – he probably disliked the clothing even more than Anne. It was a surprise, because from the start he'd seemed somewhat well-mannered, and now…not so much. But then Ash barely knew the guy, didn't she?

Anne seemed to notice the same. "Are you well, sir?"

"Never better!" George practically shouted, then corrected in a more normal tone, "Just something of a megrim, I'm afraid. No doubt it will soon pass."

Megrim? Oh, he meant he had a headache. "I'm sure there's something you can take for that." Ash looked at Georgiana. "Do you have any painkiller? Medicine, I mean."

"Thank you for your concern, but I do not need medicine!"

Ooh. As far as Ash could tell, he was foul-tempered enough that he was very uncomfortable. But then a few men (and sometimes women, but it seemed more often males) would refuse to admit they were in any kind of pain, as if it made them somehow weak.

Well, that was his problem, but she'd avoid him until he looked more normal. They were about to go into an underground city to meet some kind of non-human monarch, and she had enough problems to deal with beside his bad moods.

On the other hand, Georgiana was all smiles. Except for the brief moment when she told them off for using titles, the woman didn't seem to have any other settings. "Let's go, then."

Another door slid open in the lobby, then off they went.

IVERSLEY, UNDERGROUND

George went with the others from the foyer into a very small square room. The doors closed behind them, there was a strange sense of movement that made his stomach slide up into his throat, and ten seconds later the doors reopened to reveal an entirely different location.

As promised it was a city, and unlike anything he had ever seen before. The whole thing was built in a vast cavern that rose probably a quarter-mile above their heads, and the buildings rose multiple levels ahead of them in every direction, entirely unfamiliar right down to the materials they seemed to be made of.

It was lit as bright as day from a thousand torches set in the walls and roof of the cavern and tops of the buildings, and there were people, so many people, and more of the giants that would need to be size-changers to fit into the moving box that had brought him down here. Ah, correction; *Nobles.*

George knew his mood was foul, because while the women (even Ashlea!) were gasping in awe around him, the whole thing left him strangely unimpressed. He'd lied to them before. He didn't truly have a megrim. What he did have was a tremendous sense of melancholy – condemnation even – that had him feeling as though he'd been squashed flat by one of those Nobles he could see even now.

It had started just after they'd reached the village. He'd been feeling not quite himself all morning. Well – not the 'himself' that the world usually saw, anyway. They'd all been eating breakfast together: him, his newly discovered family, and his co-travellers, when he'd started to feel melancholy. Not just slightly melancholy: very, very melancholy.

It was not the first time this had happened. George knew that generally he came across as a friendly, cheerful fellow, which usually he was. But sometimes, without warning, it would happen. A dark, doubting cloud would fall over his mind and everything would seem awful. Hopeless.

Anything could set it off: a thought, a memory, someone saying something unkind – he'd be left feeling as if someone had stepped on him and squashed him flat into the ground.

It never lasted, thank Deias. After a day if he was lucky, or a fortnight if he wasn't, he would come back into his normal, cheerful self.

He'd endure it as best he could, hide it as best he could, and usually he could hide it well from everyone except his mother. She'd told him her father had been the same, but much worse; during a bad time he had ordered one of his sons whipped for spilling soup, and in one of his good times he'd given all the servants a guinea because he thought they were 'such fine fellows'. There was nothing that could be done about it, she said, some people were just inclined to fits of melancholy.

Well, George had never had it *that* badly, and the worst mood swings had ceased after he was about sixteen. Except for the time with Clarissa, of course. He'd been so buoyant while courting her that her defection had led to his worst dark period ever.

But this time, as George had sat at that breakfast table with the others, a darkness descended faster and stronger than ever before. Even worse than when Clarissa had left him. He had lifted a glass of water to his mouth and next thing the clear memory of that terrible time had come into his head.

"I do love you, George," she'd said, her beautiful face streaming with tears. *"But I can't live like that. I can't be poor, George, I won't! And you wouldn't be happy either!"*

He'd tried to reassure her that they'd be fine; it didn't matter if his father had threatened to cut him off if he married beneath himself. He'd find a job and they'd be happy.

She'd shaken her ringleted head. Golden like his; their children would have shared the same colouring. *"No, George. You wouldn't. We wouldn't. I- I can't take that risk."* And then she'd left him.

She hadn't trusted him to look after her. What sort of man isn't trusted by the very woman who claims to love him? A failure, that's who. Or worse – maybe she'd never loved him at all, just his social standing and his sizeable allowance from his (then) generous father.

He didn't know why that memory had come up. All he knew was that it brought with it an almost overwhelming gloom.

Then later on after they'd eaten he'd been following Teron up the stairs to his room, trying not to show his foul mood, when he'd remembered the look on his father's face whenever he saw George. Disappointment.

You're a failure, boy. Useless. Good for nothing. No son of mine.

George couldn't remember if his father had ever said those actual words, but now he heard them in his head as clear as if he'd been standing next to him.

Useless.

Then when he was in the cleanser, (a fascinating piece of technology, which unfortunately he was unable to fully appreciate at the time) those images had come back to mind. They'd mixed in with the vivid memory of his man of affairs telling him that his last chance ship, the Proserpine, had gone down in a storm off the coast of Afreca.

He'd clearly seen that same look of utter disappointment on the man's face. *You've failed me. You've failed everybody. You've made bad choices, and now we'll all suffer.*

And then all those angry words and angry faces had blurred into a stream of negativity, consuming his mind until he wasn't sure what had been real and what hadn't. All George knew was that he felt more miserable than he ever had in his life. That arrogant man, Dr Walker, had been right. He wouldn't be missed. So what if he died here in this bizarre parody of his home country? The world would be no worse off without him.

That's not true! a little voice, strangely reminiscent of his late grandfather, argued against the despair. But it was small and quiet and the melancholy was overwhelming, and quite frankly he didn't have the emotional energy to listen to it.

Then, in the middle of it all, as George had stood staring blankly at the white shower wall, a touch of sweetness entered.

It doesn't have to be this way.

It was a woman's voice, smooth and beautiful and more enchanting than anything he'd ever heard in his entire life. Had he imagined it? It was even clearer than the other voices, the ones that sounded like Clarissa and his father and every other disappointed person he'd ever known.

I'm real.

The voices were responding, now. Oh, dear. That wasn't good. The stress of life had become too much, and he'd finally cracked. At least it was a *nice* hallucination. He'd heard they could be very unpleasant.

You're not crazy. The beautiful voice came even clearer than before. *I'll show you. Come to visit me in my temple, and I'll show you. I'll free you.*

Her...temple?

My home. My throne, the voice corrected. *Come.*

And then for a moment the despair lifted like a heavy layer of fog under bright sunlight, before coming back down almost as heavily. Amongst it all George just had the same recurring thought – *go to her.* But who was 'her'?

The oddity of it combined with his otherwise terrible melancholy meant that he could barely focus on what was going on around him even now, but he felt like he was being pulled inevitably forward, like an invisible string had tied around his lungs and heart and took him to her.

Oh, Hades and Eternal Chaos. Perhaps he *was* crazy.

"I hope you don't mind that we're walking," Georgiana said apologetically. "We're but five minutes from the palace. Perhaps another time we can show you how to use the skimmers."

She pointed up to where dozens of curving rails were running overhead and moving around the buildings, chairs skimming along them like seats on a rollercoaster. Just now a couple of seated people whizzed past overhead, both looking unimpressed by the journey. One even appeared to be reading from something flat and round – their version of a newspaper, maybe.

"That's fine," Ash replied in amazement. After everything, she hadn't *actually* been expecting an entire city to be below ground. So it wasn't a huge city – nothing compared to Lunden or even Nelsonton back home in the Southern Isles – but you could get lost in here.

There were even multi-storey buildings, and while (disappointingly) there weren't any flying cars, the 'skimmers' made her think of a fun park. "This whole place is incredible. Are there other cities like this?"

Georgiana shook her head. "Not in Angland. Other cities have partial components underground, but Iversley has less than one percent above ground. Quite something, isn't it? Although I should say that we're technically only a town because of some silly ancient bylaws involving the lack of a cathedral, but we're big enough to be a city, and that's what we mostly call ourselves. Anyway, you'll find everything down here. Greenhouses, entertainment, food, public services – we even have our own water supply. There's a beautiful lake over the far end of the cavern, fed directly from a spring beneath us."

"But *you* live above ground," Anne pointed out.

"Well, we've had the place ever since it was built by my great, great grandfather. He was one of those who wanted to extend the city underground in the first place, back in the late twenty-first century. When the green belts – laws to stop all the green spaces being lost to development – meant that towns had to go up into multi-storey buildings, he suggested that they could go down into the ground instead. He got the idea from the Devil's Arse. Have you heard of that?"

Oh, to see Anne's face – that was *not* a word that she used, Ash would bet.

Ash stopped herself smiling. "No, I haven't, I'm afraid."

"It was an ancient cavern that had a village in it. He thought we could do something similar, although a lot of work would be needed first, obviously. He was laughed at, at first, but then there was all the mess with the first radioactive wars over in Eurasia, and all of a sudden everyone was keen on it. Just in case the fall-out spread, it was built as quickly as possible, and many people from the area moved in. It was just as well, because a bomb dropped right on top of us and wiped out what was there before. We lost our ancestral home. Luckily that was only one of the newer destructive bombs – it cleared the area completely, chewed the earth up into hills and valleys, as you saw, but at least there was very little radiation. But then when it was safe to rebuild above ground, only a few families were allowed to."

"Wow," Ash gasped. "Everything was wiped out?"

"Well…quite a bit. It chopped up the landscape somewhat too, but then my grandfather and everyone were safe down here. All of the forest grew back eventually, although we did have to bring new species in that would grow in the damaged soil. I rather think it's an improvement from the old pictures I've seen. Greener, more beautiful."

That explained the difference in the forest from when Ash had first gone on her 'walk'. But it sounded so sad, like how you'd see a beautiful face, then find out that there'd been an accident and they'd once looked like a different person. It just felt *wrong*, especially as Georgiana had just described what sounded like the Apocalypse, minus a few plagues.

"I'm sorry to hear that," Ash said honestly. "Did it happen all over the world? Did many people die?"

Georgiana shook her head. "I'm sure some did, dear, but that's what happens in wars. But enough on this subject. Iversley is what it is because of that past, and while we're a little isolated, living here's not at all a hardship. We are most fortunate, because otherwise the Nobles wouldn't have come to us as they did."

"Did you say that the Nobles came *because* of Iversley's isolation?" George asked. He still looked as grim and white-faced as he had since he'd changed clothes, and his hands were in tight fists at his sides.

Teron opened his mouth as if to speak – the first time since they'd left his lobby – but Georgiana cut in. "I'm sure I've no idea why they chose Iversley. But we must go, or we'll be late." She began to walk down the neat, mostly vehicle-free streets, and Teron and George began to follow.

"But did they?" Ash echoed, reluctant to follow. Something about what had just been said didn't sit right, and she wondered what Teron would have said. "Did they come here just because it's isolated?"

"Perhaps you can ask once you meet the Queen," Georgiana called over her shoulder, but she didn't slow down. Teron walked alongside, and George trailed behind. But even though Ash was curious, she also wasn't sure what she was getting herself in for, so she stopped walking. Anne obviously felt the same way, because she stopped too and stood beside her, arms folded and looking mutinous.

"I do not wish to meet this 'Queen'," she announced. "What could she possibly want with us?"

"To meet you, as she meets all new people." Georgiana's

smile was wearing thin. "She has ordered us to bring you to her, and so we must. It is a great honour! Don't you want answers to your questions?"

Maybe it was, but the fact they'd been 'ordered' – and that Dr Walker hadn't even *heard* of any giants/Nobles – made Ash very hesitant. "I'll have to agree with Anne on this one. Your hospitality has been very appreciated, but I need you to tell us why we're going, or else I think we'll just have to find someone else to answer those questions for us."

If they could get anyone to stop what they were doing and help, that was. Ash could see all around them those curving cable cars running like rollercoasters up and down and all around the buildings, and people dressed in the usual monochrome suits moved purposefully wherever they were going. Work, presumably.

There were park benches clearly for relaxing, but no one was using them. Well, one person – an older woman who sat staring blankly into the distance, hollow-eyed and with her mouth moving silently. It looked like this city too had its fringe of over-looked, not-quite-there souls, and Ash felt a pang of pity. At least the woman didn't look hungry, just a bit mad.

Here and there giants (sorry, *Nobles*) stood idly around. Ash still got the sense that they were supervising the humans. It was possible they were conquerors, but the people didn't seem at all downtrodden. Instead Teron and Georgiana seemed very proud of them, like they were a cross between heroes and tourist attractions.

"But it's the Queen," Teron said, baffled by Ash's reluctance. "Why *wouldn't* you want to meet her?"

"Are you afraid?" Georgiana echoed. "There's nothing to be afraid of."

"Not afraid, precisely," Ash lied. "But a name would be a good start. Which queen is this, again? Why would she order you to bring us to her?" In fact, Islo walking up to them this morning in the village was feeling less and less like general friendliness, and more prearranged.

"Ashlea, we've already answered that question," Georgiana replied tightly, the smile now seeming pasted on. "Come along, we're going to be late!"

"You did not give a sufficient answer the first time," Anne said from beside Ash. For once they were unified. "I would also know who is this queen who would strip people of their titles and decent garb, and take the glory for herself." She paused. "Not that this is uncommon for monarchs, I vow. But I would know who *this* queen is."

"What about you, George?" Ash asked. Through the whole exchange he had stood beside the two locals, staring vaguely into the distance with that same frown on his face. "Do you want to visit the queen?"

"I suppose so," he mumbled. "She's been calling to me all morning."

There was a long, awkward pause where Ash tried to work out how that might *not* sound crazy, but Anne had no such restraint. "When did she call to you? I've heard not a word!"

He scrubbed a hand over the side of his face. "In my head. She was speaking directly to my mind. I know it sounds mad, and perhaps I am. But I must go to her."

Ah, well. It just showed you never knew a person. They might seem perfectly polite and Regency era-snobbish, but they could be just as schizophrenic as the next unfortunate soul. And she *had* only met him yesterday afternoon under strange circumstances, so how would she have known what he was really like?

Ash said carefully, "If you feel like you must, then go right ahead, George. I'm going to find Dr Walker like we were supposed to. Lady Anne, do you want to come along?"

She'd added the 'lady' just to be contrary, but Anne brightened. "Indeed I do. Mr Seymour, I wish you well in your endeavours with your…family, and mayhap we shall meet again in the next world. Or back in the forest, all going well. But I bid you good day."

Ash almost applauded, it was such a lovely closing speech. But unfortunately it wasn't enough – Georgiana and Teron had been looking increasingly anxious, and the former lifted a hand in gesture to someone behind the two girls. Ash turned to see who, and abruptly smacked into a tree. A big, brown tree trunk with leathery bark…

Ash looked up the length of what looked to be an enormous boot, into the scowling face far above her. The giant had dark, shoulder-length hair with a thin braid on either side of his face – it was the one she'd seen in the forest earlier. **"Where do you think you're going?"** he rumbled.

The girls both screamed. Acting on instinct, Ash kicked out at the giant's foot, which was all she could reach, then dashed around him. She hadn't got ten steps when she was suddenly grabbed around the waist and swung into the air. The giant lifted her up so she was level with his face. He had brown eyes, Ash noticed dazedly. Anne was now in his other hand. Ash could see that his fingers went right the way around her waist, almost covering her torso.

"Are you going to walk, or do I have to carry you?"

"We'll walk!" Anne squeaked. She looked as if she was just short of hysterics. "Please don't eat us!"

Ash didn't say anything. She was too busy staring at the thing in front of her, who hadn't seemed so very, very, very large when she'd seen him in the forest. Good grief, his nose alone was the length of her forearm, and she could see the hair in his giant nostrils. Alien? Fairytale monster? Mutant?

He glared. He probably didn't appreciate the scrutiny, but he was dangling her in the air right in front of his earth-ball sized head. She didn't get the feeling that he'd hurt her, though being held like this was unpleasantly intrusive. She wasn't hurt, but just…urgh. Too close, too much, too scary.

"I don't eat humans," the giant rumbled. **"Not with the bones in, they stick in my throat."**

Anne began to scream hysterically, and the giant made a scoffing noise, giving both of them a little shake that made Ash's head rattle. **"Chaos. She can't take a joke."**

Ash, who was about to wet herself in fear (close thing there) laughed in that panicked way you do when you're scared but also relieved. "Ha ha ha, you can put us down, then…"

He ignored her, speaking instead to the couple below. **"Got a summons, have you?"**

"Lord Hadur," Georgiana called. "If it pleases you, would you carry them to the Queen? They are to see her as soon as possible, but I fear that they will not go unaided."

The giant growled in assent and began to walk. As Ash rocked back and forth with his footsteps, she looked down at their hosts. All she could see was the back of their heads – they were *bowing*. Maybe she should have done the same thing, played along until she had the chance to go her own way. But now she felt like a fly on its way to the spider, trapped so securely she had no other choice. Maybe it wouldn't be so bad. Maybe the Queen *would* be nice, and her intentions kind…?

"You don't have to carry us!" Ash pleaded, her voice jolted by the movements. Anne, at least, had stopped screaming and was now letting out an ongoing panicked whimper. "We won't try to run away again."

Hadur ignored her and kept walking down the main street from the elevator, covering the distance far faster than they could have run. He carried them some way along, taking the occasional turn from street to street before entering a courtyard with a very high arched roof, then heading up towards some large double doors. They gleamed like polished brass, (couldn't be gold at that size, surely?) and were high enough that even the giant could walk through without stooping.

Ash tried to relax and stop wriggling. It was hard; the giant was holding her gently but it wasn't exactly comfortable. "Please, we'll walk." Because there was no way they could escape held in the air like this!

"Stop talking."

She did, and awaited her doom in silence… quite melodramatic, but that was how it felt. As if with every long step Hadur took, she was getting closer and closer to something big. Something different and powerful enough to be scary. And she did not like the feeling.

The doors swung open as they approached and Ash heard Anne give a squeak of surprise. Ash didn't see anybody operating them. That didn't mean anything. They had automatic doors at home too. Except they weren't ten metres high and possibly solid gold…

But then they walked inside the room, and all her anxious thoughts flew right out of her mind.

❦

Anne was more afraid than she'd ever been in her entire life, and her life had been filled with some moments of intense fear, Wilfred's recent death not one of the least.

When she was seven she'd fallen into an old well and not been found for hours. She'd thought she was going to die then, but she'd been fished out at the last moment, cold, hungry, and probably wiser for the experience.

But now, she was *certain* she was going to die. Either that, or something else dreadful was going to happen, and she could do naught to change it.

By the Saints, she was being swung about in the air by a genuine giant! Anne was no fool. In all the stories she'd heard, giants were wicked. Always grinding bones to make their bread and suchlike. 'Twas bad, bad, very very bad-

She stopped herself. She was becoming overwrought, and

'twould not aid her situation. She forced herself to breathe as deeply and regularly as possible considering she was still ten feet in the air in a giant's fist, and focused on what was happening around her.

They'd gone inside the vast doors of what looked to be a palace, but unlike anything she'd ever seen before, and had made their way to their current location. 'Twas a vast, dimly lit room.

On the far wall she could just perceive a mirror. 'Twas the biggest one she'd ever seen, mayhap as wide as her outstretched arms and as high as the doors had been, and it sat almost oddly in the centre of the wall, its lower edge propped on the floor so that it reminded her of a door.

At home she'd had a beautiful little Venezian hand mirror, but had never seen anything near as vast as this here. The framing looked expensive too. Finely worked gold and silver ropes combined in a sinuous interwoven pattern, reminding Anne of climbing ivy, or less pleasantly, snakes.

For all of its grandeur it didn't look to be a very effective mirror. The surface was misty, and she could only just make out faint colours showing their reflected selves.

The giant set her down on the ground gently but far too quickly. Anne swayed a bit, then fell against Ash, catching her balance and then once more feeling the shock of only two layers of clothing. This outfit was more comfortable than her usual, that was for certain, but she felt underdressed, and it only added to her sense of displacement.

She took a distinct step closer to Ash, taking comfort in the other's closeness. Odd how just twelve hours ago Anne had despised the girl, but now George had proved useless, Ash seemed to be her only friend in the world.

Suddenly there was movement in the fogged plane of glass, and a burst of light, and then Anne was standing in front of the most beautiful woman she'd ever seen. Not just beautiful – *glorious* – and Anne fell to her knees. Not on purpose, but because the power and (majesty, could she say that?) of the creature was too much to stay standing.

Well, it most certainly wasn't Queen Marian from back home.

Taller than even George, and perfectly proportioned, the Queen was surrounded by a golden light that seemed to emanate from her very skin. Saints above, she looked just like one of those paintings of a celestial, except without the wings. Pure white skin shone even through the golden glow, hair also (unsurprisingly) like gold, and eyes that blazed amber fire. Simply magnificent. And her features – they were perfection. Not a flaw or freckle to be seen.

But the vision wasn't coming through the mirror – she appeared to be in it.

And then she spoke.

"Georgiana, Servant of Lady Alfeior, you may return to your home."

Her voice was like liquid sunlight, like a beautiful symphony of caramel and velvet. That shouldn't even make sense, Anne thought, but 'twas how it seemed. Her voice was so sensual that 'twas almost physical, and Anne couldn't focus on anything else. She certainly couldn't move.

Georgiana bowed her head so that her forehead touched the floor, then got up and backed out of the room.

"Step forward, George Seymour."

George moved closer to the mirror, his face filled with awe.

"Kneel before me."

He knelt, and the Queen said, *"You have listened to my voice, and it was the correct path that led you to this place. I know your suffering, Honourable George Seymour, and I will take it away from you and give you a new purpose in life. Henceforth you shall be known as George, Servant of the One True Queen."*

George looked baffled but ecstatic, and was murmuring his heartfelt thanks. But something pricked through the thick haze around Anne's mind, and she frowned. There'd been something wrong with that statement.

Something wrong? How could anything that came from such a beautiful, perfect creature be anything but right?

But he was some form of noble himself, was he not? Why would he want…

Then the Queen called her name and she forgot her objections.

"Anne of Covington," she said. *"You have been known by many names, and your life has been restricted, dull and dangerous. You have fit into the names and the moulds that have been created for you, regardless of who you are on the inside."*

She was right. Anne *had* been forced into all kinds of roles – even the Countess of Longford was a role she played, and before that, the perfect lady. Or she'd *tried* to be the perfect lady. But 'twas so dreadfully difficult to maintain, and so often she'd missed out on the fun that others had around her, because of who she was required to be, not only for herself, but for others. But how did the Queen know her so well?

"This journey will become a joy for you, Anne. You will be a woman for all seasons. Had you not been snatched away to this time, you would have died within twelve months of your second wedding of childbed fever. Instead, you shall stay here and live out your long days in a way you'd never imagined was possible. Henceforth you shall be known as Anne, Servant of Lady Souris of the Lesser Waters."

Anne felt power wash over her like a warm wind, and with it came a sense of joy and acceptance that she didn't think she'd felt since childhood. 'Twas as if that rich, melodic voice had taken Anne's deepest, most fervent dream, the one she didn't even know she had, and spoken it into reality. Anne felt overcome with joy. 'Twas perfect. 'Twas what she'd always wanted, but hadn't the wits to know it any sooner. She would serve Lady Souris of the Lesser Waters. Anne had no idea who that was, but who cared?

You're not a servant! shrieked inner Anne, that familiar voice now seeming shrill and irritating – and persistent. It wouldn't go away, even though the golden haze almost stifled it into silence.

You're a lady! Granddaughter of a duke!

The happy/peaceful Anne told that voice to shut its mouth. She looked up at the Queen, who was smiling down on her with that lovely, lovely, strangely familiar face, and another face popped into her mind. A young girl, less than a year Anne's junior, with similar features to Anne but with dark brown hair instead of red. Her sister Elspeth, who was all alone with people who treated her like a nuisance.

She'll be fine, the happy/peaceful voice murmured. *She's not like you. She's more placid, accepting. She will do well.*

But the damage had already been done, and now Anne had never felt so torn. On the one hand she felt as though she was on her wedding day – or how she *ought* to have felt on her wedding day, mayhap, because she hadn't been all that thrilled to marry a man twice her age. But on the other hand she recalled those left behind in her own time, and guilt and confusion slunk in to sit heavily in her chest.

"*Ashlea Jane O'Reilly*," the Queen said, and it seemed a cue for Anne to move back. She'd been on her knees the whole time, and now she forced herself to stand, moving back to what seemed a reasonable distance. Everything in her rebelled at the increased space, wanting to move closer once more, but at the same time the small, shrill inner-Anne wanted to turn and run far, far away to where life was easier, and there was no confusion.

But then Ash stepped forward, and the Queen's attention was on her instead. To Anne's admittedly biased eyes, Ash seemed perhaps a little afraid – but also excited, and as baffled as Anne had been when her late husband announced (rather prophetically as it turned out) that he would die before he would convert…but that wasn't a good memory.

Ash shuffled forward to within a dozen yards of the glass, and on the other side of it the Queen echoed her posture. If it was possible, the Queen herself seemed to be leaning closer to the other side of the glass. She almost looked as if she would break through. *"Ashlea Jane O'Reilly. I have waited many centuries for this moment. To meet one such as you."*

Ash touched her chest self-consciously. "Me?"

Anne had to agree. Her? Why?

"You, Ash. I cannot yet tell you the reason why as you would not understand, but you are the only one in innumerable years who is fit to be my namesake."

Ash frowned, that mixed expression of fear and excitement becoming more pronounced. Anne felt the same – what was the woman talking about? She quickly glanced around the room to see that George was staring at the Queen with the slavish devotion that people often had for the very beautiful, and their hosts had left. Only the large and grabby Hadur still stood at the back of the room, looking bored. But then he would have seen this before.

"I don't know what you mean," Ash replied, her tone awed and quiet.

The Queen gestured for her to come closer. *"It means that you will carry my name, and be a vessel for increasing amounts of my power. You alone among mortals will have this honour and this privilege."*

The girl looked more worried than honoured. Anne wanted to encourage her, but didn't dare interrupt the flow of the Queen's speech.

"Reach your hand out to touch the mirror."

Ash shook her head slightly. "I'm not-"

But they never found out what Ash wasn't, because the Queen kept speaking. *"Don't be afraid. I will only help you, not harm you. Even now you don't really believe, do you? You cannot believe what has happened to you; that you are a traveller through time even as I and my own people are. Touch the mirror, Ash, and I will show you the truth."*

Ash's face was a mask of indecision, and she raised her hand slowly towards the glass, moving forward. But she stopped too soon.

"Touch the mirror!"

This time it wasn't a suggestion, it was an order. Anne felt the impact of the words like a physical blow, almost knocking her backwards.

Anne watched as Ash reluctantly lifted her hand towards the glass, touching it with the tips of her fingers. On the other side the Queen mirrored her gesture, then golden light exploded from their joining to envelop Ash.

When the light receded Ash was standing back from the glass, cradling one hand in the other and staring at it numbly. The Queen looked almost smug, if that mundane expression was possible on her flawless face.

She said triumphantly, *"Henceforth, you shall be known as the Queen's namesake, and shall require no other title. You may go."*

And just for an instant, Anne felt a cold dash of fear.

Seven

NAMESAKE

"Namesake," Ash said thoughtfully. "What do you think that means?"

"She might have explained it to you before she disappeared," Anne answered grumpily. In fact, she'd been grumpy full stop from the time the queen had vanished and the giant Hadur had shuffled them back out onto the street. "And what are we supposed to do now, I ask you?"

Ash didn't know either, but she didn't really care. All she could think of was how it had felt to stand in the Queen's presence; the power that had emanated from her, how Ash felt *better* as a person for having been in that contact.

Her whole world had been turned upside down, because the Queen had been right. Even after the shock of the underground city and seeing the giants up close, Ash still hadn't really believed that she'd time-travelled. Not until she'd met the Queen – not until she'd *experienced* that power, because even seeing wasn't believing. And the gift she'd been given…

"She was a time-traveller too," George announced. He looked much better than he had before the meeting where Ash had wondered if he was crazy. Now he looked happy, but a little confused. Kind of how Ash felt. "But what time would she have come from, to look like that? To have that power?" he continued. "Perhaps the very distant future, where humanity has enough knowledge to make themselves greater than merely human. Or perhaps the very distant past, if more alter-power was available. Because that was alter-power, wasn't it?"

"Yes." Ash knew it couldn't have been anything else. It was a force that Ash's father had always claimed was far more accessible than most people believed, but he'd never been able to so much as bend a spoon. He'd thought that there was an entire realm of alter-power, and if you could find it, you could become… "…Like a god."

"Precisely," George agreed happily, thinking she referred to the Queen. "She had enough alter-power that I can see why ancient peoples might worship her as a god. Perhaps that's what the ancient gods were, do you think? People such as the Queen?"

"That's quite enough!" Anne snapped, throwing her arms in the air forcefully and almost poking out the eye of an innocent passer-by. "They are not gods, and you shall not refer to them as such simply because they glow like celestial beings! Did you hear what she said to me?"

"No," Ash replied, not really paying attention. She was too busy studying the little green tattoo that had appeared on her hand after she'd touched the mirror. The design was a green leaf bud, with tendrils curling down her finger and over the back of her hand. It was quite delicate and almost realistic, and didn't rub off. She'd tried.

"She made me a servant! She made *you* a namesake," Anne declared accusingly. "I do not see what is so special about you, Ashlea O'Reilly, that you might be chosen like that."

"Calm down," Ash replied distractedly, still studying the tattoo. It hadn't hurt at all, but even now she could feel it tingling under her skin. What was it for, she wondered? And those last words that the Queen had said to her… "You don't need to be jealous."

"Jealous!" Anne squawked, almost causing Ash to jump in fright. "How in all of heaven do you perceive that I might be *jealous* of you?"

Had Ash said that? But it was obvious. Back in that room, Ash had been honoured. She'd been chosen out of everyone to be the Queen's namesake – she'd been chosen above Anne, who was made servant to a lesser Noble. Ash still didn't know what it all meant, but how could Anne not be jealous? So that was what she told the girl.

It didn't go down well. Anne practically turned crimson with anger, arms waving around in the air again. "Do you not see what has been done to us? We had no questions answered, we were simply allocated to those oversized, unnatural creatures like some kind of- of-" She struggled to find the word.

"Servant?" George suggested mildly.

"Yes, servant!" Anne spat out the word like it was an insect in her ale. "We must flee from this horror, not *consider* it! Have we not been snatched from our homes, from our families, and for what? To serve some glowing, power-riddled, oversized-"

"That's enough," someone growled, and Ash actually took a moment to look around for Hadur before realising it was George, as his voice had been so deep and grouchy, and not at all like him. But then he softened, just a little. "I understand this is a shock, Anne, and you must realise that no one is forcing you to stay here. But we've been offered…options. That's how I see this. We have options to start anew, and I for one am considering it. How can I *not*? It's not as if I have a wonderful home to return to. I've nothing really, and nobody, not any longer. But here…"

Ash watched him. His face was brighter, like he carried some exciting knowledge that had given him a new purpose, and she knew it came from those few moments back in the palace. Power, indeed. And she had to agree.

"I'm not thinking about tomorrow," he continued. "Not now. But I want to see what's here. I've never even imagined things like this existed. I just want to see what it's all about, this namesake thing; the nobles. This city. And then once I've seen…I can decide what to do next."

The redhead's face was a picture of frustration, but George's words had made so much sense that she didn't argue, even though she clearly wanted to. She turned to Ash instead. "And what of you, Ash? Yestereve you were doing everything you could do to return to your…your whatever it was. And now you have changed your mind because your position in society has improved?"

Now *that* was a good point, and not entirely true.

But then Anne ruined it by adding, "You are truly common-born, and that shall not change. You called me lady before, did you not? You know what is right. Come, accept your lot in life and return to your home with me. You return to your home, I shall return to mine, I mean."

Wow. Just…wow. It was probably the shock of everything that had happened in the last twenty-four hours and especially the last ten minutes, but Ash didn't listen to Anne's full, reasoned argument. All she heard were those damning couple of sentences… "Accept my lot in life? *Anne*, I've just been given a new lot. You heard it. So why in Hades shouldn't I take a look into this new opportunity just like George is? Because you're dead jealous of being overlooked, and of your title and birth meaning nothing here?"

Anne sputtered impotently for a few seconds, then managed to screech, "Jealous? Stop talking nonsense!" She took a deep breath. "I shall overlook this last conversation, but you must come with me now. We shall find Doctor Walker, and then-"

See how she orders you around? She thinks she's better than you. You don't have to listen to her, Ash thought, and the thought came straight out of her mouth. "You're not any better than me," she burst out resentfully. "I don't have to listen to you."

"Don't have to- Excuse me for trying to save you! And as for the first…" Anne lifted her chin haughtily. "I am a lady born, no matter what anyone says. At my home I could have you flogged for your impertinence!"

This conversation had gone rapidly downhill, but Ash couldn't seem to stop herself. With every word Anne spoke, Ash grew angrier and angrier, and all those little insults Ash had overlooked earlier piled up into a huge, seething mass of irritation. How *dare* the girl talk to her like that?

"Back to that, are we? Well, we're not at your home, and here you're not a lady. You're nothing and nobody, *servant of Souris*. Look, your clothes have even changed colour."

They'd been sky blue, and now were a tawny beige. That was what Georgiana had meant about their colours showing their allegiances. George's and Ash's had changed too, to identical shades of scarlet, although the colour didn't flatter his paler skin tones, unfortunately. But the mention was enough to infuriate Anne just as Ash knew it would.

"Why you-" Anne spat, looking down at her newly beige clothing as if she'd like to strip it off and burn it for witchcraft. "It doesn't matter what that witch in there said, I *know* who I am. I *know* I'm a lady, and nothing *anybody* says can change that." She glared at Ash. "And no imaginary titles bestowed will make you one bit better than you are."

There was a long silence full of anger and hurt, and Ash thought of how haughty Anne had always been, and of how she'd never liked her, not at all. There wasn't anything to like. "Weren't you in a hurry to be somewhere? You'd better be going, because I'm not coming with you. In fact, I don't care if I never see you again." It was true. It had to be true, and the tattoo on her hand now felt as heavy as lead.

Anne lifted her chin, but her eyes were suspiciously shiny. "And you may fall off the ends of the earth for all I care, Cinder-ash. What of you, George?"

"My apologies, Anne," he replied, and Ash noticed the missing 'lady', "but I've already told you how I feel. If you wish to go now, you'll need to go alone."

Anne dashed a tear from her face. "Fine. I don't need *you*

either. I'll find my own way back!"

Ash and George watched as Anne's small straight back disappeared into the crowded streets, and Ash rubbed her hand uncomfortably over the new mark on the ball of her thumb. It felt heavy, like more than just colour sat on her skin. "We just spoke the truth," she said to George, "but I don't like talking to people like that. Do you think she'll be alright?" Anne was so small, and out of her comfort zone, and probably vulnerable in spite of her arrogance, or maybe because of it…

"I think she'll make her own choices," he replied finally. "And I cannot see harm coming to her in this place."

"You're probably right."

As for Ash and George, they too had to make their own choices. Right now they stood outside the palace gates on one of the larger city streets, pedestrians streaming on either side of them like water parting around a rock. Ash was getting some strange looks, but she didn't care.

She'd never felt so conflicted. On the one hand, the most glorious creature she'd ever seen had granted her almost unimaginable powers (or so she said), and in an instant Ash had revised her sceptical stance on the existence of aliens, celestial beings, elves and maybe even gods. It had been an incredible moment, and she didn't think she'd ever forget it.

But on the other hand, she felt just plain weird. She didn't feel full of unimaginable powers. She felt tired and a bit shaky, like the crash after a triple shot espresso. That's what seeing the Queen had been like; an intense high. And it wasn't like she'd even sought the high. She'd been resisting it because it felt so overwhelming, and quite frankly the whole concept of a mind-reading, giant Queen scared the mickey out of her.

But the Queen hadn't been giant. She'd been only about six feet tall through that mirror, and so beautiful in a strangely familiar way, as though she looked like someone Ash knew. Some actress, perhaps? But no one on the silver screen could match up to that level of beauty, not for a moment. It had been actually stunning; with the shock of that beauty and the power that the Queen carried meaning that Ash could barely move, even when she'd been asked to approach the mirror. But then the Queen had ordered her to touch the glass, and her body had bypassed her brain to obey.

The sensation that had flooded through her at that touch- oh! She'd felt like she'd been connected to a bolt of pure electricity, except instead of pain it brought an immense feeling of power, as the Queen had said it would. And as a reminder of the exchange, on the back of her hand was this small dark green curling tendril, like a tattoo of a newly sprouted plant.

Ash remembered what the Queen had said to her in that last blinding moment, directly into Ash's mind. 'As the plant grows, so will your power. And then I will call you back to me.'

The idea had amazed Ash, and at the time it had seemed incredibly exciting. Her power would grow! She'd get to go back to the Queen! But the further she had gone away from that mirror and that golden glow, the more confused she felt. Right now, she was frankly baffled.

"It's the oddest thing," George said suddenly, "but did you realise that you now outrank me, Ashlea?" He laughed a little sheepishly. "I will require some time to become accustomed to that."

Ash felt a flash of pride that didn't last long. "Yeah, that's all very nice, but I don't know what I'm supposed to do with this rank. How long does it last? What are we supposed to do in the first place?"

"I would have thought the Nobles would tell us." He watched the passing crowds as though he'd get a suggestion from their midst, but finally shrugged. "I am the Queen's servant, and she told me nothing except to do good. So I suppose I shall find a way to do that."

Ash figured the Queen must have told him in the same way

she'd told Ash about the plant growing. "Well, she didn't tell me *anything*," she said emphatically. "What does a namesake do, anyway?" Because so far it didn't seem much more than a useless title, perhaps a little like being knighted in Ash's time. You got to swan around telling people you were 'Sir whatever', but it didn't actually change your life.

"Anything they like, I suppose." George looked down at his newly scarlet vest, running a hand over it lovingly. Ash half expected his hand to come away covered in paint as though it had been a clever spray of colour, but of course it didn't. "So we now wear the Queen's scarlet, rather like the Anglish soldiers back in my time. And if *you* are the Queen's namesake, then I rather doubt you'll ever need to work again."

Strangely that didn't please Ash all that much. She didn't want to never work again, she just wanted to do something interesting, that had purpose; that made a difference to someone some-where and wasn't just counting down days until she retired. And she really, really wasn't committed to staying here. The more George spoke, the more it seemed like he had already made his decision. Her...not so much.

"I'd still like to-" she began, but then she felt a gentle tap on her shoulder.

"Ahem." The interrupter was a tall boy in his late teens (but weren't they all tall?) with dark auburn hair and a friendly, open face. He was looking at Ash expectantly. "Queen's namesake?"

He meant *her*. "Um...yes, I think. Can I help you?"

The boy grabbed her limp hand and shook it enthusiastically. "Indeed you can. I've been looking for you ever since I heard the news! All the other namesakes are dying to meet you!"

"They are?"

"Of course! You must realise that this is the most significant appointment-" Just then the boy saw George, who'd been looking on curiously. "You must be one of the new, lesser servants. You'll excuse me as I greet the Queen's namesake?"

George looked a little taken back at being referred to as 'lesser', but shrugged. "Certainly, once I can be assured of her safety. Who are you, sir?"

"Yes," Ash added in quickly, unsure how she felt about this new person for all of their friendliness. "You didn't say your name."

The boy blinked large brown eyes twice. "Forgive me, I thought I'd already…but then there has been a lot to remember, hasn't there? I was so excited when I saw you that I forgot myself for a minute." He cleared his throat. "I am Janeus's namesake. But if you prefer, you can call me Sam."

"Sam." Ash smiled at him politely, not wanting to seem cold in the face of his obvious friendliness. "Um…*whose* namesake?" Because it sounded like he'd said *Jay-nus*, which rhymed with a-

"Janeus," he repeated. There was a long pause, then he added impatiently, "You know, the Queen's consort?" There was another awkward pause where this time she knew she was supposed to recognise this name (and really, really didn't) and then he said, "It's a very important position, second only to yours. Have you really never heard of him?"

She shook her head, and George added, "It sounds a little like Janus, the Reman god of doorways. Because he had two faces, you know."

Sam glared at George. "Janeus is rather more significant than a mere god of doorways. But then you should find someone else who can educate you. I was sent here to retrieve the Queen's namesake only." He looked towards Ash expectantly. "If we might go now, milady?"

The formality felt rather nice, and she realised why Anne liked being treated with this kind of respect. Having it rapidly removed wouldn't have felt good at all. But she also didn't like the way he was trying to dismiss George. "Can't he come with us? He doesn't have anywhere else to be."

Sam looked pained. "It really is for namesakes only. But

perhaps you could meet later, if you have a…*friendship*?"

Ash realised with a start that he thought she and George were involved romantically. "We're not together. *Together*, I mean. We did *arrive* together-"

"We have no relationship," George explained politely. "And I have been given an imperative by the Queen, so also have no desire to intrude on your…private matters."

Ouch. They weren't exactly friends, but he didn't need to be that blunt. "But you said that you didn't know what you were supposed to be doing-"

"I do know. I'm going to the hospital." Then George ruined that moment of decisiveness by adding, "If I can find the place, that is."

George took the boy's directions with good grace, then strode off towards the hospital, resisting the urge to look over his shoulder to see if they were watching him go.

After about ten seconds he gave in – they weren't looking. Sam 'Janeus's Namesake' actually had his hand on Ashlea's arm and was leading her away. As George watched, she looked over her shoulder and smiled at him. He smiled back briefly, then turned and kept walking casually as though it hadn't bothered him to be sent off.

It did bother him, just a very little. The youth was too bold, and it had felt a little like George imagined it would feel to be made to go to the servants' entrance at a grand house. Ashlea was no doubt unaccustomed to such gentle treatment, and he hoped that Sam's intentions were pure.

But even that minor irritation couldn't dispel George's incredible sense of wellbeing. The headache that had come along with his sudden melancholia had disappeared in an instant once he'd walked inside that room and the Queen had appeared in the mirror.

She was the most beautiful person he had ever seen, that went without saying. But it was more than that. The power that had emanated from her had jumped across to him when she'd named him her servant, and he felt stronger, wiser, and happier than he ever had before. Euphoric, in fact, even though he didn't yet know what his purpose was here beyond serving her.

He'd lied to Lady Anne before, saying that he would stay only to consider his options. (Anne. He must start thinking of her as 'Anne' only.) The truth was that he'd decided to stay the very moment the Queen had spoken to him, and she had *known* him. In a way he felt like he knew her too, although how could that even be possible? Perhaps in the same way an infant might know their mother by her voice alone, somehow familiar even in a brand-new world. It was a dream come true.

To be fair, he hadn't been aware that his dream had been to serve the One True Queen, but now he knew, he wasn't complaining. That sudden, deep sadness that he'd been struck by had almost immediately been broken by her sweet voice, and he hadn't been the same since. Even his sense of time felt distorted. He could have met her five minutes ago, or it could have been five days.

The palace wasn't far from the hospital, and the directions that Sam had given proved correct. The hospital sat squatly on the corner of a large, open square. Like so much of the ground in this city, it was paved in a single piece of shining white stone. Placed all around it were strange, colourful sculptures; some depicting things that George couldn't identify, and some familiar as if from his own time. A couple of other people milled around in the square, but he ignored them. He'd already seen something wonderful.

Right in the very centre was a fountain. It was enormous and ornate, and its clear centrepiece was a gold statue of a woman, thrice life size and standing with her arms outspread, and with her glorious robes streaming away from her body, the carving so skilful they almost seemed to flutter as though blown in a breeze. It was a depiction of the Queen, and even though George had intended to go to the hospital, he found himself just stopping and staring.

She was looking at him, and just like in the mirror, her eyes seemed to be glowing with amber fire. He fancied that she really could see him, and she was smiling.

Of *course* she was smiling. She liked him, didn't she? Or else she never would have chosen him as her servant. There had to be dozens of other options, and he easily could have ended up with some lesser Noble as Anne had. But she had named *him*.

From the base of her robes water ran in a million dancing rivulets to land in the wide bowl surrounding the statue, shining even in the odd light down here, hidden away from the sun. It was the same clear, sparkling water that he'd enjoyed this morning with breakfast.

It wasn't normal for him to choose water over any other beverage, but he'd been particularly thirsty. Now he felt the same thirst, and the water looked like liquid life.

Inscribed in the dark green marble base were the words, 'Drink, and be free'.

Well, they didn't have to tell him twice. George crouched down, reaching out to scoop up a handful, then felt a gentle tap on his arm. He jumped a little in fright, and the intruder smiled apologetically.

"I did not mean to frighten you," the old man said in a musical voice, his accent reminding George perhaps of those traders he'd met from the far east – or perhaps from Italie, he couldn't tell.

Either way, it was irritating. Yet his upbringing kept him polite. "Yes, sir?"

"If you are thirsty, I have water." The man held up a small brown earthen jug, its brim shining as though it had just been filled. "It's very good. Far better than the water from this fountain."

"Indeed."

"Indeed," the man agreed. "My water will open your eyes, give you wings. I *promise* you, on my own name."

Everyone was making promises around here, it seemed. But George already had a goal, and had no interest in making any deviations from it, especially not for random strangers with dubious oaths. "By your name, you say?" he asked dryly. "Thank you for the kind offer, but I am quite content with what is already here."

He bent to drink, feeling absurdly thirsty by now, but the man just leaned in closer. "The water here comes directly from the lake," he said. "It is not good for drinking. This is the truth."

George was now feeling distinctly irritated by the man's mere proximity. There was something about him... "How very kind," he clipped out. "But as I said, I am quite content. I do not require anything further."

The old man looked at him assessingly, his very dark eyes crinkling at the edges either with humour or something else. "Very well," he replied, his accent now mimicking George's perfectly. "Do as you have chosen, George. But perhaps I will see you later."

Not if George saw him first. "Perhaps, sir. Good day."

And with that definitive ending, he finally managed to get that drink. His throat had become remarkably dry, rather like the end of a cold where one could drink and drink and never quite lose that parched feeling.

So it was some time later when he finally stood, and the old man had disappeared. George's headache had reappeared, and he set off towards the nearby hospital a little grumpier than he'd arrived. It was only at that moment George realised that the man had known his name, but George hadn't known his...

Ah, well. Surely the man had overheard someone else say it.

Up ahead the hospital beckoned. It was large and square and only three levels high, and George knew what it was because the word 'OSPITIL' was displayed in enormous glowing text from just below the top level. Assuming that the spelling had changed in a few centuries, what else could it be?

He headed towards the entrance, almost walking into another of the men who'd been quietly standing at the edge of the square. This one wore dark green rather like the marble of the statue, and didn't respond to George's quick apology, instead staring blankly at his feet as though they were of great interest.

There were clearly more than a few oddballs in this city.

In spite of multiple distractions, George finally made it to the hospital. Inside the main doors was a large, open space edged in open doors, each opening to a small square room. Probably a good place to do good – but not an invalid in sight. A woman sat behind a high, narrow table near the entrance, wearing a solid suit of gold rather like Georgiana's. She looked up at him for a moment, then turned away to whatever she was doing on the desk in front of her.

"Excuse me," he began, then realised he didn't know what to say next. Why was he here? His head felt heavy again, that headache intruding from the edges, and then there was a brief flash of warmth as though from a distance. The Queen.

Room 223, she whispered, directly into his mind.

He waited for further instruction, but there was none. "Where might I find room 223, please?" he asked the woman in gold.

"Use the lift."

"I beg your pardon?"

She pointed him towards those small square rooms at the end of the larger room – rather like he'd travelled in from Georgiana's house. "Go into one of those little rooms and say where you want to go."

Very well. He thanked the woman, then went into the room and immediately the door closed on him. He looked around.

There were four plain walls, one of which must have been the door, but nothing was happening…

"Where you want to go?" he said hesitantly, feeling foolish to be speaking to nobody.

A light flashed at the edge of the door, but nothing else happened. What…oh.

"Room two-hundred and twenty-three," he said clearly, and the whole room moved smoothly upwards. There was a *shh* noise and when the door opened again, he was outside a new hall filled with rooms. 223 proved easy to find; they were all numbered.

George walked in cautiously, then relaxed as he saw a child on the bed. Only about seven years old and hollow-cheeked, the boy slept between the white sheets in the deep sleep of the exhausted.

"Right. I'm here now." George said to himself quietly. "Now what?"

There was a chair beside the bed, scarlet with curved arms and a single swivelling stem. That looked a likely choice. He settled himself in the chair, the padded cover giving comfortably around his body, and waited for his next instruction.

❧❦❧

Anne stormed her way down the path back towards Georgiana's little lifting room, dodging clumsy pedestrians as she went. They were all too bloody tall, that was the problem; they looked right over her head and she had to constantly avoid being knocked over. And yes, she'd thought *bloody* tall.

Bloody…damn…chaos, Hades and darnation! Definitely not language befitting a lady, but today she had certainly not been treated as one! Servant indeed! And to some upstart named 'Souris', which sounded awfully close to the Frencine word for mouse. Never would Anne allow herself to be ranked below a *mouse*! They had horrible hairless tails, and they smelled.

She was reminded of the argument with Ash this morning,

and scowled. Saint's bones, she'd gone the wrong way. The little lifting room they'd come down in was nowhere to be seen, and this city was so big, and the streets all looked the same.

She wanted to see sunlight. Real sunlight; not the false light that the Witch-Queen had been surrounded by. If she wasn't an elf, then she certainly was a witch. Anne didn't care what Ash said, the facts all pointed to that conclusion. Inhumanly beautiful and powerful, but absolutely heartless. No truly good being would enslave others.

And she was a trickster. She was forcing others into servitude, and then making them think it was their own idea. Anne knew she couldn't be trusted. She made humans lose account of time, judging by Georgiana and Teron's reaction this morning when they'd been asked how long the 'Nobles' had been in Iversley.

They hadn't known the answer. All of that together spelled E-L-F, or something else wicked and inhuman.

Poor George and Ash. George was done for; utterly bewitched, and would be no use to himself or anybody else. And Ash… Anne had been so angry at her, mostly because some of those things she'd said had a basis in truth.

The hygiene thing was debatable. It was all relative, really; if one person was obsessively clean and bathed their whole selves *daily*, then of course anyone else who was more relaxed would seem 'unhygienic'. So there.

And yes, Anne did think that she was better than Ash in the sense that she'd had a much higher birth. Life had a natural hier-archy: Deias above, then the reigning monarch, then the noble class, of which she was one, followed by everybody else. Dukes' granddaughters weren't born every day, after all.

But in spite of those issues, Anne felt safer with Ash around. They were on the same side. Or they had been, before the Queen had got to her. It wasn't just Ash's attitude that had changed in those few moments. Her clothes were now the same deep red as George's, but unlike his, hers were edged with the same dark green leaf pattern as the little drawing on her hand.

Tattoo. The word even sounded savage. The plant looked like a cross between curling ivy and a climbing bean plant, minus the beans, and it was embedded *in Ash's skin.* How horrid!

But now the Queen had a solid hold on Ash, and Anne didn't know if it could ever be broken.

Anne would just have to look after herself, and getting back above ground would be an excellent start.

Anne tapped a passer-by on the shoulder. "Could you tell me how to get back-"

The woman shook her head. "Sorry. Can't help you."

She must be very busy, then.

"Excuse me, I need to go-"

The man shook her off. "Can't stop."

Goodness! These people were most *rude.* And very unhelpful.

Deciding against asking for more help, Anne walked further in what she'd thought had been the right direction, but now wasn't so sure. All the streets looked the same. Straight, filled with straight-sided buildings with very little décor, and coloured in glum browns and greys.

Then there were those strange little bridges all over the place. They were smooth half-circles on the bottom, and with little carts fitted on the top. People were sitting in the carts and speeding all over the place ridiculously fast. Weren't they afraid of falling out and breaking all their bones?

Anne shuddered. She'd rather try to ride a rabid stallion.

"Anne…" A woman's voice came from behind her.

"Yes?" Had someone noticed her plight and come to help?

"…servant of Lady Souris, you are hereby summoned."

Hades!

The couple now facing her were tall, of course, and strong-looking, dressed in the same light brown Anne now wore, but with thin black piping around the edge of the fabric. They did not look amiable.

Anne tried to act nonchalant. "Summoned by whom?"

"By your lady Souris." The man, clean-shaven and green-eyed, stepped to flank her. The woman did the same on her other side.

Anne tried to step away from them. "I wasn't aware I had an appointment, so I will decline."

Suddenly Anne felt strong hands grasp her shoulders, and then her feet weren't touching the ground. The two began to walk, carrying her suspended between them with her legs flailing.

The man stated flatly, "The appointment is *not* optional."

Back in the palace of Lower Iversley, in a small and comfortable room behind a two-way mirror, a woman sat with her head in her hands. She had long dark hair and a classically beautiful face that at this moment was twisted into a scowl, and her mouth moved in mostly silent mutterings. Whatever she was thinking about, it wasn't making her happy.

"Aegus!" she shouted suddenly, rising to her feet. Her long gown was as beautiful as it had appeared through the mirror, although was in fact green, and it let out puffs of light as she moved, bouncing up to reflect off the intricate earrings she wore on both ears.

Within three seconds a man appeared through the doorway. He was handsome, with neat dark hair in a long plait down his back and a perfectly manicured beard. Used to her 'requests', he bowed neatly at the waist, eyes lowered. "Yes, my Queen?"

"Any progress on finding the Eternity Stone?"

She'd asked this question every hour since it had gone missing, and he dreaded giving the answer just as much this time as before. "Not yet, I'm afraid. We have every Noble and human on alert-"

"You said that last time," she snapped. "Nothing new, then."

Aegus didn't answer, because he knew her well enough to know that she didn't like information being repeated. Instead he waited while she paced and raged.

"I'm bleeding power, Aegus. Look at it coming off my gown. It's as much as I can do just to break even, and you know that what affects me, affects all of us. We can't even leave this damned time without the Stone. We must find it, or we're all lost. Do you understand?"

"Yes, my Queen. It is of the utmost importance." And he *did* understand. Serving the Queen so closely might be dangerous (Janeus was the only Noble to ever cross her and not have a creatively painful end) but it had incredible rewards. They were powerful, immortal, but only as long as she was. And when the power ran out…

He didn't want to think about that. Grecia in the fourth century AD had been primitive and dirty and full of disease, as had every land before about twenty-one-hundred. He didn't want to get flung back to his original time, to live out the rest of his days like every other ordinary human, withering from age within a few decades and turning to dust.

Suddenly the Queen changed. Her hair rippled through shades of brown until it reached just the right one, and her green eyes flickered a few shades darker and murkier. Her lovely features changed only subtly, and she turned and raised an eyebrow. "Time-travellers," she said flatly. "What do you think?"

Ooh. He saw where she was going with this – and this particular time, she'd actually be close to telling the truth. "Given the circumstances," he replied very carefully, "it seems a little…reckless."

"Reckless!"

"With the likely involvement of Amaranthus, that is," he corrected quickly. "Perhaps it might be more…prudent to focus our attentions on simply finding the Stone…" His voice petered into silence as he saw the expression on her face. "Or whatever my Queen deems fit."

"My enemy," she ground out, "need not be mentioned by name in my presence. And I am well aware of his likely involvement, which means that diversification in power gathering *is* a wise option in case of further delays in finding the Stone. And as for the travellers – what happens, will happen. You *know* that the past cannot be changed."

Aegus did know this, and he knew that while he had misstepped in speaking that name, the Queen would forgive him. Somewhere around four centuries of time spent together would lend a lot of forgiveness for slips of the tongue. Deliberate disobedience however – not so much. She could be very creative in meting out revenge, and her constant dipping in the Other realm that flowed with alter-power gave her the ability to do the inhuman.

That was another way to gather power, but he didn't even think to mention it. While she was just about the most powerful being in this realm (except possibly for one, and that was still debated) she was adamant that one did not enter the Other realm, not if they wanted to remain entirely themselves.

See, there were beings that lived and moved in the Other, and even the Queen was terrified of them. They *would* share their power, but the price they'd demand was one that no one would ever want to pay…

There was a story there, but he didn't know it. He just accepted that they borrowed power from the Other realm via use of objects of power and living conduits, and also by the Eternity Stone…which was lost. Temporarily.

Aegus watched the Queen, watched her face, and knew that the Stone had to be found soon. For all of their sakes.

ASH MEETS THE OTHERS

Sam seemed very keen to take Ash to meet the other namesakes, and so she went along with it. She was keen to meet them as well, even if to find out exactly what namesakes were supposed to do. She tried asking him, but the answer wasn't quite enough.

"So…these namesakes – each Noble has only one?"

"Of course only one," he replied in surprise. "Well – one at a time, of course. If a namesake proves unworthy then they lose the privilege – but never mind about that. There are twenty-two of us, and I've counted thirty Nobles, including Janeus, who of course is not present. So-"

"Wait," Ash interrupted. "You said Janeus was the Queen's consort. Is that like a partner?"

"A husband," Sam corrected. "Except lesser in status. She chose me because he wasn't here to do it, and because I look like him around the eyes." He said that last part with tremendous pride, and she took a second glance. He was pleasant-looking if not gorgeous, with a solid, rugby player's build that was attractive enough that if she'd met him back at home she would have considered him. He wore black with gold trim in the same pattern as Ash's clothing. It seemed all the namesakes wore the fancy edging.

"She chose you because she liked your eyes?" That was a bit much, but then whatever reasons Ash had been chosen for were probably flimsy too. Except perhaps the time-traveller thing. That could be legitimate.

"And because she saw my loyalty and independent spirit," he

added, as if reciting a well-known verse. Ash could barely remember exactly what had been said to her, but clearly Sam had no such problem. "Janeus has been her consort since the very first Nobles ever existed. And I was selected to carry his name and power."

"Mmmm. Wow."

"I was one of the very first chosen, back when the original ten Nobles arrived and the government tried to destroy them. Back then, we were the rebels." Sam sounded very proud of that fact. "There's even a theory that I might be Janeus reborn – but I don't believe that, because I'm certain he's not dead." He seemed disappointed by this last part.

"Good for you!" Ash encouraged, trying to sound as if she really meant it. She found the whole thing incredible, but the part about reincarnation seemed more like wishful thinking than anything else. "I wouldn't have thought the Queen the sort to have a consort. She seems very…independent." Kind of like the sun – it was enough on its own. "Why isn't he here now?"

He flushed a little. "That's a long story. But basically, he wasn't loyal to her, so he was exiled. She still considers him her consort, though."

"Not loyal? You mean he was unfaithful?" It was hard to imagine anyone daring to be unfaithful to that glowing being – or that she would even have a partner, for that matter. And while Sam had the kind of open, honest face she usually found appealing, the choice of him as namesake seemed like a mismatch. (But then what did that make her, she wondered?)

"So they say." Sam didn't seem pleased to admit that. "But whatever might have happened in the past has no effect on us today. Here in the city we have a fresh new start, and we're making the most of it." They'd reached a short queue leading up to the cable car/rollercoaster things Ash had previously noticed, and Sam stepped right around the queue and took the first available seats. "Come on, the skimmers will take us there in no time."

She looked back at the queue nervously – at home one did *not* skip to the front – but she only saw approving expressions. Someone was bowing respectfully, and she did a double take once she realised it was *her* they were bowing to. She sat down behind Sam in the small, bucket-like seat, feeling a belt snap into place as she did so. It reminded her of a bumper car.

"Is that normal, the way they acted?"

"Of course," he said in surprise, looking back at her over his shoulder. "Why wouldn't it be?"

Because Ash had been a namesake for all of twenty minutes, and still didn't understand what it entailed. Having trim on your clothes must be like wearing a crown or something, judging by the reaction passers-by had. It was strange, being treated like that, but at the same time it made her feel really good. This must be why people want to be famous.

"Namesake House," Sam said to no one in particular, and *WHOOSH!* The chairs, hers attached to the back of his, shot off up the track. Those things moved fast, and she revised her opinion of them from 'bumper car' to 'rollercoaster'. That must be why they all were set so high in the air, except for the turn offs for stop points. A few times she thought they were going to hit other chairs, but they missed each other by mere inches. And if a pedestrian got hit by one, small as the chairs were, they'd surely be crushed.

They moved silently for all of their speed, and after a moment Sam turned back to look at her, grinning over his shoulder. "This your first time on the skimmers?"

She nodded.

"Then you'd better get used to them. They'll take you anywhere in the city within a couple of minutes. It means the city has very few vehicles so the streets are free for pedestrians."

"I did notice that." Ash was gripping at the sides of her seat, but after a while relaxed. They shot up and over and around buildings, but there wasn't the sense of movement that you got from a rollercoaster. "Hades, if one of these hit someone, they'd be taken apart."

"No one would get hit," Sam said, almost laughing. "The protective forcefields around the skimmers will knock them away, of course."

"Of course," she echoed, feeling a bit silly even though she couldn't possibly have known. "Uh…so there are forcefields. That sounds very useful."

He looked at her incredulously. "You must be even newer than I thought. How long have you been here in Queenstown?"

"Where, sorry?" Ash asked, feeling a bit like a mimic. "I thought this was Lower Iversley."

He shrugged, the gesture looking awkward with his twisted posture. "Traditionally, but I'm backing a move to change the name. Once the Queen takes Angland, she'll need a capital. I'd like it to be here, small though it is."

"Once the Queen takes Angland…?"

"You're sounding like a warped comm unit! Always copying me," Sam said with a laugh. "And you never answered my question. How long have you been here? A couple of weeks, perhaps?"

Ash shook her head vehemently. "Oh, no. Just a day, if that."

His dark eyes narrowed. "Really? You seem familiar, so I thought I must have met you before. But surely you've started using your powers?"

"Powers?" Ash's eyebrows shot up in amused disbelief. "I'd love to know what you mean by that. All I've got is this weird—um, *beautiful* tattoo on my hand, and I still don't know what a Namesake is even supposed to do. And what kind of power could I even have?"

"Well," he said lightly, "you could create things, or kill them, or do impossible feats. Maybe you could even fly."

Now Ash was the one to laugh. "That would be quite a feat." And while excitement fizzed in her veins to think of that, she'd believe it when it happened. "At the moment my only skills are making a decent pavlova, gardening – and I was good at fencing in high school."

Sam laughed as though she'd made a wonderful joke (she'd only partly been joking – she actually could do those things) then continued more seriously, "There are a few things you should know about this place, if you're as clueless as you seem to be. You've been honoured, and the Queen is the one who knows why, but you need to make sure you keep up your side of things…"

The rest of the trip likely only took two minutes, but by the time she'd arrived at their destination at the other side of the city she'd learned what she now called 'FAQs for Queenstown', as recounted by Sam.

One interesting thing was that the palace had been built not by human hands, but within a few hours by the Nobles after their arrival. And get this – the original ten Nobles (including the Queen) had come from the sky. Just dropped in without warning one day, like a meteor shower minus the flames. Not by flying, but by 'falling with style'.

Sam told her that the people hadn't known what to make of them at first. The council – never very strong in the first place, since they hadn't had weapons since the end of the Great War – had tried to control them, but didn't have a chance. They quickly surrendered and a new era was born. "That was the best thing that could have happened," Sam had explained. "Because now everyone is so happy." Yes, his actual words, and Ash hadn't seen anything yet to counteract them.

There were more like thirty Nobles now, not counting the absent Janeus, but more kept arriving from different places. That's how they got their titles; Lord or Lady plus the description of either how they'd arrived or what their powers were.

So Lady Alfeior of the Greater Waters had arrived (surprise surprise) from over the massive underground lake that edged the city. Ash could see it when the skimmers reached their highest points.

Alfeior was called 'Greater' because with her had come Lady Souris, and quite frankly Souris didn't have half the power Alfeior did. She couldn't even change size! (Emphasis Sam's, but it made Ash think again that Anne had been seriously demoted).

Their powers ranged from immense – the Queen could do just about anything, to limited – some of the weaker Nobles had limited power over illusion only. Even so, the weakest of the Nobles could easily defeat an army of humans (or so Sam said, although he was vague on how big the army would be).

And the most important of all – the Queen was to be trusted, loved and obeyed over all else.

Ash thought again of how she'd felt when she'd met the Queen, but it was beginning to feel dreamlike, hazy. Had she really reacted like that? And now Sam was talking about the power being shared with the namesakes, and listing off a bunch of names that meant very little to her, and she started to wonder if this was all too good to be true.

The two chairs slid to a halt outside of a neat garden square in a quiet area of the city, a little like those parks that had been scattered throughout central Lunden in Ash's time. Sam climbed out, then carefully helped her out onto the ground. "It's just this way."

"Ah…thank you, Sam." Ash followed him through the centre of the garden, still thinking about what had just occurred to her. "I just have a question…"

"Sure. Anything."

"What do the Nobles get out of this? Sharing their power, I mean?"

He seemed puzzled by the question, smiling politely as he set a hand to the door sensor panel. It slid open, and he gestured her inside. "Why, they get our adoration, of course. What more could they want?"

"And control of the city." And Angland too, if what he'd just said was correct.

"Naturally. This way, please."

Around about this point Ash began to feel uneasy. The euphoria clouding her mind was quickly fading, and that last thing Sam had said sounded…incomplete. With their names and 'powers' the 'Nobles' sounded like mythical gods, even if they didn't call themselves that. But who were they really? Super-heroes? Aliens? Mutants? *Were* they gods?

What made a god, she pondered?

The answer came to her clearly; a god was something that was worshipped. Although, the word 'idol' might fit just as easily there – something that was worshipped but didn't deserve to be. The people might call them something else, but the relationship they had with the Nobles sounded perilously close to worship.

Funny, Ash couldn't feel the Queen's presence at all now. Except there was one solid reminder…

She looked down at the back of her hand. The delicate dark green tattoo seemed larger than it had before, but she couldn't really be sure. Had there always been a little flower bud reaching towards her thumb?

"…and I know that you've probably got somewhere to stay already, but I'm sure they'll understand that you want to live with me. Our Nobles are connected, after all."

They paused outside another, more impressive set of doors, and Sam looked at her expectantly.

Uh oh. What had she missed? Ash smiled brightly. "That sounds lovely."

He nodded, satisfied. "Good. I'll send a message to whoever you're staying with…?"

"Teron and Georgiana. They live above ground."

"Ah, the former Lord Morley." He dipped his chin sheepishly. "Although I shouldn't mention that. The Nobles prefer that no humans are set above any others, even by virtue of a *former* title." He tapped at what looked like an earring, but was clearly something more. "Teron servant of Kari, this is Janeus's Namesake."

A mini cellphone? Or perhaps what he'd called a comm unit, Ash mused.

There was a pause, and then, "Yes, I have the one formerly known as Ashlea here. You may now call her the Queen's namesake."

Sam sounded really pompous when he said that. Most of the time he seemed as goofy as a puppy, but once he got onto the subject of namesakes…ugh.

He listened for a few seconds, and then said, "Yes. Yes. She'll be staying with me now."

WHAT!?

"Right." Then Sam dropped his hand and turned to her with a smile. "Great! Let's go meet the other namesakes!"

Evidently he didn't feel the need for 'goodbye' at the end of phone conversations like normal people.

"Sorry, Sam – what did I just agree to?"

He looked hurt. "Weren't you listening to me?"

Obviously not, or she would have known what he was talking about. "Of course I was listening to you! I just got a little distracted just now, what with so much happening." She smiled at him apologetically. "I'm sorry, I should have said so."

"That's OK." Although he still did look a bit miffed. "You're moving in with me. I've just sorted it out with the people you were staying with."

Oh. "And why's that?"

"You *weren't* listening!"

"I'm sorry, I was listening *most* of the time. Just the last few minutes, as I said, the view was amazing…" Sam still looked disgruntled, so Ash added, "Please remember this is all new to me. I just got here yesterday – I'm not even from this century!"

He looked somewhat mollified, but not entirely. "Yesterday, was it?"

"Yes!" She'd already told him that repeatedly. It seemed he

wasn't a good listener.

"Hmm." There was a pause where Ash wondered if she'd really put her foot in it, but he shrugged. "I'd thought as much. I figured you were really foreign with that colouring, but I got carried away with the fact that you're the Queen's namesake. And I'm the Consort's namesake." He gazed at her meaningfully. "Which means that we belong together. As I said before, and thought you'd agreed."

Belong together? Oh dear. And it didn't really matter whether he meant romantically or business-wise. How did she get out of this one without hurting his feelings?

"Sam," Ash began carefully, "you seem to be a nice guy, but I just can't jump into a relationship that quickly. We just met fifteen minutes ago!" Not to mention that she hadn't even decided if she would stay here. After all, her family and friends all lived back home. Funny that she'd forgotten that, even briefly. He started to speak, but she rushed on, "Maybe one day, but I really don't want to give you false expectations."

"Fine." He seemed resigned. "Will you still stay with me?"

She didn't want to, but it could work to her advantage. She could find out more of what was going on, pretend to be one of them, and look for the real Doctor Walker at the same time – the last having become a goal in the last ten minutes. She nodded. "I will…if it's entirely platonic."

"Done."

That came out quickly enough to deflate her ego. Not that she'd been very interested, but it had felt good to think *he* might be, especially after being mistaken for a boy by both Anne and George. Sam really seemed to want her to stay with him, though. Could it really be just because of the Janeus-Queen situation?

Ash studied his face, looking for signs of duplicity. His light brown face was friendly and open, with wide brown eyes, an aquiline nose and red-brown hair that flopped over his forehead. Add to that his solid physique, and he certainly didn't look at all sinister. It was hard to imagine that he might have ulterior motives.

"You do know what platonic means, don't you?" she asked.

"Of course. Friendship only," he replied promptly.

"And you're OK with that?"

He looked her straight in the eyes. "I am honestly and truly fine with that. I won't say that I wouldn't like you to consider more in the future, but I certainly won't push you for anything you don't want."

As said by every single man since Adam. However, it was probably the best she was going to get. And if he got grabby, she'd GST him. It was an extremely effective form of self-defence.

"What's GST?"

Oops. She hadn't meant to say that aloud. "It's a form of tax," Ash replied cagily.

Sam looked wounded. "Why would you tax me? Not that I am going to get 'grabby'."

She sighed. "It's a self-defence manoeuvre for women to use. Grab, squeeze, twist?"

He paled as the meaning hit home, and took a step away from her. "Please don't do that. I promise not to get even *slightly* grabby. I won't even try to hold your hand."

Unsurprisingly Sam was rather quiet the rest of the way to meet the other namesakes. They wound down various halls, and he perked up once they'd reached their destination: a wide set of doors with columns on either side, with the vague sense of bureaucracy about it.

She could see faded marks which just made out the words, 'Iversley City Council', but they were obscured by a large metal plate inscribed *IMPERIUM INFINITUM*. That sounded familiar, but she wasn't sure of the translation.

"It used to be the council building," Sam explained without waiting for Ash to ask, "but now it's the namesake headquarters.

This is our main meeting room."

"Really?" Ash asked interestedly. "What do you do here?"

"We meet," he replied.

Gee, that was helpful. "What do you talk about-" she began, but by then they were inside the room and Ash was swamped by dozens of people chattering excitedly.

"I'm Aegus's namesake. I'm so pleased to meet you," an older man dressed in yellow greeted her, giving that formal bow and shaking her hand.

"I'm Vulcana's namesake. It's a pleasure." That was a blonde teenager on her left.

"I'm Tor's namesake; so honoured!" A shaven-headed giant reached over the others on her right.

"Souris's namesake."

"Genevieve's namesake."

"Freyja's namesake."

"Alfeior's namesake."

So many people, and such unusual names! Ash was overwhelmed. But then thankfully Sam began clearing them away, then showed her to a seat.

It was in the centre of the room, at the end of a very long table made of the same dark material as the door. It would have easily seated thirty people along each side. Goodness – he'd sat her at the head. Or it could be the foot, but she was betting it was the head, from what she knew about Sam.

He settled himself in the chair next to her and waited for everybody to be seated. Meanwhile, Ash took the chance to study the others. Mostly aged between mid-teens and mid-twenties, the Namesakes' skin was of every shade of brown available, from pale olive to almost black, and both genders were represented evenly.

There was one thing in common though – every single one of them was good looking. It seemed that nobody wanted an ugly namesake.

Ash also noticed that every person wore a different colour,

and every suit was trimmed in the same distinct leaf pattern. It seemed that each Noble was represented by a specific colour, but only the namesake had the trimming.

When they were seated, Sam began, "As you all are no doubt aware, we have today been honoured with the presence of the Queen's very own namesake!"

The room filled with the hum of many voices, then died down when he coughed loudly. "Queen's namesake will be staying with me from now on. If anybody wishes to talk with her, they may come to me first."

Hold on, Ash thought. That was a bit high-handed!

Seeing the expression on her face, he added quietly to her, "It'll be too much for you otherwise. They'll all want to talk with you at length."

She didn't like his manner, but his reasoning made sense. She nodded her agreement.

"Now, does anybody have anything new to report?" Sam looked down the table expectantly.

Midway down, a young man stood. He was small compared to the others, but held himself with a confidence that made up for his lack of visible strength.

Sam called, "Nargis' namesake, you may address the room."

Nargis? What an unfortunate name!

The youth cleared his throat, his excitement clear. "As of this morning, I am now able to grow trees from seeds…within seconds!"

Chattering broke out all over the room again. That would be impressive, thought Ash, if it could be proven.

"Order!" Sam shouted, and everybody went quiet again. "Can you show us an example?"

Nargis' namesake drew a small packet from inside his vest front. He shook it upside down over his hand, and a few small brown seeds fell to rest in his palm. "Apple seeds," he said. He carefully took one and placed it in a decorative glass vase in the centre of the table. Then, holding one hand palm down over the glass, he closed his eyes.

There was a feeling almost like static, and then a plant BURST from the vase. Within seconds the roots were filling the glass vase as thickly as a bowl of spaghetti, and the plant had shot out the top to become a tree, nearly reaching the high ceiling.

As Ash watched open mouthed, several apples bloomed into cherry-sized, then fist-sized fruit, blushed rosy pink. The young man plucked an apple from the tree, steadying the thin trunk as it wobbled the small vase, and tossed it towards the head of the table.

Sam caught it one handed and gave it to Ash with a flourish.

"Wow!" she gasped, feeling the solidness of the fruit in her hand: it was no illusion. "That's fantastic!"

The youth bowed to her, clearly pleased, then took his seat.

"And that's pretty ordinary," Sam said far too loudly to Ash. She winced as she saw the young man flush in embarrassment. "You should see what the really powerful namesakes can do!"

"You'll have to show me sometime," she replied, watching as two men in untrimmed olive-green outfits carried the tree out of the room, vase and all. Another placed an almost identical vase back in the centre of the table. "But I thought that was pretty freaking incredible. Amazing, actually. I've never seen anything like that outside of a story."

And that meant her father had been right about alter-power after all. These people had clearly tapped into a vein of alter-power that gave them supernatural abilities, or else she was being well and truly conned. When she got home she'd have to apologise to him for being so doubtful.

Mind you, the only reason she believed it at all was because of the Queen, and before that the events that had led up to that moment. If she'd seen that feat back home, she wouldn't have believed it.

Ash saw Nargis's namesake smile in gratitude at her compliment, and felt irritated at Sam's lack of tact. Next to her he looked annoyed at her comment, but then covered it up with a shrug and a casual smile. "Well, it was a good start for you then. We'll show you what we can do, then give you a chance to test yourself."

"Sounds good." And terrifying. Ash had no idea what she'd be expected to do, but the idea of being more than human for a brief moment in her life sounded wonderful and scary.

What if it didn't work?

What if it *did*?

Don't drink the water.

The voice was quiet and very clear. She looked to either side of her, but no one seemed to be looking at her. Who'd said that?

Don't drink the water.

The voice came again. It sounded like it was inside her head, and it felt almost like her imagination except that it was such a strange thought to have so randomly. It wasn't the Queen, was it?

No. The Queen was…forceful, even though she had a lovely voice. Her voice and power overwhelmed. This one was more like a suggestion. But it made no sense: there wasn't any water to be seen.

"Glass of water, Queen's namesake?"

Ash jumped. A woman stood by her chair, carrying a clear jug of water and glasses.

"What?" Ash stammered.

Sam raised an eyebrow. "She's asking you if you want a drink of water." When Ash just stared at him, he added, "It's very refreshing."

Oh Hades, what were the chances of that timing? Unless it was someone else in the room playing tricks, of course. She remembered a moment too late that Islo had said something along those lines when they'd first met – that he didn't drink the water, and she'd thought it was an odd thing to say.

"I'm sure it is," Ash replied carefully, making a split-second decision. "But I'm really not thirsty." After all, what harm could be done by *not* drinking the water? At least until she found out what was going on.

The woman didn't move, and Sam persevered. "Are you sure? It's excellent quality. Very clean, from the underground lake and perfectly filtered."

"I'm sure."

Sam looked disappointed, but waved the woman on. Around them the room had fallen into cheerful chatter, the formal part of the 'meeting' apparently over.

"So, Sam. What do namesakes actually do with their time?" Ash asked. "What will I be expected to do?"

"Whatever you want." He took a bite out of another apple and crunched it noisily. "Mmm. These are pretty good. Can you guess what variety they are?"

"I'll take a guess...queens?"

"Close! They're 'True Queens'. Especially crossbred in her honour."

Was it just her, or was she was sensing a theme? And how could she do whatever she wanted? She needed *some* purpose.

Ash scanned the room. The couple of dozen namesakes were talking, eating and drinking, and occasionally doing something weird. Two places down on her left, a woman set her neighbour's hair on fire, then extinguished it without causing a hint of smoke.

And on her other side, the big bald guy (Thor? Tor?) saw her watching him and promptly changed his skin tone to merge in with the wallpaper behind. It startled her enough to flinch (and make him smile), but nobody else blinked an eye at either activity.

Hades, it was amazing. Either that, or terrifying. She was going to go with amazing. Ash watched with interest even more demonstrations of alter-power – people disappearing, changing appearance, changing other people's appearances, creating things out of thin air – until she almost didn't feel amazed anymore. Almost.

"So, now do you understand what namesakes do?" Sam

asked proudly.

"Well, sure," she said in surprise. "I see what you *can* do. But surely you don't just do this all day, every day? Do you have jobs?"

"Some of the lesser namesakes still have jobs," he replied dismissively. "But we don't need them. We have much more freedom."

A few seconds passed while Ash read between the lines, and she wasn't sure if she liked that answer. "So you don't have any duties during the day, then."

"If you're thinking of it that way, then yes, I suppose we don't. Now," he wheedled, "are you going to have a try yourself, or are you going to keep procrastinating?"

Was that what she had been doing? Suddenly every face seemed fixed on her, and she felt very small and nervous. "Um…I suppose I'll try. What should I do?"

"Anything at all," Sam said expansively. "Impress us."

Really not helpful. Ash just felt even more nervous thinking about what it would take to impress this lot, and not having the slightest idea of how to do it. "Um…"

Suddenly the youth with the apple seeds – she was now thinking of him as Nargis, as adding on 'namesake' took too long even in her head – was standing next to her. "Try cupping your hands together and imagining something appearing," he suggested. "Even just a ball of light. Focus everything on it, and you can work up from there."

"Thank you," Ash said gratefully, although she had no confidence of being able to actually *do* it. Even a ball of light…

She cupped her hands in front of her, staring down at them and trying to imagine a sphere of glowing gold appearing there, like a lightbulb or a miniature sun. Then slowly something appeared between her fingers. It did look like a faint little sun, and it shimmered and flickered and then disappeared amid the hushed silence. "Ohhh."

"Try again," someone encouraged.

So she focussed once more, this time thinking of a chandelier, then getting distracted halfway through and thinking of a disco ball. She ended up with something in between; a gold ball that shattered into glowing, multi-coloured shards and scattered across the room before disappearing into a faint glow once more. "Ohmygosh! Did you see that?"

There was muted applause, and Sam gave her an encouraging pat on the shoulder. "Well, at least you got something. Keep working, perhaps you'll master basic shapes today. We'd expect at least that much from the Queen's namesake."

Now that just made Ash annoyed again, because in her opinion she'd done bloody well, and not one person even commented as much. It seemed that Sam was the undisputed leader – for now, anyway. The gold glow winked out from her hands, and she shoved them into her pockets. "Geez, thanks."

"You're welcome." He clearly didn't understand sarcasm. "Let's have lunch, shall we? Then I can give you a tour of this city. As you said that you haven't been here before."

There was an edge to his voice that made her glance at him quickly, but there was nothing but amiability displayed on his face. "Thank you."

"Let's go, then."

But as they retraced their steps out through the wide doorway, she once again noticed the carved text, *IMPERIUM INFINITUM.*

This time she remembered what it meant. Something like, absolute power...

...forever.

TO DRINK OR
NOT TO DRINK

The couple dragged Anne for what felt like an hour through the busy streets. After the first dozen people had ignored her cries for help, she'd decided to focus on breaking herself free.

She'd kicked and bitten and scratched, but the two of them had simply picked her up, the man holding her feet under his arm, and the woman holding her arms stretched above her head. So now she was strung out between them like a roast boar on a spit, and couldn't move *at all.*

She tried to reason with them. "Good sirs…uh, and madam, I truly am quite capable of walking, and I'm certain you must be tired of carrying me. The Eternal One knows I'm small but I am not light! Feel very free to put me down…"

"You are not heavy," the woman grunted, but the sweat on her face told the lie.

Anne tried a new tactic. "I'd say it's more like you're both impressively strong." She batted her eyelashes at the man from her awkward position. "I've decided that I shall come to the appointment after all. I wouldn't want to disappoint, er, *Lady Souris.*" She had to force out that last bit. She was a good Churchian woman (mostly), and blatant lies sat very uneasy even now. "So you need not carry me. I will walk with you."

"We will carry you," the man gritted out.

"Well – 'tis really not decent, is it? You being a man and having your hands all over my ankles; I feel quite taken advantage of. If you were any kind of gentleman, you'd put me down-"

"Be quiet." The man readjusted his grip so that he was holding her knees.

Eek! Not quite what she'd meant, but she was afraid to protest anymore in case he moved his hands higher. 'Twas these indecent clothes giving off completely the wrong idea. She wasn't even wearing petticoats. He could probably feel her *legs*!

Anne fought off a blush, and tried to look dignified as they carried her along past hundreds of gawking pedestrians. Not easy, but if anyone could do it, 'twould be her, she told herself.

Eventually the tall buildings spread out, then turned into low housing units that reminded Anne of the village back home, except they were all made of a material that looked like a mix of stone and metal rather than wood. Then they were past those too, and reached the shore of a huge harbour.

Anne gaped in amazement. She'd never seen the sea or even anything bigger than Renwick Castle's man-made (and stinking) fishpond. The sea, or at least a colossal lake, stretched flat and blue into the distance where the cavern roof lowered to meet it. There, the cave's lighting faded into blackness so that the joining couldn't be seen.

An underground sea! How marvellous!

Her captors dropped her abruptly on the pebbly ground, and she landed hard on her bottom.

"Ouch! Was that truly necessary?" She scowled at them then picked herself up, brushing off the dust that clung to her skirt.

They weren't looking at her. They were kneeling before a girl who stood by the shoreline. Anne hadn't noticed her before, she'd been so taken in by the landscape, but now she watched carefully.

The new girl was tall, though not as tall as the woman who had carried Anne. Mayhap a little shorter than Ash, even, and she didn't look as though she'd seen more than twenty summers. Her colouring made her stand out next to the others. Pale olive skin and soft brown hair the colour of oak, cut straight across over her forehead then falling down to her slender shoulders. She had large dark eyes and a small, pointed nose.

Was this Souris? She did look a little like a mouse, Anne thought unkindly.

"Well done, my servants," the girl was saying. She rested one hand on each of their heads, and closed her eyes for a moment as if the touch brought her pleasure. Then she opened them suddenly, dropped her hands and said, "You may go."

They left. Anne had never even known their names.

And then the girl turned to her with a narrow smile that didn't reach those dark eyes.

Not dark, Anne thought. Islo's eyes were dark, and his were lovely if rather bold. Hers were as black as the gates of Hades.

"My servant Anne. Why did you delay in coming to me?"

✦✦✦✦

"And this one," Sam announced, changing pose, "this is a griffon. It may never have existed, but Janeus was known to have taken this form at least once during the Nobles' time in Ancient Grecia."

He morphed into a strange beast with a head like an eagle and body like a winged lion, the whole thing sitting oddly considering that they were still in the restaurant they'd sat in for lunch. She'd eaten, but he'd spent most of the time regaling her with stories of what Janeus was rumoured to have done (strange, strange man) and what Sam had managed to replicate, and alternating the shape changes with comments on how important the namesakes were to the city and to the Nobles.

"This form can't fly, unfortunately, in spite of the wings. None of the namesakes can fly, nor can the Nobles, for that matter. But of course Janeus could fly when he took this form. He was known to have taken over a hundred different forms, and that's only the recorded ones."

"Wow," she said, because he was clearly expecting a reply. "That's amazing. You do it very well." And he did, but considering he'd also done another dozen changes during the forty-five minutes they'd been at the restaurant, she was getting a little numb.

Besides, she hadn't had a chance to practice herself yet, and she *really* wanted to. Not when Sam was watching, either. In spite of his clear interest in her (or in her position, rather) he wasn't the most encouraging when someone was still learning. "I have a question…"

"Anything," he said. "I'm an open book."

More like one of those pop-up ads on the internet that you couldn't put on mute. "If none of the Nobles can fly, why did you say that I might be able to?"

Sam's eyes fixed on hers for a few moments. "Why did I say that?"

And now he was just copying her. "Yes, why did you say that?" Ash asked in genuine curiosity.

Finally he sighed, shrugging in that odd bird-lion form. "None of us have done it yet, so I figure there's a first time for everything. Besides, you aren't always going to be mucking around with balls of light. Soon, you'll be able to do something really worthwhile. Like me. Do you want to see another shapeshift?"

Deias, no. "Are you going to eat? Your food must be getting cold."

Griffon-Sam looked down at the platter in surprise, morphing back to his usual form within a second. "It's a cold platter, Ashlea. It's always cold."

"Regardless," she said with dignity. "We've been gifted this food by the restaurant owners, so we should appreciate it. Besides, I don't like eating alone," she added when he looked sulky. "Won't you eat with me?"

The small flattery worked enough for him to sit down once more, and in silence they finished off the array of bread, fruit, cheeses and meats – all grown organically in 'farms' down here in the city, without the participation of any actual animals. That made Ash feel good (no little piglets had died for this bacon-like food) but uneasy (because she was basically eating the most extremely processed food she could imagine). Mind you, the locals all looked pretty healthy, so it must be alright.

Regardless of the meal, she had to admit that she'd judged Sam and found him wanting. Had she actually thought that in other circumstances she might consider going out with him? Well, she'd changed her mind.

He clearly held a significant role here in Lower Iversley/ Queenstown, and his abilities were impressive, but it didn't justify his arrogance, self-importance and complete lack of tact when it came to anyone else's feelings. Whatever she decided to do from here on in, it wouldn't be living with this boy. Hades, she couldn't even imagine spending the rest of the afternoon with him.

"So," she said, putting down her glass of sweet beer (as he'd called it). "I can see the advantages of some of these abilities. For example, Nargis would be able to go into places with famines and create food, and if the big guy with the bald head could sneak in to hostage situations and free people-"

"Tor's namesake," Sam interrupted. "And Nargis' namesake, although I can understand the confusion. And we don't have any of those issues here in Queenstown. We've got a very safe, pros- perous environment."

Obviously. "Yes, but the rest of the world doesn't, surely," she persisted. "In my time, some countries had dreadful famines, and every country has danger. The namesakes could do a huge amount of good-"

"We do what we're told to do, and we haven't been told to leave this city. But don't worry," he added kindly. "Your interest in helping people has been noted, and we'll find something for you to do, once you've got the ability. Alright?"

"Alright," Ash agreed flatly. The funny thing was, she wasn't even that altruistic. She'd never volunteered for a charity (or anything much, really) but then she'd never really thought she was capable of much. But then to suddenly have all this *power* and not have anywhere to direct it except in displays to impress the other namesakes? It was seriously disheartening. They could have done so much good…

So much evil, too; but in spite of the strangeness of the surroundings and the apparent power the people possessed, Ash didn't really feel that they were dangerous. Wrapped up in their own self-importance, yes, but not killers.

They reminded her of some of the boys she had gone to school with, bragging about their prowess and trying to outdo each other with silly dares and drinking too much. They had so much potential, but what did they do? Nothing. What a time waster.

As Sam talked (bragged, whatever; she was no longer interested) her thoughts turned towards the other two. While Ash had certainly landed on her feet here, who knew what could be happening to Anne and George at the moment? Especially tiny, snooty little Anne, barely scraping five foot and with the attitude of a giantess…

The more Ash listened to Sam talk and saw the attitudes of the cityfolk, the more uncertain she became about Anne's safety. The girl was off on her own looking for Dr Walker and a way back home, and she didn't have the wisdom to keep her mouth shut about her feelings regarding the Queen and her new position.

The next job would be to find Anne, Ash decided. She'd help the girl find Dr Walker and do whatever was required at that end, and then not only would Anne have a way back to her home, but Ash would have an exit strategy. Not that she was planning to go home yet, but she wanted to know that she could when she wanted to.

As for George… He'd probably be fine as he was suitably enthused about his new role, and assuming he hadn't got lost on his way to the hospital, Ash knew where to find him if she needed him.

The rest of the lunch dragged on as Sam talked and talked. Then finally he began to hint at starting a city tour, and Ash had had enough. She was tired and antsy and concerned about Anne, and she was a little less than polite. "Sam, what time is it?"

He stopped mid-sentence, then after a few seconds replied, "Two fourteen p.m."

Was that all? It felt later. "How did you know what the time was?" she asked curiously. "You didn't look at a watch. Did you ask the Queen?"

He laughed. "Ask *the Queen* for the time? As if she doesn't have better things to do! No, I used my comm unit." He unclipped what she'd thought was a small diamond earring from his ear and showed it to her. "See? Comm unit. Almost everybody has them. You can contact other people or get information off the 'net, like the time."

They still had the internet, or some version of it. Interesting. She took a closer look. On the inside of the piece was a long, perforated section that presumably extended inside the ear. "How did you ask it the time? You didn't say anything. Does it mind-read too?"

He patted her shoulder like she was a not-too-bright child. "I didn't have to say anything. It picked up you asking the time, and retrieved the information."

"Does it do that a lot – give information on things you haven't even asked for?"

He shrugged one shoulder. "Sure. That's what it's for."

"I'd think that could get annoying. How could you focus on anything?"

"Oh, you get to ignore it after a while. Just becomes background noise. Good thing too, with all those ads…" He grimaced. "But then of course the Queen banned advertising when she came into power. Would you like one?"

"Ah…no thanks." The constant flow of information sounded very irritating, and she had enough to focus on for now. "Actually, I'll need to delay that city tour for a bit. I need to head off now, I have someone I need to talk to."

"I thought you were new to the city," Sam said with a hint of resentment. He probably didn't like being dismissed – and he was like a dog with a bone with that idea.

"I am," Ash replied patiently. "But I've met a lot of people in a short space of time."

"Who are you going to see?"

"My friends who I arrived with. Show them what I've learned, make sure they're settled." Help Anne leave, find Dr Walker – although she didn't think Sam would appreciate those bits.

"Hmm." He looked away, still wearing that wounded air. "I hadn't realised you were *friends*. Besides, if I were you I wouldn't expect too much from that yellow-haired boy with the stick welded to his spine."

"We're close enough to friends. And why should I not expect much from George? Is he alright?" Except for the stick, obviously. She couldn't argue with that.

But Sam only shrugged, still looking away. "You can find me back at the meeting place when you're done, or just ask anyone where to find my house. They'll tell you. Shall I expect you for dinner?"

"Ahh…" Too much commitment! Too domestic, as well. "I don't know," she answered finally. "Perhaps not tonight."

He shrugged again, at last meeting her eyes with his own dark ones. They were rather pretty, large and long lashed, and she wondered again if the impossibly wonderful (shapeshifting, unfaithful) Janeus had looked like this. There was definite resentment in those eyes, though. "See you later, then."

"See you," she echoed. "And thank you for lunch and all your help." She began to sidle away, not wanting to turn her back on him outright. He just stood there watching her leave, a hard-to-read expression on his face. In the end, she just waved, then turned and quickly walked away.

Talk about high maintenance. She'd have to deal with that one later – now she had other problems.

First on the list: find Anne.

❦

Souris walked up to Anne slowly, hips swaying, and a nasty little smile on her face. "My servant Anne!" she purred. "Where *have* you been?"

She was nobody's servant. "You need not swing your hips like a Covent Garden harlot. I do not find it appealing."

Souris snapped to attention, the smile now somewhat fixed. "Why, you have a sharp little tongue, don't you? We'll have to deal with that."

This close, Anne realized that the other girl wasn't much taller than herself. That was positively *tiny* compared to the other Nobles.

Anne held herself tall and put on the expression she used to deal with pushy merchants and impolite relatives. The one that said, *I am the Lady here. You are scum.* "I am Lady Anne of Covington, Countess of Longford, granddaughter of a duke, and widow of an earl. You will do nothing to me."

"Is that so?" Souris said, but she was still smiling, and now it looked sincere. "It may be that back in your time you were quite the little leader. You might even have been the Queen of Frencia – you certainly have the arrogance for it – but here…" She took a step forward, forcing Anne to step back. "…you are *nobody*."

Anne wasn't arrogant. Was she?

Souris took another step forward, and tapped Anne on the forehead. Anne tried to avoid her, but tripped over again. Ouch.

Twice on her backside in ten minutes.

The Noble loomed over her. "Here, I have the power of life and death over you. If I wanted to make you clean up excrement with your bare hands for the rest of your life, I could do it. You see," she said, smiling even wider, "*I* am the lady here. *You* are scum."

Anne gasped. Souris had echoed her earlier thoughts exactly.

Souris continued, "Even back in your own time, you weren't as high and mighty as you like to make out, were you? Barren, your husband executed for heresy, you about to be sold in marriage to the highest bidder yet again…"

"Shut up!" Anne cried. "My husband was not a heretic; he was a Protestor who didn't convert quickly enough, so Queen Marian made an example of him. And I might not be barren – I was only married two years!" You *witch*!

"I'm not a witch, I'm a Noble, as you never truly were. You pathetic humans, giving yourselves titles as though it makes your pitiful lives worth something, and lording it over those beneath you – well, now you shall see what it feels like to be *beneath*."

To her horror, Anne felt the ground dropping out from beneath her. With a squeal, she fell into a deep pit in the earth. Oof. She landed at the bottom hard. She checked herself for broken bones, but seemed to be mostly unharmed – except for a bruised posterior, and being well and truly stuck, that was.

Anne looked up into the bright circle of false sunlight that lit the city. Souris was leaning over the hole, her long brown hair swinging as she laughed. "Not so confident now, hmmm? Shall I add a few snakes?"

Anne gasped in horror as several long black shapes appeared on the pit floor. "Please…they'll bite me…"

"Beg me," Souris taunted. "Beg me to release you, and I might just consider it."

She'd never begged in her life! Better to die of a serpent's bite than be slave to this viper. And the play on words was unintentional. "I will not!"

"Suit yourself. I'll just add one more snake for every minute you resist me, shall I?"

So she did, and Anne braced herself against the dirt walls, and tried not to scream.

Where would Anne have gone? Ash pondered the question as she rode the skimmers back to the lift. Probably back to the bunker. Besides Georgiana and Teron's, it would be the only place around here that she knew, and the latter probably wouldn't be safe anyway.

The low chair turned down a side path towards the ground, then slowed and stopped, giving a jerk that almost toppled her onto the ground. Honestly, it was worse than a ski lift to get out of. Ash caught herself carefully, then studied her surroundings. Yep, this looked about right. A wide street: to the left was the path they'd taken to see the Queen, past all the really fancy buildings, and down a side street in the other direction should be the lift back up to Georgiana's house.

Wait a moment – that lift had been *in* Georgiana's lobby. So when Ash came out, she'd have to be careful to avoid both her and Teron, *and* Islo. That would be impossible. Surely they'd have security, probably a message sent instantly to their comm. about visitors?

Ash would have to make up some convincing story for why she had to come above ground.

I wanted to get my clothes.

I needed some fresh air.

I left something in the forest.

I was overwhelmed by the greatness of being the Queen's Namesake and needed some time alone in the fresh air. Also I left something in the forest.

That last one would have to do. But what if they asked what she'd left? Phone? Jewellery? MP3 player?

Probably best to go with jewellery. If she said it had been left in the bunker…grrr. No. Then they'd know about the bunker, and there'd really be no safe place to hide.

Lying was *hard*. It was far too easy to trip herself up.

Yeah, Ash told herself, and the truth would be so much better. *I don't know if I want to stay here, so I'm keeping my options open – also helping Anne to leave ASAP.*

Perhaps not.

Ash had just turned into the small side street that led to the lift when she was grabbed from behind. "Eee-"

Her scream was cut off by a hand over her mouth, and strong arms dragged her backwards through a doorway. She relaxed for a moment, then suddenly jabbed her elbow backwards into something soft. Her assailant groaned and loosened their hold.

She took advantage of the freedom to stamp her heel hard onto their foot and was rewarded with another groan. Those self-defence classes were worth every dollar she'd paid, after all! She drew a breath to scream again, but a voice stopped her.

"Please – it's me!"

She turned, but almost didn't recognize the man. It was Dr Walker, but looking nothing like he had in the hologram. Considerably taller, probably a clean six-feet, and very dishevelled. It looked more than just the effects of her fighting, though. If fear had a smell, then this man stank of it.

"Dr Walker?" she gasped in amazement. "Why did you grab me?"

He was still bent over in pain. "Please, don't hit me again. I just need to talk to you, and I can't have anybody seeing. Her spies are everywhere."

"Her? Do you mean the Queen?"

He nodded. "Crazy, power-hungry *frock-trotter*." He spat the last word out.

Ash didn't know what a frock-trotter was, but judging by the tone he used, it was definitely an insult. "Why would you say that? I thought everyone here loved her."

The doctor looked at her incredulously. "Because they have to! Haven't you worked it out yet?"

"Worked what out?" But she was getting a very, very bad feeling about what he was saying, and it was ringing true. *Something* wasn't right…

"That every single person here in Iversley has been drugged and brainwashed," he enunciated clearly. "By Deias, girl, the fact I'm even here talking to you is because you haven't been, at least not entirely. You didn't drink the water, did you? The water from the lake?"

Ash felt cold right down to her toes. The pieces were all fitting together, and she didn't like what was coming out. "I didn't drink the water," she answered in dawning horror. "I had a tiny sip this morning at breakfast, but I didn't drink more. Didn't like it."

"You didn't like it, the Tudar girl doesn't drink water, so you've both been saved." Dr Walker threw up his hands dramatically. "Except here you are with the highest title a human can have here – for now – and she's off who knows where. So I need *you* to help me."

"Me?" she squeaked. "How can I help you? Your recording sent me to *find* you? What was wrong with the water? And what do you mean, *for now?*"

He quickly checked outside the door once more before turning yet another incredulous glare on her. "You can help me because you have the freedom to move around, and because I was stupid. I drank the water from the lake, filtered like I always do, but it wasn't enough. They put something in it that makes everyone susceptible to mind control, that makes the invaders' power far, far stronger.

"Can't you see it? You met the Queen, yet you haven't even argued with me about what she's done. So her power has worn off, hasn't it? Without the water, it will wear off within hours."

"I suppose so…" Ash said weakly. "But-"

"But you're bloody lucky that you're not just like the others now," he cut in. "Look at me, girl. I've done all I can to avoid being sucked in, and it was sheer luck that I was setting up the control centre for the experiment when the invaders arrived two weeks ago." He gestured at himself aggressively. "I haven't bathed in a week. I can't go back to my home. I can't talk to anyone, and her bloody voice keeps forcing itself into my head!"

This was so, so different from her initial impression of Lower Iversley, and it was horrifying. It meant that every single thing Ash had assumed, everything she'd appreciated since meeting the Queen, had been a lie.

"But she made me her namesake," she whispered in dismay. "Why would she do that if it's not real? What does she *want*?"

"What every person wants," Dr Walker replied, looking at her as though she was an idiot. "Absolute power. And if you've been given a fancy title and coloured lights to throw around, then you're a pawn. It's not real, it's not going to last, and you need to face that."

Imperium Infinitum. Absolute power forever.

In that moment Ash's protests died on her lips, because she knew it was true. She didn't know who the Queen was, or why she'd done what she'd done, but it wasn't from pure motives, oh no. "Oh my Deias," she moaned. "What in Hades am I going to do?"

"Stop whining and listen to me," he said matter-of-factly. "Now, I saw the records of you being in the forest bunker last night, so I presume the recording will have filled you in. You were brought here for one purpose, Ashlea Jane O'Reilly, but you'll remain for another. Now, how would you like to fly?"

The view from above the clouds was a good one, when your eyesight could cover the distance, but this view too was excellent in its own way, although most wouldn't understand what they were seeing.

The man stood in front of a colossal tapestry in a round white room the size of several football fields. The tapestry was several metres high and wound right around the circumference of the room, and it was woven entirely of countless black and white threads. The pattern and fineness of the threads was enough that in many places the tapestry appeared to be in shades of grey, but that was an illusion that lasted only if the viewer didn't look properly.

He was looking properly. He was looking very closely, in fact, at the back of the tapestry where the pattern was impossible to distinguish, but where all the action happened. A trio of fine white threads had been pulled across from several feet apart and were now being carefully woven together at this one point where the pattern became very black.

Except for the long, unbroken edging threads (and those he wasn't going to look at until the time was just right) most threads were very short, barely two inches long and just enough to weave in well with those around them.

See, every single thread represented a life, and most lives never lasted more than ninety years, a hundred and twenty if you were extremely lucky, and then it was time to move on to the next realm. This elemental tapestry showed the entire history of the human race from start to finish, and the one who had woven it…well, he was very dedicated, and he had *a lot* of time to spend perfecting it. All the time in the world, in fact.

But the man went back to the trio of fine white threads in the middle of the little patch of black. The whole group was only the size of an infant's thumbnail, but clear to him. He touched one of those tiny threads, the one that had moved the shortest distance, and smiled. "Ashlea Jane O'Reilly," he declared, "I'm going to give you the ability to believe the impossible."

After all, great feats always started with a tiny little bit of faith.

❦

There was a long pause as Ash tried to figure out if her hearing was off, then she just repeated it back. "Sorry, did you say fly? Like in a plane?"

"No, not exactly." Dr Walker suddenly grimaced as though in pain, rubbing his hands over his temples. "Hades and Chaos, that hurts. She's right there, right there on the edge, pushing all the time. How do you stand it?"

"Pushing?" Ash echoed. "I haven't felt anything in my head at all, not like what you're saying. Not since we met her in the mirror."

"Smoke and mirrors," he muttered. "Classic trick, very clever, but she has the real power to back it up. Why didn't you drink the water, Millennial?"

The question caught her short, and for a moment she didn't answer. She recalled that voice, the quiet one that had told her not to drink, but something also told her that she shouldn't tell Dr Walker about that voice. Look at him, the way he was sweating – if the Queen *wasn't* trustworthy, then he wouldn't be able to keep his mouth shut for long.

So Ash told a partial truth. "I preferred the juice this morning," she said finally. "I'm not really one for water."

"Huh." There was a long, ominous pause, then he shrugged. "Regardless. Listen well, Millennial, because what I am about to tell you is *extremely* important. The future of Angland, and perhaps even the world depends on this."

"Well, you've come to the right person then," she said sarcastically, bordering on panic. "Why on earth would you tell *me* something that the fate of the whole world hinges on?"

"Besides the reasons I've already told you, because there's no one else! Now, as you are aware, I have access to highly restricted time travel technology. For my research, of course. So once I realised what was going on here with the invaders, I made it my goal to access the time travel device once more, which while its effect is found in the forest, the machine itself is in one of the houses of Upper Iversley."

"Really? Which house?"

"It doesn't matter which one!" Dr Walker snapped. "What matters is that I was able to use it. In a move that carried significant risk to myself, I went two years into the future to see what would happen if the invaders continued unchecked…"

Ash leaned forward, fascinated in spite of herself. "What was it like?"

The doctor tightened his lips, looking away for a moment. "Like one of your old atomic bombs had struck. I didn't see any sign of life."

Ash was so horrified that for a moment she couldn't even speak. "How is that even possible?"

"I don't know. That's the problem. There was nobody there to ask, only ruins of buildings and huge cracks in the ground, and vast areas burnt black. There was barely any forest left at all. I used my comm set to try to pick up the net, somebody nearby, *anything*. I picked up a signal, but it was blank. Nobody there, nothing working. I don't know how that could have happened. Something catastrophic, obviously."

Now the deep lines of worry on Dr Walker's forehead made sense. He must have been carrying the burden of knowing that whatever was happening here would lead to disaster, but was unable to do anything about it.

Then she had an idea. "But if you can travel through time, then couldn't you just go back and stop it all happening?"

He shook his head. "I tried that. I went back two months to warn the council what was about to happen, and to be prepared to fight."

"Did they believe you?"

For a moment he looked like the old arrogant doctor she'd met in the bunker. "*Of course* they believed me. I'm a world-renowned scientist, not some idiot waving a placard on the street." He calmed himself. "They believed me, and prepared their weapons as best they could. I even warned them about the water supply being tainted, and they put guards on the shoreline full time."

"Obviously it didn't work."

"No, and not due to my lack of effort or planning. It appears that altering past events is actually impossible, because then the catalyst to send one back in time in the first place wouldn't have happened, and therefore one would never have gone back in time at all. Which clearly couldn't happen."

"Oh." Now that *was* disappointing. Time travel was not the solution to life's regrets after all.

"So the invaders took over as we have already seen," he continued briskly. "The weak resistance put up by the council amounted to nothing once that witch had got her hold on the minds of the people by throwing around power as you've already seen. It seems people are easily impressed. And then, when I got back to this time, I found I was unable to use the machine any longer. It was broken."

A horrible thought had occurred to Ash. "When did this happen?" she asked. "The machine breaking?"

Now Dr Walker looked a little sheepish. "This morning."

"So you can't send us back once we're done?!" she cried. "You've trapped us here so we can get bombed with the rest of you!"

"We don't know that it's a bomb!" he snapped. "And besides, I can fix it, I just need time, and this thing in my head to stop distracting me. You didn't drink the water, or barely at all, and so while you keep your distance from the Queen, you'll also keep your right mind. And haven't you had a change of attitude? Not so happy to be a namesake anymore?"

"Not after what you just told me," she muttered. "So, what is it that you need? I'm not promising that I'll do it, just that I'll try."

"Good." The doctor fumbled in his pocket and pulled out a small black bundle. He was sweating profusely now, and his hands were shaking as he handed her the bundle – a small bag about the size of a men's wallet. "Don't lose this. I travelled almost fifteen hundred years back in time to get it, and while I'm loath to give it to someone so unschooled, I see no other choice. We need alter-power to defeat alter-power, and inside you'll find the means to make yourself superhuman – for a while anyway – and you can find a way. Find the Queen's weak spot, or kill her."

"Kill her!?" Ash squawked. "I'm not killing anyone. I don't even like killing flies! And what do you mean, alter-power?" She tipped the contents of the bag into her hand, revealing a small pile of what looked like junk jewellery, as well as a couple of little thumb-sized glass vials that reminded her of very expensive perfume. "What are these? I can't read the text on the sides."

"You won't be able to read them as I picked them up from the early Ottomins in Turkiye. The translation nanobots in your brain only work on spoken languages."

"Oh." That was disappointing, but made sense. The recorded Dr Walker had been unsure, but this Dr Walker had no confusion.

He pointed at the smaller, rounder vial. "So this one is for flight, and you'll only need a sip to make it work. It'll last about two or three days, I'm not sure how long, so make sure you don't go too high after the two-day mark. The other is for- *argh, my head...*"

He bent over and retched violently on the ground, sending up a splatter that made Ash take a quick step away. She might be sympathetic, but she also liked being clean. "Um...flight, in what sense?"

"Flight, like flying," Dr Walker mumbled, still bent over.

"Like a bird." And then he threw up again.

Ash looked down at the little pile of junk in her hand, then carefully put it back in the purse. Perhaps it was a hallucinogenic drug, or perhaps it was perfume after all. She wasn't saying she discounted his words regarding the Queen and the drugged water – entirely – but suddenly she felt a lot more solemn, and a little disenchanted.

"OK," she said politely. "Thank you. Um…is there anything I can get you? Some water, a cloth-?"

"No water!" he shouted, then bent over again and retched once more. Deias, whoever this house belonged to wasn't going to be pleased. "Only drink pure squeezed juice or alcohol, or milk! Nothing water-based!"

She began to apologise (one shouldn't upset crazy people) but then the sound of voices and footsteps echoed from further in the house. Dr Walker swore, and she looked at him in surprise. "Anyone you know?"

"Doesn't matter," he whispered frantically. "If I know them or not, they'll be working for her. Puppets, all of them. We must go!"

"Go where?"

"Anywhere!"

Suddenly there was a flicker of light like a doorway opening, and a woman's voice called out; "Who's there? Is that you, Osvaldo?"

'Osvaldo' said a very bad word, then scuttled out that front door like a rat, slamming it shut after him. Ash almost walked into it, then realising she was trapped, turned to smile at the house's owner. "Er…hello…"

The young woman had been extremely friendly once she'd recognised Ash's distinctive red clothing with its black, embroidered trim, and she'd invited Ash to have afternoon tea along with her own family, including three small and fascinated children. The husband was off at work apparently, down by the lake working for…oh, some Noble, Ash couldn't remember all of those strange names.

But the woman wasn't offended at Ash's intrusion, just smiled and said that Osvaldo (AKA Dr Walker) had been a bit odd lately, but wasn't dangerous.

Ash was relieved to hear that, but she'd still declined the offer of food, instead quietly putting the little black cloth bag in her pocket and heading off.

Then she realised she had no idea where she was going, went back and got directions towards Georgiana and Teron's place (there not being any public lifts up to the forest apparently) and headed off once more.

Third time lucky.

ASSISTANCE

George wasn't sure how long he'd been sitting in that red leather chair in the hospital. Quite a while, it felt like, and with nothing to do except swivel left…swivel right…full circle! Wheeee!

That was more entertaining than going to the races, and certainly more entertaining than a *ton* party back at home. He certainly didn't miss those gatherings of the rich and titled. And why did they not have chairs like these in his own time?

Because no one would get any work done, he supposed. They'd be too busy spinning in place until they were nauseous.

But that was quite enough of that, he told himself. He hadn't been a child for many years and would not act like one, no matter the temptation.

He stilled the chair's movement and looked back to the child on the bed. Eric Baker, the tag on the door had said. The name didn't sound familiar. He hadn't even recognized the name of the illness.

George had gone to the room as instructed, having realised belatedly that not only did he not have any medical ability, but he really didn't know what he was doing here. The child had looked alone, so George had thought perhaps he could keep him company until someone else showed up. It was never pleasant to be alone when one was feeling ill.

But nobody had come in to check on the child the entire time he'd been there. Not a single doctor or even assistant. Perhaps the disease was life-threatening? Perhaps the boy was going to die, and there was nothing to be done now except for someone to be company for him in the last few hours of his life.

That was an unpleasant thought. George had never got as far as having children of his own since that had always felt somewhere in the future, but he'd always envisioned himself in the same type of family he'd grown up in. Two sons: one the heir and one the spare, and a daughter to dote on.

This boy looked to be about eight years old at the most. That he might be dying alone was completely unfair. Where was his family; his mother and father?

Dash it, now George needed to go to the water closet. The Queen had said to go out and do good, but one still had to attend to one's bodily functions. He'd be quick, and then he'd be right back and ready to do good – whatever that might look like.

The water closet was harder to find than George had expected. He must have wandered fifteen minutes around the ward before finally giving in and asking for directions.

It turned out that they were just down the hall from where he'd started; he just hadn't recognized the symbol on the door.

How was he supposed to know that a circle with an arrow coming out of it meant 'men's room'? It didn't look anything like a man at all. Except perhaps the arrow could be a distorted…and the circle could be…

Oh, how silly, and how obvious. Muttering about the foolishness of it all, he walked back into Eric's room. But as he went through the door, a wave of nausea washed over him.

By Jove, his head felt strange! Like it was both too heavy and too light at the same time, if that was possible. Was it from too much spinning on the chair earlier?

The room now seemed to be filled with a smoky haze, and appeared to swim before his eyes. Perhaps one of Eric's family members had visited, and had been smoking a pipe. Or many pipes, based on the level of smoke.

Then it cleared, and he saw what was on the bed.

Having narrowly avoided being caught trespassing, and now back on the street, Ash continued on towards the lift up to Georgiana's house. She tossed up little balls of coloured light as she went, focussing on making them hold their shape.

Regardless of what Dr Walker had told her, this was *fun*, and seemed harmless. Even the brightest light she came up with made her look away, but didn't even send any light onto its surroundings. And look, she could make three coloured balls like a juggler…

She tried making them spin around each other, and it worked for about five seconds before the red ball swerved off course and into the blue ball then the yellow, exploding all of them into nothingness once more. Better than her first try, but nothing that would impress Sam.

Ha, she'd have to fly like a bird (or a plane, or…) before she'd impress Sam, and no matter what Dr Walker said, that was highly unlikely.

The road came to a dead end where the unnaturally smooth cavern's edge curved down into the ground, and there was a line of elevator doors with chutes set into the wall showing their path. There were three possible doors that all looked as though they could be the right one for her destination, so Ash randomly chose the middle one, lightly touching its surface, and the door opened.

She carefully leaned in to inspect the inside. It looked about right, so she stepped in and said, "Above ground."

Nothing happened. Did it use voice recognition?

Maybe a different phrase would work. "Up."

"Up, up and away!"

Predictably that didn't work either. Hmmm. How about…

"Lobby." The door slid shut and almost silently, the room began to rise.

A few minutes later the door reopened and Ash found herself looking out at an unfamiliar room.

Large pieces of lounge furniture were scattered around the spacious area, and an entire wall was taken up with what looked like a cinema screen playing an ancient, 3D version of a familiar comedy, 'Buddies'. But there was something wrong with it – the handsome doctor had grey hair, and his best friend's face looked as stretched as a seventy-year-old actress's. Then it came to the end of the segment and she saw the name: 'Buddies (*again!*)'.

Huh. She should go home and make a bet fifty to one that they'd make another series in their twilight years. No one would believe her, and when it happened she'd make a bundle.

Through an open door Ash could see an unmade bed, thankfully with no one in it. It was quite messy, reminding her of her older brother's apartment before he'd married (and even now when his wife went away for the weekend).

The next moment Islo walked out of the bedroom. He was shirtless and had an odd little device fitted over his mouth like a muzzle. It was vibrating: he was brushing his teeth. He caught sight of Ash standing just outside of the lift and his eyes widened.

"Hi!" Ash gave an embarrassed little wave. "I'm really sorry – I picked the wrong lift. This must be your private one, right?" This was awkward, especially after the discussion they'd had this morning where she'd said an emphatic 'no thanks!'. And now she turned up in his room?

He held up a hand, then disappeared back into the bedroom. She heard some water running, then he came back out drying his mouth, fully dressed.

"Hello, Ash. This is quite unexpected."

She fidgeted self-consciously. "Yeah…as I said, unintentional.

I was actually aiming for your parents' lobby."

Islo raised an eyebrow. "You didn't see the sign?"

"Uh, no. There were three doors, I just picked the wrong one."

"They're all labelled for private use; they belong to the family. This one is for my apartments, the right is for my parents, and the left one is for my sister."

They must be really rich. Three lifts for one family!

Ash was horrified at her mistake. "I'm so sorry! I would have taken a public lift if I'd known where to find it. Just tell me the way out onto the street, and I'll go. Again, sorry."

He held up a hand again. "It's not a problem. The doors wouldn't have opened for you if you hadn't been on the approved list of people. And anyway, I forgot that the Nobles got rid of the signs since they didn't want us using our name anymore. But where are you going?" Islo gestured towards that distinctive outfit she was wearing. "Queen's business?"

She decided to forget her planned lie. He had been interested in Anne, and she didn't think he'd cause trouble for them. "Um…sort of. I was actually looking for Anne. You know, the little redhead?"

"My memory isn't that short. I met you all this morning, remember?"

"Of course. Anyway, I think she's gone back to the forest for some time alone. It all gets a bit overwhelming, you know? All the Nobles and power and stuff."

He didn't look convinced. "So you were going to find her, then 'have some time alone' also?"

"Yes." Time alone to figure out what in Hades was going on, and what she should do next. Defeat the Queen, indeed…

If he was still doubtful, he didn't show it. "Are you coming back to stay here tonight?"

The comment reminded Ash of that last conversation with Sam, and she deflated. "I'm supposed to be staying with this guy

I met today, Sam. He's Janeus's namesake; do you know him?"

He snorted. "Oh yes. I know him. How did that happen?" Then he rolled his eyes and said, "Of course, the clothes you're wearing tell the story. So the two of you have set up together already, have you?"

"No! Not at all." Islo clearly wasn't that keen on Sam, so Ash felt free to be honest. "I got roped into it. One moment I was admiring the scenery, then the next I'd agreed to move in with him. I didn't want to hurt his feelings by saying no, especially after he'd already told your father."

There was an expressive pause where Islo tried unsuccessfully to hide his smirk. "If that doesn't work out, you'll always be welcome in my home," he said casually, then at the expression on her face elaborated, "in my parents' house, in a bedroom of your own. We already went over that this morning."

"In that case, I'm very grateful. Thank you." She might take him up on that tonight, actually. The idea of going back to stay with Sam wasn't all that appealing. "Is that because I'm the Queen's namesake?"

He shook his head, a little smile on his face. "For my parents it might be a reason. But for me? Hardly."

Ash just looked at him. Why would he help her, if not because of the Queen? Everybody else seemed to. They didn't know each other. There was no good reason for him to put himself out for her. Except...he'd never seemed as enamoured of the Nobles as his mother and father. Was it possible that he was free?

Even as Ash thought that, she realised that Dr Walker's warnings must have affected her. Free? That implied that the others were controlled or somehow prisoners, and she wasn't sure if she believed that. Drugged water...? It was possible...

"Islo," she asked carefully, "do you usually drink the town's water? I hear that it's very refreshing, although I can't say I've much of a taste for water."

There was a 'ping!' moment where she *saw* the lightbulb go on over his head. Oh wait, that was a coloured light she'd accidentally conjured up – but he didn't notice, instead smiling crookedly. "No, as a matter of fact I don't. Too many *additives* for my taste."

Oh Deias, him too. And if he said it…

Ash said a very bad word. "So the water is drugged, then."

"Shh!" Islo said urgently, looking around as if someone was already reporting on them. "I never said anything like that! And you shouldn't either!" He pointed mutely at the green tattoo on her hand, mouthing something that she took as 'eyes are everywhere'.

She stared down at the tattoo. It looked as harmless as her coloured lights, except that inexplicably it appeared to have grown. She would have sworn it had only covered the ball of her thumb before, but now the tendrils reached over her wrist. And the little flower bud she'd noticed before now had distinctly red petals.

This? She mouthed back.

Yes!

Ughh. That wasn't good. She stared down at it once more, then carefully pointed to her eyes and ears and the tattoo again and made a questioning gesture. Islo shrugged, then nodded.

"But of course you can stay for dinner," he said loudly. "Anything for the Queen's namesake."

Shoot, shoot, shoot. Was he saying that the tattoo was somehow bugged? Ash supposed it was possible with the increases in technology – but then you brought alter-power into it, and she had no idea what the possibilities were. So it seemed that the only ones not entirely enamoured of the Queen were Dr Walker, Anne, Islo…and her, after all.

Ash didn't know if she entirely believed what Dr Walker had told her, since the parts about magic potions were obviously far-fetched. But there was something terribly wrong with this whole situation, and she was going to find out what it was.

"Thank you," she replied loudly, then realised she sounded like an actor on a bad soap (case in point still playing on the big screen). In a more normal voice she added, "My friend Anne should come for dinner as well, so we can discuss each of our days. They've been very…momentous. And perhaps you can bring some of your friends?" Anyone else like him who hadn't been drinking the water?

"Anne is most welcome," Islo replied courteously, "although I do not believe any of my friends are available tonight. Perhaps on further notice."

Oh. She didn't know if that meant there *were* others who were busy, or that there weren't any at all. "And perhaps Anne can stay here tonight," Ash added on inspiration. "In her own room, without milk."

He grinned, getting the joke. "I believe Souris will have already made plans for Anne's accommodation, but if there are none then Anne is welcome here." And he silently and exaggeratedly nodded.

"Wonderful! Um…I'll just go and get her." Ash made a 'where is she?' gesture, and Islo shrugged. He made a gesture that looked like starbursts, and after several moments of clear confusion, he just sighed.

"Ah, chances are it's fine. I just wanted to be extra careful, because you never know who's listening. As for Anne, I've no idea where she is, of course. But perhaps she could have gone for a walk in the woods?"

Ah! Back to the bunker. Of course. "Mm," she agreed noncommittally. "Perhaps." Then she gave Islo a big, silent grin and a thumbs up, and headed for the door.

It turned out to be the wardrobe, and the second door was the bathroom. The third door took her outside to the small village of

Upper Iversley and the late afternoon sun, and she found she was feeling both excited and scared.

Find Anne, don't drink the water. And then…who knew?

Two hours later, Ash was knocking on that same door to be let back in. She'd been all around the woods several times, and had finally stumbled across the bunker. It had been empty, and the Dr Walker hologram in the bunker was no good either. She hadn't been able to make it appear for more than a few seconds, and then it wouldn't say anything, just flickered and disappeared once more.

Furthermore, the surveillance screens still showed the view of the entire forest, so unless Anne had painted herself green and was hiding in a tree, Ash knew that the girl really wasn't there.

As Ash stood on Islo's doorstep, she felt a knot of worry clench her belly. What had happened to Anne? She was so little that *anyone* could have taken her. They'd just have to pick her up and walk off with her. She could have really annoyed someone, or just been an easy target, or just got lost. Look how easily Ash had been lost, after all.

After what felt like ages (but was probably only thirty seconds) Islo opened the door. He frowned when he saw the look on her face. "Are you alright? Did something happen to Anne?"

Ash stepped inside, closing the door after her. "I couldn't find her, and I've no idea where she might be. She's so tiny, Islo; I'm afraid she wouldn't have a chance if somebody wanted to hurt her."

He studied her pensively, his own expression reflecting the worry she felt. "Anne doesn't seem the type to take well to being a servant either, especially if she doesn't, er, *drink*."

"You've got that right!"

"The message came across the comm that Anne was assigned to Souris, so if you can't find her, it's a decent bet that Souris has her. You don't need to worry about her being hurt; the Nobles almost never physically harm their humans. It would be wasteful and there are ways to control other than using physical pain."

Somehow that wasn't comforting. "*Almost* never? What if the human was really arrogant and disobedient and annoying?"

"As you think Anne is sure to be? Again, there are other ways to punish than physical. Souris will probably be so excited to have an actual blueblood under her control that she'll be boasting for days. She won't damage her new toy. Much." Islo added the last word as an afterthought.

Ash was confused. "I thought they hated humans being titled. Why would Souris be happy to have Anne?"

"The Queen always assigns titled humans to the lowest Nobles. It's like punishment for mortals who've had the presumption to call themselves nobles, even if they were born with a title like my sister." He shrugged. "Personally I think the Nobles – the big ones, I mean – are bored."

It seemed criminal that anyone could be bored with that much power available, but it was something else he'd said that caught her attention. "Your sister is titled? I didn't realise you even had a sister!"

For a moment, Islo looked sad. Then he explained, "My older sister Gaira. She was to take the title after my mother. Unlike my mother, Gaira didn't give in to the Queen easily. So she was punished by being given to Souris. She is very good with illusion, Souris, and spiteful."

Ash felt for him. It must be terrible to have a sister, who he clearly felt responsible for, in the hands of someone who he didn't trust an inch. And who was good with illusion… That was interesting. "What title was she to inherit?"

Islo raised his eyebrows. "We're related to George Seymour, remember?"

"Of course I remember, but what title is it? I don't know all the details of George's life."

He spoke clearly and slowly. "Lord Seymour. Viscount

Morley."

"Your *sister* was to be a lord?"

He shrugged. "Sure. She is older than me by two years."

"Oh...well, that's different," Ash remarked. "In my time only men can gain lordships, and the definition of a lord is that they're male."

"How strange! I heard it used to be something like that, but it would be rather unequal, wouldn't it?"

"Of course, but it was tradition for hundreds of years. And a female lord was just called a lady. Does that mean that your sister is a lord rather than a lady? Do you even still have ladies?"

He nodded. "I'm not sure how things worked in your day, but now, if not for the Nobles, my mother would be Ll Georgiana informally, but Lord Seymour and Viscount Morley formally."

"El Georgiana?" It sounded like the name of a Mehican restaurant.

"No, *Ll*. With a double L. It stands for lord and lady, I believe."

Weird. "That's interesting."

"And my father is- *was* Llan Teron, and my courtesy title was Llan Islo." He looked a little embarrassed by the last.

Ah-lan Islo. It sounded like they were all strange last names. "Wow. Is that why you have three lifts? If you don't mind me saying so, you must be really rich!" Ash flushed, realising she'd sounded vulgar, then shrugged. "In my time you would be, anyway."

He shrugged a shoulder. "Lifts are pretty commonplace; we're a bit odd because we use stairs too. But Father always worried that the power would give out and we'd be stuck, and didn't want to use the evac chutes like everyone else. But it's having land above ground that's the great thing: this house has been in our family ever since the rebuild, and the land itself before that. Building is now restricted to underground except in special cases. We need the green space for fields and so forth. Food's got to grow somewhere, you know."

"But what about all the greenhouses underground? Your mother mentioned them earlier."

He grinned. "The greenhouses grow a lot of fancy lettuce, sure. But grains don't grow well down there. We *do* use fields. There's forest all around, but the fields are beyond that."

"Oh." Ash thought about it. "But that sounds pretty depressing, to live down there all the time. No sunshine."

"People can come up if they want to. All of this forest is public land. Or at least, they used to be allowed to. Not so much anymore," Islo admitted. There was a depressed silence, then he asked, "Why is it that you didn't seem to know what I meant when I mentioned the water this morning, but you did this afternoon? Are you just a very good actor?"

"I only just found the town this morning," she replied for what felt like the fifth time. Hades, Islo could be a slow learner. "Remember? I didn't know about any of this."

"Ah. Right."

There was a long, awkward pause where Ash could have sworn he didn't believe her, so she abruptly changed the subject. "What about you, Islo? Why didn't you...*drink*? Aren't you assigned to a Noble?"

He gave her another long stare, then shrugged. "As I said, I don't like the water. And I was assigned to Lord Kadeon, but he never bothered to meet me or make me do anything. I suppose he had better things to do than play with his puppets, and so after the first couple of days the effect of the Queen's presence faded. I think I've built up immunity to the water by now. I only drink it boiled, and haven't had any problems since the first week. I was taken in then – but everyone was. I've been meeting with others like me – there are only a few of us, but numbers are growing – and biding my time."

So they could boil out the drug like one of those nasty water-borne bacteria at home. How simple. "Aren't you afraid someone will find out?"

He made a face. "I'm doing my best to be invisible, and not do anything out of the ordinary. Except for taking you home this morning, that is."

Ash nodded. "I'm really grateful you did. I don't know what would have happened to us otherwise."

Islo gave her another one of those strange looks, then laughed. "Yes, because I'm so generous and forward-thinking. So, do you want some dinner? It's after six, and I've already eaten, but my parents will be glad to have your company. After all, you are the Queen's namesake."

So everybody kept telling her. She thought briefly of Sam, then resolutely put him out of her mind. "Dinner would be wonderful."

George froze where he stood like a deer before a hunter. The *thing* on the hospital bed looked at him. He looked back, unable to move.

It was horrible. Greenish-grey and hairy, it reminded him of a fairytale troll. Where did it come from? Where was Eric? Damnation...had it *eaten* him?

Or maybe, George thought hopefully, Eric was just hiding.

He hadn't even come into consciousness. How could he have hid?

But George ignored that last nasty thought and looked for something to use as a weapon. Nothing. As a last resort, he darted over and picked up the red swivel chair. He raised it between himself and the thing, and waited, desperately wanting to run, but not willing to leave the boy to die.

It didn't seem as if it was going to attack. It was just sitting there placidly, looking at him as though it found him interesting.

But George's sight was growing blurry, and fear twisted in his gut. Would it strike while he was incapacitated?

Then the troll on the bed wavered, and there was another beast sitting where it had been. What was going on?

George tried to turn and run to the door, but his body wouldn't obey him. It stubbornly stayed where it was, standing five feet away from a full grown Afrecan lion.

Anne spent the afternoon and evening huddled against the sandy dirt wall of the serpent pit. She had not even been able to sleep: 'twas difficult to do so when she was stiff with terror and afraid to move an inch for fear of a slow, painful death.

The first one had bitten her about half an hour after Souris had put her in the pit. In truth she was surprised it had waited that long. She wasn't an expert in serpent poison, or in anything actually, but did not some poisons take hours to work? Hours of slow, horrible pain…

So now there were two tiny red marks on her ankle, and Anne waited to die as the poison spread and the bite mark began to feel numb. Then another serpent bit her.

Some time after the third bite Souris came back. She looked down at Anne and asked, "Ready to beg me?"

Anne answered with an Anglo-Saxon hand gesture she'd seen her brothers use. Souris snarled, and left. Anne hadn't seen her since.

The evening turned into night, and the pit slowly filled up with serpents. Long, slender and black, they slithered over each others' bodies and Anne's legs. She came to the point where she was standing almost waist deep in the creatures.

Once she got over the initial mind-numbing horror (which took about fifteen minutes; in spite of anything Ash might think, Anne was quite hardy) she found that she could look at the situation objectively. She began to count serpents as a way to measure time, and then later, pondered her situation. 'Twas not what she had expected.

For example, why weren't the bites swelling up? She had twelve now, having the time to count them. In fact, that first bite had almost faded to nothing, and the most recent bites had hardly hurt at all.

Mayhap the poison was numbing her entire body. Anne experimentally pinched the soft flesh of her upper arm. Hard.

"OUCH!" That had *hurt*. So why hadn't the serpent bites?

She looked down at the writhing mass sliding around her hips. They looked real, and she could feel them moving against her borrowed, insufficient garb. But they weren't *heavy* at all; they didn't squash her the way she would have thought. Mayhap 'twas just another sign of her numbness, the poison working? If so, 'twas not a very good poison.

She'd lost track of time at eighty-eight serpents, and amazingly the pit was able to hold them all. Mayhap they weren't really poisonous, and she might wait for the pit to fill, then climb out on top of them…?

Abandon foolish hope, Anne told herself. This was not some heroic ballad where there would be a miraculous escape, and instead she would likely be dead by morning. But better to be dead than a slave.

Ouch! Yet another bite…

She sighed in resignation and slumped back against the wall.

🙢❧

Ash rolled over in bed, eyes wide, and stared at the dark ceiling of Islo's parents' spare room. One of them, anyway; the house was a very good size. Both Georgiana and Teron had been more than welcoming, and absolutely ecstatic that she was the Queen's namesake. They couldn't do enough for her.

But it all felt so wrong, knowing what she now knew, what Dr Walker had said and what Islo had confirmed.

They didn't do it because they wanted to; they did it because they were compelled to. Brainwashed into happy compliance in their service to the one true Queen. That put a real damper on her enjoying their hospitality.

And now she just couldn't sleep. She'd believed Dr Walker when he'd told her about the disaster to come to this area, but the idea that she was the only one who could stop it happening was so ludicrous and frightening that she'd just rejected it completely.

And now it was all she could think about. It seemed guilt caused insomnia, and that guilt also destroyed her enjoyment of the little coloured lights she'd been creating. They now seemed silly and pointless.

She couldn't even brush off the responsibility onto Islo, because *she* was the Queen's namesake, for better or for worse. She had to make a difference, but how?

Ash hadn't asked for any of this! She just wanted to live her normal, boring twenty-first -century life, and never have to know that all life would be gone by 2157. Or at least all life in and around Iversley. Er, Queenstown. Whatever.

She could just forget it all. Find Anne, go back to the bunker, make Dr Walker send them home, and live to a ripe old age. None of this would ever touch her, provided the lovely doctor didn't try to steal her back for some reason.

But the hologram was gone, wasn't it? She didn't know where Anne was, and the actual Dr Walker was a nervous wreck. He'd said that the time machine – wherever it was – wasn't working. So leaving it all behind was a lovely thought, but actually impossible at this point.

Ash looked to the bedside table where the little cloth purse sat, illuminated gold in the glow of the clock. It was comforting that they still used both clocks and bedside tables. It made her feel a little hopeful to know that some things wouldn't change.

The clock read *1:44.* She'd gone to bed almost four hours ago on the offer from Georgiana, as she'd stayed longer for dinner than she'd expected. Teron had offered to contact Sam regarding her whereabouts, and she'd taken him up on that offer, pushing down any sense of guilt over Sam's response. It wouldn't kill him to have to wait a bit…or a lot.

Dr Walker had made some pretty bold claims over the contents of that purse. One of the vials supposedly would make her *fly*…but only in her mind, no doubt, while lying on the ground giggling like an idiot. She'd always liked the idea of flying like a superhero, but it had always sat firmly in the realm of fantasy.

But still the same idea niggled – what if they *did* work? She could just drink the vials. See what happened. The worst that could happen was that they *wouldn't* work and she'd have a tummy ache, right?

Actually, logic reminded her, that wasn't the worst that could happen. The worst would be that she could die a horrible death, go insane or be permanently maimed from consuming something never intended to be inside a human body.

That last thought made Ash roll over, resolutely determined to sleep and deal with all this mess in the morning. But that resolution lasted only two minutes, and then she was staring at that same cloth bag again.

After all, some of the people here could actually time-travel, and that was something she'd thought was myth. She had seen a boy today who could shapeshift into a bear, although possibly an ass would have been more appropriate. What was a little high-flying compared to that?

She quietly pulled the vials out of the purse and set them on the metal table with a little *chink*. With the light of the clock behind, they really looked like liquid gold. Now, it was the tall slender one he said was for flight, yes? No, the shorter round one. Argh!

It wasn't Ash's mind that made the decision to reach over, take one of the vials and open the lid, more her morbid sense of curiosity. A pleasant fruity smell wafted out, with a hint of something that reminded her of pineapple.

Just a little taste…

Like a child forced to drink their medicine before allowed dessert, she quickly lifted the vial to her lips and took a teeny tiny swig. Then before she lost momentum she grabbed the other vial and did the same – after all, she couldn't remember which was which. Then she carefully set the lids back on and waited for something incredible to happen, or for her stomach to seriously rebel.

Three…two…one…

Eleven

A DARK SECRET

That hadn't been so bad. Ash cautiously felt her body to check for boils, paralysis, limbs falling off. The usual. Everything seemed attached as normal, and she felt…good, actually, except that the clock was now reading *9.31*. She'd slept all night!

The sound of the door startled her into full wakefulness. Thinking quickly, she grabbed the vials from the table top and stuffed them and the purse under her pillow just as Georgiana walked in.

"Good morning!" Georgiana chirped. "I saw on the monitor that you were awake, and came in to tell you that breakfast is ready whenever you want it! Also, you're welcome to wash in the ensuite; it's all yours!"

How could the woman be so happy, *all the time*? It was unnatural.

Oh, that was right…there was something in the water.

"You don't have any coffee, do you?" Ash asked huskily. Her voice always sounded rough in the morning before she'd had a drink. "Or a cup of tea? With freshly boiled, purified water, please." She added the last as a precaution, feeling like the world's fussiest guest but also not prepared to take any risks.

"Of course! I'll have a cup made for you!"

"Thanks. I'll have a shower now, thanks."

Georgiana left, presumably to fulfil Ash's every desire. For coffee, anyway. The woman had always been pleasant, but now with Ash's new title she was absolutely *fawning*.

It reminded Ash of that movie where one character says, "What kind of sycophant are you?!" and the other replies; "What kind of sycophant would you like me to be?" It had been funny in the movie, but in real life it was kind of sickening.

It bothered her as much as the knowledge that they'd had some kind of monitor in her room overnight. Hopefully they wouldn't have seen her drink the vials.

Ash hadn't thought she'd drunk very much, but the taller, slender vial was practically empty. The smaller round one was still mostly full of that golden liquid that reminded her of runny honey, and the odd text on the side now made sense. *Flight*, it read in elegant italics, and the empty one now read *Far-sight*.

She froze. Had someone sneaked in during the night and swapped the vials? Because she knew she hadn't been able to read them yesterday.

Carefully she put them back in the cloth purse and took the whole lot into the bathroom for her shower. It wouldn't do to have them found by a dedicated servant of the Queen like her host.

Looking in the mirror after she'd washed, she noticed something disturbing. The small tattoo that had just reached her wrist the night before was now stretching up past her elbow.

It had also sprouted small red flowers like orchids. Last night she was sure it had been a dark, forest green, but now it was more of a turquoise green. Beautiful, but that wasn't the point.

Tattoos shouldn't spread like a vine…or a virus.

They ate breakfast in another room. Instead of the kitchen, this time a table was beautifully laid in what was clearly the formal dining room. Ash commented on the change, and Teron said, "Only the best for the Queen's namesake."

So when they were merely visitors from another century they only merited the kitchen table? She was beginning to hate that title. Well, she'd done what she could. She'd drunk those mysterious vials, and now she just had to wait for them to work. Or not poison her, at least. So far, so good.

Ash carefully avoided the sparkling glass of water by her plate.

After they'd eaten, Teron announced, "I've just been given wonderful news. Ash, the Queen has summoned you again, and she wishes to see you *in person!*"

"Why?" Ash blurted out in horror, thinking of how she'd been so impacted by the power felt through the mirror. Dr Walker had said that as long as she kept away from the Queen and didn't drink the water, she'd keep her right mind, and personal contact would *not* help.

But then she saw the bemused expressions on her hosts' faces and quickly corrected, "I mean, I only saw her yesterday! Surely she has better things to do than waste her time on someone ordinary like me!"

"But you're her namesake," Teron said, baffled. "You were chosen from all others on the planet. Why would you even question this request?"

Now that was a question she didn't want to answer. "Good point," Ash replied with false heartiness. "When does she want to see me?" I.e. how long did she have to escape?

"Right away."

Damn. DAMN. "Really. Lucky me. I, uh, need to go to the bathroom first. Excuse me."

The bathroom was no help; not even a small window for air. There were only tiny vents in the ceiling that even Anne would be hard pressed to fit into. In despair, Ash sat on the closed lid of the toilet and put her head in her hands. What was she going to do?

Go to the Queen. She cannot harm you.

What?

Go to the Queen. She-

"I heard you the first time." Ash muttered. It was that little voice again, the one that had told her not to drink the water.

"Who are you?" Ash asked quietly.

A friend.

"How do I know I can trust you?" Because usually when people heard voices in their heads, they should go and contact the nearest specialist, not *obey* those voices.

You don't know. You can only make the decision to trust and see how it turns out. Time will tell.

Well, that was completely useless! Ash was in a very dangerous place. She needed guarantees, not maybes. But the voice had been right about the water. Probably she should listen this time too.

"Are you alright in there?" Georgiana called through the bathroom door. "It won't do to keep the Queen waiting."

Ash made a split decision. She would trust the voice. The worst that could happen if it was wrong was that she'd be a mindless slave, but hey! At least she'd be happy, and not notice the world ending.

Hadur, the same large, hairy Noble that had carried her previously, led her, Georgiana and Teron to the Queen. He looked at Ash with something like contempt, or possibly pity, but at least he let her walk.

This time instead of going through the ornate golden doors to the mirrored room in the underground city, they passed them and headed towards a small door in the back. The others left her at the door with encouraging smiles, and Ash walked in alone. The room was dim again. It made it that much scarier, not being able to see what was ahead of her.

Be brave, Ash. You have nothing to fear from her now.

That was comforting. The voice hadn't forgotten her, even if it wouldn't give her much wanted guarantees.

Then the lights came on, and Ash was standing face to face with the Queen.

Anne woke up with a start. For a moment she knew not where she was, since she could feel pebbles under her stiff body and could hear the sound of water close by. Then she saw the serpents under and around her like some hideous mattress. How had she managed to sleep in the middle of *that*?

Wait- there was something wrong here. Firstly, that she was still alive. She pulled her leg out of the black mass and checked it. No bite marks. And had she not felt pebbles? She was in a *dirt* pit.

Anne looked around. Upwards was a circle of light. Sideways, sandy dirt walls. Downwards, piles of black serpents. She stood up fully, closed her eyes and leaned back against the wall again.

Oof! She was on her backside again on a pile of stones. Her eyes shot open, and she was still sitting in the middle of the pit, nowhere near the walls. How had she fallen through the serpents? She hadn't even felt them.

She tried again. She closed her eyes and walked forward towards the other side of the pit. One step, two, three… Her footsteps crunched with every step. Seven, eight... The pit wasn't that wide!

She opened her eyes and again she was standing in the middle of the dirt hole, about five paces wide from one side to the other. She looked down. Still serpents. By the Rood, that one just went *through* her leg!

What sort of sorcery was this?

Taking a deep breath, Anne closed her eyes again and dropped to her hands and knees. She didn't feel snakes, just the smooth round shapes of dozens of stones under her palms. Eyes still glued shut, she waved her arms around in every direction. No serpents! They seemed to only be there when she had her eyes open. 'Twas as if the power that had created them was weakening.

She carefully crawled in the direction of the city sounds. From the day before, she remembered that solid, flat stone streets had led directly onto the pebbly shore. If she could but reach the solid stone, she'd know that the pit wasn't real.

A few minutes (and sore hands and knees) later, Anne hit solid rock. "*Yes!*" she cried out loud. She'd reached the street. She opened her eyes to celebrate…and found herself back in the pit.

No! This time she wouldn't give in. She could still feel the stone under her feet, and the serpents, though they looked solid, barely registered touching her skin anymore.

Anne stared hard at them. She could just make out the outline of the street paving beneath them; but 'twas like looking through dark glass. They weren't truly there, at least not any longer. They didn't truly bite her.

She wasn't in a pit, for 'twas all sorcery and falsehood, Anne realised in dawning amazement. She only wished that Ash was nearby to share the discovery (and for Anne to say 'I told you so') for Anne had *known* there must be some form of witchcraft in this place!

"Servant Anne," a voice called. It was Souris again, back to gloat. She obviously didn't know the spell was wearing off, or she wouldn't have sounded so confident.

Anne turned toward her voice, at the last moment remembering she was supposed to be in a deep hole, so made sure to turn her face upwards. It was very strange. She could see Souris above her looking downwards, but at the same time she could see in the corner of her vision Souris standing directly in front of her.

The Noble seemed confused at Anne's movement from across the shore, but then she recovered herself. "I see that your night in the snake pit has brought you some humility."

Anne wasn't so sure about that, but she tried to look suitably contrite. "Indeed it has."

"Then ask me nicely, and I shall free you," Souris said.

Anne sighed. "Please let me out of the snake pit."

"Please, *Lady Souris*."

"Please, Lady Souris." See, Anne could be humble when she

needed to be.

With a wave of Souris's hand, the now-sheer walls of the pit disappeared. The Noble stood there in front of her, hands on hips. "You see now what power I have. You are helpless before me."

Anne mumbled something that must have sounded right, because Souris continued, "But just in case you still have any ideas of escape, let me show you what I do to those who continually defy me." She gestured dramatically down the beach.

All Anne could see was a girl sitting on the ground. She had flaxen hair and a dull expression, and wore plain clothing in a similar style to all the other cityfolk. Nothing dreadful or out of the ordinary.

In that moment she recalled that Souris had read her thoughts the day before, and would know that Anne wasn't fooled by any of this show of illusion. She panicked, sucking in a deep breath, but the Noble didn't seem to notice. And if she had known Anne's thoughts, she didn't show it in her speech or actions.

"Come closer," Souris said triumphantly, "and I shall tell you of this worm's terrible crimes against me."

Anne followed her towards the girl. Closer, she could see that she was not overly old, no more than in her early twenties. She reminded Anne of Georgiana, somehow. Mayhap 'twas the odd combination of brown skin and flaxen hair. These people truly needed to take care of their skin! Apart from that, all appeared correct.

"This one thought herself noble, as you did," Souris said with a dramatic hand gesture towards the girl. "She refused to bow before me. So I have given her this terrible punishment until she begs for mercy. And yet she refuses, don't you, Gaira?"

The flaxen-haired girl looked sorrowfully up at the two of them. It still wasn't clear what the punishment was supposed to be (no more smiles?) so Anne just made what she thought was the appropriate gasp of horror. "Oh, by the Rood."

Anne felt it sounded forced as she wasn't the best actor, but it must have been the right thing to do, because Souris nodded grimly. "Yes. I have made her this dreadful creature of merely skin and bone, without any flesh, and I will keep her in this cage, eating but not filled, drinking but still thirsty, and unable to die until she is completely my creature."

That sounded disgusting, and was probably reason enough for Gaira to look so sad. The only problem was that Anne didn't see any of it, or even the cage Gaira was supposedly in. Then Souris moved, and the artificial sunlight struck the girl full on the face. For a moment, Anne could see the outline of her skeleton imposed over the skin of her pretty face. She recoiled in horror.

The Noble saw Anne's reaction and nodded in satisfaction. "And I will do the same to you unless you obey me without question."

"You'll do to me what you've done to this girl," Anne echoed flatly. "Just as I was imprisoned all night in the serpent pit."

"As I just said," Souris agreed. "Do you doubt me?"

Anne didn't answer, instead focussing on the girl in front of her. The brief moment of artificial sunlight had shown Anne the apparent punishment, but also its falseness. Gaira was no more harmed than Anne had been last night, and there was no doubt that the curse of living death was all in the girl's mind. Now Anne knew what to look for, she saw it for what it was. A lie, and not even a very convincing one.

Anne walked up to the girl. She could still see the bone on one side of her face, but now it looked even less realistic. She reached out to brush the girl's cheek, and felt soft flesh.

Gaira flinched back. "Why are you touching me? How did you get inside the cage?"

"There is no cage," Anne replied softly. "It is a deception on your mind. Smoke and mirrors, if you would but believe it."

The blonde shook her head in dismay, and her voice came out in a hoarse whisper. "You're calling this pain my imagination? I assure you it's quite real."

Anne turned to Souris. "I do doubt you. I doubt you can do any harm at all, except to the mind. And 'tis now apparent that you cannot touch mine any longer."

The Noble's jaw dropped, and her face twisted in hate as she realised that Anne was in earnest. "We'll see how long that lasts, little girl. I'll see you writhing in agony."

No doubt she'd try. But for this moment, Anne was focused on Gaira. "Come with me now. We'll walk away from this place together, and you'll see that Souris has no power over you."

Gaira didn't just look disbelieving, she was offended. She shook her head again. "Don't taunt me! I can't walk through solid bars, even if you can."

"There are no bars!"

But to Anne's dismay the girl turned deliberately away, wrapping her arms around her bent knees and ignoring Anne completely. The bars were on the inside of Gaira's mind; where only the Eternal One – and the Nobles – could reach.

Anne turned to see Souris standing right in front of her, red with fury. "How dare you disobey me! I warned you of the penalty for that."

"What?" Anne asked scornfully. Her failure to convince Gaira wasn't just upsetting, it made her angry. "You shall make me believe I'm in a serpent pit again? A vat of boiling oil? A theatre full of Morris dancers?"

Suddenly there appeared a massive serpent, its body as thick around as Anne's waist, poised to strike. She started to cringe away, then checked herself. "No," she said firmly. "'Tis not true, and I am not afraid."

The serpent lunged towards her, and she saw its immense hinged jaw close over her head. She felt nothing. "Still not afraid."

Souris was livid with anger and panicked all at once. "Stop, or I'll make you sorry!"

Anne laughed at her. "You can do nothing real to me, can you? You have not even the strength to stop me leaving. That's why you have your human slaves do it for you."

Souris sneered. "Of course I can-"

Anne brushed away the transparent monster that rushed towards her. The illusions didn't even appear solid now, more like the 'ghosts' she'd first seen in the forest. Either 'twas because Anne didn't believe it, or because Souris was panicking, but the result was the same. "I'm going to leave right now, mouse, and you shall not stop me."

She turned to do so, but found the man who'd carried her there blocking her path. He shook his head. She went to step around him, but he grabbed her arm.

"Come now. We've done this before, have we not?" Anne told him lightly. She took advantage of his surprise to knee him sharply in the family jewels.

He bent over in agony, and she stepped neatly around him and ran as fast as her legs would carry her.

❦

The Queen looked different today. Smaller, less terrifyingly inhuman as she sat on a Grecian-style couch in the suite of rooms Ash was led to. She had dark hair and wore a simple green and silver gown, and a rather fabulous set of chandelier-like earrings.

In fact, Ash only knew it was her because there was no one else in the room – and that beautiful face remained the same. She wasn't just lovely, she was fabulously beautiful, like a combination of the most gorgeous film stars Ash had ever seen.

Mind you, Ash thought, the Queen could change her appearance, couldn't she? Perhaps she really looked like a troll.

One thing was certain though; the power the Queen had used the day before was no longer present. Her voice, when she spoke, was pleasant: husky and perhaps a little familiar, but it lacked that supernatural perfection of before. "Hello, Ash."

"Um…hello." Ash wondered if she should kneel, but no one

said anything, and so she just stood in place, feeling scared and confused and a little bit stupid.

In the silence the Queen continued, "You're wondering why I look different today, no doubt. And no, I don't read minds. But I have become very good at guessing from expressions and context. You want to know why I called you here too, I presume?"

Ash nodded, relieved at the thought her private (possibly treasonous) thoughts weren't being read, but also nervous that she was so easily read.

"I look different because I don't need to impress you anymore." The Queen waved a hand around the room. "You see me as I am. Well, mostly. It's nice to not have to try all the time, isn't it?" She didn't wait for Ash to respond, adding, "And as for why you're here, well, I wanted to have a chat with my newest namesake. It's a lot to take in, and I realised that you're probably feeling at sea, what with being a time-traveller to boot. How are you finding things?"

There was an expectant pause where Ash realised this time she needed to reply. She fumbled out, "Um…different. I like the…" What, power? Handsome but pushy boys? Warnings of doom from Dr Walker? "Food," she finished lamely. "I need more practice with the power."

The Queen looked briefly startled, then laughed. Her voice was like a bell. "Oh, you *are* funny. I'd forgotten that."

"You had?" But they'd never met before…

She shrugged. "Enough time passes and you forget everything. Do you know how old I am, Ash?"

Ash shook her head silently.

"Neither do I. I lost track at around three hundred and forty-four, but even that was an estimate since we moved around so much in the early days. People are afraid of power, Ash, and they're even more afraid of women with power. That's why it's so important to make friends early on with the locals. The namesakes are part of that, of course. We show by sharing power that we are to be trusted, and everyone is a lot happier."

Ash tried to take in what had been said. The Queen was a time-traveller, she'd known that, but to be so open about it… "So that's what the namesakes are for? Just to make friends?"

"That, and a few other things." The Queen stood, casually walking towards Ash. Her gown rippled as she went, moving like flowing water under light, and Ash caught a glimpse of what might have been a tattoo on the underside of her arm before the fabric covered it once more. She stopped a few feet away, eye to eye, and Ash had to resist the urge to step back or look away.

The Queen's eyes were green today. Not muddy green-brown like Ash's, but a clear, lovely jade. Naturally.

"You're not my first namesake, of course." As if prompted by Ash's thoughts, the Queen pushed up her left sleeve to reveal the tattoo that had caught her attention earlier. It was rather like Ash's, had Ash's been a whole vine rather than just a branch, and was finely detailed and covered in large red blooms. "See these flowers? I have one for each namesake. There are eighteen in all. You're the nineteenth, right here." She tapped a little bud reaching out over her hand, right where the same image was on Ash's hand.

Ash stared down at bright red blooms disappearing under the Queen's sleeve, and a horrible thought occurred. "What happened to the others?"

"They died."

Oh Hades, the Queen had killed them. She didn't just control people, she killed them too-

"Mostly of old age, although there were a couple of premature deaths. Who would have thought that someone could choke to death on a piece of bread?" The Queen looked disgruntled. "What did they think they were, a pigeon? People need to *chew* their food before they swallow."

Relieved, Ash laughed awkwardly, and the other woman laughed with her. "But that won't happen to you. You, of all my namesakes, won't die of old age."

Ash caught her breath, and suddenly she wasn't laughing anymore. "Are...are you going to kill me?"

"Oh, Deias no!" The Queen laughed. "I said that all wrong, didn't I? What I meant was is that you won't die. You can't, see? Because I'm still alive."

It still wasn't making any sense. "So...I die if you die? Or you die if I die...?"

"In a manner of speaking." Suddenly the Queen was much closer, and Ash took a nervous step backwards. "You don't understand what I mean when I say I've been waiting for you for a long, long time, and that I knew this moment would come. You don't understand when I say that it doesn't matter what comes next for you, because it's been preordained. Even everything down to meeting Janeus..."

Ash stared at her open-mouthed, still not understanding, and the Queen's voice became gentler. "I'm sorry about Sam, by the way. He's rather too pushy for my tastes. Would you like me to get rid of him for you? We'll find you someone much nicer. Easier."

Was she talking about killing Sam? It was an extreme response to his general annoyingness. "Ah..."

The Queen made a dismissive gesture. "Or not. We can leave him in his current position for now, but if he causes trouble then he can move along elsewhere. It really is up to you, Ash. You are my one *true* namesake."

"I'm sorry," Ash said finally. "I still don't understand what you mean."

The Queen sighed. "No, you don't, because I didn't. But how can you understand if it's not explained to you? Ash, I'm going to tell you a great, terrifying truth. And you can believe me or not believe me, but it's not going to make any difference in the end. You can't change the past. Or rather, you cannot change *my* past, because it's already been written."

"What is it?" Ash whispered.

And the Queen told her.

Lights and sound and smells whirled all around George like he was caught in the centre of a storm, and it was too much for him to take in.

He staggered across the room (was he even in a room anymore?) in the direction the door might have been, and hit something hard. The sensation flared up in his vision like a bright white light, and the word 'POW' appeared briefly before vanishing again. The lion was long gone, as was the troll – and presumably the child too – and the hospital room may as well have disappeared too.

What had happened? Had he been snatched away again?

"Curse you, Doctor Walker," he tried to say, but it came out more like 'Criss… drruhduhwhuh', and then he took two staggering steps forward and-

POW.

Oops. Found the door? Or some sort of floating carousel, complete with dancing clowns, white-faced and with brightly coloured laughing mouths. Somewhere in the depths of George's disturbed mind he managed to hope that this was all a hallucination.

Giants he could handle, but clowns…? This was the most terrifying sight yet.

After the Queen finished speaking, she stopped and waited for Ash's response. And waited, and waited. "Well?"

"I don't believe you," Ash said abruptly. "You can make yourself look like anyone at all, and you've got enough power that

you can lie. I don't believe you."

"You don't want to believe me," the Queen corrected. No matter how she'd made her face look when she'd given that announcement, Ash still couldn't think of her as anything except the Queen. They weren't the same. They *couldn't be* the same. "Although most of this time is a blur, I recall feeling the same way. I don't seem like a real person to you, do I? You can't identify with me. You don't understand why I do the things I do."

She cocked her head to the side, mirroring Ash's movements. A true mirror now, only one that was perfected beyond anything Ash could manage even on her best day. "You judge me, young Ash, thinking that I'm doing wrong just because I've taken steps that you'd never dare to take. You can't see yet that it's for the good of everyone.

"I've tried the free will thing. It never works for long because people just *refuse* to do what's good for them, because they're afraid or just contrary. Can't you see that?"

The Queen was now an almost exact replica of what Ash had seen in Georgiana and Teron's bathroom mirror this morning, only somehow shinier and prettier and with an irritatingly patient expression.

But with what she'd said – that *she* was Ashlea Jane O'Reilly, just a couple of hundred years and a whole lot of power down the track – Ash couldn't believe it, and she couldn't accept it.

"I still don't believe you," Ash said again, and her voice was almost a whisper. "You're playing some kind of game with me, and I don't know why. You need to stop it." Stop looking like *her*, change her face back to that extra-lovely visage, anything but this horrible, unwanted clone.

And anyway, if they were the same person in one space, shouldn't the universe have exploded or something?

She said so, and the Queen laughed in scornful surprise. "I realise you're practically a child, but don't be so foolish. This is just our timeline crossing over for a brief moment. It'll happen again, but next time you won't be so surprised."

Ash was silent, and suddenly the Queen burst out with, "Chaos, you're so *stupid*! You don't have any ambitions, do you? No dreams, no desire for anything *greater* than a simple little life with a handsome man and a white picket fence. No plans to make a mark on the world, nor to ever be more than fading memories in the minds of your *two point five children*. And you accept it! You never even try to become anybody, content to be absolutely mundane!"

"I'm not content to be mundane," Ash countered in almost a whisper. "I have plans. I just need to…"

"Get away from your dull but easy secretary job? Drive off in your 1992 blue Cortina until you find somewhere that life feels like it has a purpose, hmm?"

The job…the Cortina…how did she know?

The Queen – the other Ash – stared at her in disgust, that façade of kindness now gone. "Yes, of course I remember those details. I forget the faces and the names of the people I worked for, but I remember the sense of being bored stiff. And I remember that when I was you, I would have done anything to get back to that time and that place, Hades knows why. But greatness found me, and will find you in spite of your efforts to avoid it."

"How did this happen?"

"Why would I tell you that? I wouldn't want you to inadvertently sidestep your fate. You can try to avoid it as I did, and as I know you will," the other woman said, shaking her head scornfully. "But you can't outrun your destiny. So run along, young Ash. Do whatever it pleases you to do, and know that it'll not make any difference. Either way, you lose. Or rather, you win, because you get to become me. Lucky, lucky you."

No. No, this nasty lookalike couldn't win. She wouldn't; Ash wouldn't let her.

But even as Ash had that thought, she realised that she had nothing. She had coloured lights, and the other… the Queen had an army of giants and the minds of a city.

Ash felt so impotent that she found herself choking out, "Deias, I hate you!"

"Don't hate yourself," the Queen mimicked in Ash's voice, then her face began to change back to that lovelier, supermodel perfection. "But I got rather bored of having our features. Pleasant, but hardly worth a second glance, don't you think? I mean, if you could look like anyone in the world… it wouldn't be *you*, would it?"

As Ash fumed helplessly, the Queen added, "You can run along now. Go entertain yourself with coloured lights, or even, if you wish, try to find a way to bring me down. That's the next step, isn't it? You and some dubious gift given by Doctor Trotter…no, Walker. That was it. Enjoy whatever he gave you, young Ash, and know that whatever you do, you can't change your fate. Your future is my past, and it *cannot* be changed."

As if on cue Hadur's tall figure appeared once more, and Ash barely felt the hand he had on her shoulder to escort her out.

⁂

After the girl left, the Queen sat down again on her chair with a thump. The expression on her face was both petulant and calculating, but Aegus pretended not to see either, schooling his own face into obedient pleasantness.

"Ha," she said to no one in particular. "Take that, Amaranthus. Do you think she believed me, Aegus?"

He almost dropped the tray he'd been carefully holding. It seemed she actually expected an answer, and he fumbled to provide one that would be true yet flattering. She had an excellent nose for lies, and a short temper with those who told them. Ironic, really, and brought to mind that saying about pots and kettles. "I couldn't say, my Queen, as I was not present." There, a good answer.

"I know I got a hook in," the Queen continued gleefully, clearly not having paid attention either way. She was becoming more and more reckless since the loss of the Eternity Stone, he'd noticed, and was attending less to the things that previously she'd considered vital. Directing the servants, for example. "Chaos, the young are so *entertaining*. Hard to believe I was ever like that."

It was hard to believe. The Queen seemed to have stepped fully formed into her powerful self right out of sea foam, as the old tales went, without going through any awkward childhood. Of course, anyone who *had* known her back then wasn't able to tell. Or so he'd thought, until a day or two earlier.

"My Queen," he said carefully, directing her attention to more important matters. "It has become a matter of concern that several of the servants are no longer being actively directed, and thus the power is causing issues-"

"Issues? What issues?"

He thought of those he'd seen wandering aimlessly around the city and shuddered. "Insanity, for one."

"Huh." She seemed to think, then shrugged. "I'll have someone direct them in the next day or two. Now, how goes progress on the Eternity Stone?"

Well, they hadn't found it, had they? "We've tried a new route," he replied. "Searching out those unaffected by the water in order to question them. I believe we are close to finding the last few."

"You *believe*," the Queen snapped suddenly, her good mood gone. "Which means you hope, which means nothing at all. What am I going to do, Aegus?" Another rhetorical question, because she immediately continued, "I could revert back to blood sacrifices, of course, but that makes a terrible mess and I wouldn't be able to leave without the Stone, so it'd be a waste of time and potential long-term gain."

"Would it give you enough power to find the Stone?"

She tapped her fingers glumly on her richly embroidered

knee. "Perhaps. Perhaps not. The Eternity Stone is like…is like an eel in custard. Or that might not be the right metaphor – but something difficult to catch, anyway. It was a sheer miracle I found it the first time." She pouted. "Besides, I don't *like* killing people if I don't have to. It makes me feel like some kind of monster."

"You'd never be a monster," Aegus said smoothly, because it was what she expected to hear. "Not one as beautiful as you."

His queen shrugged off the compliment. "Of course I wouldn't. But I don't want to *feel* like a monster. I'll give the girl a few more hours, then I'll gather what I can. If I can't find the Stone from that, this one last time…"

Then she'd get serious, it went without saying. And perhaps one or two – or more – of the local townsfolk might go missing. The Queen didn't enjoy killing, Aegus believed, but over time she'd become very pragmatic. If it was her or them, she'd choose her. He understood that, and respected it, because he felt the same way.

As long as it didn't become her or *him*.

He pushed down that horrible thought, smiled comfortingly, and went to get his monarch a goblet of wine.

Twelve

OUTLAWS

In an almost perfect repeat of the previous day, Ash was standing dumbly out in the streets of the city centre. This time she was alone, and the knowledge she'd been given made her feel numb. Either that, or she'd be screaming.

The Queen, that amazing, powerful, not-quite-real being, claimed to be *her*. From the future, after a whole lot of time travelling and power-gathering until she bore only the slightest resemblance to her past self. And she'd been so *careless* as she told Ash, as if she didn't know how upsetting it would be! Or as if she just didn't care…

The Queen had known about Dr Walker. She'd known about a lot of things, including the rather old, ordinary car Ash drove, and the dull, ordinary job she itched to escape from but lacked the direction in which to move.

"Lots of people don't like their job," Ash told herself. "It was a guess. It had to be a guess."

Yeah, but naming the model of the car Ash drove? Lucky guess…

One thing was for certain. If it *was* true, then the Queen was nothing like Ash. Looks aside, Ash wasn't sure she even liked the woman.

What had she said about Ash's next move? Something like: *Try to bring me down…you and Doctor Walker…but know that whatever you do, you can't change your fate. Your future is my past, and it cannot be changed…*

The tattoo on Ash's hand and wrist had grown further still since she'd last looked, and now curled right up her forearm. As she watched yet another bloom opened, and she imagined she felt a throb of pain.

A tear trickled down her cheek, and she dashed it away, turning from the tattoo. That, she couldn't deal with, not on top of everything.

"Queen's namesake!"

Oh, Deias, it wasn't-

"Ash!" Sam came to her almost at a run, his expression both relieved and annoyed. "Where have you been all this time? I thought you'd come to serious harm!" She opened her mouth to reply, but he carried on. "Well, perhaps not really, but it's just not *done* to disappear for hours at a time, without any indication of where you've been. We namesakes-"

"I was with the Queen," Ash said quietly, and it cut his rant short.

"Oh. The whole time?"

She shrugged, not wanting to have this conversation. What had the Queen said – Sam was too pushy, and they could replace him if needed? Deias, he was *annoying*, but being a namesake was clearly everything to him. Ash hadn't yet reached the point where people's feelings meant nothing, although apparently she would reach that point, if the Queen was right.

Well, it was hardly like the Queen would be mistaken. She knew; Ash didn't. So either she was lying for some unknown reason (and by Hades, why would she want to lie about something like that??) or she was telling the truth.

Oh Deias, please let it be a lie.

"What did she say?"

With a jolt Ash realised Sam was asking about her conversation with the Queen. While it was on the top of her mind, she did *not* want to repeat it. It might make it seem more real. "Uh…general namesake things, I suppose."

"Right." Sam was looking at her with a hint of disbelief, then shrugged and gave that usual friendly smile. "Well, if you're going to be a namesake, I suppose you will need to meet with your Noble once in a while. Everyone does, except for me, of course, Janeus being off who knows where. Now, for today I've planned-"

"Please," Ash interrupted with more force than she'd intended. "I'm tired today. I need to think, and I need some space. We'll take a rain check for tomorrow?"

For a moment there was a flash of something dark in his expression, then it settled into mere disgruntlement. "What are you going to do today? Where are you going to go?"

She wanted to say it was none of his damn business, but he was already annoyed, and she felt like she had no energy for arguments. "To see my friend Anne, perhaps. And as I said, to think."

"I can't speak for the thinking," Sam said with some satisfaction, "but that Anne is in trouble. I heard over the comm that she's gone missing. Ran away from Souris not twenty minutes ago, the silly girl. It's not as if there's anywhere else to go."

That snapped Ash out of her depressed confusion. Last she'd seen Anne (and argued with her) Anne had been on her way to find Dr Walker, and had been determined to avoid her new 'lady'. After all of that, how had she ended up with Souris?

The memory of being picked up by various Nobles came back to mind. And there was the answer – it was hard to run away from someone who was four times your size. You'd either need to know some very good hiding places, or else be able to fly like Dr Walker promised. Ha.

"Is she alright?!"

"How should I know?" Sam retorted in surprise. "Last I heard she'd gone missing, and it's not my responsibility to find people who lose their Nobles. That's Souris's problem to deal with."

"And where is Souris?"

"I don't know. Down by the lake, probably-"

"And which way is the lake?!"

Sam pointed in a vague direction, laughing. "You're not really going to try to find her, are you? Ash…?"

But she'd already taken off at a run. It would be a miracle if she found Anne before anyone else did, but she had to at least try.

❦

Anne was well into the city when Souris's servant stopped chasing her. He probably realised 'twas a fool's errand; he might have had longer legs but he was also half-crippled from that well-placed knee.

Anne paused to catch her breath, and waylaid a passer-by. "Where might I find the Queen's namesake?" she asked. Even though they'd argued, Ash would be a better choice than George. She seemed less bespelled, and hadn't mentioned hearing voices in her head.

Poor George.

The man shrugged, then pointed vaguely in the direction she was already headed. "That's the palace, that big red building. Try there."

Anne ran. She had to get to Ash as soon as possible, before the witch queen put even more spells on her mind. 'Twas just like that poor girl back on the shore, the one who sat like a numpty all alone because she thought she was some sort of living dead stuck in a cage. 'Twas as false as those serpents had been, and Anne now strongly suspected that everything was. Power, yes, but the power to *look* powerful rather than actually be so.

The palace was so close now, and Anne moved back into an awkward trot. It didn't look much like a palace to her, unless palaces were intended to be in that horrid shade of red, with the trimmings overly gilded. Rather, it made Anne think of some form of Hades-

229

"Got you!" The rough hand closing around her arm came as a complete surprise, and clearly angry, the man made no effort to be gentle. "That'll teach you to run from your Noble!"

Anne tried to kick him again, but he was dragging her along and she could barely keep her footing. Saint's bones, why did she have to be so *weak*? And why did they all have to be so enormous, she thought helplessly? 'Twas hardly fair!

She struggled furiously, screaming like a madwoman the whole time, and then he slapped her hard around the side of the head. Her head rang and she was briefly stunned, and bright lights flashed in front of her eyes. 'Twas like when she stared at the sun for too long as a child, and took days for the headaches to stop.

Someone was screaming, and it wasn't her. As Anne's vision cleared she realised the screams came from the man who'd grabbed her. He'd let go and was slapping at bright flames that consumed his head and shoulders.

'Twas like the Biblical burning bush, because the flames burned but he didn't blacken, not one jot – and the one who'd set him on fire stood not ten feet away wearing the Queen's scarlet, with an expression of horror on her face and hands bright with flaming illusion.

"Ash, you saved me!" Anne exclaimed happily. "Now let's flee this cursed place before anything else goes wrong!"

But Ash was moving towards her – then past her towards the man now rolling madly on the hard ground – with that same expression of horror. "Deias, he's burning alive!" She touched his shoulder and the fire faded. He still lay there whimpering pathetically, and Anne sighed.

"Ash, he's quite well. You didn't *truly* burn him! Now come!" She grabbed Ash's arm, and when the woman didn't budge, tugged again frantically. "Make haste!"

Ash finally turned and they moved away together in what was hopefully the direction of the moving rooms to the forest.

"How can you be so cold?" Ash whispered as they walked. "He was in such pain…"

"No, he was not."

"Yes, he was! He might have struck you, but now he'll be maimed for life-"

"Will not!"

They were still arguing even as they found the little moving rooms and made their way up to Islo's home, then went straight out the front door without even consulting the owners. 'Twas very rude, mayhap, but necessary. In spite of the argument, they'd moved in unison towards the forest, both seeming to know 'twas the safest and most secluded place for them to be.

"I told you, 'tis nothing but the lowest sorcery!" Anne insisted once more, not that Ash seemed to be listening. "Your fiery hands, Souris's power – 'twas not real. Why can you not accept that?"

"If it wasn't real, then why was he screaming?"

"Because he *thought* 'twas real," Anne explained patiently. "And he was most upset about it, I'd vow. But if you'd looked at him for a moment longer, you'd have seen he had no burn marks. Even his garb was unharmed."

"Then that's just as cruel," Ash began, then stopped. "Well, I suppose it's not as cruel. And you say you saw no marks on him?"

"Yes," Anne said for the tenth time. Mayhap now they were safe in the forest, Ash could actually listen. "No marks. Nothing. Just like the tricks Souris played."

Ash lifted up her hand and a small white flame appeared, dancing harmlessly over her skin. She turned and threw it towards a nearby tree, where it raced up the trunk and quickly engulfed the branches. "Oh, excrement," she said (only she didn't say *excrement*, but a rude word rhyming with 'knit'). "I've started a forest fire." She rushed up to the tree and patted at the flame, and it died out almost immediately, leaving behind a faintly blackened trunk. "See, it *is* real!"

But that wouldn't fit with what Anne had seen. "Try again," she suggested. "Take away the blackness. I vow you're the one putting it there."

"That's just silly," Ash shot back, but then the burnt area vanished, and she frowned. "Oh. You were right."

"Naturally. You should listen to me more."

Ash grunted most unbecomingly, but Anne took it as agreement. "I thought you were looking for Dr Walker, then Sam told me-"

"Sam?"

"My…the Queen's consort's namesake." Ash didn't seem too pleased about that. "But as I was saying, Sam told me you'd gone missing and were being hunted by Souris. Or something like that. How did you end up with her?"

"Well…"

And Anne told her everything, from being snatched by Souris's servants, to the serpents, to the girl with the cage in her mind. Ash listened and reacted as expected, but there was something not quite right about her. She seemed extremely weary, as though she'd been worn down by whatever had happened to her.

"So that's why you say it's all illusion," Ash said slowly once Anne had finished. "And it makes sense. The Queen told me…" She paused and for a moment Anne thought she would cry, but then she finished quickly, "that she did use mind control. She as good as admitted it, said it kept everyone happy. Except for a few unlucky ones, it seems."

"Of course she does!"

"Oh, and I found Dr Walker." And now Ash seemed to become even more flat. "Whether illusion's used or not, there's real power there, and people are messed up. Anne, he said…" She paused, trying again. "He gave me… He said the time machine's not working."

Time machine. Anne ticked through the bizarre things she'd heard in the last day or so until the term's meaning came to mind, and then hit the roof. "What?! Why?! That cannot be true! He swore-"

"It's the Nobles," Ash interrupted tiredly. "It seems like their presence is stopping the time machine working properly. Remember, there were supposed to be twelve of us. There are only three. It was sheer bad luck we even got here at all."

"Then we must get rid of the Nobles!" If they could find a very large sword, mayhap, or a gallon of some clever kind of poison...?

"That's what Dr Walker said." And then Ash laughed. "He thinks that because we didn't drink the water – that's what causes the mind control, by the way – that we can defeat the Queen. Or me, rather, because I'm the namesake, and you were supposed to be off being controlled by Souris."

"She's a truckle-headed mouse-wit," Anne said with satisfaction. "And I *knew* that water couldn't be good for anyone. I'll be sure to tell everyone never to drink it again."

"You can't do that!"

"Why ever not?"

❧

"Because," Ash began, then stopped. She was *going* to say 'because then the Nobles will know we're not controlled', but the Queen had already known. She'd known about the conversation with Dr Walker, and about the gifts he'd given Ash, and which she'd drunk. What an idiot. "I'm lucky my stomach hasn't been eaten through," she muttered.

"I beg your pardon?"

"Because we need to keep under the radar," she said instead, then corrected when Anne clearly didn't understand: "Avoid their notice. Besides, it wouldn't work. Everyone's already controlled anyway."

"You and I are not," Anne pointed out. "And Dr Walker."

Kind of. "And Islo, but you mustn't tell anyone that."

"I wouldn't tell." But Anne looked quite pleased about that last piece of information. "What did Dr Walker give you? An invisibility cloak? Hundred-league boots?"

"Nothing as fun as those." Ash fished out the bottles from her pocket, but saw that she'd lost the far-sight one. There was only the short, round flight vial sitting on its own in that small cloth bag, along with those assorted bits of junk jewellery. "Supposedly this'll make me fly like a bird."

"Truly?" There was a moment where Ash waited for Anne to excitedly ask for some herself – but then the girl shook her head in scorn. "Poor man, he must truly have injured his mind. Of course no human can fly. We don't have wings."

"Or rocket packs." Ash ignored Anne's quizzical expression, studying the small bottle still mostly full. "Maybe it's meant to be anti-gravity?"

Anne stared at her blankly (the word 'gravity' probably being unfamiliar to her) then asked, "Did you drink any?"

Ash admitted that she already had, with no signs of flight to be seen, and Anne nodded decisively. "Ah, well. 'Twas a fanciful thought, but at least no harm was done. You've not been poisoned. Was that all he gave you?"

"All that's worth mentioning."

"Hm. Well, we shall simply have to move forward with what we do have."

"And what's that?" Ash watched her curiously, for once not minding Anne's decisive nature as today she felt very *indecisive*.

"Our own natural wit and wisdom. And you are currently the namesake, which while I do not know the purpose of such a thing to that witch-queen, I trow will be most useful in our quest to return home. Has Mr Seymour seemed at all less enamoured of this place?"

Ash shook her head. "I haven't seen him since yesterday, same as you."

"Hmm." Anne pondered that, then brightened. "Islo! You said his mind was not controlled, so we shall see Islo."

So Anne hadn't been mortally offended by his approach yesterday after all. Finally gathering her thoughts, Ash replied, "Yes, I think that's a good idea. But Anne-"

"Yes?" And it was a sign of how far they'd come along that the girl didn't even add, 'lady'.

"You're currently a fugitive. I think I should go back to see Islo, get some food for you, and find out what our next step is."

"And what, perchance, should I be doing during this time? Hiding in that dreadful little underground room?"

Ash hadn't even thought of that, but... "Now you mention it..."

Anne wasn't stupid. She accepted that she was in danger, and even perhaps that she should stay hidden in the forest, but insisted on coming back to Islo's, just for a meal. Ash thought perhaps she still had an interest in that direction, although it was none of Ash's business.

As for what was her business, she couldn't keep her mind off what the Queen had said. It was crazy, the idea that they were the same person at different stages of their life's thread, overlapping by some bizarre means.

Crazy, yes, but Ash had seen so many supposedly impossible things since arriving here, and had no idea what to think. The Queen could have lied, of course. But why?

They'd settled into quiet conversation as they walked back to Upper Iversley, and Ash had told Anne a little bit of what had happened this morning.

"So you went back to see that witch again," Anne said curiously, "and she looked different. Was she still very beautiful?"

Except when she'd looked like Ash, yes. "I suppose so."

"Hmm. I suppose that with power such as hers, she might look however she chooses. Why be plain when one can be fair?"

And point proven. Without meaning to, Anne had repeated that main point Ash held onto as evidence *against* the Queen's words. The Queen could look like whoever she wanted to, so merely looking like Ash was no proof of anything.

"Although I must admit she reminded me of someone, even through that golden glow. Mayhap all golden-haired women look the same, in some way. Just as all men with moustaches seem to blur together in my mind-"

"Do you think it was the hair?" Ash blurted out hopefully.

"The hair...?"

"The hair. That made the Queen seem familiar."

Anne paused, then shrugged in a very teenage way. She might be five hundred years behind Ash, but she was still sixteen. "No, not truly. I've never seen anyone with hair that colour, although you say, that was not her true colouring. Mayhap something about her manner, or the bones of her face?" She shrugged again. "Although it did seem as though I had met her before. Seems that in this small area there are many relatives of George's. Who's to say she's not one of them?"

"But she said she was a time-traveller," Ash persisted. "She said she was...just like us."

"Except that we hold no power and do not control an entire city," Anne pointed out reasonably. "Not so very much in common. But mayhap you have the right of it, Ash. I may have met her earlier, in my own time."

That wasn't at all what Ash had said, nor what she'd wanted to hear, but by then they'd reached the small village, and the time for talking was over.

They made it back to Islo's house without incident and without seeing any Nobles. On the surface that was good, but Ash couldn't help wondering where they all were. It wasn't that easy to hide twenty or thirty giants, even in a city the size of Lower Iversley, and even if they could change size they were still distinctive enough on their own compared to the locals.

But it was probably better not to dwell on that. Instead Ash focussed on what Islo was saying as they stood in one of the empty side rooms, his parents still away.

"You've taken enough risks bringing her back here," he said quietly. "I won't tell, but anyone can just look at her and know immediately who she is. The colour of her hair and her dress-"

"Good point." Ash squinted down at the offending items and wiggled her fingers, imagining that Anne's hair and dress were coloured very plainly. There was a moment of confusion, then Anne stood there with hair as dark as Ash's, and a plain white outfit. She looked like a nineties gospel singer.

"What did you do?" Anne asked, nose screwed up in confusion as she studied her new clothing.

"Hid you," Ash replied, exhilarated. She was good for something more than coloured lights! And burning people… "Even if it's only illusion, it'll work on anyone who's been…*drinking*."

"As long as the hair change isn't permanent," the younger girl announced. "I shan't be able to return home like this."

"It's just hair colour. They'll still recognise you, surely," Ash pointed out.

"Ashlea. Women of nobility and character do not colour their hair…unless it looks most natural. Which this does not." Anne twisted, looking at the underside of her wrist in surprise. "Oh, and you've given me one of those odd markings like the one you have. Is that truly necessary?"

The tattoo looked like a tiny violet, and it curled out to create a second bloom even as they watched. Ash's was red and resembled an orchid, and was significantly larger. She hadn't even been *thinking* of adding a tattoo, though… "Ah…"

"Illusion will fade," Islo cut in smoothly. "Although I'm not sure if this use of the Queen's power is wise. It'll make it easier for her to find you."

"She already knows where I am anyway," Ash said flatly. "She knows where everyone is."

"She can't be all-knowing and all-seeing. Or why have I been left alone?"

"Who knows," Anne interrupted, having lost interest in the illusion she wore. "'Tis certain she carries more power than Souris, whose servants couldn't even catch *me*. Now, someone mentioned breakfast?"

It was closer to lunch, really, but Ash didn't quibble over details. There were a few minutes spent directing Anne how to use the 'ready cook' – which to Ash looked like a cross between a microwave and one of those automatic coffee machines, and which produced food or drink with the right combination of letters. And if the ingredients were there, of course.

Surprisingly Anne loved it, not even mentioning the possibility of witchcraft, and Ash even found herself distracted. It was lucky she didn't have one of these at home, because if she had access to good food at the touch of a button then she'd get *so* fat…

Then she remembered why she was here, and pulled Islo aside for a quiet chat.

"So what you're saying is that you can't go home until the Queen stops influencing Dr Walker, so that the machine will work," he summarised. "And you want to free him, or else get rid of her entirely."

"Um. Yes."

There was a pregnant pause. "And you came to me," Islo elaborated, sounding rather like Ash had when approached by Dr Walker. "Because you want to get rid of the Queen. Don't you know that I'm barely keeping myself out of her control?"

"I'm sorry, I didn't know who else to go to," she said desperately. "You must know something. Anything. A weak spot, even. Anne thinks it's all fake anyway-"

"Just because it doesn't last doesn't make it weak, Queen's namesake. I see that clearly enough. And what can we do against her when the whole city is controlled?"

"Don't call me that. And I don't know. You're the one who

lives here. Don't you know someone who might know something helpful? Anything?"

Islo folded his arms, looking thoughtfully out the window. There was nothing much to see, Ash thought; just grass and forest in the distance. But then he said, "There's one thing, but it's probably nothing."

"Anything. Anything you've got."

"Well, a few weeks ago I ran into an old neighbour, Solomon. He lives down the other end of Upper Iversley. And he doesn't…drink. Not now, anyway, even though he's supposedly servant to…Angus? Can't remember the name, starts with an A or E or might have a G in it... But back then I was just coming out of the initial stupor, and he was acting like a mad thing. He was rushing around all the houses, looking in the bushes and saying, 'she's lost it, it's gone' and things like that."

"Lost what?" Ash asked in fascination.

Islo shrugged. "I don't know, and I didn't think anything of it. A lot of people were acting strangely. It seems that if you drink the water but your Noble doesn't ask anything of you, you go a little crazy. But then last night I heard my parents talking. They were saying that whoever found 'it' would get a wonderful reward, and would be like the Queen. They seemed really excited about it, but once I asked them, they acted like they had no idea what I was talking about."

Oh. "Maybe they forgot."

"No, they were definitely hiding something from me," he said grimly. "So…something's missing, possibly an object of power, and whoever finds it will get a wonderful reward. It's not much, but…"

"It's something," Ash finished, noting the flat disappointment in Islo's face when he'd admitted his parents had lied to him. She considered asking him why he thought the 'thing' was an object of power, but came to her own conclusion. What else could the Queen possibly value except more power and ways to get it? "So you think this Solomon will know more?"

"Probably not, but it can't hurt to try."

The Queen squinted at her reflection in a small hand mirror. Her real reflection, flaws and all. While it was nice to be perfectly beautiful all the time, she had to see her real self, if only to see how much damage had been done by the loss of the Stone.

Damn it, another grey hair. There were more and more of those every day. If they didn't get hold of the Eternity Stone soon… well, she wouldn't think about that. They *would* get it.

She pulled the hair out and glared at it balefully. It was just one more physical sign of how she was losing control of her dominion, and she hated it with a passion.

But only for so long would she let things go. They'd looked so carefully, chosen this time period and place from among many other possibilities, and for a while it looked like everything was falling into place.

But then the Eternity Stone had disappeared – no coincidence, she knew. *He* had done it. He was following her, stalking her as he always had. She wouldn't let him ruin her plans this time. This time, she would win.

She'd been listening with half an ear to all the information that hummed around her; the voices that carried towards her on currents of power. Perhaps she could have saved power by not using those currents, but they were too valuable to her. Like now…

So *that* was who that last person was. And who had she assigned to be his Noble?

Just then her servant came in with a platter for the mid-morning meal, and she narrowed her eyes at him. "Aegus!"

He jolted visibly and the platter wobbled dangerously, but was caught again. The fact it had wobbled at all showed his own mental state, in her opinion. Back in the fourth century AD he'd been the best goblet-bearer she'd ever met, and since then he'd remained so. Most of the time. His other duties as a Noble, however…

"Yes, my Queen?"

She allowed him to set the platter down in front of her, ignoring the range of delicacies cooked up by some desperate-to-please local. "I know who the last person is," she told him ominously. "He's one of yours. Have you not been following up with your servants?"

"Ahh…"

"Of course you haven't," she finished for him. "And it's a mistake you won't make twice. Now, I've already sent someone to fetch them, but- what? Why are you staring at me like that?"

Aegus glanced away quickly and the Queen caught another glimpse of herself in the hand mirror. Her true self, lines and jowls and all. Chaos. She looked almost…*middle-aged*. She quickly snapped a new image over top – her favourite – and then glared at her servant, putting power into the glare until she saw him begin to turn a little red from lack of oxygen.

Once she was sure he'd understood the severity of the situation (i.e. that he must not *ever* mention her state to anyone whatsoever) she eased off and smiled, just a little. "Now, do you have any good news for me? Anything at all?"

Aegus swallowed almost imperceptibly, then brightened. "Janeus, my Queen. The twins think that they might have found him in Eurasia, in the seventh century AD."

That was good news. Very, very good, because when she'd sent him away that last time she hadn't thought he'd *stay* away so long. She hadn't thought she'd have to set his own children to finding him either, but then that was life. It didn't always go how you'd think, case in point her arrival in Iversley. Except… "We still need the Stone to bring him here." She pondered that for a while, tapping her fingers on the armrest. And to find the Stone, they needed enough power for a finding spell.

The Queen pondered her options once more and settled for the easiest one. She had in her possession an object of power, one she'd found back in the distant past. It could collect power from one soul, or from many, but she'd never used it, unsure of what it might do to her as well as for her. The traveller had only been namesake for a day and so using the object would only provide a short burst of power, but it might be enough to find the Stone without having to do something more *monstrous*.

"Right," she said aloud, mostly to herself. She didn't need Aegus's help, but she'd never lost the habit of thinking aloud. "I'll send out for a collection, then. Ensure that they're brought directly to me."

"Yes, my Queen."

Because what else could he say? *Everyone* said yes to the Queen, and that was how it should be.

FAR-SIGHT

Ash headed down the main street of Upper Iversley, trying to look nonchalant. It was hard though, as she felt as if her intentions must be written all over her face. She had never been great at acting. The few people she passed didn't seem to notice, instead all nodding respectfully when they saw her clothing.

Oh, that was right. Nobody actually *knew* she was trying to take out the Queen...emphasis on *trying*. Except the woman herself, unfortunately.

Ash reached the address Islo had given her. It was a large, rather squat grey house in the same style as all the others, but unlike them it managed to look decidedly unwelcoming.

She stopped at the main door and stared at it a moment. *Don't bother knocking*, Islo had said. *He never answers, so just go right in.* So overcoming a lifetime of training, she opened the door and called, "Hello? Solomon?"

There was no answer. After another moment of indecision Ash just went inside, closing the door after her. It was a similar setup to Islo's place, with a large lobby with stairs leading up to a second level balcony, and multiple doors presumably leading through to other rooms.

She called again. "Hello?"

A man leaned down over the upstairs balcony. He was big and dark-skinned, with short grey hair and sharp green eyes that stood out even from this distance. "Up here! Quickly!"

Did he mean *her*?

"Yes, you in the red," he snapped, rolling his eyes. "Who else would I be talking to?"

It would have been funny if he hadn't looked so worried, and that worry spread over to Ash. She quickly stepped inside, and just like at Islo's, the door slid silently shut behind her. "Are you Solomon-"

"Questions later, namesake. Come up here before you catch your death of cold."

It was a very Anglish, old-fashioned thing to say, and rather than make Ash hurry, it made her slow down. "Cold…?" It wasn't even slightly cold, instead edging on too warm for these long sleeves, had they not been so thin.

"For the love of poached eggs, just get up here, will you?"

She moved, climbing the narrow staircase to the upper level and then following the quickly moving Solomon down a hall and through a door, then through a second door into a small inner room. It reminded her of an old darkroom for developing photos, and appeared to be empty of anything except a closet and a couple of old chairs.

He stood behind one of the chairs, gesturing for her to take the other, and after only a brief pause she did so. He sat opposite, and they stared at each other suspiciously for a few moments.

Ash finally broke the silence. "You do know who I am, right?"

"Hmm. Teron's lad sent you."

Solomon had an interesting face, she decided. It was more Asien than Afrecan, and those eyes made her think of a cat she'd once owned. Well, the neighbour had owned it, but Ash had fed it sometimes, so it had felt like hers until it had been hit by a truck.

"Um…yes, he did. Because I don't *drink*."

The man stared at her for a few long moments. "Is that meant to be code for something? Or you just won't touch alcohol?"

"Water," Ash got out. "I don't drink *water*."

"Oh. You might have said that in the first place. And it's all very well to say it, isn't it? But it simply shows that you've been schooled in the right words."

She tried to make sense of that. "So you want me to prove that I'm not being mind-controlled?"

"You don't think you're being controlled, but the Queen, she manoeuvres. She manipulates. She's bloody brilliant; shame she's got the ethics of a crocodile. Now, what was it that you wanted to talk to me about?"

He'd changed subject so quickly that Ash scrambled to keep up. "You think that I'm being controlled, but you still want to talk?" Here in this cupboard-like room?

Solomon shrugged, almost smiling for a moment. "There's always someone watching. Here at least I know that the outside cams can't get any pictures, and that there aren't any audio devices. Anything more than that I can't help with. So what do you want, girl in red?"

"It's Ash. And Islo said that you might know about something that the Queen wants. Something that she's been looking for ever since she arrived here."

"You're talking about the Eternity Stone, of course." His voice dropped even lower to just above a whisper.

She was? "I am?"

"It's the only thing she's been looking for that I've heard of. And I only heard it because the giant she assigned me to didn't mind his tongue. Besides, I'm at the palace two days a week working in the kitchens, would you believe. Did you know that if the power isn't used, you can sometimes hear their thoughts?"

Now that was a horrifying thought, made worse when Ash remembered that quiet little voice that had warned her against drinking the water. Who, who was it? Not the Queen or her friends, because surely they would want her drinking it. Would want her easily controlled.

"I did not know that," she replied carefully. "But this...immortality stone-"

"Eternity Stone," he corrected in a whisper. "And don't go shouting about it. The Queen's rabid about it. Absolutely rabid. Whatever it is, it's extremely valuable."

"So you *don't* know what it is," she said in disappointed realisation.

Solomon sniffed. "I know it's small enough for a person to carry easily, and that the Queen is sunk without it. Find it, and you'll be able to use it against her."

"Use the Eternity Stone how-"

"Don't speak so loudly! Anyone could be listening!"

Ash looked sceptically around the tiny room within a room. Who could possibly hear? Well, there were such things as bugs (electronic, not winged) even at home. Better safe than sorry. "How do I use the...thing?"

"I don't know. You could start by finding it."

"How can I find it when I don't know what it looks like?!" She was just about bursting in frustration. "What colour is it? Is it an actual rock, a jewel?"

"Power," he replied decisively. "You'll feel the power, I reckon. It comes off her like buzz from a broken comm unit, if you know what to look for. And you do, don't you, namesake? You feel the power when it's there."

Ash shrugged. "Doesn't everyone?"

"Some do more than others." He studied her face through those bright green eyes. "I don't know why the Queen's letting you run around in that namesake red when you're clearly not under her control. But then she didn't notice me, either. The Nobles aren't all-powerful. Not quite, or not yet. But we can use your position, girl."

It was the same thing Dr Walker had said, and Ash hadn't liked it any better then. It was too much pressure.

"I don't know the city," she argued. "I don't know *anything*. I don't mind helping – if I even can – but don't put this all on me!"

Solomon shot right back, "We don't have the opportunities

you do. You're the Queen's namesake. You've even got a bleed'n flowered dress like she does! For now, you're top human in Lower and Upper Iversley. It might not last, but while it does you need to *use* it. Anyway, I'm pretty certain I'm being watched. It's probably only a matter of time until I'm caught out doing the wrong thing, saying the wrong thing."

Understandably he looked depressed at this thought. Ash sympathised; she guessed it was also only a matter of time until the Queen got sick of Ash's messing about and brought her in. If this massive man was afraid... well, what could *she* ever hope to achieve? Maybe she should just leave, take Anne and get as far away as she could.

"My dress isn't flowered. And it's not really a dress, either, it's a long shirt."

"That was all you took out of what I just told you?" he asked disbelievingly. "Besides, haven't you looked at yourself lately?"

Ash opened her mouth to reply, but suddenly, like a movie playing in ultra-fast-forward, six men in the Queen's red burst in through the door. *Ash and Solomon fought to escape but were easily subdued. The soldiers took them to the Queen, who declared a death sentence over Solomon, and the soldiers took him away... And for collaborating, Ash was painfully stripped of her tattoo (!) and status and then thrown into prison indefinitely, into a tiny little box almost too small to stand in. And the Queen laughed, and said, "It doesn't matter what you do, namesake, it'll all lead to the same place..."*

Then the images all played backwards faster than Ash's eyes could follow, and she was still sitting in an old chair in a small dark room opposite Solomon Kingsbury, who was still waiting for her response to whatever they'd been talking about. The whole thing – whatever it was – had happened instantaneously.

Ash's eye twitched, and she gasped.

"What? What is it?"

She shook her head incredulously, a little embarrassed at her reaction. "I think I had one of those crazy moments you were talking about. Where someone else's thoughts run through your head…or more like a waking dream."

She expected him to dismiss her, but instead he stared at her intently. "You mean a vision?"

Ash laughed awkwardly. "No one has *visions*." No one who wasn't smoking something illegal, anyway.

"No one should be able to turn themselves into a giant and control the minds of an entire city, either. But if you have enough power you can do anything, and I felt power working just then. Felt it in the air. What did you see, girl in red?"

"Just a strange little series of events." But Solomon was still staring at her like she had something important to say, so she continued, "Like I said, sounds crazy, but I just saw the Queen's soldiers come to take us away, and you'll be killed and I'll be imprisoned." She felt her face heat and couldn't look to see his reaction. She added, "I'm not usually this weird. Maybe I ate something that was off."

He moved to the edge of his chair, his hands white-knuckled on the armrests. "*When?*"

Wow, he was taking this seriously. "Well, we were in this room-"

"We've got to go." Shaking his head frantically, Solomon leaped off his chair and reached into the closet door.

"What?" Ash heard a *click,* and craned her head to see what he was doing. The back of the closet was opened to reveal a dimly lit passage.

"In here. NOW!" He hissed the last word when she didn't move immediately.

She couldn't see why they had to hurry, as she was pretty sure her 'vision' had been just a result of stress or her new diet, but she obeyed anyway and climbed in through the small space. On the other side, the passage was made of the same wood as the house, and lit by a strip of glowing paint along the ceiling.

He climbed after her, and had just locked the inner door from the inside when there was a BANG! It sounded like the dark room had been invaded, and she could hear men shouting something like, "Where did they go?!"

Ash gaped at Solomon. His eyes were so wide they almost bugged out, and he quickly moved in front of her. "Follow me!"

They raced along the passage as silently as possible, which was maybe why Ash heard the exact moment their escape route was found.

"In here!" a voice shouted, and like a dose of nitrous oxide to a car, they put on a jolt of speed.

Solomon was well in the lead, and she followed him down staircases and around corners. The sounds of pursuit became fainter but he urged her on. "Keep going! They'll be right behind us."

Fear lent Ash wings, and she pushed herself to keep up with Solomon's long-legged run through the increasingly elaborate tunnels, leading ever downwards. The walls became brick, then rock, all lit by the fluorescent paint on the ceiling. Although she couldn't see where she was going, she had the sense of a huge weight over their heads. They must be deep in the ground now.

After about half an hour Solomon finally stopped.

"Have we lost them?" she gasped, red-faced and sweating from the unusual exercise.

He paused, head cocked to listen. "Yeah, we have."

Oh, thank *Deias*. She wasn't used to long-distance running.

"We should be safe here," he said. "It's practically a labyrinth, they won't find us this far in."

"Where exactly are we?"

"Between Upper and Lower Iversley. In the rock beside the cavern. Forced to run like rats, by that vicious, inhuman Queen." He spat dramatically on the ground.

Ash took a step back. Spitting was gross, even when their lives were threatened. "What happened up there? How did you know that...that thing I saw was real?" she asked tentatively.

"Thing?"

"The vision."

Solomon raised a grey eyebrow. "Are you serious?"

"Well...yeah. I could have just been having a hallucination or something, but you listened right away."

He laughed abruptly. "I don't know where you're from, but here, we take warnings like that seriously. With the sort of power that's flying around, prophecy or premonition or whatever you want to call it, is no surprise."

"So you think it's actually alter-power?" Ash asked in surprise. She had wondered if it was just an advanced technology that could affect minds. Very, very, very advanced. After all, didn't primitive tribes always think explorers' gadgets were magical? Or that might have just been on TV.

He shrugged. "Alter-power, alien technology, whatever. It is what it is, and you'd be a fool to ignore it."

He was saying what she'd thought but hadn't wanted to voice even to herself. Even with her father's obsession with alter-power, it was hard for her to accept the supernatural as a real part of life. But here, she *would* be a fool to deny it.

Whatever had happened, it had been real. As real as the giants, as real as the time travel.

OMD. I just predicted the future.

"They would have killed you," Ash said aloud. "That's what the...picture showed." Even now she couldn't call it a vision. Visions were for gypsies and priestesses and crazy religious people. Not for sensible, normal Ash O'Reilly.

Solomon nodded. "Yeah. Would you believe I knew one of them? I recognised his voice, and he'd been a friend. But not anymore – he'll do anything for *her*."

Ash stared at him in pity. A friend trying to lead him to his death? That was just *awful*.

"Well, they won't get a chance to now," he continued. "I'm out of here. I'll take these tunnels as far as they go from the city.

There's nothing here for me anymore."

"But what about the Resistance?" Ash asked in dismay. "Taking down the Queen?"

He laughed again, scornfully this time. It wasn't like he was laughing at her though, more like at himself and the whole sad situation. "There is no 'Resistance'. Islo was foolish to give you that idea. There are only six or seven people trying desperately to stay sane in the middle of this madness. It's a losing battle."

Ash's hope plummeted. "Then why did you offer to help me, if you thought it was useless?"

"Who knew? Maybe there'd be a miracle and you'd get some-where." More contritely, Solomon added, "*I* can't do anything except die, probably painfully. But you – you can predict the future now, flower-girl. That's got to be good for something. You could make a real difference here."

"But I'll be alone!" she cried. "I don't even know how to get out of here!"

He sighed. "Just go left, down the first staircase, then right, down two staircases. You should come out in the upper levels of the lower city."

So what... she'd go by herself, find the immor- *Eternity Stone,* whatever it was, and defeat the Queen?

Well, she was sure she could manage the bit about going by herself. Thanks to Mr Kingsbury, it was guaranteed. As for the rest of it, Ash's best hope was probably to perhaps distract the woman enough that Dr Walker could fix the time machine, and Ash and Anne could go home...and maybe George too, if he changed his mind about staying here.

Or maybe if Ash couldn't distract the Queen, she'd just beg for mercy, because that little prophecy had implied that the Queen wasn't so happy with her right now. She didn't know what she'd done wrong, but to end up in prison it must've been *something.*

"Fine. Thanks," Ash said grumpily, but she was talking to empty air. Solomon had already gone.

And that was when she looked down at her red namesake suit and saw the new design on the hem of her long shirt. It was a delicate little violet, just about the same size as that tattoo she'd accidentally left on Anne's wrist when she'd tried to disguise her.

Ash stared for a couple of seconds, completely still, then took in a great, gasping breath.

Namesakes. The Queen's dress, that lovely, elaborate dress that seemed to change along with her illusions, always had ornate flowered patterns on it. *One for each of my namesakes*, she'd said. The same as the tattoo on Ash's arm.

It doesn't matter what you do, the Queen had taunted. *It'll all lead to the same place…*

Ash sat down with a thump on the rocky ground and tried not to throw up.

After a while Ash managed to get up. It was easier if she just refused to think about that new flower design on her clothing, or even the tattoo on her own wrist that had now grown past her elbow.

She managed to follow Solomon's directions and found herself looking out over the city. The doorway she had come out of was on a rooftop, partially built into the rock of the vast cavern. To her right was a metal staircase leading several storeys down to the street below, and she could see all the way to the underground lake that was the city's contaminated water source.

She was at least as high as those skimmer tracks that wound around the city.

This must be a tall building by this city's standards. Oddly, in spite of the room available down here in this cavern, few buildings were more than three storeys high. The couple Ash *could* see were a thin tower in the distance, and closer by, a five-storey red building, all strange curves and thin windows.

Actually, the last one looked familiar. With a start, she realised that it was the place where she'd twice met the Queen –

the 'palace'. It was only a few blocks away, and that was far too close.

Well, she wasn't going to stay up on this roof. In the bright red she was wearing, she'd stick out like a fly in yogurt. And she couldn't go back into the tunnels either; they were such a maze that she'd get lost for sure and probably die of dehydration. Or worse, come out in some random person's bathroom or bedroom.

So it was down the stairs for her – all eight narrow, nausea-inducing flights. Had she mentioned that she didn't like heights?

It was a slow descent, and Ash distracted herself by debating which way she'd head when she reached the street. Left would take her in the direction of the Queen's palace, which had the considerable deterrent of having the Queen in it. Forget going left then.

The other way was towards Islo's…maybe. If Ash went there, she could tell him and Anne about what happened with Solomon, what he'd told her about the Eternity Stone and the 'knowing the future' thing.

Maybe that was from one of the vials she'd drank last night, the one she'd drunk dry, perhaps? It had had an odd name. Far-scape?

Far-*sight*, that was it, and it had come straight from the slightly crazy Dr Walker.

Ash didn't think it was the Queen's power. For all Ash had been promised as a namesake, she hadn't been nearly as powerful as the other namesakes. And the flash-forward had felt different to how the Queen's power had felt, if that made sense.

It was hard to explain, not a physical feeling, but like it was from a different power source, a gentler one. No flashing lights and illusion; just pictures in her head like a film played too fast.

Then out of the blue it was happening again. In fast-forward, *Hadur grabbed her at the door to Islo's house. He took her straight to the Queen, who said that for plotting against her Ash would be stripped of her tattoo and status and imprisoned indefinitely. The tattoo was torn from her flesh (ouch, again) and then she was alone in a tiny boxlike cell in the basement of the palace, almost too small to stand up in. "It doesn't matter what you do," the Queen said with a sneer, "because you can't avoid your fate…"-*

In the blink of an eye Ash was back at the base of the staircase, her foot raised to walk towards Islo's house. She let out a deep breath, tried not to panic, and then turned in the opposite direction. Not Islo's house, then.

But in that moment she understood that it wasn't *physical* far-sight; it was the ability to see the far-reaching consequences of her actions. Only the future didn't look too good at the moment.

So much for wondering if the Queen really knew or cared what Ash was up to – she clearly did, and didn't like it. And according to far-sight the scary Hadur had to be close, and if he caught her, there'd be same result – tearing off the tattoo like a wax strip, then the same imprisonment in that strange little cell like a golden box.

It reminded her of a video she'd seen online once, of a cat that pushed its friend into a cardboard box and then sat on the closed lid, seeming to forget what was underneath it. That had been funny, but the image of the tiny cell wasn't. Not at all.

Better to go left then, Ash decided. She'd turn at the next side street, avoiding the palace. Then *twenty steps to the left, and another giant grabbed her, a blond one this time with a moustache as big as her leg, and just as clearly 'the muscle' as Hadur had been. He took her to the Queen who said, "Thank you, Kari," and then her tattoo was taken, and she was imprisoned…*

Back at the foot of the stairs, Ash was shaking in fright. Doom to the left, doom to the right! And that other giant had to be less than a minute away.

She turned and bolted back up the stairs the way she'd come, just reaching the roof as a huge blond figure came into view. It was Kari, the second giant from the vision. For a moment she froze with fear – but when he saw her, he lunged at her with a roar.

She dashed back to the entrance of the tunnel, and in spite of his size he couldn't reach her over the edge of the building. She squealed as there was a near-miss with his giant grabbing hand, and cringed back into the tunnel entrance, and then he started to shrink and disappear from sight.

A moment passed and then Ash heard what could only be him in human size: heavy steps stomping up that same metal staircase towards her.

Run! Automatically she turned to go back into the tunnels, but then the far-sight kicked in again. She saw herself *lost for days then finally stumbling out, desperately thirsty, right onto the Queen's doorstep. Same story as last time.*

Then what should she do? Ash asked herself in despair. Jump off the building?

She'd meant it sarcastically, but in another rapid-fire series of images she saw *herself running across the flat roof, leaping off into thin air, and then arms spread, soaring upwards like a bird.*

"No. No!" She turned once more for the tunnel entrance and that same vision of being lost in the tunnels came to mind, so loud and clear that she couldn't ignore it.

She turned again back out towards the building's roof and back to where the footsteps on the stairs had become loud enough that she knew the giant was only a flight or two away.

Her options ran through her mind like quicksilver. Let him catch her and end up stuck in a little golden box, or run into the tunnels and end up in the box a bit later, or....

But then Ash saw herself *hesitating too long, and Kari changing back to giant-sized once he reached the rooftop. He reached her within a few strides and she dodged his footsteps, skipping around him until he growled in anger and lunged for her. She stepped back – right into thin air. Then she was falling, and she stretched out her arms and screamed; and suddenly the air beneath her was lifting her just like a bird on a strong wind. Up and up and then she was just floating there in the air-*

But even then, Ash couldn't make herself do it. She couldn't run off that ledge, because no matter what the pictures in her head had showed, they were just pictures. They didn't feel real, and she couldn't make herself believe them.

Besides, the Nobles were brilliant at messing with people's minds. If it was wrong then she'd be a human pancake – and maybe that was the plan all along.

But then the vision became real life as a fair head came into sight at the top of the stairs. As predicted, when Kari saw her, he started growing back to giant size again.

Ah, Hades.

He was already running towards her, and he'd reach her within seconds. Too slowly Ash turned, and even though she'd been forewarned, she couldn't stop herself from playing through those same actions.

One, two…four strides and he reached her, ducking down to swipe at her with one of those ridiculously large hands. She dodged him, then dodged again with the agility that had made her so good at fencing in high school.

He almost stepped on her – probably not on purpose – and she grabbed onto the fabric of his trousers, using it to swing herself around and behind him. She didn't know where she was going; just trying to get away-

Ash felt air under one foot. In an instant of clarity, she realized she'd come right to the edge of the roof without meaning to.

And the momentum from her swing meant she couldn't even try to catch herself as…over…she…went.

❧❧❧

It was like trying to catch a scared mouse in his bare hands – one that was too fast to catch and which he wasn't allowed to kill – and by the time Kari realised the little sneaksby had disappeared, she'd already fallen off the roof.

Chaos, he hoped the girl wasn't too important to the Queen, because he was going to be in trouble now.

It was a long fall to the ground, and humans didn't tend to bounce.

THE SECOND BOTTLE

"AAAAAAAAAAAAAAARGH….gh?"

Ash opened one eye just a crack. The pearly gates didn't greet her – and she could swear that there was nothing underneath her – so she cautiously opened both eyes.

Far above was a grey rocky ceiling lit with that usual luminescent glow that faked daylight. It wasn't rapidly receding, so she carefully checked one side, then another. There were buildings, and there was a brick wall, and underneath her was air…

Ash squawked in surprise and flapped her arms (rather like a chicken, she thought in hindsight) and suddenly she was moving upwards. Not like someone was pushing her, but more like she was weightless.

As she rose, she spun gently until she was upright and the edge of the rooftop came into sight. Kari the Viking giant was still standing there, giant moustache and all, and she rose until she was eye-level with him. They gaped at each other for a long, long moment where Ash didn't dare to look down, and then she rose past him too.

It didn't really hit her what was happening until he bellowed up at her; "HEY!" as if she'd stepped on his foot or something. She glanced down and met his eyes again. He looked furious, and so baffled that she just had to laugh. *Me too.*

But then Ash made the mistake of looking down. The ground was excessively far below, and the tiny, doll-like figures of a few humans were staring up at her from the miniature streets.

A surge of fear hit, and she raised her arms in panic as if she could somehow escape from the height. All that did was make her fly faster. She shot upwards like a bird, or a plane, or another unnamed superhero, until she'd almost hit the cavern ceiling.

"Oh my Deias," Ash moaned, and it wasn't entirely fear. It was awe as well, because this couldn't be real. She couldn't be flying, because people couldn't fly.

Just like they couldn't use illusion, or time travel, or see visions, or transform into extra-large versions of themselves…

"Perhaps I am really flying," she murmured. But there was no perhaps about it, and as she realised that, her fear left. In its place there was a sense of peace and awe.

She was flying, against all apparent laws of physics.

Flying.

Ash lowered her arms from where they were pressed against the cavern ceiling, bringing them down by her sides, and she began to slowly float downwards. She raised them again, then once more she was floating upwards.

Arms down… arms up…arms down again, and then just to make it interesting, arms to the right. Predictably she began to move sideways, and then an awkward downwards gesture flipped her into a somersault.

"Oh, my, Deias," she breathed once more. "I really am flying!"

Wheeeeeeeeeeeeeee!

Goodbye, giants! Goodbye, namesakes and drugged water and underground streets!

Ash ducked and dived and spun in spirals like a bird let out of a cage. It was the most amazing, exhilarating and surreal experience she'd ever had. It was as easy as walking – a flap of her arms would take her higher, and pulling them back into her sides would cause her to drop. She just had to angle her body to steer.

Ash flew up until she was just below the high cavern ceiling once more. This close she could see it was artificially smooth, without the hanging stalactites that she'd expect in a natural cave.

Far down beneath her the whole city was laid out in miniature, whole buildings smaller than her handspan, and now with two giants looking up at her, one dark and one fair. They were as small as action figures from up here, and the real humans like insects.

Her fear of heights was nowhere to be found, and she laughed again with the joy of it all.

The relief of her narrow escape caught up with her. "Ha!" she shouted down at Hadur and Kari below. "Hahahahahahaha! You can't catch me!"

She heard a faint "You'll have to come down some time!" and then suddenly a *whomp* of something bright and glowing hit the cavern ceiling right by where she was resting, rather like a sticky meteor.

Oops. She'd forgotten about the other abilities some of them had, and she'd actually written these two off as being all brawn and no brains.

Ash jolted in surprise, then pulled her arms into her sides and dropped like she'd seen birds do at the beach, before stretching out into a sharp curve that took her over the other side of the city, probably as fast as the skimmers could.

So much for that fear of heights she'd always fought. But it wasn't a fear of heights so much as a fear of falling off heights.

No, that wasn't it either. It was a fear of crashing into the ground at high speeds, and ending up ten feet wide and an inch thick, that was the problem.

That had been the real reason she'd gone bungee jumping to celebrate her eighteenth birthday, to try to defeat it. It hadn't worked though; it had almost made the fear worse, besides apparently proving to her parents that she *wasn't* grown up enough to look after herself.

And now the fear was gone! Ash spun a corkscrew just for the fun of it. She felt like Percy Pan and every flying superhero in one, only with a slightly better outfit.

She floated around a little longer, then remembered that she had been given the vial for a reason. Dr Walker had said she had about two days until the ability to fly wore off, and she shouldn't waste those days here above the city.

Ash dropped a little lower to study the buildings beneath her, taking care to avoid the area where she'd last seen the two giants. Because she could only see roofs from up here, and because the city was unfamiliar anyway, she really didn't know what she was looking at.

But a glowing Jollywood-style sign caught her eye. On closer inspection it read; 'OSPITIL', and she stared at it in confusion for several moments before realising what it meant. *Hospital*, and spelling must've changed somewhat since she'd looked at a dictionary. Either that or the 'H' had fallen off.

Something pinged in Ash's memory, and a moment later she remembered Dr Walker's instructions back in the bunker. She was supposed to find him either in the government buildings or in the hospital, and in return he'd send them home. But that was another Dr Walker who'd told her that, and the government buildings were full of Nobles. He hadn't seen *that* coming.

Well, it wasn't like she had anything better to do. Checking for Nobles, Ash gently dropped down onto the ground in front of the main doors, landing just a little shakily. She straightened her hair self-consciously as a few bystanders studied her curiously before turning away. They were obviously used to showy displays of power.

Aside from the curving shape of the architecture, the 'Ospitil' was pretty much like those of her own time. They'd managed to tone down the smell of medicine and cleaner, and the foyer was empty and shining barring one single desk. A woman sat behind it, her neat gold suit clashing nicely with the bright white of her surroundings.

She looked up as Ash approached. "Who do you seek?"

Ash opened her mouth to say 'Dr Walker', but instead found another name coming out. "George Seymour, if you've got him."

"One moment." A single second ticked by, and then; "Last seen room 223. You'll need to take the lift."

'Last seen?' That was a strange response, but she'd correctly asked for George. "Uh, thank you."

Ash turned to move into one of the many lifts, but then the woman called after her. "I'm sorry, but you need to wait here for a moment. There's...a problem with Mr Seymour's room." The woman wasn't a good liar. She'd obviously been listening to something on her comm set, and her suddenly tense expression and posture screamed subterfuge.

Ash surreptitiously checked for a security guard; there wasn't one in sight. "Sure," she replied cheerfully. "Just as soon as I've checked with George."

The receptionist stammered in confusion. "Uh...I think perhaps you should-"

But Ash was already in one of the lifts, and the doors closed before the woman finished speaking. "Room 223!"

She barely felt the lift move, but then the doors reopened and she was in a new area, an open space with doors scattered all around. Each held a small, silver symbol which might've been a number, but was impossible for her to tell.

Luckily, here was someone who could help her. The young man stood further down the corridor with his back to her, wearing a dark grey-red suit she hadn't seen before, and with vaguely familiar fairish hair.

Ash cocked her head to the side. Surely not... "George?"

The man didn't budge, didn't even turn his head. Not George, then, but perhaps he could give some directions.

But when she drew alongside him, she realised she'd been wrong. Well, right and wrong, because it *was* George, but he probably couldn't help her, or anyone. He was staring blankly at a spot on the distant wall, and didn't move except for the occasional foot shuffle.

"Um…George."

No response except for a slow blink. Deias, he was even mouth-breathing. This was a new development, and not a good one.

"George! Hello…" Ash waved a hand in front of his face, then when that didn't work, poked him gently in the chest. "What, are you sleep-walking or something?"

His eyes cleared for a moment. "Have we met?"

Ash's jaw dropped in offense before she realised he was being serious. But even that brief responsiveness vanished, and it was like he couldn't even see her there. He wasn't manic like Islo had warned humans could become if the power they'd been drugged with wasn't directed by their Nobles. He was just…absent.

"Oi!" She grabbed him by the shoulders and gave him a good shake. "George! No! Wake up!"

She poked him again, hard, but there was no reaction. None, and that was what made her really worried.

If he'd told her that he wanted to stay here in this version of Iversley, she would have accepted that. She wouldn't have agreed, but she'd have accepted it, because he could make his own choices.

But he wasn't even responding. There was no way he was like this of his own free will.

Gritting her teeth, Ash did something she hadn't done since she was about ten years old and angry with her younger brother. She grabbed George by the skin under his ear, and pinched hard.

George didn't flinch. Ash let her hand fall away, revealing a red mark already forming on his skin, and her shoulders slumped. She couldn't get through to him.

Then Ash turned to *see the two human-sized Nobles come rushing into the hall towards her, and she was too slow to run, with nowhere to fly, and they caught her and took her to the Queen-*

Right. Time to go.

"I'm so sorry, George," she told him earnestly. "I'll come back for you when I can, I promise."

With one last regretful look, Ash turned back towards the lifts. She'd almost reached them when the doors opened and inside were both Hadur and Kari, both about six feet tall.

They ran out towards her, and she *flew* in the opposite direction. Back past poor dumb George, and down to the stairwell at the other end of the corridor.

The Nobles were close behind. It was creepy how they followed; without making a sound except for their thundering footsteps. A few 'oi's or 'come back here, you's would strangely have made her feel better.

"Stop, in the name of the Queen!"

Ah, there it was. Futile orders shouted by lumbering henchmen. Ash happily ignored them.

Then a flash of far-sight warned Ash that Hadur was about to knock her down in a leaping tackle. She swerved to the side, and he landed on the hard ground with a satisfying *thump*.

And then she saw that someone was about to come out of the stairwell…

A man opened the door from the other side and was almost trampled by one flying namesake and two hotly pursuing Nobles.

"Sorry!" Ash called after him. She zipped down the spiral staircase without touching the ground, then accidentally (ow) opened the swinging door to the outside with her head. Then she shot up into the air as fast as she could go.

She was well out of reach when another flash of far-sight came. Now that was clever – too bad it wouldn't work. Kari was about to grow full size, and *throw* human-sized Hadur up into the air after her.

Forewarned, she dropped suddenly and as predicted, Hadur went flying overhead, his grasping arms missing her entirely. She waved at his scowling face as he went by.

He shifted back to giant size on the trip down and landed

heavily on his feet in the centre of a wide street, sending humans scattering in every direction.

Ash coasted up to the roof of the vast cavern and surveyed the scene below. As before, it seemed like her fear of heights had disappeared. They couldn't throw high enough to reach her here, but in a city this size, there had to be other ways above ground besides the lifts. Surely they wouldn't risk being trapped if there was an electrical failure.

So, at one side of the cavern was Islo's place with *that* exit to aboveground. On the other side, buildings were crammed right up to the cavern's smooth, rocky wall. The lake was to her far right, and there was no way to get out there unless she could somehow breathe underwater.

Perhaps at the far end of the cavern from the lake, she wondered. There seemed to be some sort of gap there.

Ash flew closer. The rocky ceiling grew low here, and the ground rose up to meet it. It looked like she was about to be cut off, but no, the roof curved sharply down and then up again leaving a tunnel of about three metres in height.

She skimmed through, and then she was flying out towards the distant patch of bright daylight that made up the cavern mouth. Grass grew sparsely at first on the dusty ground, then thickly as she neared the exit.

Ash shot out into the open air like a cork from a bottle. The brightness of real daylight was almost overwhelming after the artificial lights of the underground city.

"Woohoo!" she shouted, spiralling upwards into the beautiful blue sky.

She stopped just short of a fat cluster of cumulus clouds. Beneath her, the cavern mouth looked surprisingly insignificant in the bright green grass of rural Angland, set amongst a patchwork of crop-filled fields. It was an idyllic scene with the small town of Upper Iversley in the distance, edged by a small cliff and thick forest on two sides. From up here, you wouldn't even know that thousands of people lived and worked beneath the ground.

Then Ash noticed something unusual about the landscape beneath her. All around the village of Iversley the land was faded, more muted in colour; like a fine coating of talcum powder sprinkled over a quilt. The colours weren't as intense as they should be, and the effect stretched as far as the underground city would.

She flew closer to look, dropping to a body-length from the ground. How interesting… Right *here* where the colour was muted, the grass seemed to be covered in a thin frost. And *here*, the frost stopped suddenly, and the grass was bright green again.

Going closer towards the town, she saw that the frost covered everything. Every tree, rock and blade of grass. She'd never noticed before only because there was no area free of the frost to compare to.

Rubbing her fingers over a tree leaf, Ash realised it wasn't real frost. It wasn't at all cold – she actually couldn't feel it at all. It didn't even come off on her finger, seeming to have soaked into the landscape like dye.

What *was* this stuff? Something about it made her think of power, but it wasn't the kind that you could borrow from. Instead this was more like the mark of someone else's power. A power-stain? She'd never heard of such a thing before, but that was what came to mind.

Ash flew back to where the frostline started. She settled on the grass at the border, and saw in amazement that it was changing. The layer of whatever-it-was was spreading, covering blade by single blade of grass.

Then she recognized the pattern.

The fake-frost area was like a target with Iversley as the bulls-eye. No, more like a nuclear bomb site with the town as ground zero.

It was the area of the Queen's influence, and it was growing.

George was trapped. He was in some sort of prison, but he couldn't see it or even see himself. He couldn't see anything except a grey fog and the confusion that filled his mind.

It was so bad that half the time he wasn't sure of his own name or where he was.

Then he'd remember; he'd remember that he was the Honourable Mister George Seymour and he needed to get back home, but then the confusion would swamp his mind again, and he'd forget it all.

All he knew was that he was imprisoned, with no way out.

Somebody, help me! he cried out.

Then like a candle in a dark room, a spot of clarity appeared.

I'll help you, a little voice replied.

And they did.

❧

Ash sat on a grassy slope, staring grimly down at the little village below. The edge of the frost-covered area was a few hundred metres away, and from here she couldn't see its movement. But it was moving, that much was certain.

This was all too big for her. When the Queen had told Ash that horrible secret, she'd basically accused Ash of thinking too small, and it was true.

Ash didn't want to be the dividing wall between peace and chaos. She didn't want to be the only person who could defeat a tyrant. Deias forbid, she didn't want to *be* that tyrant, and with every new conversation she just grew more and more confused.

The Queen was a liar, there was no doubt about that. And even everyday people would tell little lies if they thought it was easier. Ash had done no less herself on occasion.

But at what point did the little lies become big ones? Where did you draw the line?

She saw how it could happen. Every event could lead to a new decision, new power, with more decisions leading from there, and then she'd end up in a place she'd never thought she could be.

Ash had almost been able to dismiss the Queen's claim. In fact, she'd almost made up her mind about it until that conversation with Anne.

Sure, the Queen seems strangely familiar, Anne had said in her own particular way. *Not the colouring – something else. Maybe I've met her before?*

Uh, Ash had thought in a panic; maybe Anne had been talking to the Queen right then!?

But Ash didn't like the Queen. She definitely didn't want to *be* the Queen, but what was there to be done? If it was true, then Ash couldn't escape it. If it wasn't true, then hooray! But the Queen would have no real motive for keeping her safe.

Then a thought popped into her head. *Does it matter if it's true or not?*

Well yes, it did matter very much. That was just what she'd been thinking, that she didn't want to be-

Do what you know is right, and you'll never become that person.

That idea caught Ash right in the middle of her misery. Do what she knew was right?

On every occasion. And if you've acted against your conscience, then go back and make it right.

Huh, that was actually really wise. She'd been raised to love her neighbour and to follow the Good Book's teachings – including not worshipping false gods (thank you, Nobles) and not murdering or committing adultery et cetera, but that also included the more subtle, ordinary human flaws like hatred, envy, lying…

She sure hadn't followed them perfectly, but she had the general idea, right? She knew when she was doing something she shouldn't be.

It's called a conscience. But if you keep ignoring it, you'll stop noticing when it prompts.

Ooh, Ash really needed to stop lying, even just little ones. See, if she *never* lied, and *never* wanted to be anyone except herself and certainly never, *never* thought it was OK to present herself as a kind of goddess and control people's minds, then she couldn't become a person like the Queen, no matter how much power she gained. Because her character, who she was on the inside, wouldn't change.

Wow, that was brilliant.

Thank you.

Now that definitely wasn't Ash's thought. She paused, and she felt the unseen other person pause too while she debated her reaction to yet another voice talking straight into her head. It was the same one who told her about the water, wasn't it?

Yes.

Ah. The one that had stopped Ash from drinking the water, but then had barely spoken up since. It felt vaguely male, and not at all like the Queen. But was it – he – friend or foe?

Friend, of course. Most definitely a friend. But if I were your enemy, I wouldn't tell you so, would I?

That was a fair point. "Can you hear me when I speak aloud?"

Of course.

Oh. "Are you stalking me?" Ash asked suspiciously, hearing her own voice echo across the empty grassed space. "What do you want?"

You say stalking, I say taking an interest. And not just in you – in everything around here. Suddenly a very clear image popped into her mind of the surrounding landscape ravaged and blackened, and the sky a sickly red-grey. It was like she was seeing Dr Walker's pronouncement made real, and a moment later the landscape was green once again. *I have an interest in seeing that this land remains beautiful, for its people and for its own sake.*

It seemed they shared the same interest then, except that she also wanted to go home.

You'll go home, I promise.

"Let me guess, I just have to do exactly what you tell me first?" She'd heard this one before.

There was a pause. *I'm not trying to control you. In fact, I'd much rather that whatever you do, you do it freely. But if you're asking for direction, then I can give it to you, and it will be your best option.*

He said that with such confidence.

Yes.

Ash looked around once more at her lonely location, and the little town before her hiding so much underground activity. The giants hadn't come after her yet – chances were they didn't yet know where she was – but it was only a matter of time.

And her options were limited. Either she stayed here forever at the mercy of those more powerful (and accepted that everyone else would stay in the same situation) or she ran away, and accepted she'd never leave this time again, or she tried something new. Because the last option of finding the Eternity Stone felt impossible.

Not impossible.

Did he know where it was, then?

I always know where everything is.

She sighed. Who did he think he was, Deias? "Alright, what're you suggesting?"

The voice told her.

Nope. Nope. Nope.

Half an hour later Ash was considerably further away from Iversley. She'd flown non-stop from the time the voice had made its suggestion, and had only just begun to run out of energy. It seemed flying was actually a kind of exercise, and you needed the strength to keep it up.

But the more she'd flown, and the more of this future Angland she'd seen – complete with a another city visible in the far distance

– the more she'd lost motivation. Where was there to go?

But I don't want to get locked into a little box! she cried out mentally. If she went back like the voice wanted her to, that was the only thing that could happen. She'd seen it over and over-

Have you tried now? the voice enquired mildly.

It – or 'he', as she thought of him – had been silent for some time, and she'd almost thought he'd abandoned her.

Just because I'm quiet doesn't mean I've forgotten you.

Ash paused mid-air and thought about going back. Not really considering it, but letting the idea of it run through her mind. She imagined herself flying back in through that tunnel and- and here, as hoped, the far-sight took over.

The two giants were waiting at the tunnel entrance, and they looked puzzled to see her, but they took her to the Queen as requested. And the Queen looked puzzled as well, but just smiled and ripped the tattoo away like pulling off a sticky plaster…and then Ash was free to go.

As always when Ash had been caught up in far-sight, the scene reversed rapidly through her mind, leaving her once more aware of her surroundings. There was a long silence.

"Why," she asked finally to the empty air, "did it change this time?"

There was no reply from her invisible friend, and she couldn't help wondering if he was playing some game with her all along. What could he be but just another kind of power-user, maybe even one of the Nobles himself?

But that didn't sit right with her, and she stared back down at the distant patch that marked Upper Iversley.

Do the right thing all the time, and you'll never become like her.

Well, there was only one thing to do then. So Ash went and did it.

Ash flew back into the city the way she'd come in. The two Nobles, now full-sized, were on their way out of the cavern mouth as she approached. She set down at their feet.

"I'm ready to see the Queen now," she told them. Her voice sounded far more confident than she felt.

Hadur and Kari exchanged confused glances. "You do not wish to fly away again?" Hadur ventured. "Or kick one of us in the face?"

"Hey!" Ash said indignantly. "I never kicked either of you in the face." She'd kicked Hadur in the ankle.

"Only because you couldn't reach," he retorted.

That was true. Normally she would have gone for the weak spots, but he was just too damn tall.

"Sorry about that," Ash said, not feeling sorry at all, "but I was scared. That's why I left. Now I'm ready to face my, um, destiny." Provided said destiny didn't include torture and/or imprisonment.

"Good," Kari said. This close up she could see that he looked even more Viking than Hadur, with blond plaits pulling his hair away from his face, very blue eyes, and a sizable moustache. "We were tired of chasing you."

They didn't move, so Ash said impatiently, "What are you waiting for?"

"Are you *really* not going to try to escape again?"

She stared up at them incredulously, and Hadur shrugged. "Come on, then. But you'd better not be playing with us."

It was on the tip of her tongue to ask, *or what,* but her bravado didn't go that far.

Kari drew something out of his pocket. "You need to eat this," he instructed.

Oh, great. Why wasn't she surprised? In his large hand was a small pile of something white. She picked up a piece. It looked like bread, and she told them so.

The Noble shrugged. "Just eat it. It'll help."

"With what?"

Another shrug from Kari, and a blank stare from the glowering Hadur. Ash decided then and there that if *she* was the

Queen, she'd not bring these two in as help, because Hadur didn't know how to smile, and Kari was annoyingly vague.

She thought about turning and flying away, but far-sight showed that Kari might have the moustache of an eighties popstar, but he had a quick reach. *This* time they wouldn't miss, and they'd be less kind.

Then she thought about actually eating the bread, and…

Oh. *Ohh.* Alright, then.

The bread was bland and chalky, but once Ash had eaten the last piece she felt a tingle of alter-power spread from her belly to settle in her arm. The tattoo itself felt heavy on her skin, as if it was now sitting on it rather than in the skin itself. Far-sight had been right, of course, and the visions of the tattoo being pulled off now made much more sense.

The feeling grew more intense as they walked back to the palace. Why they had to walk, Ash didn't know. It was five of her steps to one of theirs. Couldn't they just carry her like last time and get there ten times faster? It was just delaying the inevitable, like pulling a sticky plaster off slowly rather than in one quick rip.

The tattoo had taken on a life of its own. It pulsed and throbbed up her arm and shoulder, the tendrils of vine feeling like tentacles on her flesh. Quite frankly, it was horrible. Ash was looking forward to having the perverse thing removed. Even if it did hurt, it had to be better than having an octopus plant in her skin.

Suddenly irritated, she picked up her speed and left the others behind. If this was going to happen, it was going to happen soon.

She nipped inside the main doors of the palace, then headed past the mirrored room to the room she'd last seen the Queen. The door was closed, so she knocked on it loudly.

An unfamiliar Noble answered. He was human-sized with a neat dark beard, and carried that aura of power that they all did. For a moment he looked at her in surprise, then recovered himself.

"We're expecting-"

"Good," Ash cut in, stepping around him.

And there was the Queen in the second form Ash had seen, the beautiful dark-haired human one. But her expression was startled, then amused. "Where are my Nobles?"

"Here, my Queen," Hadur called from the doorway. He'd clearly been running, and didn't look pleased about it. "She moves fast."

"And since when has your speed been your only strength?" she countered.

The two now-smaller giants both were silent. "Ask her," Kari said finally.

The Queen turned to Ash, who was still holding out her arm with that horrible tattoo. She stared at the tattoo, then at Ash's face, and her expression turned calculating. "Well."

There was something going on here that Ash didn't under-stand, and the memory of that nasty little golden box popped back into her mind. But she held still, chin lifted. "I thought you wanted the tattoo. You can have it."

"Of course I can have it," the Queen replied. She stepped closer, her hand on something at her side, but she didn't move to touch Ash yet. "I would ask why you ran, but I already know you were taking advantage of that short-lived ability to fly. Yet here you are back."

"You're surprised." In spite of the Queen's words, this seemed obvious to Ash, and a sense of elation ran through her. She wasn't following the script. No matter what was true or false, she'd stepped outside those expectations. "You didn't expect me to do this."

The Queen jolted almost imperceptibly. "Don't be silly," she said smoothly, stepping forward and grabbing Ash's wrist. And Ash knew what was coming, but she couldn't help gasping in surprise when the Queen dug her nails in underneath the edge of the design.

For a moment it felt like being stabbed with little needles, and then *riiip!* With a sound rather like a zip being pulled too quickly, the tattoo was gone.

Ash screamed.

"Oh stop it," the Queen said dispassionately, the tattoo writhing in her hand like a worm pulled from compost. "That didn't hurt at all."

Ash just stood there, face crumpled. Well, actually it *had* hurt terribly. Now it didn't – there wasn't even a mark on her skin – but at the moment it was pulled, it had hurt like her skin was being torn away as well. "Was that it?"

"Yes, that was it," the Noble replied testily. She stood at an angle, one hand slightly hidden behind her green and silver skirts. The tattoo was now winding itself around her other arm, settling into the bare skin and becoming flat and metallic. It had five blooms now, Ash noted, and they didn't look any different from the others the Queen wore. "You may go."

It seemed too easy, and Ash couldn't help but think of that little golden prison. The Queen's other hand was still hidden behind her skirts. Might have been a coincidence, might not. But she felt so unsafe here, like Daniel in the lions' den, and the hair prickled on the back of her neck. "Oh. OK…thank you."

She turned to leave, but the Queen called after her. "I wouldn't bother trying to access my power anymore, by the way. You won't be able to use it."

No more coloured lights and setting people on fire? Ash looked back at the other woman, really looked at her. She was smirking, but her face was pale. Something was off. "But what you said last time – that it doesn't matter what I do, because-"

"It'll all turn out the same anyway," the Queen finished flatly. "Whether you're my namesake or not. That's fate, isn't it? Now go away, Ashlea Jane O'Reilly, before I lose my temper."

But that wasn't enough. What wasn't being said, and why wouldn't Ash be able to use her power?

"I said, go!" The Queen had no more use for her, it seemed.

Ash left. She walked back out into the city, wondering what she'd missed, what the Queen was going to do with that tattoo, and what purpose it had even served.

But she wasn't sorry she'd come back. The tattoo's removal had been painful, but now Ash felt so free and light, as if a chain weighing her down had been loosened.

No more power. But even as she had that thought, she raised her arms in the air and her whole body lifted as though on strings.

No, she still had power, even if the use of illusion was gone. She wouldn't miss that. In fact, she felt *stronger* without that power, without the tattoo.

Then Ash noticed one more thing that finally made sense of the Queen's last words. Her clothing had changed from scarlet back to that sky blue, and even the little violet had disappeared.

She'd been demoted.

Fifteen

GAMES

The Queen stood in front of the small basin of water that she kept in her private rooms. Sometimes a wash basin, today it was being used for a finding spell. Although it *wasn't working*.

"Damn it to Hades!" she shouted suddenly, and heard something clatter to the ground behind her. Kari had dropped the tray he'd been carrying, and was hurriedly scooping it up. "Where's Aegus?"

Kari looked blank. "Shall I find him, my Queen?"

Chaos, that one was half-witted. Why had she taken him again?

Oh, that was right. He'd sworn his undying loyalty, and after Janeus's unfaithfulness, the opposite sounded pleasant.

She sighed. What could Aegus do anyway except make guesses in answer to all of her questions, the same as he always did? "Maybe you can help me."

The man panicked. "I can?"

"Tell me..." Why the finding spell wasn't working yet. Why the golden soul-catcher had refused to catch. Why the new damned tattoo was *itching* on her skin and was driving her crazy!

The Queen didn't bother finishing her sentence, instead turning back to the scrying pool in front of her. She'd taken all the power she'd leeched from the time-traveller and had forced it into the water, the same as she'd done with all the other namesakes she'd had, once she'd grown tired of them.

And the tattoo should have sat quiet and silver on her skin, just like the others; a link to its original owner that would continue to give power until the human died.

But in spite of all her focus, the water hadn't shown her the location of the Eternity Stone, and the tattoo still itched and wriggled and shimmered from silver to colourful to a strange pinkish bronze.

I've picked up a virus, she thought in distaste. Because there was only one reason why all of those things would have gone wrong, and why she hadn't been able to do this one simple thing.

Interference from an old enemy, one who could follow her movements through time as easily as she picked information from a simpleton's mind. It looked like Amaranthus hadn't forgotten her after all.

The Queen turned back to the scrying pool, its surface still murky and unhelpful. It was true that the traveller hadn't done what was expected. That was a problem, but it could be worked around. Unfortunately for someone in this room, the workaround wasn't a kind one.

"I strongly believe," she said aloud, "that sometimes difficult decisions must be made for the good of all. Do you agree, Kari?"

The man just looked relieved to have a question he could answer. "I do, my Queen. You are always right."

And he was stupid, but right about that last part. She walked up to him, one hand again hidden in the folds of her skirt. "And you are *most* loyal to me, are you not?"

"I am, my Queen!"

Well, that much was true also. "Thank you."

In a swift movement that Kari wouldn't have even noticed, she brought her hand up and slammed the object she'd been holding right into his face. The little golden box hit him in the mouth, and there was a fraction of a second when his skin moulded like rubber around it, and she saw the realisation in his eyes.

Then in a shimmer of bright power, his life force was sucked into the box and his big form fell to the ground, empty and useless. So not much of a change, then.

Now she could call Aegus. After all, someone needed to clean up the mess.

The Queen quickly moved back to the scrying pool, sticking the soul keeper into the water up to her wrist. She closed her eyes and focused on the Eternity Stone, focused on its shape and its size and its purpose, but mostly on its power. *Show me where you are*, she instructed the water.

The surface of the pool rippled and she smiled in satisfaction. Bad luck for whatshisname, but sometimes only a death would create the power needed for success.

And then she saw where the Eternity Stone was.

"AEGUS! AEGUS! AE-"

He reached the room before she even finished shouting his name. "My Queen?"

She rolled her eyes when he spotted the body and blanched. "Don't act all squeamish; it was better him than you. I know where the Eternity Stone is."

"My lady?" Her excitement was echoed in his expression. "Shall I send out a search party?"

"Already done." She'd contacted her people directly. She couldn't *believe* it had been there all that time, so very very close. The *thief*. How *dare* they! "They've been sent to collect the carrier, and not to alert them of the Stone at all costs. They don't understand what they hold." Idiot – but lucky for her, or they'd have been long gone.

Aegus didn't answer, and after a few moments she turned back to see what the problem was. His face was pale, but he wasn't staring at dead Kari anymore, but at her. "Sashy..."

In spite of the spell's success, that sound of that nickname made her furious. Only her nearest and dearest had ever used it, and no one since the last time Janeus had left. "What did you call me?"

Her servant cringed and bowed, as he should. It seemed that his long years of service hadn't entirely made him forget his position. "Forgive me, my Queen, but you're...*leaking*."

She looked down at her gown. The silver on green shimmered just like it always did, but now it was shimmering away into the air, little pulses shining like heat waves as they escaped from the hem of her gown. "What in Hades-"

She hadn't even felt the power leaving her, but now she did, and it centred on the new tattoo on her arm. It still sat badly on her skin, hard and copper in colour, but she'd overlooked that because of her excitement at locating the Eternity Stone. The tattoo was like a nail in a tyre, to quote an old saying.

The Queen swore, then swore again, picking at the edge of the tattoo, trying to remove it the same way as she'd added it on. But these marks weren't made to be removed from their creators, just added, and it felt like it had tied itself into her very soul. Her skin bled, and the tattoo wouldn't go.

So she tried once more to make it like the other tattoos, but that was no good either, because if she could've done that she'd have done it already. She tried to stop it, spoke all the invocations she knew, but it was no good. The flow of power from her to the empty air was increasing. She could see the waves spilling out in all directions, seeking a human home.

"Why is this happening?!" She was panicking and Aegus could see it. She could see the mirroring panic on his own face.

And now when she looked down, she could see that even the silver of her gown was changing colour. The Queen's body, testament to a thousand namesakes and a *lot* more dubious power sources, was bit by bit being changed from the silver of power to that wrong, useless, leaking-

"I can fix this," she said manically.

The Stone, that would fix everything. Using all the resources she had, she sent out another message, this time an urgent one showing exactly where the Stone was, and who held it.

BRING IT TO ME NOW!

All the power wasn't gone, not yet. But it would be gone within a few hours if this wasn't stopped. How to stop it, how to stop it…

Her gaze fixed on Kari's body once more, and then past it to where a terrified-looking Aegus stood in the doorway. That might work, although she'd hate to do it after all those faithful years of service. Better him than her, though.

She switched into a gentle tone. "Aegus, my dear, you're loyal to me…"

But showing he was more observant than Kari, the man had already fled.

❦

Ash had been demoted back to new-blue. She wasn't namesake anymore, and the Queen didn't seem to want anything to do with her. She wasn't trapped in a box, thankfully, and the tattoo was gone.

And that meant…no more Sam. She internally celebrated, then felt a little bad about it. It wasn't his fault he was pompous, pushy and annoying – or perhaps it was, but even the worst kind of person had feelings.

Speaking of pompous, George was still at the Ospitil wandering around like a zombie. Now Ash wasn't being chased anymore, she could go back and see if she could help him out.

She skipped the hospital's lobby this time, instead flying outside to the right level and trying to find an open window. It was around about where the big OSPITIL sign was attached to the building, only all the windows appeared to be sealed.

She was starting to think she might have to break something – or risk the receptionist again – when a flicker of movement caught her eye. Someone was up here, up where the massive letters were fixed onto the building. Each rested on a broad metal beam, and a series of glowing tubes ran up the length of each letter, creating the glowing sign effect. Between each beam was empty air right down to the ground three storeys below.

That would be fine with her now gravity wasn't really a problem, but it wasn't so good for the average, non-flying person. Even if that person was in a zombie state and didn't know what they were doing.

"George," she called cautiously, coming to rest on the metal beam between the letters. "Is that you?"

But then the movement was behind her, and a *hard blow struck her neck, burning her, and she fell tumbling to the ground, barely able to pull herself up in time to stop the hard collision. She felt something crunch when she hit and then someone was landing next to her and she turned painfully and saw it was George…*

Ash pulled away a moment too late. She felt a sharp, burning pain graze her neck like a heated poker, and then she was falling from her perch. But this time she managed to pull herself up and fly around to land on the far beams rather than hitting the ground. Something about the pain made it hard to fly, and she gripped onto the upright wood with one arm, touching her neck with the other. It didn't feel damaged, but her skin still burned.

Three beams away from her stood George, right outside the place she'd fallen from. He had changed his clothes, now in black with a brown jacket, and he was standing on that beam as though he didn't need any support, hands empty and eyes bewildered. "Ash? What are we doing here?"

She shook her head. The pain on her neck was fading, but she watched him warily. "George, I'm here to find you, but you just attacked me! How in Hades should I know why?"

He didn't correct her language, a sure sign something was wrong. Instead he just shook his fair head, staring down at his hands in confusion. "I'm sorry. I didn't mean to hurt you. Are you alright?"

Ash sighed. "Yeah, I'm alright. It's probably not your fault, anyway."

"They did something to my hands." George was still staring at his open palms as if he'd never seen them before, and taking pity Ash leapt lightly from one beam to the next until she was only arm's length away from him.

"Show me."

He reached out his hands to her. She leaned forward and next thing, lightning fast he grabbed her wrist tightly and the pain was searing, and he wasn't bewildered George anymore. He was laughing, and he wouldn't let her go even though she screamed.

Finally he released her and she saw the distinct red handprint left on her skin, and like last time, the pain seemed to incapacitate her. She wanted to fly away, to flee, but she felt like her ability had left her once the pain had arrived. She could feel it; she could feel that if she tried to fly it wouldn't work and she would fall, but she was so desperate to get away from this new and unimproved version of the boy that she almost wanted to try.

"You'll fall," he mocked as if he could read her thoughts. Maybe he could. "Just try flying. You'll fall."

A stab of fear went through Ash, and she stumbled back, falling through the gap. She waved her arms about desperately and managed to rise just enough to grab hold of the beam again.

This time when he reached down to grab her, she tried to let go, thinking that falling would be better than another burn, but he was too quick. He grabbed her wrist again and pulled her, flinging her up and against the beam, and she grabbed hold of it to keep from tumbling again.

This time the burn was briefer, and she looked at him in horror and betrayal. "You don't know what you're doing," she sobbed. "But you'll be sorry. Stop it, George!"

"I'm following orders," he said mockingly, grey eyes glittering. Had they always been so cold and merciless? "And I won't be sorry. But make it a bit more fun, won't you?"

He turned to the glowing tubes that were climbing the beams

and grabbed one of them, pulling a three-foot-long piece out of the wall. It didn't spark or crack, just sat there in his hand like a bizarre sort of light saber. He broke off a second one and threw it to her, and she caught it just in time, staring at him in confusion.

"Go on, fight me," he told her, swinging the tube at her head. "Didn't you say you were good at fencing?"

Had she told him that?

But this time she didn't even need far-sight. She ducked out the way, and he didn't seem upset. He laughed, showing that he'd not even tried. She didn't want this. She didn't want to fight him. Ash looked down at the ground longingly, but still felt heavy and very gravity bound. She didn't dare try to fly.

When he swung again far-sight finally kicked in, and she jumped sideways, blocking his strike with her own tube. But he still hit her on the shoulder, and she gasped. That would bruise.

They kept on like that for a few moments – him swiping at her and sometimes hurting her, and her being purely defensive, not wanting to harm him and still bewildered by his attack. It reminded her a little of fencing back in high school but she couldn't summon the moves, instead just trying to keep out of his way.

Finally one of her defensive blows slipped and hit him on the neck, and he stumbled and almost fell off the beam, but caught himself at the last moment.

Ash could have struck again and knocked him right off to fall to the ground, but she wouldn't. She didn't. Instead, she turned and ran desperately in the opposite direction, making small jumps from one beam to another until she reached the last one. Then she scrunched her eyes shut, thought about being as light as air, and leapt.

She fell, but waved her arms around wildly and began to rise again slightly. Frantically she waved them again, flapping like a bird and thinking about how she'd been able to fly before, how far-sight had shown her that she could, and she began to rise back high into the air once more, but she was oh-so-tired.

You'll fall, she heard George's whisper again, and right at that moment Ash felt herself drop a little.

But that was also when she understood the problem – it was her, all her. It was whether she *believed* she could fly. The ability was there, but doubt hindered it.

At that moment something clicked into place, and it was like whatever had been holding her back fell off and she felt light again, light enough to fly away.

But there was still that red handprint on her wrist.

❧❧❧

I'll help you, the little voice had told George. Then a door had opened in the middle of the fog and a little man had stepped out of it, gesturing for George to come closer. George had just enough presence of mind to step through and then it closed after him, and the scene changed.

Before, he'd been in a grey fog filled with horrible creatures, but he had known he was in a hospital room. Now he was standing on the balcony rail *outside* the hospital room, a wobble away from certain death. The little man reached out with a smile and helped him down into thin air…

…And then with a jolt, George was right back inside the hospital room where he'd first become confused. But now the room was bright and clear, and covered in these strange, shifting patterns, and he saw that there was nothing on the bed at all. Nothing.

"The boy?" George asked in puzzlement. "Have I lost him?"

The man who'd come to help him smiled, seeming vaguely familiar. "He left hours ago, George, but you didn't notice."

"Oh." George looked at the hospital room once more, and then at the direction the man had come from. It was like the entry into another world: like the room dissolved into the most enormous beautiful garden he'd ever seen, with what looked like a vast glass city in the centre.

He could turn and walk back into the now strangely-coloured hospital room, or he could follow the little man where he beckoned into this new, beautiful place.

With a shrug of his shoulders, George followed.

❦❦❦

Ash fluttered to the ground far from the hospital, tired and disheartened. That couldn't have been George, not truly. He never would have hurt her like that.

He *couldn't* have. Those burning hand prints weren't something he could do on his own, and now she thought of it, he hadn't spoken correctly either – he'd even called her *Ash*. Clearly he hadn't been in possession of his right mind.

The thought of George being played like a hand puppet crossed her mind, and she shuddered. It was awful, but she had no idea what to do about it.

But at that moment Sam walked around the corner with several other namesakes, and his eyes lit up when he saw her. "Queen's namesake," he called.

Damn. Ash smiled at him awkwardly, since dealing with Sam was the last thing she wanted to do right now. She remembered a moment too late that she'd ditched him the night before, and he seemed the sort to make a fuss. "Oh – hi, Sam. Sorry about not coming back last night. I was with a friend longer than I'd planned, and it was easier just to stay with them."

He must have been in a good mood today, because he brushed it off with a grin. "No problem. Actually, we were about to go play a game where we get to use our powers. It should be a bit of fun. You should come with us."

She gestured down at her blue clothing. "You obviously haven't noticed I've been demoted. I don't have any powers."

"You can fly," someone pointed out. "We don't know anyone else who can do that."

"We've all seen you," Sam agreed, still smiling. "So there's no need to be coy. Namesake isn't what colour you wear, Ash. It's who you are, and you're still the same person as you were yesterday, aren't you?"

His tone was light, but it made her think of the Queen's words. It was who Ash was… Damn it. "I don't think-"

"We've got uneven teams," someone else said. It was the girl who'd lit her neighbour's hair on fire at the meeting. She didn't look like a pyromaniac, more like someone Ash would have gone to school with. Friendly. "Besides, we've never played with anyone who can fly before."

Ash looked at all those smiling faces, a few of which she recognised. *Don't disappoint us*, they seemed to be saying, and she relented. There was no far-sight warning, and she was still feeling shaken from what had happened with George, so her general unsettled feeling had to be wrong. She was probably getting paranoid from just being attacked by someone who was almost a friend, and temporarily misplacing her flight ability.

"Have you got some other pressing engagement?" Sam prompted. "Need to fly up to some floating house, or something?"

That didn't make sense, and wasn't even funny. Ash smiled politely. "I suppose I could come for a while." She'd make a showing just to keep them happy, then leave as soon as possible…as soon as she knew where she'd be going. "But you'll have to teach me all the rules."

"Not a problem, Ash. Right this way."

✳✳✳

Anne was readying herself to leave for the bunker when it happened.

"Look at your dress," Islo pointed out in surprise.

She glanced down at herself. For a moment she did not see what concerned him, then it made sense. "Oh, it's turned blue again. I suppose Ash's little illusion couldn't hold itself once she left."

"And your hair," he added, frowning. "It's back to that flaming red."

"You needn't look so displeased about it." She'd thought he *liked* her hair, even if most people didn't.

"It'll make you stand out too much, that's all." Islo tapped his fingers on his leg thoughtfully. "How do you feel about wearing a hat?"

'Twas most ironic, since Anne had felt such freedom upon throwing her coif away at the beginning of this journey. She sighed. "Why not."

❧

The namesakes all walked together through the city streets, so Ash did the same. Their chatter faded out around her as she became lost in thought. Thoughts of George, of the Queen, and wondering why any of this was happening. What was true, what was false…

"*Ash!*"

She looked up in surprise to where Sam was trying to get her attention. "Oh, sorry. Were you talking to me?"

He grimaced. "I was trying to. What has you so distracted?"

I might have met my future self, and I don't like her very much. And nothing makes sense… "I was wondering about your power," she replied instead. "If it's real or not."

"What do you mean? Of *course* it's real."

"But Souris only uses illusion," Ash pointed out. "That's what I mean by not real. And why would the namesakes have more power than a Noble?"

"Souris can't even change size," the big bald guy said, lip

curled in distaste. "Her namesake still works a regular job, because they can't do anything."

Ash tried again. "I know that when I had some of the Queen's power, and I actually managed to use it, it wasn't real. I set someone on fire, but it wasn't real fire. It didn't really burn them."

"Did they scream?" the pyro-girl asked curiously.

"Um...yes. But I didn't enjoy it," Ash added hastily. "I just wanted to know if that was only me, or if it was everyone."

"Fair enough question," Sam said lightly.

They'd reached another building now, one near the edge of the cavern, and they began filing in through the single door. Inside was a room as big as a tennis court, with a slanting roof about ten metres high at its highest point. Set around the walls were massive posters – maps, diagrams, and what looked like inspirational pictures of some of the Nobles.

Above those were ornamental weapons: shields, swords, an axe or two, in the same way others might have picture frames. The occasional potted bush against the walls completed the scene.

Sam continued, "And if you're even asking, it means you've seen that some of the Nobles' power *is* illusion. Although some would say that if you make someone think they're on fire, then they may as well be for the pain they'll feel. But the answer isn't simple."

"Oh?"

"Nobles have various powers, and their namesakes will echo those, in a way. Some real, some not." Sam pointed to pyro-girl. "Jess there, she's Mortimer's namesake. And what are his abilities?"

Ash wasn't sure if she was expected to answer, but Jess/pyro-girl answered for her. "Fire, and death."

"You *kill* people?"

Jess grinned. "Nah, but I could probably make them think they're dead, if their minds were weak." She lifted her hands, and her palms glowed red hot. "And same story, I could make people think I was burning them. But they're not real powers, just illusion. Your words, not mine, but Mortimer's the one with the real power."

"As it should be," someone said, and there was a general chorus of agreement.

"Wait a second," Ash cut in. Something in her mind had gone *click*, and she was beginning to feel angry. "This Mortimer can burn people with his hands for real? But how's he with illusion?"

Jess shrugged. "Dunno. He's got some, I suppose. Plenty of Nobles do."

Illusion enough to disguise himself as another person…all except for those cold grey eyes. But why would Ash be targeted like that?

Sam cleared his throat. "As I said, if people think illusion is real, then it may as well be. Any burns Jess inflict will hurt, as long as the vict…the *person* thinks that they ought to hurt. Quite a thing, isn't it?"

But Ash was still thinking of Mortimer, a Noble she'd never even met until just now, and the ongoing pain in her wrist and shoulder. That was real, and it went further than just pain. For a while it had stopped her being able to fly. "Quite a thing," she echoed distractedly.

Around the room the namesakes seemed to be organising themselves for the game. Someone opened a cupboard and out came some long white sticks that reminded her of fencing sabres, only vaguely plastic in appearance. She wondered what on earth they were intended for.

Back at the entrance – which was also the only exit – Nargis' namesake was touching the two miniature trees that sat on either side of the closed doorway. As she watched, the branches grew up and towards each other until they covered the door like a wall…or bars.

"Now that," Sam said lightly, "that's real enough to stop anyone moving past. See for yourself."

Ash moved over curiously, touching the branches. They felt real, but then so had the apple of the previous day. "It's not just a really good illusion. It *does* seem real. How is that possible?"

"Because I had something real to start with," Nargis (as she was now thinking of him, as adding 'namesake' was too long-winded) replied in his soft voice. He held up his other hand, and a pineapple materialised from nothing. "Catch."

She stuck out her hands in automatic response, and for a moment the pineapple felt solid as she caught it. But then it turned sheer and shadowy, and fell through her hands.

"That's because it came from nothing, and you know it's not real," the boy explained, frowning. "Most people never realise the difference between illusion and reality. How do you?"

"Good question," Sam said from right behind Ash, and she jumped. He laughed, and it was a nasty laugh. "How *do* you know the difference, Ash?"

"You all seem to know," she retorted, stepping away from him. Game or not, she was beginning to feel uncomfortable, especially with the knowledge that it hadn't been George who'd attacked her. Hooray, George didn't hate her...but oh dear, a Noble did. "So why wouldn't I? And what about this game of yours. Are we going to play or not?"

One of the namesakes handed Sam one of those long sabre-like sticks, and he grinned, swishing it through the air a couple of times. "Oh, we'll play." In a sudden, sharp movement he swung the stick around *and held its humming point against her throat-*

But Ash had already moved. She'd shot upwards the moment far-sight had warned her, and she clung against the high ceiling like a spider, staring down at him in dismay.

The tip of what was clearly a weapon swished harmlessly through the air, and Sam scowled. "You are fast, aren't you?"

Lucky for her, she was. "That's not funny, Sam. Those look sharp, and you could have hurt me!"

"And wouldn't that be a tragedy," someone muttered off to

the side of the room. Ash looked at the group in shock but couldn't tell who'd spoken. All around the room Nargis was still moving, and those harmless-looking little pot plants set around the walls were growing into monsters tall enough to cover the walls and create a net over the ceiling – and thick enough to stop her from escaping upwards.

Ash went cold from head to toe and began urgently looking for an exit. It seemed like the only one was the now-covered doorway, and the whole room was sealed…except for right up high above the plant barrier covering the ceiling. Did people still use air vents here?

Down below Sam still held the white sabre-thing, and the others all had the same. They were all armed, all except her.

"The whole point is that they're sharp," he called up to her. "Pun intended. Where is it, Ash?"

"Where is what?!" This was so surreal, but she wasn't going to have to *fight*, was she? She was again nastily reminded of that twisted not-George and his instruction to 'fight me'… And how she'd fumbled and forgotten her moves.

"Don't play stupid, because it's not holding up. The Queen knows you have it, and if you return it immediately, *maybe* we'll let you live."

Well, that was a sharp about-face from wanting to move in together. "I still don't know what you're talking about, and I don't appreciate the death threats!" There, up above the growing netting of branches was what looked like a tiny little window. They were underground so she didn't know where it would lead, but if the door wasn't an option…

Ash looked down to where the namesakes were grim-faced – all except for pyro-Jess, who seemed to be enjoying the whole thing. But then her Noble was a bit of a monster, wasn't he? Noble of death and fire and burning hands, et cetera.

They were serious. They were all serious, and her life really was in danger.

As she had that thought, far-sight confirmed it – showed her the plants growing lower and lower and forcing her into their reach, and how ruthless they would be with those swords. '*Silver-tungsten,' Sam said, 'as light as plastic, as strong as titanium; and sharp enough to cut through bone…'*

Ash turned and flew across the room, over their heads, to where a couple of old-fashioned swords were fixed to the wall, crossed over each other decoratively. She tugged at the handle of one, bracing her feet against the wall in an effort to remove it. She wouldn't go down easily!

"Don't waste your time," Sam shouted. "They're fixed to the wall! Just tell us where the Eternity Stone is!"

Was *that* what this was all about? Overcome by relief and anger, Ash turned on the lot of them. "You think I've got the Eternity Stone? And you call me stupid! Sam, I only ever heard of the thing yesterday, and I *definitely* don't have it!"

"The Queen says you do," Tor's namesake called up to her. "So you do."

Or so they believed, enough that they'd search her dead body for it if they had to.

The sword didn't budge, and she realised in horror that it was welded on to the wall.

And then far-sight gave a warning and she ducked sideways, and suddenly one of those white sabres was stuck in the wall right by her face, still vibrating from the force of the throw that had sent it up here. She stared at it in shock, then down at the namesakes. One of them whose name she couldn't remember was now minus a weapon.

"Nice one," someone muttered to the one who'd thrown it. "Now she's got it."

Good point. Ash grabbed the new sabre by the handle and with a brief tug freed it from the wall. Above her head the branches were growing thicker and lower as she'd foreseen, and she knew she only had minutes before she ran out of space and was forced into the namesakes' reach. She thought of that little window-space up by the ceiling and began hacking frantically at the growth above her.

It gave, and Ash cut with renewed vigour. Nargis kept trying to make the branches grow back, but she was faster, and finally she started to force her way through, but got stuck halfway like those poor princes in the old Sleeping-Princess fairytale.

It was ironic because Sam had mocked the other boy for having a weak ability, but the truth was that most of them had nothing but illusion. If they had had more, then they'd have been using it now rather than simply wandering down underneath like idiots.

Oh Deias, but they weren't all stupid. Below her someone had gone to get a ladder, and the others were boosting each other up in a human pyramid. They'd chosen this place because of the weapons, no doubt, and because of the roof. They knew she could fly, and they knew they'd have to keep her in, and right this moment she was feeling like a fox trapped in its den with the hounds baying for its blood.

Ash began to cut more urgently where the branches trapped her legs. It seemed to be giving a little, but not fast enough. Beneath her the human pyramid was nearly at her height, Sam at its top with that too-sharp sabre. Then finally, finally she forced her way through the plant barrier and sped for the little window thing a few metres higher up. It was clear plastic, and on the other side seemed to be air. A kind of vent after all, maybe?

Below her Nargis had begun to redirect the branches, moving them away to help lift the others up towards her, and to block her new exit. But they moved slowly, and she began desperately kicking at the vent's plastic cover.

"You're not the Queen's first namesake, you know," Sam called. Gone was the goofy, friendly guy, and in his place was a stone-cold killer. "For a moment there I thought you'd be good enough. But you're just like the others were: unworthy of the honour given to them."

Talk. Talk could distract them from immediate slaughter, Ash thought desperately. She had some fencing skills and far-sight to aid her, but those wouldn't be enough if they all attacked at once and if she was trapped in place.

She glanced down. They were almost on her, looking very serious indeed. "What happened to the others?" she asked quickly. "I thought I was the only one."

"There are always others," Sam answered, tone heavy with disgust. "But they're gone, and so will you be. And it's what you deserve for the way you treated me, pretending you didn't know me!"

"Oh my Deias!" Ash shouted, losing her temper. "You *really* hold a grudge! I didn't want to move in after knowing you only one day, and now I'm bloody glad I didn't, because you're crazy!"

"Knowing me one day?!" he shouted back, and now he was almost at her level, the others below him boosting him up. "Don't pretend you didn't know me before, as if I'm so easily forgotten?"

He stood on two others' shoulders, pushing himself upright and taking a swing at her. She deflected it easily, those almost-forgotten fencing moves coming back into play, and she realised she had to move. They'd trap her in this corner.

She pushed off the wall like a swimmer doing a tumble-turn, making sure to cut some of the branches holding them up as she did. The tower of namesakes swayed, and for a moment Sam looked like he'd fall.

"I've never met you before yesterday," she insisted. "Never! This isn't necessary, Sam! I don't have what you need!"

"Liar!"

Moving as one, the whole namesake tower swayed towards her and her eyes widened as she realised they'd fall. Well, with a little prompting they would...thank you, far-sight. As foreseen, Ash ducked around them and gave someone at mid-level a good kick in the shoulder. They yelped, and suddenly the whole thing was collapsing sideways. Ash flew in the opposite direction, intending to go around and go for the little vent again, but an idea occurred to her.

The door would be an easier escape route.

Ash feinted as if she'd head for the vent, but at the last moment tumble-turned and went for the door. She could see them understanding where she was going, but they were all too slow, all too caught up in each other. And yes, there were a few injuries from those sabres being thrown around, but they weren't her problem.

Nargis was the only one who wasn't caught in the tower, and he ran for the door even as she sped for it, his face intent and sabre in hand.

"Don't do it," she warned him.

"Anything for my Queen," he retorted, holding the weapon aloft. But he had no skill, and she realised he'd probably never used it properly before. Would never have needed to.

He was so slow and awkward that she could cut his throat in an instant if she was so inclined. She might even need to do it. She had bare seconds before the others recovered themselves, and then she'd be trapped for sure. But all she needed was one sharp thrust to cut through those branches and get out the door. Hades, maybe they'd even fall away by themselves once the boy was dead…

Do what is right, and you'll never become that person.

She wanted to do the right thing, but she also didn't want to be killed by these idiots. Some help, please??

A picture of the vent came into her mind, but this time of her *gently lifting the cover off, then forcing her way into the small space. It felt like being born when she finally came out on the other side, but she was free and safe…*

That'd do. Ash swerved at the last moment, the movement meaning she caught a slash of the sabre's razor-sharp tip across her leg. They hadn't been like that at high school, that was for sure. Fencing was meant to be a sport, not a way to reduce the population.

But she headed upwards once more and reached the vent within moments. With a little tug, the cover lifted off, and she paused at the opening to glance down to her attackers. Most of them had managed to stand again and were watching her with impotent rage. They knew she was going to escape.

"You idiots," Ash shouted down at them, her voice trembling with fury and adrenaline. "Don't you know the Queen's using you? She'll kill you as soon as it suits her to do so!"

A few of them frowned, but Sam glared at her with as much hatred as if she'd run over his pet puppy. "The Queen will *never* kill me," he spat, "because I stand in place of her Janeus. But you, girl – you're expendable. So enjoy your extra five minutes of life, because I swear that if we don't get you, the others will."

There were *others* gunning for her? Ash had no response to that. She forced herself to turn her back on them, then shoved herself headfirst through the vent. It was a tight fit; if her hips had been any bigger, she wouldn't have made it.

Then she was through the vent and outside in the cavern once more, still trembling from the violent encounter, but free…for now.

PURSUIT

George stood in the new, beautiful world, staring at his surroundings in amazement as he'd been doing for several minutes.

This was easily the most incredible location he'd ever been in. Calling it a garden was an enormous understatement – unless it was a garden for kings, or even for gods.

The little man who'd led him here waited patiently, perhaps accustomed to this reaction from guests.

"I beg your pardon," George said finally. "We've not even been introduced."

"Oh, I know who *you* are," the man replied with a smile. "George William Seymour. And we have met before, although you may not recall it."

There was something about that smiling face with those bright dark eyes, not very much hair but no less confident for the lack of it... "The fountain," George said in sudden realisation. "You offered me water."

"I did. And you chose not to drink it."

There was a pause. "Was the-"

"Yes."

George hadn't even had a chance to finish his question, but there was no doubt that the answer had been given. Yes, the water from the fountain had contributed to that fog of confusion. "But all the things I saw," he persisted. "Were they real? Any of them at all?"

"Power," the man replied succinctly. "You were tied to the so-called Queen after your meeting with her, but the power used to tie you wasn't being directed. That can result in some extremely vivid hallucinations, or a complete absence of mind."

So-called Queen, eh? And thank Deias those monsters hadn't been real! Even the memory of the still made George shudder.

There were many things George could have said next, including that if the man had been more forceful about the danger of the fountain, or if the water offered had been more attractively presented, then perhaps George would have made other choices. But it came down to this: George had made his choice, and the man had come back for him anyway.

"Thank you for bringing me here," he said instead.

"You are most welcome, George." And the man seemed to mean it. "My name is Amaranthus, and we will meet again many more times before you reach the end of your journey. But here is not where we will stay."

George was still caught on the man's wording – end of what journey? Did he mean George's return to his own time? "It isn't?"

Amaranthus shook his head. "One day you'll come back to this garden, but for now, I think it's tea time." He waved his hand, and a doorway appeared, hovering above the grass. Through it was visible a little sitting room, with comfortable couches and a table in its centre. Someone had left a teapot, and perhaps that was a plate of scones?

George's mouth watered, and he didn't bother to ask about how this was even possible. He'd been freed from a kind of madness – that was good. He'd been brought to a garden away from any kind of mental influence – that was even better. And he was being offered decent Anglish food – that was best.

"Tea sounds lovely, thank you."

Ash shot out into the space of the cavern, still shaking with adrenaline and anger, and even a little hurt.

She'd not thought the namesakes were friends, exactly, but they'd always been friendly. She *knew* that they were all to some degree controlled by the Queen, but Sam in particular had seemed so normal, even somewhat likeable. That he would turn around and try to kill her had been a horrible shock.

She remembered what Solomon had said about knowing one of his attackers, and suddenly understood how that must have felt.

Ash headed out of the cavern using the same exit from earlier and moved into the space under the forest canopy, heading towards the bunker. Better to be down here, dodging trees, but unseen. Up in the air, she'd surely be an easy target, and the trees were mostly large and well-spaced.

She was some way along before she realised she was still holding the sabre. She considered ditching it but decided to keep it for now. It would probably come in handy, at least as a threat.

A little further along, Ash realized she wasn't alone. The namesakes were still following her at a distance, their noisy footsteps clearly audible compared to her almost silent flight. They were barely in sight, well behind her, but they knew where she was. That mean she couldn't go to the bunker to check on Anne after all, since she risked leading them straight there.

Ash veered away and picked up speed. But then when she glanced back, she saw five enormous figures moving through the trees ahead of the namesakes. She caught a glimpse of Hadur's familiar scowling face and her stomach wrenched in fear.

A branch smacked her in the face, sending her skidding sideways, and it took a few moments to regain her balance. *Face forward, Ash!*

She was well out of their reach, right? But if anyone had a projectile weapon then they'd get her with no trouble. Actually, it was strange how these people didn't use guns or tasers or-

Something like lightning skimmed past Ash's face and slammed into a nearby tree, sending a heavy branch flying. She screamed and swerved again, almost hitting another tree in her panic. The forest was meant to hide her, but it was just another obstacle when they already knew where she was – and when they'd decided to pull out the big guns.

Going for the first patch of blue sky she could see, Ash shot upwards. Branches whipped at her from every angle, but within seconds she was above the forest canopy, shaking off leaves as she went.

She went up and up, making sure to fly in a random spiralling pattern, until the flashes of light/lightning attacks stopped. Maybe she was too far away now, or maybe the Nobles couldn't see her through the thick canopy. She saw them, though; their huge forms shifting the foliage as they moved. Somehow they were keeping pace with her on the ground.

Then Ash saw two of the namesakes and a Noble, a giant woman, break away from the others. A moment of far-sight showed Ash that they were going to the bunker to get Anne. Ash hadn't realised they even knew the bunker existed, but that brief vision showed Anne *glancing up in surprise as the bunker door was opened, then violence…and death. One down, the Noble said…*

Ash gripped the hilt of her sabre tighter. "Oh, no you don't!"

❧

Anne had had her fill of waiting. There was naught to occupy her in the tiny underground room. She'd obediently returned here after partaking in a decent supper at Islo's home, and that had to have been at least, oh, a half-hour before. Thirty whole minutes with absolutely *naught* to do but watch the moving screens that showed the forest.

Not that there was much moving now. It had seemed so fascinating the first time she'd seen it, almost like magic, but now Anne had grown accustomed to the novelty and 'twas simply dull. Trees, trees, a stream, more trees….and nothing happening at all.

Just then a trio of people entered the far screen – two regular folk and a female Noble who stood at twice their height. Anne sat up straight, her boredom forgotten, and watched the screen avidly.

Next to the giant, the humans were easy to overlook: a man in brown and a woman in dark purple. To Anne's surprise, both carried thin swords, even the woman. How odd. Back home, females were not permitted to use swords at all. A small knife was considered sufficient for womanly needs.

Anne watched in fascination as the three crossed first one screen, then the next. They were moving quickly, and they seemed to be heading for her own little hiding place. But they couldn't know where she was, could they?

Could they?

Two seconds passed as Anne considered the point. Then she let out a slow breath. "As a matter of fact, they could," she muttered aloud.

She, Ash and George had assumed that the bunker was secret, but mayhap 'twas not at all. Its location might be common knowledge, and if she was caught here, she'd have no way of escape.

'Twould be back to Souris, and then would be a simple matter to force Anne to drink some of that tainted water. Then she'd be a poor, pathetic slave as all the others were, and really, that couldn't be borne.

So with no plan in mind except to escape, Anne left the bunker. And no sooner had she made it behind the first thicket of trees than the odd trio arrived at the bunker entrance.

Anne shrank back behind the shrubbery as the giant woman bent down, tore the entrance cover off, and threw it away. The first human began to climb inside.

Then suddenly, a blue streak plummeted out of the sky and

slammed into the giant's back, knocking her over. Then the blue-clad figure lifted another of those thin swords and struck the giant in the neck. *Poof!* The Noble disappeared in a wisp of smoke.

Anne was frozen in place. That was Ash who'd come from the sky, wielding a sword like a seasoned warrior! How was such a thing even possible?

Anne watched wide-eyed as the other two humans, who'd frozen briefly in shock, recovered and turned on Ash in unison. But they were too slow, and somehow none of their blows even landed. Within mere moments, they were both dispatched with that same puff of smoke.

Anne's jaw dropped painfully low. What manner of creature were they – genies? Spirits?

And however had Ash become so quick? The girl had never been so agile before!

Her enemies defeated, Ash crouched down over the open bunker hole. Her features were twisted in fear. "Anne!" she called down. "Are you OK?"

"I'm here!" Anne ran out of her hiding place, gasping in amazement. "That was marvellous! I did not know you were such a skilled warrior!"

Ash stared at her for a moment, then abruptly threw her arms around Anne's neck and burst into tears. "Hhhmmmai-iesssseee...."

"I appreciate the sentiment, but I cannot understand a word," Anne told her finally, pushing her away. "Why does everyone seem to have swords? I want a sword."

Ash's face crumpled again. "They were going to *kiiiillllly-ooooooouu,*" she wailed.

So Anne had concluded. "Well, t'tis most fortunate that you came along when you did, although Saints know how you managed it. Were you dropped from a height?" A moment later, revelation dawned. "By the Eternal One, have you learned how to *fly?*"

Ash was still bawling in a most unattractive manner and didn't answer the question. "Oh my Deias I can't believe I killed theeeeemm! It felt like cutting ham; it was really grooooossss…"

By the Rood. Anne expected that killing a human would be distressing, but they'd started it, hadn't they? Arriving with weapons as they had. And these attackers had not bled at all, so could they even be considered human? "How did you know they would disappear as they did?" she asked curiously.

"I didn't!" Ash wailed.

Oh. Anne would have queried further, but Ash suddenly paused mid-sob, an odd expression on her face.

"Are you well, Ash? Do you need the privy?"

Anne had been jesting a little, but Ash turned to stare at her intently. "Anne, you need to run away NOW. As far as you can!"

"What – whatever for?"

"Please don't argue with me. Just believe me when I say that I can see the future and if you don't run away immediately, you'll be dead!" Ash pointed into the trees. "Run as far and as fast as you can!"

Now Anne might be at times proud and stubborn (she'd admit that herself) but she wasn't stupid. This, she told herself as she dashed away, was why 'twas a good thing to accept the supernatural. Why, she knew a person or two who would have argued and insisted on a reason for being told to leave so abruptly…

Still, to claim she knew the future, indeed. Why, Ash must think Anne a right simpleton. The veriest fool knew that one needed a crystal ball or other unsavoury objects in order to see the future. It likely would help to be a gypsy, also-

Behind her Anne heard shouts and the sounds of swords clashing. Somebody called, "She's getting away!"

Uh oh.

Never mind her modesty. Anne hitched up her skirt over those blue trousers and literally ran for her life.

Ash made it above the trees just as her pursuers came into view. It was a different group than Sam's gamers, but they were armed in the same way: circa 1500AD.

She'd known they were coming, just like she'd known they would have killed Anne without a second thought. Far-sight was proving itself to be invaluable. Ash was only glad she'd been able to stop them, and she was still buzzing with adrenaline from that last, incredibly lucky fight.

Ash had never fought anybody in her life. Not for anything that mattered, since the fencing she'd done in high school had been all in fun even though it had taught her some handy skills. Apart from that, the closest she'd come to true hand-to-hand combat was accidentally tripping someone up on the train and them giving her a dirty look. That was it. She just wasn't the fighting sort.

But with far-sight she knew all their moves before they made them, and she'd felt as powerful and as fast as some sort of super-human. No move had been too difficult. It must have been a side-effect of one of the vials, because that sure wasn't her naturally.

The fight against the three at the bunker had been only too easy. Ash hadn't thought, just reacted, and she certainly hadn't known that they'd vanish when she 'killed' them.

She'd fully been expecting blood, gore and screaming, which was horrible but not as horrible as letting them chop Anne's head off as they'd been planning. And then they'd just *poof!* Disappeared like characters on a cheap video game.

It was very disconcerting, because where had they gone? Had they ever really been there in the first place?

And the fact that they wanted to kill her at all – it was so sudden. She had thought everything was fine (relatively speaking) because the Queen had taken her tattoo away, but then this? Talk about stressful. When she got home she'd probably need therapy.

Ash flew deeper into the woods, dropping down below the canopy once more to hide herself as she skimmed close around hundreds of tree trunks. If the namesakes insisted on chasing, then she'd lead them in the opposite direction to where Anne had gone. Hopefully they'd all go after her and leave Anne alone.

Ahh, why were they still following her? It was a thought, but it was also a plea to the unseen person who'd spoken to her before.

Silence.

Hello, mystery man! Answer me pleeeease?

Still silence, and if Ash hadn't been so scared and hyped-up then she'd have been angry. How on earth was she supposed to know whether to trust that quiet voice when it came and went so easily? She'd gone back to the Queen as she was told to, and yes, the tattoo was gone, but now everyone was trying to kill her. It wasn't so much of an improvement, more a sideways step.

She'd killed someone. Maybe. It wasn't really killing when they just vanished, was it? But Ash had already grimly resolved that she'd do whatever it took to return herself and the other two home, and if it meant using the sabre... She wouldn't think about it, but that was another topic to add to her future therapy sessions. How to kill baddies without feeling guilty.

Pictures flooded her mind a moment before an ambush from the trees above, and as the new attacker dropped down, Ash dispatched the woman with a sharp slash across the neck. She vanished in a puff of smoke, and then Ash was surrounded.

She shot upwards, ducked a blow from behind and followed it up with a double strike to the man's head and chest. Then - *ouch* - someone caught her shallowly across the right shoulder, because with an attacker on each side, she couldn't dodge both strikes even with far-sight.

She stabbed one in the belly and one in the chest. *Poof...poof.* There was no blood, just faint mist left behind where they'd fallen.

But the shallow cut on her shoulder seemed permanent. It

stung like blazes, and she could feel blood running down her arm and seeping into her vest.

More namesakes were coming. Nobles too. Ash moved into an odd, numb state, where she concentrated on dodging and weaving and parrying blows, striking where she could. She was fully focused on the blade and its movement. Her opposition stopped being men and women, and became just human-shaped targets.

But there were too many. Even with far-sight she couldn't take on more than one or two: she had no shield and they weren't like movie villains who only attacked one at a time. At any moment they would all come in a horde and get her, and her little sword too.

The moment Ash saw that she was about to be overwhelmed, she shot upwards again, out of the trees, then headed uphill. The remaining group of about five humans and the same number of Nobles spread out as they moved to follow her.

She picked off the Nobles first. One in front and one behind, but thank you far-sight – if she moved *here* like *this*, then one of them would (to his own horror) accidentally kill the other. She finished off the first one while he was frozen in shock from his mistake.

With far-sight (although *they* didn't know about that) Ash was clearly winning. She flew low again so they had to follow her, faster and faster and round and round, dodging and slashing and moving to separate them from each other so they'd be easier to deal with, and always moving towards higher ground.

She felt like she had all the energy in the world, like her fear and anger had triggered the adrenaline rush of a lifetime. She was the ultimate fighter. She was a knight, a legend…

Then all of a sudden the rush faded, and she was *tired*.

Ash started to move away, out of reach now the trees were spaced well apart, and one of them threw his sword after her in frustration. It arched into the air, missed her by a mile, then fell straight back to its point of origin. *Poof*.

Then there were just two, and the unfortunately named Nargis' namesake was one of them. Ash stared at him in surprise. She hadn't recognized anyone she had 'killed' yet thank heavens (who knew what had happened to Sam and the others) and this could be difficult.

He took advantage of her pause to throw something on the ground. She squinted at it, and half a second later a tree shot into the air, Nargis clinging to its branches.

No, not a tree. It was a beanstalk as massive as from the classic fairytale, and in barely an instant it had grown ten metres into the air where Ash was hovering. The boy was hanging onto one of the oversized broad leaves, his sabre in his free hand, and with a set expression he reached out and took a clumsy swing at her.

He missed by two feet, but Ash reared back anyway. "Why?" she asked tiredly. "I thought we were on good terms." Before the last murder attempt, anyway.

"That was before you betrayed my Queen!" he spat. He made another lunge at her but nearly lost his grip on the beanstalk. The sabre fell from his hand and to the ground below.

She should just leave, Ash thought. It was clear that he wasn't in his right mind – none of them were, and fighting back would feel like murder. "You're the only one who used your power, and you can't fence to save your life. Give it up, Nargis. This whole fighting with swords thing doesn't make sense."

"It's the only way to bring true death to someone like you," he answered vehemently. "And I'm not Nargis, I'm his namesake!"

Oh, who *cared*. "Why do you need to kill me? I told you I don't have the Eternity Stone!"

"The Queen says you do-"

So therefore Ash must have it. Right.

The boy threw out his hand, something green appearing from thin air and spinning towards her, and Ash dodged what turned out to be a net of vines. He lifted his arm again in a fierce movement, and the broad leaf he was clinging to broke suddenly.

He fell so fast he didn't have a chance to scream. Less than a second later, another wisp of smoke was fading into the air.

One left. Feeling sick, Ash watched the woman as she stopped only a few metres downhill. This one gave off the buzz of power that made Ash think she was a Noble, but she was only human-sized and a small human at that – perhaps only a few inches taller than Anne.

This woman was slim with big, very dark eyes, pointed features and brown blunt-cut hair swinging around her narrow shoulders. She didn't attack immediately, instead studying Ash with narrowed eyes as she moved around the hill.

She was obviously looking for the right angle to attack, and Ash wouldn't give it to her. Not after all that fuss she'd just gone through.

"Why are you still here? You've clearly lost!" Ash shouted down at her.

The woman ignored her and kept circling below.

"Go away," Ash shouted again. Now she was out of the heat of battle, sticking a sword into this woman would feel too much like murder. She didn't want to 'kill' anybody else, bloodless or not, unless absolutely necessary.

The little Noble ignored her, instead just kept circling around Ash at a safe distance. Her eyes were fixed on Ash's trousers.

Trousers? Oh, the pockets which were the only ones Ash had. Clearly, the Noble wanted the Eternity Stone, and she thought Ash had it.

Hades, that thing must be incredible if they were all going to such effort to get it. Ash wished she *did* have it, because then-

Pockets. The only thing Ash had in her pocket was that little parcel Dr Walker had given her, the one with the vials and the…the…pile of junk jewellery.

Ash shot up much, much higher until the woman below her was the size of a doll, then with shaking hands pulled out the little velvet bag. It was hard work too, since she still held the sabre.

Inside the bag was the partly full flight vial, as well as three or four other things she'd taken for junk. There was a black thing the shape of a tiny hourglass, a string of little blue beads…and a little silver rock the size of her thumbnail. She could feel the alter-power buzzing off it even from here.

"Oh, Deias," Ash moaned. "Oh, Deias…I've had it all along."

Poor, stupid Dr Walker, telling her to find something that he'd had in his possession. Poor stupid *her*.

Ash carefully put all the objects back in the bag, all except for the Stone. She held that tightly in one hand, wondering what to do with it. Funny that it didn't really feel like much now she held it, but still, it was what everyone had been searching for.

Just then the sound of thunder filled the air. Somehow while Ash had been distracted, thick grey clouds had covered the sky. They were moving over Iversley at a phenomenal speed, coming right towards her, and bright flashes of lightning lit up their midst.

That didn't look good, and it didn't look natural.

There was a light touch on Ash's back, and she glanced over her shoulder to see the Noble was right there behind her, smiling a vindictively evil smile.

Ash screamed and dropped the stone.

It plummeted towards the forest hundreds of metres below, and within moments Ash couldn't even see it anymore. She lunged after it, but the Noble was there first, diving through the air faster than seemed humanly possible. But she wasn't human, was she?

One moment Ash was shooting downwards at full speed, trying to catch the other woman in what seemed like the biggest lost cause ever, and the next, bright light filled her vision and thunder echoed in her ears.

She stopped flying and spun in the air, stunned. Her whole body tingled and ached.

"Ow..."

She'd been struck by lightning.

❧❦❧

By the Rood, they were catching up. Anne ran through the forest as fast as her legs and borrowed garb would allow, dodging tree roots and rocks and the occasional hidden pothole, but 'twas not enough. They were faster, and she could hear their footsteps and even their whispered voices.

Her pursuers spoke to each other, but their voices echoed quietly through the air. One of them seemed to resonate through her very skin, sending up a chill every time he spoke. He wanted to kill her. She could see her own death in the next few seconds...

"Left. Keep up speed, she's tiring."

The other one didn't respond, but she knew that he must be following. Desperately Anne ducked behind a good-sized stand of trees, pulling her long, narrow skirt into her sides and pressing up against the trunk. She just needed them to carry on past her. Please, please, carry on past her.

Suddenly a white light shone, as bright as a thousand full moons. It shone right through the trees and everywhere around her, leaving flashing spots across her vision even though she squeezed her eyes tightly shut.

"There she is."

Anne gasped and started running again, still blinking away those spots. She came out onto a steep, open slope with no trees and only loose leaves scattered about. Nowhere to hide, and certainly not from someone who could see through solid objects as this one could.

"I see her, Master Mortimer. She will make a fitting sacrifice to your greatness."

'Twas the servant, and his words made Anne's heart just about leap out of her chest in fear, but she didn't dare turn around to see how close her pursuers were.

Was her end to come so harshly and quickly, and at the hands of such as these? There was nowhere to hide but the occasional flax bush, and 'twould be a waste of time. She may as well give herself up now rather than hide there-

Hide in the bush, someone whispered. *I'll cover you.*

Anne's heart leaped again. This voice was different from her pursuers, but she'd heard all kinds of voices, in her mind and out, to simply accept that this one was trustworthy. *Why should I trust you?*

Why trust anyone? The whole earth isn't full of people who want to harm you, Anne of Covington. There are those who would help too.

An image of Anne's half-sister Elspeth flicked into her mind. The girl's colouring followed her own mother, green eyes and dark hair, but her features were very similar to Anne's. She trusted Anne implicitly, which was why Anne had to return. Because she cared for the girl, and Elspeth needed her.

Exactly.

But the owner of the voice didn't even know Anne! Why should they care for her?

And right then, when she hardly had the emotional strength to consider such a thought, Anne tripped. She tripped over a rock and over her stupid narrow skirt, and fell face-first into a good-sized flax bush.

Hide, the voice said again. *I'll cover you.*

And because Anne could hear her pursuers right behind her, hear their breath in her ears, she obeyed.

Several seconds passed where she hunched in the sparse greenery, her hands wrapped around her knees and her whole body tense from fear. She could still hear them. It sounded like they'd been right on her heels the whole time, but no one came into sight.

How odd. Surely she hadn't imagined her pursuers…?

It's how he uses his power, Anne. He makes you desperate with fear, when in truth the danger's not what you think.

So she wasn't being pursued?

I didn't say that. Don't move!

Anne froze, and that was when the first man came into view. He was human, pale-skinned compared to the other locals she'd seen, and with dark hair rather like Ash's. Forgettable. Anne couldn't have even said what he was wearing, because then the second man came into view.

This one wasn't any taller than the first, and no more elaborately dressed. In fact, he was plainly clothed in grey, brown and black that wouldn't have been out of place on a peasant in Anne's own time, and he wore his light brown hair in a queue at the back of his neck.

But what made him unforgettable was his cold, grey eyes and the sense of power and *evil* that emanated from him. He carried a curved dagger in one hand, its grey hilt studded with black gems.

This one must be the Noble. *Master Mortimer*, the first man had called him. But he'd have to be blind not to see her here, crouched awkwardly behind the straggling flax bush. She could see them, so how could they miss her red hair and blue garb?

Don't move, the voice warned her again quietly. *Trust me.*

So Anne didn't move. 'Twas less about trust and more about intense, crippling fear, but she didn't move an inch, not even when the Noble walked right past her hiding place, then turned and walked back again.

"I thought I saw her here," the human servant said in confusion. His voice wasn't nearly so terrifying now, and Anne realised that for the first time she was hearing it in truth. Those dreadful whispers had been as false as Souris's serpents.

The Noble stopped in front of the flax bush, looking around him with narrowed eyes. Then he raised one hand in front of his face. For a moment it glowed red, then white, and the whole clearing filled with that bright, bright light once more.

It shone right through the long leaves of the flax bush and into Anne's eyes, but this time she kept them open. She stared at the Noble even through that painfully intense light, and he stared right back at her.

Trust me, the voice said again. *Be silent.*

It took all Anne's strength not to move, not to even squeak in fear, but she did it. And several long seconds went by, and finally the Noble shook his head. Not in disagreement: more in the way Anne's late husband's hounds would when they were confused or had lost interest.

"We've missed her," the Noble said instead. He sounded displeased, but the expression on his face hadn't changed at all. "Carry on north-east."

They left, and several more minutes passed where Anne wasn't able to move. She sat in that flax bush, waiting for them to return, to say it had all been a game and yes, they were indeed going to kill her, but they never returned. 'Twas only her, all alone in the forest, and the invisible presence of someone who felt a lot like a friend.

"'Twas illusion that I thought them so close," she said aloud, very quietly. "But they would have killed me in truth."

Yes.

But she didn't drink the water. She shouldn't have been fooled by such weak magicks-

Not so weak anymore. The Queen's been sharing her power.

Truly? She hadn't seemed the kind to share.

She's not, and the sharing wasn't on purpose. But this area has become far more dangerous for you, and for everyone. Power that was merely illusion has become truth, and weak illusion has become strong.

Anne felt a chill up her spine. "Is that how you speak to me? Because you have gained power from the Queen?"

The invisible presence seemed to laugh. *I don't need her power. But if you wish for a safe place, I can help you.*

"Where?"

The voice told her, and she just sat in silence for a few moments. "'Tis a jest, yes?"

They just laughed again. *You wait and see, Anne. You wait and see.*

Finally the light receded and Ash's ears stopped ringing. She was hovering in the air far above the forest. Above her the sky was blue with the occasional cloud, and below her the forest was green and lush.

There was no sign of the storm, no sign of the Noble, and no pain from the lightning strike, and Ash was baffled as to what had just happened. She'd almost say it was illusion, but she hadn't been drinking the water. The Nobles couldn't have that power over her from such a height, surely?

'Nobles can't fly', she remembered someone saying. Well, they'd been wrong.

Then she remembered what she'd just done.

"Oh my Deias," she moaned again. "I've lost the Eternity Stone!"

She'd dropped it like a big brunette *idiot*, because who held something of such value *in their hand* from such a height? An idiot, that was who! And now the Noble was gone, and there was no doubt she'd have the Stone and whatever power went with it.

There went Ash's bargaining chip.

"Well," she said to herself pathetically. "Maybe they'll stop trying to kill me now."

Or maybe not, because they hadn't been that friendly. And there was still poor Anne…

Far-sight kicked in again, sending a sudden stream of images into her mind. Ash *searched the forest for Anne and finally found her, hunched inside a flax bush. 'That's a terrible hiding place,' Ash told her, but the girl shrugged. 'Worked well enough.' Ash told her about the Stone being lost, and they argued a while, trying to work out their next move. But then the Nobles came. They weren't like anything Ash had seen before, and they had no mercy…*

Aaaaaaaaaaaarrrghhh. Forget the Eternity Stone – it was time to move.

"I was right," Ash said a few minutes later when she finally found Anne, not very well hidden in a large bunch of flax. "That *is* a terrible hiding place."

Anne gaped at her, then shrugged. "Worked well enough. Did you just fly?"

"Yes, but-"

"Verily, how marvellous! I-" And the girl would have launched into that spiel as far-sight warned, but Ash cut her off.

"We'll talk about it later. We don't have time to talk now, because we need to escape. There are others coming for us."

"Oh." Anne's shoulders slumped. "We do not have time to talk about my wonderful, miraculous escape, then."

"No." And Ash had already grabbed the girl's arm, pulling her along in the opposite direction from where the Nobles would be coming. It was a shame Ash wasn't stronger, or she'd carry Anne.

Anne struggled to keep up, but she didn't stop chattering. "And I suppose we shan't have time to speak of your miraculous flight, either…"

Ash looked for the best direction to head in. Uphill, perhaps, might lead them away faster. "No."

"Oh. 'Tis a shame. And 'tis a shame I cannot fly either, because that would *truly* be helpful right now."

Ash stopped so suddenly that Anne ran into the back of her leg, kicking her Achilles heel painfully. "I'm so stupid!"

"Do not be hard on yourself. I think you've done remarkably well considering."

Gee, thanks Anne. "That wasn't what I meant." Pulling out that little black bag once more, Ash held up the little round vial she'd only half-finished. Its contents gleamed gold in the sunlight. "You can fly, Anne. But for it to work, you need to believe that you can." Just like pixie dust or digital currency.

The redhead perked up like a dog hearing the word 'walk'. "I do believe!"

"Really?"

"Of course! I saw you fly, didn't I?"

Anne stuck her hand out for the vial, and Ash handed it over almost reluctantly. It had taken Ash so much time to come to terms with the anti-gravity thing, it didn't seem fair Anne could take to it so fast.

The other girl took the vial, then spread out her arms, scrunching her eyes shut. "I believe I can fly!"

Ash bit back a smile. "Um…you need to drink it first."

"Oh." Anne scowled at her, then pulled off the cap and took a swig.

"It might take a while to get used to the idea," Ash said nervously. If this didn't work then she didn't know what she'd do. Try to carry the girl, maybe; but she didn't like that idea. Anne was small but sturdy. "Like I said, you'll need to-"

"Beliiieeeeeeve!" Anne shot up into the air like a small, redheaded rocket, dropping the vial as she did so.

Ash's jaw dropped, then she sighed, shaking her head in amused disbelief. She picked up the vial and followed Anne into the air.

THE NEW PANTHEON

Some time later when they'd reached a safe distance (and Anne had recovered from the initial thrill of flying and was no longer laughing like a loon) they settled on a hilltop. It was far enough away that they could barely even see Iversley anymore; just a little distant green spot.

"I confess I'm disappointed we didn't grow wings," Anne admitted. "I'd thought it lovely to resemble a celestial, do you not agree?"

"Have you ever owned birds?" Ash retorted. "They flap their wings and feathers get all over the place. If you had wings, you'd leave a trail of fluff everywhere you went. And how would you get dressed with those things sticking out of your back?"

"'Twould be worth it to be so beautiful," Anne said staunchly. "But still, does it not seem to you odd that we have the power to fly, but our bodies seem not at all intended for it?" Ash would have responded, but then the girl continued, "Mayhap true power is about doing those things that nature would call impossible, so we know it's not us that does them, but the power within us."

"Wow, that's deep, Anne."

She nodded modestly. "I know."

They each recounted what had happened since they'd last separated, and Ash described how the Noble's illusion had been enough to make her drop the Eternity Stone. "And it felt so real," she marvelled. "The Queen had that kind of influence, but only when we were face to face since we didn't drink the water. I could swear I hadn't had any water, unless that coffee Georgiana gave me this morning wasn't properly purified-"

"'Twas not your coffee; 'twas something else." And then Anne told her about the little voice that had hidden her from her pursuers, and how the Queen had been 'sharing' her power.

"Hmm. I wonder why that happened." And it seemed that 'the voice' had been speaking to more than just Ash herself, although there wasn't time to speak about it now.

Anne shrugged. "As do I, but we have greater troubles. This small Noble you described, the one who now has the Stone, sounds just like Souris."

Ash's eyebrows shot up. "I thought she was useless except for illusion."

"Most of them are. Were, I mean. But it seems that now their power is real."

"Yeah." Ash thought again of that Noble with the burning hands, who Anne had just escaped from and who probably had pretended to be George. Poor George, who if he wasn't crazy now, might even be dead. "Hades, I wonder why the Queen keeps them around. Some of them are real a-holes."

"Ladies do not say that word," Anne said primly. "But I must agree."

"You don't even know what that means."

"Your tone tells me it is something impolite. Is that not correct?"

It was, of course. Ash scratched at her arm irritably, then winced at the sharp pain. She'd really been hurt, but hadn't even realised until that moment.

"By the Rood, Ash. Is that your own blood?"

Ash looked down at her shoulder. It was soaked in dried blood and looked rather gruesome, although it mustn't be too deep if it had healed so quickly. "It's not as bad as it looks. Besides, I did worse to them." She tapped her sabre knowingly.

"Mm."

"What's that supposed to mean?"

Anne gave her a knowing look. "You are aware that when someone is killed, they do not customarily disappear into smoke?"

And what you would know all about that, Ash was about to say, then remembered that Anne's husband had been executed. Ash didn't know if the girl had seen it, but back then had been a different, bloodier time. "Yes, I did know that."

"So…where did they go?"

"I don't know," Ash admitted. She sighed heavily, looking out over the green landscape before them. There were large swathes of darker forest right around them, and light green grassy lawns, and patchworks of fields in the distance. But then Islo had said that not everyone grew their food underground.

"This place looks very different from when I lived here," Anne noted, looking at the same scene. "'Twas quite flat, and with much less forest and more fields."

Ash sighed again, thinking once more of Dr Walker's words about the area being flattened and lifeless within two years. "And we've only got two days to sort it out," she muttered.

"Why two days?"

Ash explained how that was the longest they'd be able to fly, and the redhead's eyes widened in understanding. "So that was why he said it."

"He?"

"My invisible friend." Anne frowned. "I know not why I thought him male, just that he seemed so. But he said that we could visit him in the next day or so, and we'd find safety."

"Oh?" Ash hadn't been so blessed, even though she'd *begged* for help. Even so, if there was a way out of here, she'd take it. "And where does he live?"

There was a pause, and then Anne raised her hand, pointing one finger upwards.

Ash looked up reflexively, but of course there was nothing

above them except blue and white. "Are you saying he lives in the sky? Or just a very high mountain?" Not that Angland *had* any very high mountains, not even after whatever war had carved up this landscape.

"He said to follow the birds upwards." Unsurprisingly Anne sounded a little defensive. "I do not jest."

"I believe you. Except-"

Several moments went by and Ash still didn't finish her sentence. Instead she froze with her mouth half-open, rather like the local half-wit back home. It hadn't been his fault as he'd been kicked in the head by a horse, but Ash didn't have any such excuse.

"Are you quite alright?" Anne asked.

"Far-sight," Ash said with eyebrows raised. "Whew. That's a good one."

Anne tried to recall what far-sight was, then remembered. Some form of prophecy, it appeared, and one that made the user look rather silly. "What did you see?"

Ash just shook her head. "You're just going to have to watch this one for yourself." She pointed down into the valley, into the thick mass of trees below them. The upper town of Iversley was at the other end of the valley, and past that was the cliff they'd climbed down that first day, and the forest where the under-ground room was.

"I cannot see anything."

"Just wait," Ash said, scrunching up her face as though expecting a blow. "It'll happen."

It? Anne would have asked what the girl meant, but then she felt it wash over her: a buzz, like vibration and heat and *potential* all at the same time.

"What was that?" she gasped, rubbing her goose-pimpled

arms.

"Power spill. You know how you said the Queen was sharing her power?"

'Twas not Anne that had said it, but the invisible friend. Nevertheless… "Yes…?"

Ash gestured down before her. "She's sharing even more. Who knew she had it in her."

Then Anne saw movement in the distant trees below, and suddenly a human head and then shoulders and torso burst through the canopy. The man - for that was what 'twas - grew and grew until he was twice as high as the tallest trees, and bigger by far than the largest Nobles Anne had seen. The enormous man's skin colour changed from warm brown to darkest blue, sprinkled with gold, and then he threw up his arms, sending gusts of wind and cloud swirling around him in a roaring maelstrom of sound.

Anne's jaw dropped, but Ash just looked resigned. "Looks like a weather god, right? But wait; there's more."

Anne crossed herself, briefly forgetting she was in fact Protestor.

Then another giant shot up through the trees, like the first, bigger than any Anne had seen before. 'Twas a beautiful young man with golden skin and hair, and eyes that burned like red hot coals. He looked like the sun made flesh.

"Should we be concerned about this?" Anne asked warily. It seemed most dreadful to her, but Ash had barely responded. "The Queen-"

"Is on her way," Ash said, scrunching up her face again. But this time it looked as though she was trying not to weep. "I suppose this is how the world ends. This lot destroys it."

Anne wanted to weep with her. "'Tis just the two. Surely they can't do that much damage."

But more and more giants were appearing, colossal in size and bursting with power. A vast woman stretched her arms out, and dozens, then hundreds of woodland animals spilled out into the forest below.

"Goddess of the hunt," Ash murmured. "I wonder if those are real animals."

The new giants were staring at their glorious selves in wonder, and testing their powers without caution. Then the sun giant turned a blast of his fire onto the weather giant, who roared and threw an answering lightning bolt. The others watched with interest as the fight unfolded.

Anne was more terrified than fascinated. "What did you mean before, about the world ending?"

"Just being dramatic." Ash paused. "But there'll be no life here, and it'll reach so far that even a comm unit couldn't pick up a signal. So I suppose it's an end for Iversley."

"All those people." And although Anne had liked very few of them, her heart felt like it was going to break. "And George. Poor George."

At that moment, as if to confirm Ash's prediction, the earth shook. The two girls lifted up into the air to avoid being knocked loose by the tremors, and even the giants looked disturbed.

Streams of birds burst from the forest canopy, heading straight up into the sky. Not just one flock, but hundreds, as if every single flying creature in that entire wood was now escaping in that one direction, up into the clouded sky.

"Follow the birds," Ash murmured under her breath. "Anne, are you afraid of heights?"

"How should I know?" Before today she'd never been higher than the towers of Renwick Castle.

"You're about to find out. Let's go."

Anne didn't think twice. She nodded, and the two of them headed upwards into the clouds, leaving the trembling ground far behind.

They flew as fast as they could after the flocks of birds that were fleeing into the first layer of fat, fluffy clouds. The girls followed them through the damp fog, gaining on the flocks until they drew alongside. The birds paid no attention to these strange new creatures. They just flew frantically upwards in that one direction.

A few minutes later, Ash saw why.

"Look up there!" Anne pointed.

In the distance above them was a little house. It had four wooden walls, windows and a small porch: plain but with a nice homelike feel to it.

The problem with it, in Ash's opinion, was not the décor. It was that the house wasn't attached to anything. It just sat comfortably alone in the air, high above the clouds.

"It's got to be an illusion," Ash said in disbelief. To be so high up here, so high that even she wouldn't look down for fear of wetting herself, and without any form of motor or structure?

Despite whatever chaos went on far beneath them, the atmosphere up here was still and quiet, and cold. The house didn't look scary as such, but she was hesitant to go in somewhere that apparently defied physics.

They also didn't know who was in there. What sort of person lived in a house miles above anything solid? It could have been a particularly freakish Noble, or *anything*. The gingerbread house of folklore was brought unpleasantly to mind.

"Why must it be an illusion?"

"Because..." Ash waved her hand expansively. "Look at the birds!"

The birds were flying in droves up to the house and disappearing under its overhanging eaves, but the space only looked big enough for a few. They were either packed in like sardines, or there was a back exit that the girls hadn't yet noticed.

"Sometimes things do not make sense," Anne said, moving closer to rest on the porch. "It does not mean they are false. You may do as you wish, but *I* will go inside. After all, I had an invitation."

Hades, so she had, if you could count mental messages from unseen people.

"Or," Anne added, "you might wait outside on the porch until your ability to fly runs out. Those appear to be your options."

Ash came to rest beside her on the porch. "Just give me a moment to use far-sight, will you-"

Too slow. The other girl had already reached up and knocked sharply on the front door. It swung open, and Anne dashed inside.

"Hades," Ash muttered, then ran after her.

She found herself inside a large, warm lounge room. Strangely, it appeared larger inside than out, and she could see several doorways leading into other rooms.

A fire flickered in a grate, and four fat armchairs were arranged in front in a comfortable huddle. Anne was currently embracing the occupant of one. Then she pulled away, and Ash saw who it was.

George stood, having accepted Anne's embrace a little awkwardly, and when he saw Ash he gave a hesitant smile. There was no hint of guilt or that same mocking spirit that he'd had before, and she noticed one other thing.

"Your eyes aren't grey," she said. "They're blue. Quite blue."

⚜

George stared at Ashlea in surprise. He'd not seen her in what felt like an eternity, and even longer since he'd been in his right mind. A comment on his eye colour wasn't what he'd expected. "Indeed they are," he replied politely. "And yours are …?"

"Hazel," she said with a wry smile. "Or close enough to it." She raised a hand to touch her neck gingerly, and he realised that these two must have faced as much difficulty as he had. There were dark brown stains on Ashlea's clothing that might have been blood, and perhaps a bloody handprint on her neck, because how could such a shape be created otherwise? "George, I'm glad you're not dead."

"I'm glad I'm not dead too," he agreed, still staring at that bright red handprint. It almost looked like a brand. "And that you are not dead, also. If I might be so bold…what *is* that on your neck?"

"You don't know?"

"Of course he doesn't know," Lady Anne said staunchly. "Did we not agree that 'twas most likely the Noble Mortimer in disguise?"

"We did," Ashlea replied, but she was still staring at him from that distance, and there was wariness in her eyes. "As I said, I'm glad you're not dead…if you're even you. I've had a lot of run-ins with people who are *very* good at disguises, so I'm going to need you to prove it."

"Prove…?"

"Your identity," she elaborated. He took a step towards her, and she very deliberately stepped back. "Now, please."

"Oh." George was at a loss. "What do you require? I am the honourable George Seymour, son of the sixth Viscount Morley, brother of the seventh. I was thrown by a horse named Star, was assaulted by you with some form of burning liquid, and then slept on the floor in an odd little room full of moving pictures. My brother's descendants apparently spend too much time in the sun, and they've given up their title in order to please a time-traveller with more power than she knows what to do with. I-"

Ashlea had been relaxing as he'd spoken, particularly when he'd mentioned that horrible toxic-spray, but she tensed up at that last sentence. "You're calling the Queen a time-traveller? What do you know about that?"

"She told us she was a time-traveller. When we met her yesterday morning, do you not recall?"

"But last I heard, *you* were over the moon about her. You wanted to obey her every whim!"

"I…" George didn't know what to say, not without spilling out the whole sordid story. And while his host had been so, so kind, he still felt rather dumbstruck that it had happened at all.

Right at that moment his host walked into the room holding a plate of lightly steaming scones. "Of course he did," the man said kindly, "but he could hardly help himself. Now perhaps you might give poor George a rest, and direct your questions to me?"

"Ah…"

"And have a scone," the man added. "They're really quite good, if I might say so myself."

Ashlea still looked uncertain, but Lady Anne stepped forward. "I know who you are," she announced. "You saved my life today."

"Perhaps," their host allowed. "But only because you chose to listen to me. Not everyone listens."

He set the plate on the small table between the armchairs, and George waited for the girls to sit before seating himself again. Only Ashlea was still standing there with that same expression on her face, like she wanted to relax, but couldn't trust her surroundings. He'd not known her long, but even back in her men's garb she'd not looked so exhausted and bedraggled. And was that a *sword* at her side?

"I don't even know who you are," she said finally, speaking to their host.

The owner of the house was a kind looking man in his sixties, small and slim, and of indeterminate ethnic background. He was brown-skinned, his hairline was less receding than non-existent, and his black eyes twinkled warmly from a comfortably wrinkled face.

But the most distinctive thing about him, the thing that George would always remember when he thought of this man, was his smile. It transformed his face in such a way that one couldn't help smiling back. He always seemed so pleased to see people, and was no different now with Ashlea and Lady Anne.

"I'm known by many names, my dear," their host answered Ashlea, "and I'm not least your friend, but you may call me Amaranthus. This is my home, and I am so very glad you made it."

"Oh." There was a pause. "Thank you." Finally Ashlea looked at George, still standing in front of his own armchair. "Why are you still standing?"

"He's waiting for you to sit down," Lady Anne said. "Make haste, I'm *starving*."

Finally they were all seated, and Amaranthus busied himself pouring tea. Ashlea kept looking between him and George, and didn't touch her drink.

"It's not like the water we drank back in Iversley," George explained. "It won't harm you."

"*I* never drank anything down there," Lady Anne said knowingly. "Neither did Ash."

"You didn't?" George looked down at his lap, trying to sort out those confused memories into something that made sense. "In truth, I remember little beyond arriving at the hospital. Ospitil. What happened to the two of you?"

There was a long silence, then Lady Anne said, "*Now* do we have time to talk about my miraculous escape from death most horrid?"

Apparently they did, because she launched into a vivid and dramatic tale of being taken captive by an underwhelming Noble, spending the night in an imaginary snake pit, meeting another of George's relatives…and yes, narrowly escaping death.

Oh, and apparently she could fly now.

Ash nodded at George's querying glance. "It's true."

"Oh." In spite of everything he'd experienced today, he felt a sudden sense of envy. They could *fly*? "I must say my day hasn't been half as interesting as yours." He frowned. "A little more insane, perhaps, but that couldn't be avoided."

❧❦❧

Ash watched with a hint of suspicion as George sipped at his tea – from what looked like Anglish china, if that was possible to find here. The boy sitting in the chair seemed so much like the George she'd first met, right down to the rumpled blondish hair and the snooty accent.

Come to think of it, his voice had been different when he'd attacked her. When the *lookalike* had attacked her, she meant.

And while she mostly believed that this was the real George, and while she would *love* to believe that this little house was really a place of safety and this little smiling man with the long name was really as kind as he seemed, she'd been burned too much to just accept. (Both literally and metaphorically).

"So tell us about your day, George. Where *did* you go?"

Ash could see him debating how to answer. He wouldn't want to make himself look bad, surely.

"Out of my head," he replied finally. "And almost out of a window, right up until Amaranthus stepped in."

Then George told them about how he'd begun having intense melancholic thoughts right after the first meal with Georgiana and Teron, and how he was reminded of everything that had gone wrong in his life. "Right down to Clarissa," he said, and then blushed from the collar upwards. Ash didn't push, but Anne felt no such restraint.

"Who is Clarissa?"

His fiancée, as George explained, or at least until his father threatened to cut him off (money, not body parts) if they didn't break up, the girl apparently not aristocratic enough for the son of a viscount. Clarissa hadn't liked the idea of being poor, so had broken it off anyway.

George was proud enough that he'd walked away from the family regardless and had tried to go it alone in business. He told the story as though it were a year or two ago, so Ash guessed he would have been no more than eighteen. Young to consider marriage, and young to go into business.

Too young, as he said, or without the wise advice that anyone needed. He'd put all his eggs in one basket – goods in one ship, the Proserpine – which had been thoughtless enough to sink, killing almost everyone on board.

"It wasn't your fault, George," Amaranthus assured him. "It was the storm, not your goods."

George nodded, and it seemed like it was something he'd been assuring himself of lately. Clearly he carried a lot of guilt over that, and the Queen had used it. She'd got a hook in, speaking into his mind and making sure to send in lots of happy feelings as she did so. And since he'd drunk the tainted water, by the time they all 'met' the Queen through the mirror, he'd been well and truly caught.

"I don't really understand what happened after that," he said thoughtfully. "It's like remembering a dream well after you've woken and when the images have faded. I remember confusion, and some horrible images, and perhaps an argument with both of you…or Anne alone, perhaps. I saw things…"

❦

George had seen things, alright; before their host had come and saved him from stepping out the window and becoming a gentleman-shaped pancake. Things that led to madness, but he couldn't shake the feeling that they were real, in some realm, somewhere.

He'd seen a giant spotted cat sitting on a throne of skulls, and a beautiful/horrible white creature with vast wings like a butterfly, and a whole realm of not-real beings that were trapped behind a barrier like glass, and couldn't reach through.

But they burned to come through, burned to reach him, and they had thread-like tentacles shooting off in every direction, reaching into so many places, but by some miracle not touching him. *Namesake*, they said, and he knew that whatever the Queen had created, she hadn't come up with the idea by herself.

He'd seen a tapestry as big as a country, all in shades of black and white; and a thousand crystal coffins standing upright and with those inside *breathing*, and a little…tiny…

✺

"Eternity Stone," George said suddenly. "I saw a powerful object called the Eternity Stone, right before Amaranthus came and brought me here. I think someone was looking for it, or did I imagine that too?"

Ash's heart sank. "It's a real thing."

"Ash lost it," Anne said, daintily putting down the rest of her scone. She hadn't waited to eat, Ash saw. "She was startled into dropping it. Souris has it now."

"Oh." George's face fell.

"I'm sorry," Ash said guiltily, "but I didn't know what it was. I was completely out of my depth with it, and she made me think she was right behind me-"

"Souris doesn't have the Stone," Amaranthus cut in. They all looked at him in surprise, but he busied himself with spreading some brown paste on a cut scone. "You really should try the fig and apricot jam, Ash. It has the figgy taste but without the seeds. I do believe you'd like it."

He was probably right since Ash *did* like the taste of figs but couldn't stand the texture, but that wasn't the point. "What do you mean? I saw it drop; I saw her chase it before she hit me with lightning. By the time I could take anything in, she was long gone."

"I'm sure you saw something drop. But I am even more certain that the Eternity Stone is in this room. It arrived along with the two of you. I would ask if you could sense it, but I see that you can't if you don't know what to look for. It's a kind of buzz, sounds like music heard from a great distance, and it distorts the air a little. Like a heat wave, only very small."

"But Ash told us that Souris chased it," Anne pointed out, saying exactly what Ash was thinking. "Why would she chase it if 'twas not the right one?"

"Because she didn't know what it looked like. Her leader wasn't one to share her power." Amaranthus shrugged, smiling slyly. "Until recently, that was, and the Eternity Stone is the greatest power of them all."

Deias, that news was almost too good to be true. Two seconds later Ash had pulled out that little black bag once more and was frantically emptying its contents onto the table.

There was the little round vial that still had a little liquid in it, a funny black hourglass thing the size of her little finger, and a short string of blue beads.

"There's nothing here," she said in intense disappointment. "Just the same junk."

Amaranthus gave her a knowing look, and reached out as though to touch the black thing. "Are you really so obtuse, Ash?"

That was the Eternity Stone? A little black hourglass with what Ash could now see was a string of beads attached to one end. It looked like a booby prize from a Christmas cracker.

She reached out to touch it and suddenly the scene changed.

Ash was standing in an enormous round room, as big as a soccer field and all bright white. She couldn't really see the floor or the ceiling, although she could see it was there. But she couldn't see anything except this vast grey patterned *thing* running all the way around the room, and saw no one else except for a little man, right over the other side of the room.

It was Amaranthus. He waved at her, and suddenly she was standing beside him, although she hadn't meant to move.

Maybe Ash should have been bothered by the sudden change, but there was something about the room and about Amaranthus that made it hard to get upset.

Besides, close up she could see that the grey thing wasn't grey at all. It was some kind of fabric, a tapestry; and it was black and white only. The tiny threads and the distance had just made it seem grey.

The questions *why am I here?* and *what are you doing?* warred in Ash's mind, and she ended up saying, "Why am I doing? Argh! I meant-"

Amaranthus laughed. "I know what you meant. What I am doing is keeping track, and why you are here…well, you touched the Eternity Stone, and I took advantage of that to bring you here in the space in between seconds."

Ash glanced down at her hand and saw at the tip of one finger a faint black shadow with the hum of power coming from it that she'd not even noticed until now. "That hasn't answered my question. What is the Eternity Stone?"

He told her.

"Oh," Ash said blankly. "That's why the Queen wants it, then."

"Why everyone wants it," he agreed. "Those who live in your realm, that is. Those who live in the Other have no need of such things."

"Is that where we are?" Ash whispered, suddenly in awe. "Not even on Earth anymore?" She looked down at the little dark shadow with a new appreciation. *It'd take her anywhere? Anytime?* And then the thing about not aging…

"In a manner of speaking," Amaranthus answered vaguely. He turned to the tapestry, which was quite frankly a mess, and touched his finger to a tiny white thread that jumped an inch or two across the fabric, centring on a spot with other black and white threads, like the centre of a spoked wheel.

A small image of a girl appeared, like one of Dr Walker's holograms. Floating text over her head read *Ashlea Jane O'Reilly*. It *was* Ash, and she looked baffled.

"You wanted to know what I was keeping track of," Amaranthus said. "It's everything. Here's you right now."

The hologram-girl's eyebrows shot up in an exact reflection of Ash's face, and text floated out from her tiny head. *Hard to believe*, it read. *Is my hair really that bad?*

Yes, it's you. No, your hair isn't bad at all, it's just curly.

"My mum always says that," Ash muttered, fascinated. "So you *have* been stalking me."

"You and everyone else," Amaranthus said cheerfully. "If you want to see it like that. I see it more as taking an interest."

Ash raised her finger to the tiny thread and followed it back to its origin an inch to the right. As she did so, the hologram image changed rapidly, growing smaller and younger until finally it was a baby, and then it disappeared. Then she moved her finger back to the left until she once more saw herself as she was now.

"Oh my Deias," she muttered. "This is my life, isn't it? This is everyone's life." And what kind of person was Amaranthus that he could do this – that he'd even *want* to do this?

Suddenly she realised that she could have a very big question finally answered. Where the thread led next…

"Or," he suggested, moving her hand away from that thread, "you could look at this one instead."

This thread was as fine as Ash's own, but was coloured black, and appeared only briefly before being lost in the mess that was the tapestry. She tapped her finger on it and a new image arose.

This was another woman, similar to Ash in colouring, but with silky dark hair rather than curls, and a classically lovely profile that Ash couldn't compete with.

Unfortunately that beauty was marred by the snarl of absolute rage on her face, and written thoughts came flying out in every direction, almost obscuring the name floating above.

Eighteen

BACK TO THE BEGINNING

$\mathcal{P}$erhaps it was a sign of the food's quality, or of their general states of mind, but they didn't immediately notice the fourth person leave.

"Where did Amaranthus go?" Lady Anne asked in surprise.

George looked, but didn't see the man anywhere. "He's done it again. He has a habit of disappearing, you see."

Ashlea didn't comment. She sat frozen with her hand stretched out towards the Eternity Stone, fingertip barely touching it, and eyes staring blankly.

"Is she quite well?" George asked Lady Anne in a hushed tone.

Anne shrugged around a mouthful of blueberry preserve. "She does that at times. I believe she must be having a prophecy, or some such thing."

"Oh. Would you like another cup of tea?"

"I won't say no."

❦

Seyen "Sashy" Johannis.

Ash stared at the text floating over the woman's head, but it didn't change. "Sashy," she said aloud. "Is that even a name?"

"It is when it's a nickname for Seyen Johannis," Amaranthus replied cheerfully. "But don't use it to her face, because she really doesn't like it."

The hologram woman was still screaming in rage, those

336

thoughts coming fragmented and fast from her tiny little head. *Let her go? How could they let her go? She doesn't know how to use the (censored) Stone…how hard can it be to kill one stupid girl…blood on the floor, on my shoes, Chaos-damn it - I'm at half-full-*

Ash jerked her finger away, and the fabric was once more just a series of twisted threads. "Urgh. That can't be…"

"Yes."

"Oh." Thoughts raced through Ash's mind, and she was glad that her own weren't written in the air as they'd been before. Only they may as well be to this man. "So why did she lie to me about…about being *me*?" she asked in a small voice. "What was the point of that? I wasn't even sure if I should believe her, and all it did was confuse me…"

"And take away your will to fight?"

"I suppose so." Ash poked at the Queen's thread again – more raging with an even redder face – then moved to her own thread, showing her in this very moment. "But why? What was the point?"

Amaranthus gently moved her hand away from the thread just as she would have followed it further to the left to find where she went next. "Well…from experience I would say because she wasn't sure what to make of you, because she wanted some kind of control, because she identified with you in some way as you're both time-travellers and perhaps you did resemble her in her youth…and because she thought it was amusing."

"I don't see how that's funny." And Ash didn't. She'd spent the last day thinking it couldn't be true, but then that it could only be true, because in some horrible, horrible ways it made sense, and why would the woman say so if it wasn't true? "What do you mean, in her youth?"

He raised an eyebrow. "She's not twenty anymore, Ash. No matter how she might look."

"Oh." The Queen had been ageless rather than young, and startlingly lovely. It had been an act, of course. According to that little recording, she had a few personality issues. "Why didn't you tell me earlier?" she asked suddenly. "You said that if I always did the right thing and never went against my conscience, then I'd never become like her. You could have told me then."

Amaranthus looked her in the eye. His were impossibly dark, and like an old-fashioned camera, she could see her reflection tiny and reversed. "Ashlea Jane, you hold one of the greatest objects of power that's ever existed. Do you really think that just because you won't become Seyen Johannis, that you can't become something equally as bad?"

"I'm not going to go around twisting peoples' minds!" Ash's voice softened. "And if you think I'm so untrustworthy, why haven't you taken away the Eternity Stone?" Her heart sank as she guessed a likely reason. "You're going to take it away, aren't you. Will you at least let us go home first?"

"I don't touch the Stone. Ever," he replied gently. "You may do whatever you wish, while the Stone is in your possession. You could go directly home from that lounge room, if you wanted."

That was true. They could go straight home and bypass the mess below them. It wasn't like Ash could do anything about that anyway, right? If all life was destroyed in Angland, it wasn't *her* Angland. Or Anne's, or George's. Or even any of their descendants.

Hades, Ash would probably go back down to the Southern Isles and have her kids there. No one would ever have to find out about what had almost happened here…

"And then what? What do I do after that?"

Amaranthus spread out his hands, palms up. "Whatever you like, Ash."

"There you are." Souris finally spotted the small silvery shape partially hidden in the bush it had fallen into. It was muddied from its hard landing, but she could sense the power coming off it.

She carefully picked it up, rubbing it clean on her shirt. "There you are, my lovely," she said again, using all the power she'd gained in the last hour to hide herself and the Stone.

And it was a lot of power. Souris had only been with the Nobles for about twenty years. She'd joined with them back in Reme, 30 BC, because she'd made a friendship of sorts with the Queen's daughter Jenessa.

They'd been calling themselves gods back then. At first Souris had believed them, since they had the power to prove it, but then she'd started to realise things didn't add up. Then finally they'd revealed the truth – they weren't gods (although hey, feel free to worship) but they were very, very powerful time-travellers who liked to *pretend* to be gods. And Souris could join them, and have a long life and little bit of power, and all she'd have to do was pledge her undying loyalty.

Well, the little bit of power just meant she was inferior to every other Noble, and as for the loyalty… If the Queen wanted the Stone so bad, she should have come and got it herself rather than letting all the Nobles and namesakes know who had it.

And because of the massive power spill (possibly related to the loss of the Stone, or maybe something else – no one was saying) everyone who already had a little power suddenly got a *lot* more.

Souris had a lot more. A huge amount, in fact, and her piddling illusions had become solid enough to be real. Real enough to fool that time-traveller, anyway.

She almost pitied her. Not only had the girl not known that she held the very item that would've given her untold power, but she'd dropped it. *Dropped* it like a big, stupid fumble-fingers.

Souris snickered in delight, ignoring the nearby flash of light. Just another former namesake throwing about their power, at least until someone managed to kill them to get it back. Now, once

Souris sorted out where she wanted to go, she'd start over. Perhaps pick up a few useful sorts to act as her servants, but she wouldn't make the Queen's mistake. The Queen had surrounded herself with so many, had invested in them and shared her power, but Souris wouldn't.

No, it would be all hers.

Except, it wasn't working. The Eternity Stone gleamed in the faint sunlight, humming with suppressed power, but it wouldn't take her anywhere. It wouldn't do *anything*.

Souris cursed under her breath, rubbing it furiously like one of those djinn lamps Freyja was so fond of. Maybe there was a password?

"Come on, stupid thing!"

Poof.

Suddenly the air was white and fragrant, and Souris was staring out through white-crusted lashes. Some kind of scented powder filled the air, and it was on *everything*.

The stone had cracked open to show a hollow centre. Underneath its hinged lid read, *You've been power-puffed!*

Chaos. It wasn't the real Stone at all.

✿

"Ash." Someone was shaking her shoulder. "Ashlea."

She looked up into George's concerned blue eyes. "What?"

He moved back, affronted. "Well, did you have one?"

"A prophecy," Anne explained from the other armchair. "When you have a foolish look on your face like that, it surely must be a prophecy. Or possibly wind, but I thought it the other."

"I don't have *wind*," Ash got out. Well, not then, anyway. "I was…"

Where *had* she been? Now it was just the three of them in the little, physics-defying room, and even the other doorways had disappeared. There was just the one exit now, the same one they'd come in by. "How long was I gone?"

"Mere seconds," Anne answered. "And you didn't *go* anywhere, you simply had an odd expression-"

"I get it, thank you," Ash cut in. She looked down to where the Eternity Stone still sat on the table between the scones and the teapot. It seemed a lot less harmless and cheap now she knew what it could do.

It had occurred to her not to believe Amaranthus when he'd told her its function, but she'd had enough of being doubtful. All it did was slow her down. "It wasn't far-sight, anyway. I was talking with Amaranthus."

"In your head?" Anne asked doubtfully.

In the space between seconds. Or a few seconds, as it had turned out. "Kind of. Not really." Ash paused. "He was telling me about the Eternity Stone and what it can do. We can use it to get home."

"Wonderful!" George exclaimed. "So it's a time-travel device?"

"Mmhm. It'll take you to any time, any place, or so Amaranthus tells me."

"Even better!" Anne cheered. "I *can* go home! Does it do anything else?"

"Yes. Apparently it stops you aging."

They all went silent, staring at the little shape on the table.

"I should take it," Anne said suddenly. "Once we're back home, I'll die soonest, anyway. Because I was born so long before you, and you keep saying how life is better for you in your own times. Don't I deserve it?"

"I think not," George cut in. "A red-haired woman who doesn't age in 1556? You'll be burned as a witch before you're forty. I'll take you both home, then I can use it to *really* make a difference in the world. I'll go back and fix my mistakes, and then start on everyone else's-"

"You can't."

Anne and George turned to stare at Ash. "And why on earth

not?" George asked mutinously.

"Amaranthus told me that we can't change the past. Because if we change the very thing that made us who we are, we'd never have the incentive to go back and change it. It's an impossible cycle. Unless you start talking about split universes and alternate timelines…and he said those are fairytales.".

"What's the bloody point in time travel, then?" Anne cried, flushing red when they looked at her in surprise. "I can say bloody. You do all the time."

Ash's heart was pounding. She'd not expected this reaction to what was meant to be good news. "Yes, but- never mind. Look, we'll use the Stone to get ourselves home, but then…"

"Then we go back to our ordinary, rather depressing lives and pretend we never had access to anything more extraordinary?" George said sarcastically. "Perhaps you wouldn't mind such mediocrity, but I won't have it."

He leaned forward and tried to snatch up the Eternity Stone, but instead knocked it off the table. Ash reached out and caught it, thinking, *Deias this is awful*, and *I don't want to fight with them*, and suddenly she wasn't in the chair anymore. She was over the other side of the room, by the exit. The other two stared at the empty space she'd been, then turned slowly to where she now stood.

"Now Ashlea," George said placatingly, "Let's not make any rushed decisions. I admit I got carried away-"

"You can't take the Stone," Ash said, knowing at that moment she was absolutely right. "I have to take it, because I already did. They told me that I did."

"Who's *they*?" Anne cried. "That makes no sense!"

But Ash didn't answer her. If Iversley's past – her future – was what she thought it was, then suddenly a whole lot of things were making sense. "I'll do it," she said instead. "Then I'll come back."

"You're not going to leave us here!" George burst out.

But Ash just shook her head. "I'm sorry. I'll explain it later."

The Eternity Stone hummed in her hand, warm and full of potential, and Ash thought of one person who'd insisted that they'd met before.

⟡

"Don't-" George cried, but Ashlea had already vanished.

He and Lady Anne looked at each other in horror.

Damn me, he thought. That hadn't gone the way he'd expected.

⟡

Iversley, 2 weeks earlier

Islo stepped inside the lift from his room down to Lower Iversley, buzzing with excitement. The new arrivals were down in the city square, and they were the most fantastic beings that he'd ever seen.

They were amazing even without their exceptional heights and supernatural powers. They called themselves 'Nobles' and said that they came in peace, or something. And their leader...wow. Just, wow. What a stunner!

The lift door slid shut, then...

Pop.

There was no sound but instead the feeling of empty space being suddenly occupied.

Islo turned slowly to his left to see another face about two inches from his own. He yelped in surprise, and the other person screamed, and then *he* screamed because quite frankly it was becoming terrifying.

The person stepped back, hands in the air. It was a girl, pale-skinned and dark-haired, and probably pretty if she hadn't looked so horrified. "I'm sorry I'm sorry I'm sorry! I thought you were someone else!"

"Who did you think I was!? And how did you get in here?!" The girl didn't answer, and Islo stared at her suspiciously. "You can't be one of *them*, because you look too ordinary. Who are you?"

"I'm Ash," the girl finally answered, and it took a few moments before he deciphered her weird accent to understand what she'd said. "And you're Islo. I didn't recognise you at first with the…" And she made a gesture over her hair and teeth.

He touched his multi-coloured forelock defensively and closed his mouth. His hair and the three diamonds in his teeth were top-fashion, not that *she* would know. That blue matching suit she was wearing was the plainest outfit he'd ever seen. "Do I know you?"

Ash stared at him with a frown. "You know, I don't think you do. But you will."

"What, are you a time-traveller?" Islo was joking, since of course time travel was both rare and illegal, but her guilty expression gave her away. "You are! Have you met me in the future? Was I really old? Did I ever become president?"

Her eyebrows shot up. "President? Of what?"

"Iversley, of course. What else?"

"I didn't know Iversley had a president."

Islo grinned. "It doesn't…yet. But I'm working on it."

"Oh, for goodness sake. You might still become president, Islo, I have no idea. I met you when you were sixteen or so, with your hair all one colour. How far away is that?"

"I'm sixteen now," he replied. What kind of time-traveller was this?

"Oh." The girl paused. "Well, you were sixteen when I met you, too. So it's got to be less than a year. Probably only a few weeks, based on what you told- will tell me."

"A few weeks?" That was disappointing. "So what's the point of it all, then? You *did* come to find me, right?" Here in a lift, on his way to see the Queen. "You know, I've got a very important appointment right now. I'm going to meet someone who's practically royalty."

"Oh my gosh," Ash said in that strange, quick accent of hers. "You're going to see the Queen of the Nobles, right? For the first time?"

"*Yesss,*" Islo replied slowly and clearly, as though speaking to a slow-poke. "I already said that."

"Actually you didn't," she muttered. "But no problem. Alright, Islo. I have a very important message for you. In fact, I came back in time to tell you. Are you ready?"

"Yes, yes, I'm ready!"

"Don't drink the water."

He waited for her to say something else, but she just looked at him expectantly.

"Was that it?" he asked. "What water?"

"The drugged water that's going to make you easily controlled by the Nobles. You need to not drink it… No, that's not right. Drink it purified or boiled only, and within a week or so you'll get an immunity and it'll stop affecting you. And then, when my friends and I show up in Upper Iversley looking centuries out of place, you need to offer us hospitality."

One, two seconds went by, and then Islo let out a deep breath. Yeah, he had a time-traveller appear straight in his lift, but unfortunately she seemed a bit unbalanced. As if he was going to ever let her in his house. "Sure. Hospitality. I'll definitely do that…but do ya mind if I get out of the lift now? I don't want to be at the back of the queue."

❧

At the back of the queue? Islo still meant to see the Queen, and Ash's heart sank as she realised her warning had been pointless. He'd still go, and he'd still get caught up in that mind control and assigned to some Noble who'd treat him like a servant…

Wasn't that what happened anyway?

Oh yeah, it did, even if just briefly before he *did* get used to the drug, but it didn't stop her being embarrassed that he thought she was crazy.

Ash stepped aside then followed him out of the lift and into Lower Iversley. The streets were different than she last remembered, busier and more colourful and with a sense of excitement that hadn't been there last time. It bubbled in the air, and she realised in surprise that it was the Queen's power. If Ash didn't know better, she'd be sucked in herself.

"Look," she said, speeding up to match Islo's longer steps. "I'll just say it once, and then I'll go away and you won't see me for a while. The Nobles, their Queen – things are going to be very different here very shortly, in a bad way. I'm going to come back in a few weeks with two friends. A guy about your age with blond hair, and a short redheaded girl in a big green dress, and we'll come from the forest-"

She hadn't thought he'd been listening at all, but he stopped suddenly enough that she almost ran into his back. "A redhead? How old?"

"What- she's sixteen, but that's not relevant-"

"I really like redheads," Islo commented, beginning to walk again. "There's something about that hair colour that's just…amazing. Does she have that really pale skin too?"

Ash curled her lip. She was about to ask him why Anne's looks mattered at all, then realised this could work in their favour. "You'd think of her as very short and pale," she replied casually. "Maybe if you don't remember anything else, you might remember to look for a tiny redhead?"

"Hmm, I might do that."

Geez. Boys. Ash bit back 'you don't have a chance with her' and instead said, "Well, that's all I've got for now. You'll see the rest of it for yourself."

"If you say so."

But then they reached the crowded city centre, and she lost his attention again. Ash could feel the warm, fizzing power that meant the Nobles were nearby. A burst of panic rose in her, but she reminded herself that while she knew what was coming next, the Queen hadn't met her yet. Probably.

"One last thing," Ash said abruptly.

Islo gave her an impatient look over his shoulder, but waited.

"Islo, you mustn't let me know we've met before, or that we had this conversation. Because I won't remember-"

"Yeah, yeah, sure."

"No, seriously, I won't know what you're talk…"

Damn it, he'd gone. He'd walked right into the crowd and left her behind.

Ash struggled for a moment between irritation and amusement, then settled on the second option. That was why Islo (in his future, in her past) had kept hinting that they'd met before, and that she'd given him instructions. Because she had.

Except he hadn't listened properly, had he? She'd specifically said *not* to make hints…

Someone shoved Ash hard from one side, and she turned on the person with a scowl. "Careful!"

It was a child in a sort of hovering car with handles like a supermarket trolley. They tootled their toy horn at her, and the parent pushing them didn't even seem to notice, instead continuing on into the crowd.

All those faces were pointed inwards, lit with the same excited anticipation. They weren't dressed how they'd been last time she was down here, either. Now instead of the monochrome vest and trouser sets, both men and women wore calf-length skirts and tights, with patterns and accessories and weird hairstyles like Islo's.

This was how the future was supposed to be…right down to the flying car, which had surprisingly pointed sides.

"Rude," Ash muttered, rubbing her shoulder where it had knocked her. Her mood had slumped even further; it was hard to be here when she knew what was just around the corner. The Nobles, wherever they were, were already planning to take over the place, and soon this city would look very different.

She slipped her hand into her pocket, patting the Eternity Stone anxiously. Now she'd done what she'd planned to do, she should probably head back to the little flying house, but didn't want to face the other two yet. Or she could just go straight home…

"Go home, miss? You just got here!"

Ash's stomach did a somersault. She knew that voice… "Sam?"

Like Islo, Sam was dressed differently than last time she'd seen him. He didn't have a sabre, for starters. Ash's hand went automatically to her hip where her own had been, but she'd left it back at Amaranthus's house.

The Sam of two weeks past grinned, auburn hair flopping over his dark brown eyes. He tossed his head to flick it back. "Have we met, miss?"

Grrrr… It wasn't fair to hate someone for something they hadn't done yet, but it was all Ash could do to not punch him in the stomach. "Uh…"

"Because you just said my name," he added helpfully. "And you were talking to yourself about heading off, when you just got here. You haven't even gone to see the Nobles yet, have you?"

Hades, she'd been thinking aloud again? "What did I say?" she asked weakly.

Sam grinned again. "Something about a flying house…?"

"Ah ha ha…my little joke."

"Except you're not joking, are you?" His tone was still friendly, but there was something knowing in his eyes, and it made Ash's smile fall flat. "You really are telling the truth. Or your version of true, anyway."

A horrible thought occurred that she wasn't the only one to time travel, but she bit it back. This Sam wasn't like the other Sam she'd met. The irritating overconfidence was the same, but he was dressed in subdued tones, with a neat black shirt. The only spot of brightness was his comm unit, which was studded with white crystals where it curved around his ear.

"Why would you think that?" she asked guardedly.

He nodded towards the crowds still moving inwards towards the unseen Nobles. "Besides the power that the giants have been throwing around? Because…I can smell a lie." At the expression on her face he threw back his head and laughed. "Oh, come on. I'm not a dog. I just meant that you're not a good liar. That's a good thing, by the way. I hate liars."

"Who doesn't?" Ash quipped. She'd got over the initial surprise of seeing him here, but with the memories of his attack fresh in her mind, she just wanted to get away. "Um…you'd be wanting to see the Queen, I suppose. I won't stop you."

"We'll go together," Sam said cheerfully, taking her arm. "You're new to the city, right? I'd remember if I'd seen you before. I always like to help out visitors. What's your name?"

Ash awkwardly tried to pull her arm away without seeming rude, but he'd got a good grip on her, pulling her around the side of the crowd. Deias, he'd done the same thing when she'd been made namesake too. Latched on and dragged her around as if he owned her, until she'd managed to get away. "Are we going the right way?"

Her diversion worked. "Just taking a shortcut. I know the direct route to the council meeting rooms, and they're meeting with the Nobles' leaders now. I can get you in to see the Queen, no problem."

Argh. Ash dug her feet in until they finally came to a stop. "I've already met the Queen," she said firmly. "I appreciate your kindness to a…a *stranger* like me, but I think she's got enough to do without seeing ordinary people twice, right?"

"You've already met her?" He was still smiling, but a hint of suspicion crept in. "What powers did she give you, then?"

Ash desperately searched her memory, trying to recall what she'd heard everyone say about the Queen's initial arrival. *Come down from the sky… Amazed everyone by throwing around power… Shared their power.* And the Queen had said that was how they made friends…

But her tattoo was gone, and she sure as Hades wasn't a namesake right now, no matter what would happen or had happened. "Um…"

"You don't have any powers, do you?" Sam said, his smile fading. "Because you've never met her. You told another fib. Come on, you can be honest."

"I did not lie," Ash said with dignity. "I *have* met the Queen, and once was enough. Besides, I can fly." Two separate statements, both true, although not as related as she made them sound.

"Prove it, then."

They'd reached a quieter area a little higher up from the city square, and now Ash could see that the crowd was actually a mass of queues all based around the red building that perhaps would become the 'palace'. Now it was functional…and busy. Two Nobles stood on either side of the doorway, and the locals were queuing to go in.

And behind Ash and Sam was a high wall which might have made up part of the building.

She lifted her chin, then lifted her arms. Up, up…and over the wall.

Goodbye, Sam.

On the other side of the wall, Ash found herself in a courtyard. It was occupied by a female Noble that Ash hadn't seen before. She was huge (as always) and dressed rather like a Viking dominatrix, leaning back against the wall with arms folded and a grin on her face.

Several men and a woman came running out the front doors. They didn't get too close to the Noble, just huddled around the doorway watching her angrily. There was a definite look of the bureaucrat about them.

"You do not have the right to be here!" one of the men shouted. "This is government property!"

The Noble smiled at them cheekily. Ash couldn't help liking her, and feeling like the bureaucrats were interfering. After all, weren't the newcomers so much better than mere humans? It was only right that they could come here...

No. She shook herself out of it. She hadn't even had a sip of water, and she was still affected by whatever alter-power was at work.

The giant reached down and touched a finger against the stone wall. It rippled like water, and a gate appeared. A gaggle of teenagers poked their heads through, wearing mischievous expressions to mirror the Noble's.

They darted through the new gate into the courtyard, ignoring the futile shouts of the people in the doorway. One of the young men lifted his hand and several flagstones lifted into the air and began whirling around madly. The bureaucrats cowered and backed up into the doorway, and the Noble laughed.

Ash didn't find it funny. She'd always hated bullies.

Then the Noble shrank down to human size, seemingly tired of playing. She pushed past the flustered bureaucrats into the building, the teenagers following behind her.

Ash waited a few moments, ensuring they hadn't seen her, then studied the courtyard, looking for an exit point where she wouldn't just run into Sam again. How did he manage to be so *annoying*?

"Hey! Hey, flying girl!"

No. It couldn't be…

But it was. Sam moved into the courtyard, a narrow gate swinging shut behind him. His eyes were fixed on her, his face bright with excitement. "Chaos, you're a dark horse," he said with a laugh. "Didn't see that one coming, did I?"

"And yet I find I don't need to impress you," Ash snapped. "If you'll excuse me-"

"You have *really* got to meet some friends of mine," Sam continued as if she hadn't spoken. He stopped right next to her and leaned into her side, his tone low and confidential. "With a power like that, you'll be unstoppable. We have the biggest plans for this city. Will you join us?"

"Us?" Ash cried. "Who is *us*? The namesakes?"

"Not namesakes," he replied, puzzled. "I don't know what those are. I meant the *rebellion*."

"The what?"

"Rebellion," he whispered. "But keep your voice down! I saw your expression when I was talking about taking you to the Queen. She's been here less than two days, but we see where this is all going. They'll take over the whole city, these giants, and then the world. People like us will be the only ones who can stop them. Your abilities will be invaluable."

Ash blinked at him for several moments, dumbfounded. Sam was talking about rebelling *against* the Queen, and he seemed entirely sincere.

What an idiot.

"You've known me less than five minutes," she said in a low, urgent tone. "Don't be so open with strangers! You need to go home, Sam. *Don't* see the Queen. Don't drink any of the town water, and *don't* join the Rebellion. Just keep to yourself, and *maybe* you won't end up..." *A crazed, murdering psychopath,* she almost said, but bit her tongue at the last moment. "End up annoying people a lot," she finished instead, taking hold of the Eternity Stone where it sat in her pocket. "Goodbye."

Pop.

Ash had thought mostly about getting away from Sam – Deias, how could one person be so contrary and annoying? – but she also had been thinking about the Queen, and feeling confused and angry about the whole situation.

So it was no surprise when she found herself jammed up in a corner of a very crowded room, people's shoulders and heads blocking her view. But something else was in there. Something shiny, and bright, and *lovely…*

"Wonderful people of Iversley," the Queen's voice rang out across the crowd, and the alter-power in that sound hit Ash almost as hard as it had that first time. *"Your hospitality has warmed my heart, and has shown me that my Nobles and I have a place amongst you. This will be my home, and you will be my people."*

Ash felt the waves of goodwill softening her, putting the same dopey smile on her face that all the others wore. But she fought it, tightening her fingers around the Stone once more. She knew she should leave, but…just a moment longer.

"Come to me, my people. Come to me one by one, and make your pledges."

Craning to see over the crowd, Ash rose just very slightly in the air until she had a view of the proceedings. There at the other end of the room stood a stunning, glowing woman, twice as tall as the crowd surrounding her. She was flanked by two men who were taller still, handsome and long-haired, in old-fashioned warrior dress.

'Sashy' had arrived.

"She's so beautiful," a woman near Ash murmured.

Ash looked her over with a critical eye. The Queen – Seyen Johannis, Ash reminded herself – was all in gold, as she had been that first morning when they'd seen her in the mirror. Golden hair, golden skin, eyes like amber flame, but unlike that morning, the long, intricately patterned gown was in bold scarlet.

From her ears hung a pair of elaborate earrings so huge that they looked like chandeliers, but it was hard to see details from over here. Ash vaguely remembered them from when she'd met the Queen in person. Honestly though, when faced with someone like her, you didn't pay much attention to anything as unimportant as jewellery.

But the Queen certainly wasn't as awe-inspiring as she had been that day. Ash looked closer and saw that the gold sat over Seyen's skin and hair like a layer of shiny cellophane. Fake, and entirely separate.

The vials must keep her safe from the full effect of the Queen's power, Ash realized. Either that, or the Eternity Stone.

Now Ash knew what to look for, she could see the power shimmering over the Queen's body like concentrated heat waves. The waves seemed to be most intense around the woman's enormous earrings, and Ash wondered if anyone else could see the shimmer of power coming off those ugly accessories.

Hades, they looked almost like bunches of grapes: irregular collections of coloured stones and shapes that didn't seem to belong together, and certainly not with the woman's gold gown. Heavy too, judging by the way they pulled at her lobes.

Ash cocked her head to the side, squinting, and the power-waves shimmered and moved like whirlpools with those earrings as the centres. She followed their shining lines down over the Queen's neck and shoulders to where the threads of power connected with the elaborate curling pattern over her gown.

Head to toe, the Queen was a patchwork of power lines. And all leading back to those earrings…

Those earrings were objects of power, all nicely bundled up in easy-carry form. Ash would bet on it. And if the Eternity Stone let the Queen bring her people across time and space, and kept them from aging, then the rest of the her power had to come from somewhere.

The Stone was warm in Ash's hand as she stared at what was surely the Queen's remaining source of power. She pondered what would happen if the woman was to lose those earrings as well.

Would that defeat her?

Just then Seyen Johannis turned and met Ash's eye all the way across the crowd. Just for a second, but it rattled Ash enough that she grabbed hold of the Eternity Stone once more.

Pop.

THE QUEEN'S EARRINGS

"I knew you'd come back," Lady Anne said staunchly for what must have been the fourth time. "'Twould not be in character for you to abandon us so, over a simple argument."

"Well, I wasn't so certain," George countered finally, then realised it sounded less like an apology on his part, and more like an insult towards Ashlea. "I beg your pardon. What I meant to say, was that my behaviour was appalling, and I thought I would deserve no less." An exaggeration, but he'd learned that when it came to apologising to women, more was better.

The taller girl let out a short laugh. "You'd have to do more than give me a hard time before I'd leave you here."

"It was the thought of all that power," he felt compelled to explain. "It simply went to my head, like being a little bit mad."

"Or mayhap how some respond to the promise of great wealth," Lady Anne added breezily. "At least we now know why Islo invited us in so promptly, and why Sam turned against you. You might have been gentler with him, Ash."

"Sam was a pain in the neck, and he tried to kill me because the Queen told him to, not because I was rude to him," Ashlea countered, then paused thoughtfully. "But probably that wouldn't have helped."

"Sam tried to kill you?!" George cried. Suddenly those brownish stains on her clothing made horrible sense. "When?"

"Earlier today, and he and his friends had swords," Lady

Anne piped in. "But surprisingly Ash managed to fight them off. Oh, and a Noble made himself look like you and also tried to kill her. Ash seems to have any number of enemies."

"Appeared to be *me*?"

They explained, and even though George knew it wasn't his fault, he still felt guilty. "My word, how dreadful. I wish that I could have been of some use."

"Are you any good at fencing?" Ashlea asked. "Because otherwise you'd be toast."

He didn't understand the reference, but he got the meaning. "I'm not so dreadful," he said lightly. He wasn't that wonderful either, but the girls didn't need to know that. "But your wounds, Ashlea. Perhaps we can find some way to bind them-"

Lady Anne was standing over Ashlea, studying her neck. "'Tis not so bad now, I trow. The handprint is rather silverish, as though it has healed somewhat. What have you been doing?"

Ashlea touched her neck in surprise. "You're right, it doesn't hurt anymore, and neither does the cut. It must have been-"

"The Eternity Stone, of course, because what else would have had such an effect?" George again felt a pang of envy that she'd been gifted it, but pushed the feeling back. She'd faced physical danger that he hadn't (except for the madness making him almost fall to his death) and the Stone had healed her. Lucky, lucky Ashlea. "Speaking of which, I was thinking very carefully while you were gone-"

"In the ten seconds I was gone, you mean?" she asked sceptically.

"It felt like a long ten seconds." And it had. He'd seen his future, and it involved either falling a vast distance or having to explain to Amaranthus how he'd lost the Stone. "As I said, I was thinking, and I came to the conclusion that while it would be wonderful to simply return home, we cannot in good conscience do so."

"I completely agree."

"Please hear me out," George persisted. "We- or you, rather, hold an object of incredible power, and down below us, some wicked people are destroying the area. We simply *must-*"

"Do something about it," Ashlea interrupted. "Yes, I already agreed."

"You did?"

"She did," Lady Anne piped in. "As do I. So we are unified, and *we* can fly, although you cannot. I'm certain that there's *something* we can do."

Both girls looked at George expectantly.

"Well, I don't have any ideas," he said. "It was only ten seconds. But I do know one thing; we mustn't use the Eternity Stone down there."

"What?" both cried out at the same time.

"Whyever not?" Lady Anne asked.

"Because of something I heard them say," George replied. "Back down when I was..."

"Insane?" Ashlea suggested.

"*Confused*. I heard someone say that the Stone must be unused, because otherwise the Queen would surely have found it by now. It must give off some kind of signal when used, do you understand? So if we use it now, then there'll be no doubt of where it is."

Ashlea let out a heavy sigh. "You must be right, because the Queen turned and looked at me. It was just for the barest moment, but I left right away. But she never noticed that I had it up here, because I never used it up 'til that point."

There was a glum silence. Perhaps it was time for plan B after all – to die dramatically and pointlessly in a dashing last hurrah.

"Although," Ashlea said slowly, "there was one thing I noticed. Have either of you ever seen the Queen's earrings...?"

Ash had a plan. 'Twas not the greatest one Anne had ever heard, but 'twas better than sitting up here and eating scones until their flying ability ran out.

"Luckily," the girl was telling George, "we didn't use up the whole vial. Here you go." She handed over the small round bottle (which Anne thought *she* had finished, but was clearly wrong) and he took it as though he was holding a live serpent. Mayhap the Honourable George Seymour wasn't entirely fond of heights...and they hadn't even left the building yet.

"Thank you." Ash turned away, and then as Anne had noticed him do before, he watched her surreptitiously.

Oh. Look at her *face*, George.

Well, he was a male after all, and if the girl insisted on wearing those dreadful skin-tight breeches and that barely-there doublet then of course he would look. Ash was no beauty – her height and sun-browned skin prevented that – but in her own way she was quite eye-catching.

Anyway, who could say what someone like Mr Seymour would find attractive? He was from almost three hundred years ahead of Anne, after all. Mayhap they liked their females tall and sun-browned and bold, and 'twas not as if George was that handsome himself.

Anne had the utmost respect for him, but in truth he was simply too roughly formed to be truly comely. Not slim and pale and elegant as were the boys she admired (with Islo as an obvious exception), but broad and brawny and also rather brown. He'd be a good match for Ash physically.

Anne giggled to herself at the thought. As if the son of a viscount would marry a peasant!

What a good jest.

George finished the vial in one sip, double-checking he'd drunk all of it. It was hard to imagine that a spoonful of sweet liquid would remove gravity's effect on him, but he wasn't going to miss a drop. "Tastes a little like honey."

"Really?" Ashlea queried. "I thought it was more like fruit. Oh, well, as long as it works. Go on, see if you can fly."

He felt a tinge of panic. He'd stood at the edge of the occasional cliff, had once even gone into the crow's nest onboard the Proserpine while it was in port, but otherwise hadn't much experience with heights. "Er…aren't you supposed to do something first? Bestow me with powers, or something?"

Ashlea quirked an eyebrow, barely hiding a smile. She had a dimple in her left cheek, which was strangely adorable, and not at all relevant to the situation. "Sure, why not." Stepping forward, she tapped him on the forehead with one finger. "I hereby bestow on thee the power of flight. Go forth and be like the eagle, George Seymour."

"You needn't be sarcastic," he mumbled. He'd felt a touch of warmth shoot through his body at the contact, but that didn't necessarily have anything to do with her words.

"I thought 'twas most poetic," Lady Anne said. He'd almost forgotten she was there. "But 'tis not the words spoken over you that make the difference, George. 'Tis what you believe, see?" She raised her arms into the air. "I believe I can fly." And then as she'd said, she floated up – right until she hit the low ceiling. "Ouch."

George sighed. If a five-foot-tall sixteen-year-old could do it, then so could he. He raised his arms, feeling a bit silly. "I believe I can fly."

Ashlea giggled, although what was so funny, he didn't know. "You have to sound like you mean it."

"I believe I can fly!" This time he raised his arms above his head, imagining he could touch the ceiling. To his surprise, a moment later his fingertips touched a hard surface.

"It actually worked the first time," Ashlea admitted. "But I just liked hearing you say that." Then she sang, "I believe I can touch the sky…"

"That's not possible," George pointed out, "as the sky is simply air, so cannot be touched."

She mumbled some nonsense like, 'Tell that to ah-kelly,' but then asked, "How do you feel?"

George glanced down at gap between the floor and his feet, and gave a startled head shake. "Fine," he replied. He felt better than fine; he felt lighter than air. It reminded him of the first time he'd gone into the local lake as a child and discovered to his surprise that he didn't sink in the water. It was like that, but infinitely better. "And you say this should last two days?"

"That's what Dr Walker said."

George nodded, looking down again at the gap between his feet and the floor. That was two feet; what was two thousand?

Two minutes later, the three of them were standing on the house's front porch, looking out over a simply astounding view. Unlike the others, he hadn't come in this way. "Please tell me that's snow."

"Oh no," Lady Anne replied cheerfully. "'Tis the clouds. Think of how high up we must be!"

"I am," George said. And that was the problem.

Anne continued, "If we were to fall from here, unable to fly, I can only imagine how damaged we would be upon landing."

He swallowed. Not helpful, Lady Anne. Not at all helpful. "Perhaps we might use the Eternity Stone after all-" he began, but she was already running right off the porch and into empty air.

"Last one down is a gross lubberwooooort!" she called as she went.

By Jove, George didn't know if the girl was flying or falling, but she was disappearing at great speed: a quickly receding patch of blue and red.

He felt a touch on his hand.

"It's funny," Ashlea commented, not meeting his eyes, "that even though I've flown so far this last day, and I *know* that I'll be able to soar right off this ledge rather than fall, it still feels like I'm contemplating suicide." She gave him a quick smile. It seemed to sit oddly on her face, then George realized that he'd hardly seen her smile since they'd met. There hadn't been a reason for it, he supposed.

"Perhaps we might commit suicide together," he said lightly. "Can't be gross lubberworts, can we?"

She stared at him in shock for a moment, then laughed outright, grabbing his hand tightly. "Let's do it!" And then she jumped right off the safety of the wooden porch, dragging him with her.

Oh Deias oh Deias oh Deias oh Deias oh Deias- George was so frightened that he couldn't make a sound. The air rushed past him on every side, and he squeezed his eyes shut and thought *I believe I can fly I believe I can fly I believe I can fly*…and then added, *I believe I can touch the sky*, as an ode to ah-kelly or whatever god would save him from a squishy, dramatic death.

"See, this isn't so bad, is it?" Ashlea shouted in his ear. "We're not even falling fast anymore, see?"

He cracked an eye open to see that she was exaggerating, and that they were about to be consumed by a giant, fluffy mass of dampness. "I say, what's this-"

A cloud. It was a cloud, and it wasn't anything to write home about. It rather reminded him of a cleaner version of Lunden's thicker fogs. However, once they were on the other side of the clouds, and the view was unobscured…

"I do believe I could enjoy this," he shouted, because they were still moving with enough speed that the words were snatched away as soon as they left his mouth. "Must we go so fast?"

"Got to catch up with Anne," Ashlea said, but she spread her arms a little and slowed, so he slowed with her.Below them was a green landscape, with hills and valleys and what must have been fields, so tiny-looking that they seemed to belong to a toy set. And those bright flashes of light and black patches, they must be tiny little explosions.

Oh, dear.

⚘

In spite of Ash's high-speed dive, she didn't catch up with Anne until they were close enough to the ground to clearly see the chaos. George came in just behind her, which would have made him a gross lubberwort, had any of them cared. As it was, they just stared at the destruction arrayed below them.

There were patches of burned forest, with colourful, incredibly enormous people fighting not-so-enormous people, and all of them throwing around iridescent bolts of power as carelessly as small boys throwing pebbles. And through it all, huge cracks widened in the shuddering ground.

It seemed to Ash that Dr Walker's idea of the world ending might have been just a misunderstanding of what had happened here – a supernaturally powered battle that had wiped out the landscape.

"Where is she?" Ash murmured, studying the scene intensely for the familiar form of the Queen. It was impossible to find anyone or anything around here, it was so chaotic. Now Ash understood why in war the two sides usually wore different colours – because a mix-up would be easy in such a situation. How many people lost their lives to friendly fire?

As they watched, an enormous piece of earth detached from the ground and rose into the air like a floating island to rest about a hundred metres up, complete with trees and dangling roots.

"Uh oh," Ash said to no one in particular. "Maybe we should split up to look for her."

"Not much good if we get lost," George retorted. "You have

the Eternity Stone."

And it went unsaid that if the others were caught without it, they'd be in trouble.

"Fifteen minutes," Ash urged. It wouldn't be her first choice either, but better than helplessly wandering around in their little huddle, unable to see or do much. "We'll split up, ask the people in the houses what they know, then meet up again."

"I doubt they know anything," Anne said, her red eyebrows set low and worried. "They're probably all curled up under their beds." Luckily for the townspeople, the giant battle wasn't actually *in* the middle of Upper Iversley, rather off in the forest.

The others were hesitant, but after a few minutes of searching for the Queen with no success, they decided to split up after all. Ash would go into the underground city, Anne to Islo's house, and George to do an aerial search.

Ash didn't really know how much she could find out in only fifteen minutes, but she'd give it a try. "One more thing."

The other two turned curiously.

"I have the Eternity Stone, as you said. But I also have far-sight. So…" Ash swallowed, wondering if she was doing the right thing, but also knowing she'd never forgive herself if something went wrong. "So I was thinking that one of you should take the Eternity Stone. Just in case you're in danger, because you won't have the warning that I have."

She took it out of her pocket, shoving it at George before she could change her mind. "See you in fifteen."

In Lower Iversley, the streets were far quieter than they should have been. It was a very different environment from when Ash had used the Eternity Stone to time travel to two weeks earlier when the Nobles had first arrived, and even more different from when the Queen had been in control.

Every now and then a random, panicked person or two would hurry past, but where they were going was a mystery.

There were no giants down here that Ash could see. Wanting to keep a low profile, she came down to rest on the ground and walked the main street, carefully checking in each side street for familiar faces.

She turned the third corner and almost ran into a familiar young man. Nargis's eyes were shadowed and his posture weary, but he jumped at the sight of her, seeming like he was tossing up between running or fighting.

Then he looked down at his empty hands, then back at her. "Are you going to kill me?"

"I wasn't planning to," Ash replied warily, although a big part of her was relieved that he was still alive. Last she'd seen him, he'd fallen off that beanstalk and disappeared in a puff of smoke. "Are you going to try to kill me again?"

He shook his head. "I don't even know why I did the first time. I'm so sorry."

The boy sounded sincere, so she decided to believe him. "You did it because your 'Queen' was making you, I suppose. I won't hold it against you, Nargis."

"Nargis? My name is Drew!"

Oh. Well, that was a *much* better name, Ash thought. "Sorry. Drew. I just…never mind. Where did you go, anyway? You disappeared after you fell."

"I don't…I don't know," he replied, his forehead furrowed in confusion. "One moment it was all I could do to kill you – sorry! – and then suddenly I woke up in the namesake meeting room, as though I'd never left. There were others there too. I don't know how we got there."

"Illusion?" she suggested.

"But I felt like I was *there* when- when we were trying to…"

"Kill me, yes, I get it."

"But I don't understand," he said in confusion. "I felt like I was going around the city as normal – until I wasn't anymore."

Ash held up her hands, palms out. "If you don't know, then I sure don't. What were you training for?"

"Um…" He looked sheepish. "Taking over Angland, I think."

Naturally. "I would hope you're not doing that anymore?"

Drew shook his head emphatically. "Just trying to find my family, and trying not to get stepped on by anyone."

It was a good goal. "Do you know where the Queen is now?"

"Above ground, I think. But…do you know what happened?" Nargis- no, *Drew* lifted his hands, his expression bewildered. "There was this buzzing sound and a whole wave of heat, and then some people turned into giants and I couldn't grow things anymore."

"There was a power spillage, but I'm surprised that yours seems to have left you."

"I don't care. I'm glad. I just want to know where my family is, and I want to get out of this alive."

"Join the club." Ash wished him luck and went to leave, but Drew called after her.

"Queen's namesake – whoever you are. Sam's gunning for you. I just thought you should know that."

"Gunning…with a gun? Or trying to kill me?"

"The second."

Ash sighed deeply. "He didn't get any extra power, did he?"

Drew's face told the story. "He's huge."

Oh, great.

Back above ground Ash moved quietly between the few houses, heading back to the place where she was to meet George and Anne. The forested floating island still hung above them, and the sound of battle filled the air.

And that was when *she saw a giant so huge he could've picked her up in one hand. It was Sam, and he'd changed: had grown a beard that waved like tentacles all around his hatred-filled face, and his teeth were sharp and vicious. He came after her…*

Uh oh. That *really* wasn't good.

Ash turned and raced down one of the side alleys, desperate for somewhere to hide. A second later she heard those giant footsteps coming towards her. She caught a glimpse of a hideous, colossal figure a moment before she shot past a stunned-looking George and Anne, both of whom had obviously just come back to the meeting place.

"Watch out for Sam!" she bellowed at them, then took off into the air. She went up and up until she was well above the buildings and had almost reached the floating island. Massive clumps of tree roots were hanging out of the base like a bunch of weeds pulled from a garden.

Giant Sam came racing after her, *STOMP STOMP STOMP*, and while she'd thought she'd be out of his reach, she hadn't counted on him being able to jump.

Ash had barely reached the bottom of the island when he leapt for her. He swiped his clawed hand so close she felt the air rush past her side, and there was no time to get higher. Scrambling for a hiding place, she pushed into the bundles of roots and messy hollows underneath the island, trying to get in deep enough that he wouldn't be able to reach her.

As if in slow motion, Sam made another leap but missed her by a body-length. He couldn't reach her.

Thank Deias, he couldn't reach her!

But then he bent down and broke off a tall spire that stuck out from the roof of a nearby house. Perhaps it had once been a receiver of some sort, but now it was a weapon. It looked like a mere stick in his hand, and with murder in his eyes he leapt once more, poking the sharp spike at her hiding place. It smashed past the tree roots, nearly impaling her, and she screamed.

"Down here, you great beast!" George yelled.

He zoomed past close to Sam's giant foot. Sam tried to stamp on him but George was too quick; then Anne flew in from the other direction, taunting him.

Sam turned away from Ash to find an easier target. Gripping

the spire tight between both hands, he stabbed it towards the ground, right at George. But George dashed aside just in time and the spire stuck right into Giant Sam's foot.

A shimmer of power burst out of the wound like air from a popped balloon, and Sam visibly began to shrink. But he didn't seem to notice. With a grunt, he pulled the spire out of his foot and kept swinging it, trying to hit George who was now hidden in the bushes, or heading back for Ash who was now far out of his reach.

Ash felt the strange floating mass of land shudder above her, and a flash of far-sight showed it falling back to the ground with a violent *boom*. She scrambled out of her hiding place, heading straight for Anne and George who were now dodging a merely twice normal-sized Sam…although the tentacle-beard had remained.

"Get out, get away!" she shouted at them. "The island's coming down!"

All three of them shot off in different directions, and the still rapidly shrinking Sam seemed at a loss for who to follow. Hatred in his eyes, he finally took a step towards Ash as over him, the falling island's shadow grew larger and darker and then…

❧

The mass of earth fell with a resounding thud, sending dust in every direction. A spray of pebbles peppered George's back – and even a good-sized rock of two.

"*Ouch.*"

"Are you alright?" Ashlea called. She landed next to him, covered in a fine film of brown dust and with her face creased in concerned lines.

"Quite alright, thank you," he managed to say. "You?"

"I'm fine, but it was a close call. I think Sam might be dead."

"You think?" Lady Anne muttered from behind him, sounding disturbingly like Ashlea. "I vow no creature who could withstand that much earth landing on their head."

She was right, of course, but Ashlea's face fell and George hastened to distract her. "We need to find the Queen, remember? Did anyone find out where?"

"I couldn't find her below-" Ashlea began, but Lady Anne interrupted, pointing.

"There's the Queen!"

And indeed, there she was, but not as George remembered her.

She now loomed above the trees in her elaborate gown, dark-haired, distinctly middle-aged, and furious. She was also wielding a huge, jagged piece of glass as she faced a dark-skinned man twice her size. He kept hitting her with conjured balls of blue fire, but she shrugged them off and attacked aggressively with what might have been a piece of an enormous window.

Dodging another fireball, she leapt under his outstretched arm and stabbed him in the neck. He staggered back, lifting a hand to the wound…then shrivelled to nothing in front of their eyes, disappearing into the forest below. A glow of escaped power left his falling body and was absorbed back into hers.

"Oh. My. Deias." Ashlea gasped the words like a prayer.

This was madness; the fight between these powerful people so violent and visceral that it made George cringe. But Amaranthus had said these new giants weren't illusions, they were real people, and the illusive powers couldn't kill them. Nothing short of actual physical attack would do that, and there were no decent weapons in sight.

In unison, the three time-travellers moved closer together where they hovered above the battlefield. The Queen looked up and saw them. Her expression twisted into a snarl, and she lifted the glass shard, pulling back her arm as if she was going to throw it at them.

She was most certainly about to throw it at them.

Eek! With the Eternity Stone still clutched in his palm, George grabbed each of the girls by one hand, scrunched his eyes shut, and thought desperately, *Take me back!* Back to somewhere where they weren't about to be decapitated by flying debris…

There was a pause as if the universe considered the request, then George thought more clearly: *Back to the start of the fight.*

Then there was a sort of…shift in the atmosphere, and he opened his eyes.

The three of them hovered in the same place they had been before, but now there were considerably more players in the battle below. Still with a huge piece of glass in her hand, the Queen was storming towards a golden young man with glowing red eyes. He, like the dark-skinned man who hadn't yet died, was far larger than her or any other Nobles George had ever seen. The size difference made the Queen look ineffectual, like a terrier attacking a Great Dane.

"She's going to kill him," Ashlea cried urgently. "Far-sight showed me. You need to get us over there now!"

George scrunched his eyes shut and did as she asked, remembering what they'd planned earlier. If only it would work…

It did work. Now they were much closer, with everything below frozen in place like a painting of an ancient battle, but this battle was unlike any before.

"What on earth did you do?" Lady Anne asked.

"What Amaranthus did with me," Ashlea replied, gripping George's hand tighter where he held the Eternity Stone. Where they *both* held the Eternity Stone, and for once they'd managed to work together. "Moved us in the space between seconds."

Time had essentially stopped; had frozen everyone except themselves. Still holding hands tightly, the trio moved closer.

The motionless figures in the fight, big and…bigger, were contorted into various attacking and defensive positions, their faces twisted into fierce or fearful expressions.

In the distance George could see the above-ground village of Upper Iversley, oh-so-different from how he'd known it in his own time. Several human figures were frozen in fleeing position, minuscule in comparison to the nearby giants, who were stepping over and around them with little regard for who they might hurt.

"Wow…" Ashlea gasped.

Lady Anne pointed with her free hand towards the village. "Look, the Noble with the blue hair is about to step on that boy. He hasn't seen him."

George could see that even from this distance, the expression on the boy's face was so horrified it was almost comical.

"Good timing for him, then. We should go move him just in case." Ashlea moved towards the boy, tugging at the others' hands.

George resisted. "If we stop the Queen, then shouldn't the giant shrink to human size? He won't be in any danger then."

"But what if it isn't immediate?" Ashlea asked. "That boy could be crushed! Anyway, time's effectively stopped. So it's not like we're in a hurry."

That was true, George conceded. Giving in with a sigh, he moved with Ashlea and Lady Anne towards the village. After a minute they reached the boy, and Ashlea reached down to pull him out of the way with her free hand.

The next happened very quickly. Ashlea reached to grab the boy, and then somehow her hand slipped out of George's grasp. There were a few seconds of utter panic where she seemed to disappear, and George realized she'd moved into time without them.

He quickly released the artificial time hold, then saw that Ashlea was frantically trying to help the boy dodge the clumsy footsteps of the oblivious giant, who caught up in fighting a much larger giantess right over the top of them.

There was a muddle of shouts and attempts to grab Ashlea's hand, and then the moment George got hold of her, he thought *stop,* and finally there was peace. They were once again in the stillness of stopped time, holding hands and shaking with adrenaline.

"Whew!" Ashlea gasped. "That was close!"

"What did you think you were doing?" George snapped. "You pulled right out of my hand!"

"It was an accident!"

"Verily, she's unharmed now," Lady Anne said.

"Why is everybody standing so still?" asked the boy, who was still holding Ashlea's other hand.

They all stared at him in shock for a moment, then there was another muddle of arguing and time shifting while they moved the bewildered boy safely away from the fighting, then were at last back to just the three of them.

Lady Anne began to giggle.

"What's so funny?" Ashlea asked, but when George laughed too, she joined in.

"You must admit that was worthy of a theatre farce," George said, then grinned widely when she agreed.

"I do have the knack for the ridiculous, but I daresay the two of you help me with that."

"Why Ashlea, your speech is improving," George commented in surprise. "You sound far less…colloquial. Perhaps our superior manners are rubbing off on you."

Ashlea's eyebrows shot up, and she looked quite unimpressed. But then she inclined her head back towards the main battlefield where the Queen still stood, frozen and terrifying, in the centre of the scene. "Don't we have something we need to do?"

JUSTIFIABLE THEFT

Ash made her way across the battlefield with the other two until they reached the motionless Queen. But proximity didn't improve Seyen Johannis's looks.

She was frozen in mid-leap at the sun god's neck, her face locked in a terrible snarl. Her red and silver dress was ragged, and her visible skin was patterned with metallic tattoos much like the one Ash had worn. Ash could actually see the frozen power dripping off the hem of her gown and dissolving into the air.

The heavy earrings appeared to be the same size as when Ash had first seen them. They looked very small against the Queen's giant-sized body, but shone brightly with twin coronas of swirling power.

"You two will have to take the earrings," George whispered. "My hands are full."

It should be strange that he felt the need to whisper, for surely the Queen couldn't hear them. But Ash couldn't help thinking that she knew they were there – and the moment time was unfrozen, she'd do her best to kill them all.

They moved closer until they were within arm's reach of the woman's head, and in unison, the girls reached out to take the earrings. Ash gently unhooked the first palm-sized bundle of stones and pulled it away from the Queen. It hummed gently in her hand.

"It's warm," Anne whispered, cradling the other earring in her own hand. Then without even being asked, she handed it to

Ash.

Ash studied the two earrings intently. Like the Eternity Stone, they looked so unimportant. How could they hold such power?

But she knew that they did. She could feel their weight in her hand in more ways than just physical. The alter-power that emanated from them seemed tainted, but maybe that was because Ash knew who'd used and misused them for so long.

She felt a little sick at the thought, but she gripped both the earrings tightly in her free hand as if afraid they'd get away on their own.

"Naught has changed," Anne commented, looking around the still frozen landscape. "They're still giants."

"Perhaps they haven't yet been able to. We're still in the same moment of time, after all," George suggested.

Ash gripped onto the earrings nervously. The plan was going exactly as intended, but was it supposed to be that easy? Now they just had to check that without her earrings, then Queen lost *all* her power, then they could take the objects up to that little floating house and leave them there. "Maybe we should release the time hold, just for a moment. See if everything starts going back to normal."

They took a good few steps back, then George must have released the time hold, because everything began to change rapidly.

Within seconds the giants shrunk down to human size, disappearing into the trees, and the earth stopped shuddering, the cracks and furrows moving back into place. Ash physically felt the spilled power suck back into the earrings she held, and their strange buzzing increased tenfold.

"Huzzah!" George said. "It worked!"

And then suddenly they were underneath the canopy of the devastated forest, and the now human Seyen Johannis was staring at them from ten feet away, her face twisted with rage. She looked *old*.

Uh oh.

"Take us back to the house!" someone shrieked, and it might have been Ash.

"The Eternity Stone," George said in horror. "It's gone from my hand…"

"What?! How is that possible?" But Ash realised even as she spoke that the earrings had vanished, although Deias knew where to. Their presence was gone; that warm buzz of power…gone.

"I don't know. One moment I had it and the next-"

But then they saw the Eternity Stone. It was spinning in the air between them and Seyen as though George had thrown it and it had forgotten gravity along the way. *Come and get me*, it seemed to say.

The next few moments seemed to be in slow motion. They dove for the Stone, but Seyen Johannis had seen it too. It was a race for power, a race for *life*, and Ash couldn't focus on anything except that Stone. She reached for it, and Seyen reached for it, and then-

And then a blur of colour appeared; a figure rushed in between them and grabbed the Eternity Stone. For a moment the girl – because that's what it was – turned and winked at Ash in triumph, and then she was gone as quickly as she'd appeared.

Without their target, Ash and the Queen ran into each other full-force like rugby players diving for the same ball.

"What in Hades was that?" someone shrieked.

But Ash knew. She'd seen the girl's dark hair, pretty face and green eyes, and she knew that the time-travelling Queen had gone full circle. And Seyen Johannis would have to know it too; she'd have to remember it from her own distant past.

Slowly they both got up, staring at each other. The ex-Queen looked human, close up, ordinary in a way she hadn't before. It was age, and it had hit her hard in the same way it hit everyone. Lines around her eyes and her mouth, a drooping jawline, grey-speckled hair…

And none of it would have mattered if she hadn't been so obviously insane. She lifted one shaking hand, still gripping a remnant of that broken glass, and pointed at Ash. "You!"

Her? "Um…I did *not* know that would happen," Ash said, taking a step back. "Although really, you should have."

"This is all *your* fault," the ex-Queen ground out. "*You* have done this to me. You and that interfering old…" She advanced towards Ash with murder in her eyes.

In hindsight Ash didn't know why she didn't just fly away. Perhaps it was the pressure of the situation or her panic over losing the Eternity Stone, but she just stumbled backwards, hands in the air, wishing desperately for her sabre.

Then suddenly George was between the two of them, holding up a piece of rubble like a shield. "Leave her alone!"

Seyen turned on him. "Oh, so now you choose to act like a man?"

She lunged at him with the glass, then swerved abruptly to the side, aiming for Ash. Ash barely dodged the blow and the Queen snarled and turned on her again, swiping at her throat with the glass. Ash shrieked and dodged under the other woman's arm. Why oh why did *she* not have a weapon?!

Seyen stabbed at her, then again, each time barely missing, and then a big body knocked her out of the way and suddenly George was kneeling there white-faced, the piece of glass sticking out of his neck.

The ex-Queen screeched in triumph and pulled it out, and a fountain of red spilled in its wake. George slapped his hand over the wound and keeled over.

"George!" Ash heard Anne scream, but Ash was too busy avoiding yet another stab, and then *WHACK!* Anne hit the Queen on the shoulder with a broken branch. She was probably aiming for the head but couldn't reach any higher. Anne hit her again, and then Seyen knocked the branch aside and lifted the bloody glass again.

"Amaranthus!" Ash shrieked, and in her head was screaming *HELP HELP HELP HELP HELP!* She threw herself bodily at Seyen's back…

…and the Queen disappeared.

Ash fell to the ground, winding herself and almost flattening Anne. Huffing for breath, she scrambled up and looked around. But the Queen was nowhere to be seen. She'd disappeared into thin air, without even a wisp of smoke to show her departure.

"Where did she go?" Anne gasped, her voice very small.

"I don't know." Ash looked around numbly. That was an anti-climax. Oh, but- "George!" She spun around to see him still kneeling on the ground, his hand slapped over his blood-covered neck. "Oh no!" She needed something to staunch the wound… "Anne, give me your jacket!"

"Don't bother," he groaned.

"No!" Ash shouted. She wouldn't let him die! "It's not too late! We'll do something for you! Amaranthus! AMARANTHUS!"

"No really," George said again, his voice sounding a little funny. "I don't think I'm hurt." Then he slowly moved his hand away from the wound. There was no spraying blood, no cut visible at all. Just the blood that had already been there. It was already drying.

The girls stopped in their tracks and stared, Anne with her blue jacket hanging off one arm.

"What happened?" Ash asked finally. "I thought you were…" *Dying.*

"I was," he replied, his eyes wide. "I think Amaranthus must have healed me. I think I felt him touch my neck, just for an instant…"

Anne broke into a smile, and Ash again felt herself holding back tears. Wow. "You saved my life," she told him.

George smiled slowly, looking very pleased with himself. "I do believe I did."

"And you almost died doing it."

"I wasn't expecting that part, but yes. That woman was much stronger than I'd anticipated."

Ash was still teary. "But that makes it even more special. You now have permission to irritate me as much as you like."

George's eyebrows shot up. "Do I now?" Then suddenly he looked stricken, and he began patting his pockets frantically, then searching the forest floor. "Hades! We've still lost it. We've lost the Eternity Stone."

"You didn't see the girl appear and take it?"

The other two stared at Ash in surprise.

"I saw no one," Anne answered. "Simply yourself and that witch, crashing into each other like a couple of drunken cart drivers."

Elegant as ever, Anne. "There was a girl," Ash tried to explain. "She appeared for the barest second, and she took the Stone. The Queen and I both saw her do it. That was why she was so angry, because she knew it was gone." She quickly described the girl's colouring, and her theory of how Seyen had originally got the Eternity Stone.

"That's rather clever," George commented.

"Thank you-"

"Too clever. Too clean. Are you *certain* it was a younger Seyen Johannis?"

"Who else could it have been?" Ash asked in irritation. "And aren't we focussing on the wrong issue here? The Nobles have all vanished, and we've lost our way home."

"We've lost the easy way home," Anne corrected. "Dr Walker said he'd send us, remember?"

The doctor had promised, after all. But Ash had been wrong about the Nobles all vanishing in the same way that the ex-Queen had. They found six of them scattered around the upper and lower city. Dead, unfortunately, which meant they couldn't answer any questions.

People were pouring out of the houses into the open air, emptying the underground city as though the whole of Iversley's population was trying to congregate in the upper town's small centre.

There were shouts of confusion and excitement as people, in their right minds for the first time in weeks, met and talked over the bizarre occurrences. Yet nowhere in sight was a single live Noble, large or small. Everybody seemed to be just garden variety twenty-second-century human.

"We should tell them what happened," Ash said to George. Now the real trouble was over, she felt tired and a little bit pathetic. She wanted someone else to sort out the mess.

George nodded. "What's a little public speaking after what we've gone through today?"

He rose up into the air, and all eyes turned his way. "Excuse me! Excuse me! May I have silence?"

Eventually the murmuring crowd quieted, watching George expectantly.

He began, "You all may be wondering what has happened over the last month, and why you haven't been feeling quite like yourselves…"

George went on to summarise the invasion and mind control, and how it had all been brought to an end.

Ash thought he did marvellously. He might be a chauvinist and fixed in his ancient mindset, but he really was a good guy, wasn't he? She'd miss him, just a little.

She'd even miss Lady Anne, annoying, condescending little brat that she was. Anne did have her good points. Admittedly they were mostly that she listened to Ash under pressure, but still, that was something.

This had been a wonderful adventure, if Ash ignored the violence, weird food and overuse of alter-power. She felt like an alien abductee, knowing that she would appear back in the forest just down from her aged blue Cortina, still at five in the evening.

So much would have happened, yet no time would have passed at all.

And she wouldn't be able to tell anybody! The most defining three days of her life, and the people who experienced it with her would be either not yet born, or long dead.

Ash looked at George, who was still up in the air speaking to the restless crowds, and thought of him buried six feet deep, just a pile of dry bones. It was an ugly thought.

Cheer up, Ash, she told herself. *Maybe he'll be cremated.*

And anyway, said that insidious little inner voice (and no, it wasn't the Queen or Amaranthus. It was just annoying inner Ashlea) *you don't know if you'll get home yet, do you?*

At that moment she spotted a familiar bald head in the crowd. Oh, yes she would. She would make sure of it.

Dr Walker made eye contact with her, blanched, then tried to hide. Ignoring the gasps of the people standing nearby, Ash flew up into the air and shot after him. She dropped directly in front of him, blocking his escape.

He took a step back. "Good to see that you're still alive. It seems I did the right thing giving you the vials, hmmm?"

Ash put her hands on her hips and advanced. When she was nose to nose with him and he couldn't go back any further, she said, "You're going to keep your promise."

The doctor wiped his sweating forehead. "Promise? What promise?"

"You said that if we found out what was wrong, you'd send us home. So, when are you going to do it?"

Dr Walker tried to step around her, then slumped when it was clear there was nowhere to go. He dropped his voice to a whisper. "The time machine isn't working. It needs serious adjustments…"

"Have you tried it in the last fifteen minutes?"

"Well, no-"

"Then you don't know, do you? The Nobles screwed everything up." Ash looked up at George again. He was now trying to explain exactly where their captors had all gone, with little success – probably because he didn't know the answer himself.

Ash looked at the doctor narrowly. "You don't know where the giants have all gone, do you?"

"No! But I do have a theory."

"Go on."

He lifted his chin. "Well, it seems that if some kind of alter-power had brought them here in the first place, the removal of that power might act as a sort of reverse slingshot effect. That is, sending them back to where they came from. Except for those already dead, naturally."

Ash considered that. The same theory might explain why the namesakes she'd fought had vanished once 'killed' – it might've been simply that they were running on alter-power released by the Queen, and removing it also sent them back to where they'd come from.

"It'll do," she said briefly. "You might think about telling other people that – after you've sent us back home."

Dr Walker's eyes darted around, checking the people next to him. "No need to be so loud! Let's talk about this privately…"

An idea suddenly occurred to Ash, one so obvious yet so important that she actually stopped in her tracks. "Oh my Deias. You never had permission to bring us here at all, did you?"

"I do not *need* permission, I'm a world-renowned scientist-"

"So you didn't," she cut in. "You broke the law, didn't you? You never should have taken us from our times, or messed around with time travel at all."

"Sshhhhhh!" he said frantically, holding a finger to his lips. "I'll look into sending you back, I swear I will, but you need to-"

"For truckers' sake," a nearby woman said loudly. The middle-aged woman wore a slightly battered business suit, and she was staring at Dr Walker in disgust. "Did this girl say you took her from another time period, Osvaldo? I thought you learned your lesson with the last lot!"

Suddenly the doctor was surrounded with angry Iversleyans, all confused over their current circumstances, but also quite sure that Dr Walker *really* shouldn't have been messing with illegal time travel…again.

There was even a comment that he might've brought the Nobles in the first place, but Ash put a stop to that. "I'm pretty sure he had nothing to do with them," she said firmly. "That was just bad timing. But for George and Anne and I – we need to be sent back to our own times, and it needs to be soon."

"I can do it!" he shouted suddenly. "Just stop *shouting*! I promise I will do my utmost to send you all back. Just give me a day."

Ash had a flash of far-sight – the first she'd had in a while – and saw herself *spending the night at Islo's, getting into her own clothing, going back to the bunker to meet Dr Walker, saying goodbye to George and Anne, then all of a sudden she was standing on a forest path in front of a sign that read 'CARPARK 2 MINUTES'.*

Right where she'd started.

So that was that, then. It would be depressing to say that final goodbye, but it had to be done. The foresight that the machine would work was good enough for Ash. "I'll take it." She turned to leave, and then had a thought. "On the bright side, Doctor, you'll have plenty to write about, won't you?" From his jail cell. Time travel *was* illegal…and they were very illegal immigrants, about to be deported home.

"Now actually, that's a good idea…"

She turned her back on him and flew back to the others, leaving the doctor and the crowd behind.

George was back on the ground with Anne, talking to Islo of all people. They looked up as she arrived.

"Dr Walker says he'll send us home tomorrow," Ash told them. There were cheers from George and Anne, and Islo promised to give them a night of hospitality that they'd never forget. Ash thanked him, not detecting any innuendo in his comment, and said that she'd hardly forget her time here. It was the most...*interesting* of her life.

They spent the last night with Islo at his parents' house. It had been largely spared from damage, but the Georgiana they met there was very different from the one they'd first known. She was very shaky and prone to tears, especially since her daughter Gaira had come home and told of what had happened to her.

Her husband wasn't much better. It must be leftover from that intense mental bondage, Ash surmised. In contrast Islo was acting very adult, looking after his parents and helping reorganise the mess as well as they could. They were already talking about bringing the old government back together, just as it had been before the brief invasion.

The next morning was fine and warm. For Ash, putting on her now-clean jeans and jacket felt conclusive: like saying a definite goodbye to everything that happened here, and goodbye to George. And Anne, of course.

Ash sighed as she helped Anne into her snug corset. Ash had met her regency gentleman, and now she was going home. Well, it wasn't like she'd had a grand love affair or anything, just a little crush on someone entirely unsuitable who drove her crazy half the time anyway.

But she wasn't going to be the same timid Ash that she'd always been. She wouldn't be a secretary anymore, for starters. She was going to do what she'd always wanted, and study gardening. She'd always secretly wanted to be a landscaper, but her family had always considered it beneath her.

Anne would laugh at the idea something was beneath peasant Ash...but the class system of the twenty-first century West was built on money and education, wasn't it? As George would say, codswallop to that! She'd do what she wanted.

Anne squeaked as Ash pulled the corset a little too tightly. "Sorry."

They had a late, slow breakfast, talking about everything and nothing at all. Nobody truly knew what had happened to the Nobles. Ash had shared Dr Walker's theory, and she thought it was a good one…or good enough anyway.

Either that, or their missed years had all suddenly caught up on them, and they'd turned into dust. Kind of a disgusting thought, but better than thinking that they were all out there plotting revenge.

George thought they might have sneaked off in the chaos.

Anne was vehemently hoping that they'd all died, or had been turned into toads.

Ash thought that unlikely. She'd actually seen Sam wandering around the city, and while he deserved to be a toad, he still looked quite human, if a bit untidy. He'd looked at her blankly, as if he'd forgotten the various murder attempts.

Maybe he had, but if he was still alive, then most of the others would be too. After all, they'd jumped back in time. Sam had never turned into that tentacle-ogre, and had never been squashed by a falling island.

Shame, that.

Dr Walker messaged Islo's comm at around eleven in the morning. Ash, George and Anne said their goodbyes to the family, then walked back to the bunker where they'd been told to meet.

The doctor was waiting by the open hatch, looking smooth and well-groomed as could be, with a cell-phone-sized device in his hand…and a couple of official-looking types behind him, making sure he returned things to where he'd got them from.

"You're finally here," he complained. "Now if you'll all say your goodbyes, I'll send you back to where you belong."

Ash's eyebrows shot up. "Aren't you even going to apologise for what you did? For kidnapping us and almost getting us killed by a bunch of super-powered giants?"

Doctor Walker rolled his eyes, then when one of the watch-dogs behind him cleared their throat, sighed. "Sorry for bringing you here without warning and getting you caught up in a giant coup," he said mechanically. "Now, do you want to go home or what? I spent all night fixing the machine, and my time is valuable, you know."

That was likely the best apology they'd get from the man. And so it was time to say a final goodbye: one of Ash's least favourite things.

Ash turned to the other two time-travellers. Their expressions were as resigned as her own must be. They had to go their separate ways.

"This has been a very strange few days," she told them. "But I know I'll never forget either one of you." She leaned forward and gave Anne a quick hug. Anne surprised her by hugging her back tightly. Her eyes were distinctly wet.

George stepped forward, and taking her hand, kissed it gently. "I wish you well, Ashlea."

Ash's heart gave a little flutter. She gave in and hugged him too. Then George hugged Anne, and nobody said anything else. What could you say to someone you'd been through so much with, but knew would never see again?

Three silent seconds later, they were still standing there. George turned to Dr Walker and asked, "Do we need to do someth-"

He vanished, and the whole world lurched for one awful moment. Then it righted, and Ash found herself standing on a forest path, staring at a sign reading 'CAR PARK 2 MINUTES'.

Oh. It had worked. What a relief, but also, somehow, a disap-pointment.

She probably ought to go back to her car, but she couldn't; not quite yet. It would feel so final, like she was permanently closing the door on this adventure.

Ash raised her hands from her sides curiously, then felt a jolt of joy as she rose gently off the ground.

The adventure wasn't quite over, because she still had a little flying time left. One last turn around the forest, she decided, and then she'd finally go home.

Just then, Ash had the strangest image come to mind. It was of her, George and Anne in modern clothing, all sitting at her dining room table and eating lasagne. George was on a mobile phone, and Anne was saying that the boy at the library had been impertinent in calling her by her first name, but was blushing while she said it.

Ash blinked. That seemed like far-sight, sort of, but how ridiculous could you get? It was clearly her tired brain making things up.

She shook her head, spread her arms, and went off for one last flight.

⁂

Amaranthus stood in the tapestry room, studying a little cluster of tangled white threads. It might look like an accident to the casual observer, but in fact it was the best possible outcome at this point. He should know; he'd checked. "I think that went well, don't you, Bets?"

"It was most enjoyable," the girl cheered, beaming. She was small, with dark brown hair and very green eyes, and she was most emphatically not Seyen Johannis. Quite a lot of people weren't, as it happened, in spite of Ash's belief otherwise. "They did look startled, though. I wish I could tell them the truth."

"Later," he said firmly. "They'll find out in time."

"In time: good jest." Bets grinned again, then turned and stepped into a bright doorway leading out into a garden. Once she was through, the doorway vanished.

Amaranthus smiled crookedly, tracing the threads to where they moved next.

Heh, that joke never got old. Unlike some other people…

Ash had been flying for a few minutes, keeping out of sight beneath the tree line, when she saw something red in the distance. She slowed, and the red blob came into focus.

It was someone's hair. Someone very short, pale-skinned and wearing a dark green dress…

"Anne?" Ash said in disbelief.

"Ash!" The other girl looked up at her with wide eyes. "What are you doing here?"

"I think it's more like what are *you* doing *here*? We're in my time."

"She's right, I'm afraid." George's voice came from behind Ash. "I flew above the trees and this is most certainly not Iversley, not in any time that I recognize, anyway."

"George!"

"In the flesh. And would somebody please tell me what the blazes is going on here?"

Ash knew. Clearly, that earlier image hadn't been her imagination after all. "Um…Dr Walker sent us all back to my time."

George said a rude word that even Ash recognised.

Anne looked stunned. She squeaked, "But Amaranthus said we'd use the Eternity Stone to get home."

"I guess he was wrong," Ash said apologetically. "So I suppose you're both coming home with me."

There was long, awkward pause, then Anne said, "Well, at least you are somewhat schooled in acting as my maid. No doubt you shall be an acceptable host."

"Could hardly be worse than the giants," George muttered.

Ash held up her index finger. "You're welcome to stay with me, *but*, if you treat me like a servant, you're out on your aristocratic backsides."

"I beg your pardon," George said, affronted.

Anne put her hands on her hips. "When have we ever mistaken you for a servant? A boy, yes; although one can understand the confusion, if you *must* wear breeches!"

"Oh, good," Ash murmured to herself, heading for her car.

This was going to be *fun*…

…and it looked like she had her new flatmates.

Epilogue

Seyen Johannis sat up on the dusty ground. Over dry hills in the distance she could see a plume of smoke and the outlines of a few crude huts.

She dragged herself to her feet. Ah, her back hurt so! It was a foreign feeling, and very unwelcome. She looked down at her hands. The wrinkles and liver spots on the backs of her gnarled hands told the same story. Was this what being old was like?

Well, yes, she told herself. Because she was old, and that was how it felt.

Curse Amaranthus for taking everything she had and leaving her here. Curse him!

She wanted to shout it aloud, but there would be no point. Now powerless, all she had was her voice and this old, old body. She'd been a great queen, a goddess, and now she was a shrivelled old woman in the middle of nowhere. Nowhere to go, and nothing to do or see.

Seyen began to move towards the settlement. She knew she'd be in no danger there. Her enemy could be counted on to at least put her somewhere where she'd be sure to live out the rest of her now much shorter life. He was perverse like that; no quick easy deaths for his enemies. He wanted them to 'change their ways'…but instead, she'd just wait to die.

As she walked, she saw a lean, yellow-brown dog of no particular variety, standing on the side of the road and watching her with intent, pale eyes.

Seyen tensed and picked up a large rock. Old woman or not, if it was going to attack, she'd attack right back.

"Sashy?"

The word sounded wrong coming from the dog's muzzle, but she recognized the voice at once.

Her heart leapt. "Janeus! Janeus, my love. You've come back to me."

The story continues in

Mountain
of Glass

Across Time & Space book 2

Three time travellers kidnapped from across five centuries squashed together for six months in a two-bedroom cottage, on one income.

Confused? So are they...

After barely escaping the Queen's grasp in 2155 AD, Ash, George and Anne find themselves reluctant flatmates in the twenty-first century – no ID, no money, and apparently forgotten by friends and enemies alike. But then another bizarre twist of fate leads the trio out of Ash's time and into…well, that's the question, isn't it?

Because they're not alone, and they're not unseen, no matter where or when they are across history. And those who are watching them do not forgive or forget…

Dear Reader,

I'm going to assume you've actually read *The Eternity Stone* and don't mind if there are spoilers in the next few paragraphs. If you *haven't* read the book and *do* mind if there are spoilers, please stop now, because I'm about to tell you how the story came to be.

OK, you've been warned. Read on…

This story might seem like it's just about arguing time-travellers (and it totally is: I love a good argument) but the heart of it came from a dream. A literal dream, as in one of those things you have while sleeping.

I dreamed about powerful, dishonest, multi-coloured giants falling down to earth like meteors. They landed in a little village with a huge, futuristic city hidden beneath the ground, and convinced some of the locals to be their 'avatars' – an idea that later became 'namesakes'.

That was where the dream ended, but it had caught my imagination. Who were the giants, and what did they want? Finding the answers to those questions eventually became *The Eternity Stone*, which along with various other dreams and ideas, stretched out into a seven-book series released over six years.

I hope you enjoyed reading this story as much as I enjoyed writing it. If so, please take a moment to leave a review at your favourite retailer.

M. Marinan

9 781990 014185